To Seduce a President

by

Mark Reutlinger

To Seduce a President

Cover Art by *The Wild Rose Press, Inc.*

The Wild Rose Press, Inc.
PO Box 708
Adams Basin, NY 14410-0708
Visit us at www.thewildrosepress.com

Publishing History
First Edition, 2025
Trade Paperback ISBN
Digital ISBN

Previously Published 2018, Sister-in-Law, Black Opal Books
Published in the United States of America

Dedication

For Analee and Elliot

Praise for *To Seduce a President* (original edition):

"You can't help rooting for Suzanne, a truly enchanting character. I couldn't put it down."—*Pepper O'Neal, author of the Black Ops Chronicles.*

"A gripping thriller of corruption and a sophisticated conspiracy to subvert the American presidency, written with flair, skill, and a lawyer's focus…The character development…is enthralling."—*The Big Thrill, magazine of the International Thriller Writers.*

"I loved this book!…It is action-packed, full of danger and suspense. I like how the story takes you back in history so you get to know all of Suzanne's layers and what led her to her decision. There are some surprising twists to the story and near the end of the book had me in tears. Highly recommend!—*Reading by Deb.*

"A fast-paced, highly engaging plot, with lots of twists and turns, intrigue and titillation to ensure that the reader does not want to put the book down…I had great fun with this book."—*Geza Tatrallyay, author of the "Twisted" trilogy.*

"A distinctive storyline, well-conceived plot, and captivating characters." —*Kris Miller, TopShelf Reviews.*

"The only person you are destined to become
is the person you decide to be."
—*Ralph Waldo Emerson*

PART 1: THE PLAN

Chapter 1

Lloyd

Carl Bucholz, Jr., president of the National Rifle Association, looked out over the thousand or so member delegates assembled from around the country at the Washington, DC Convention Center. He felt less than confident about how this unprecedented meeting might progress. But it was his job as president to move it forward, and that was what he was determined to do.

The meeting had only a single item on its agenda: What should be the NRA's response to the anti-gun proposals that Patrick McNeil was certain to put forward once he was elected president?

The delegates assembled in Washington were intent on finding a way—any way—to prevent the catastrophe they believed McNeil's election would represent.

Bucholz first welcomed everyone to Washington and to the special meeting. Then he got down to business.

"As you know," Bucholz's voice boomed through the microphone, the hum of a hundred conversations gradually diminishing, "the Democrats have nominated Patrick McNeil for president."

At the sound of McNeil's name, a chorus of boos and shouted obscenities threatened to drown out Bucholz's remarks, and he again gaveled for order. He waited for relative quiet and continued.

"As you also know, Mr. McNeil is proposing several

legislative and executive initiatives that would severely restrict our rights as citizens under the Second Amendment." The volume of protest rose again, but Bucholz soldiered through it. "With Congress about evenly divided between the parties, there is every chance that if Mr. McNeil is elected, those proposals will become law. And furthermore, because the Republican Party has seen fit to nominate a man who, while sympathetic to our cause, has little chance of defeating Mr. McNeil, we must assume a McNeil presidency is on the horizon." More boos and shouts of obscenities. Bucholz ignored the din. "We are gathered here," he said, "to decide how this organization should respond to that threat."

Bucholz looked out over the assembly and hesitated—well aware this could be a messy business—before clearing his throat and announcing, "This matter is now open for debate and discussion. If you wish to speak, please so indicate by raising your hand and wait until a microphone can reach you."

One after another, delegates offered their suggestions for consideration. Some were restrained ("Begin a new ad campaign"), others less so ("Filibuster the damn legislation to death"). But then a balding man in his early fifties, red-faced and angry, rose to his feet, grabbed the proffered mike, and offered his own remedy for Patrick McNeil's anti-gun proposals.

"My name's Lloyd Kilpatrick," he began in stentorian tones that only barely penetrated the murmuring of the crowd, reflecting hundreds of private discussions. "I'm a delegate from East Tennessee. It's my belief that when and if this asshole McNeil, in fact, gets elected and takes the positions and makes the proposals that President Buchholz here has suggested, it would be a direct attack on the Second Amendment of the American Constitution. That would amount to nothing short of treason!"

On Lloyd Kilpatrick's shouting that last word, the murmuring in the hall suddenly ceased. He now had the delegates' full attention. President Bucholz's jaw dropped. It dropped farther as Kilpatrick continued. "Now, if someone in high office commits treason, there's only two possible ways to deal with him.

"One way would be to convene the proper kind of tribunal, whatever that may be, and try him, convict him, and hang him."

The murmuring began again, but this time its tone was quite different, excited rather than conversational.

"And the second way," Kilpatrick went on, "the second way would be to skip the time and expense of such a trial, not to mention the possibility that some pantywaist court or jury might be suckered into an acquittal, and to shoot the sonofabitch now!"

The murmuring became louder and quickly turned into shouting, with several variations on both "He's right!" and "He's crazy!" To the delegates' credit, most of the shouting was of the latter variety. Bucholz pounded his gavel for order, but to no avail.

Lloyd Kilpatrick's voice rose above the general din to conclude, "Now I ain't saying I favor one way or the other. I'm just pointing out the alternatives."

But it was quite clear to Bucholz and everyone else which "solution" this fellow Kilpatrick favored. He just didn't want to risk arrest for inciting a riot or conspiring to assassinate a—future—president.

President Bucholz did his best to restore order and

to get the meeting back onto a more rational track. Whatever might be his opinion on Lloyd Kilpatrick's two alternatives, he was smart enough to know the kind of public outcry that would result from headlines in the nature of "NRA Proposes Assassination of President," or variations on that theme.

One just didn't make such statements in public, at least not these days—the public was too skittish about that kind of thing.

So President Bucholz banged his gavel, shouted into his microphone for order, and finally, as a last resort, drew from a shelf on the lectern a small starter's pistol and fired a blank round into the air. The pistol had been intended to be used as part of a demonstration later, but the president decided that there was a far greater need now.

That got everyone's attention, even Lloyd Kilpatrick's.

"That's better," Bucholz said when the crowd had quieted down and a semblance of order had been restored. "Now this is an open meeting, and we welcome comments and suggestions from anyone. But when it comes to the kind of thing that the last speaker suggested, I think we have to draw a line here, folks. We are not here to break any laws, or to propose that anyone else break them."

Most of the delegates accepted this, nodding in general accord with the president. Lloyd Kilpatrick, however, apparently was not through quite yet.

"I disagree, Mr. President," he shouted. "When the laws are unjust, or they threaten to take away our freedom, our constitutional rights, the safety of our families, it is our patriotic duty to disobey those laws and to act in whatever way necessary to protect ourselves."

The general murmuring began again, with Bucholz again gaveling for order, trying to shout over the din. The uproar was becoming louder, and it appeared a fight might soon break out between Kilpatrick and several other delegates near him.

Bucholz decided things had gone far enough. Again he could picture the headlines: "NRA Meeting Ends in Brawl Over Assassination Proposal!" He shouted into the microphone, "Would Security please escort Mr. Kilpatrick from the auditorium. He may return when he is prepared to keep his comments within the bounds of proper and lawful proposals."

Two burly men dressed in military-style uniforms made their way toward Lloyd Kilpatrick. But the delegate from East Tennessee apparently recognized when he had made his point and should take his exit, so he walked out to the aisle, met the security men on their way to him, and left the hall quietly. Meanwhile, the meeting returned to its topic, with no one now willing to raise any issues that might suggest someone be shot, no matter how much they might agree with the theory that almost any problem could be solved at the point of a gun.

Next time I run for an office, Carl Bucholz, Jr. thought as the discussion continued, *it's gonna be for the damn Rotary Club.*

Chapter 2

Jamil

Two days later, the NRA meeting had ended and Lloyd Kilpatrick was still in Washington, DC. He had often traveled to the nation's capital on business—he was a salesman for a furniture company, and a very successful one at that—and he usually avoided returning home as long as he could. He enjoyed the amenities of DC that he could not enjoy at home—not the Smithsonian, or the Capitol, or the various monuments, but the great call girls, readily available and of a quality appropriate for clients such as diplomats and congressmen. Almost as fine, maybe finer than those he enjoyed on his trips to New York. Of course, the fact that his wife was a thousand miles to the west was the other important quality of a stay on the East Coast.

Lloyd was relaxing in his modest hotel room with a few room service beers when the phone rang. He picked up the receiver, wondering who could be calling him there. He hoped it wasn't Mara. His wife would start asking whether the NRA meeting was over, and if so, why wasn't he headed home yet.

"Yeah?"

"Mr. Kilpatrick?"

"Uh-huh. Who's this?"

"Mr. Kilpatrick, my name is Jamil Kahn. I am an

NRA delegate from Milwaukee, Wisconsin. I wonder if I could come up and speak with you briefly."

Lloyd considered this. Was this guy selling insurance? A newspaper reporter? A disgruntled delegate intending to start a fight over what Lloyd had said? And he sounded like a foreigner.

"Whattaya want to talk about?"

"About your remarks the other day, Mr. Kilpatrick."

Lloyd was afraid of that. "Yeah? What about them?"

There was a pause on the other end of the line, then: "Let us say I was impressed by what you had to say, and I have a proposal that you might find very interesting."

Impressed? Proposal? That might be a different kettle of fish, although Lloyd had no idea just what species of fish this Kahn guy had in mind.

"Okay, c'mon up."

"Thank you, Mr. Kilpatrick. I'll be right there." Jamil Kahn hung up.

So did Lloyd, scratching his head and wondering.

****

Lloyd threw several empty beer cans into the wastebasket, together with a few stray newspapers and spent bags of beef jerky and pork rinds.

There was a knock on the door. Lloyd opened it to find a thin, dark-skinned man in a neat gray business suit, a white shirt, and muted red tie. He looked very Middle Eastern.

The man put out his hand. "How do you do, Mr. Kilpatrick?" he said in slightly accented English. "I am Jamil Kahn. I appreciate your taking the time to speak with me." He was not carrying a briefcase, or for that matter a gun, Lloyd was relieved to see.

Lloyd stepped back silently to let Kahn enter. He

was still wary and said as the man passed by, "You ain't selling insurance or anything, are you?"

Jamil Kahn laughed. "No, no, nothing like that. But I am here on very important business, and I suppose in a way you could say it is a kind of insurance—protection against possible catastrophe."

That was a little too subtle for the delegate from East Tennessee. "I'm not sure what you mean," he said, "but go ahead, sit, and let's get this over with." Lloyd's distrust of people who looked like his visitor was tempered by his curiosity as to why he was visiting.

Kahn accepted the invitation and took a seat on the sofa.

"Can I get you a beer?" Lloyd asked, remembering his manners.

"No, thank you. I'd like to get right to the point of my visit, if you don't mind."

"Go right ahead," Lloyd said, taking a seat opposite his visitor. He was anxious to find out what that point was.

"As I said on the phone, I am here to talk about your remarks from the floor of the NRA meeting the other day. At that time, you suggested that should Patrick McNeil be elected President of the United States, and should he then carry out the kind of program that he has outlined in his campaign, he would in effect be committing treason. Is that correct?"

"Yeah, I guess that's what I said." Lloyd was still unsure what this Arab-looking guy was up to.

"And you further suggested that one way, perhaps the most efficient way, to deal with treason of that sort would be to—to remove Mr. McNeil from office by means of...let's say...direct action."

Was this guy trying to trap him into admitting some kind of crime? Who the hell was he, anyway? "So what if I did? I didn't say I was gonna do anything about it. I just said that was one thing someone might do. No crime in that." His tone was belligerent.

Jamil Kahn only smiled and nodded. "Yes, yes, absolutely. You only suggested someone might decide to take such measures. Now what if I told you that someone was, in fact, prepared to do just that, and they would like your help in doing it?"

Lloyd had heard of entrapment, when the police or feds set up some crime and convince some innocent goof to carry it out, then arrest him. Well, they weren't going to catch him in their trap.

"Are you asking me to get involved in some kind of plot to assassinate the president? I don't want any part of that!"

Kahn smiled again, seeming unperturbed by Lloyd's negative response. "Please let me finish. There is a group of people—I am not in a position to name them, but let us say they represent a very powerful organization— there are these people who, for their own reasons, would wish to…let's say…take the kind of action that you suggested at the NRA meeting."

"You mean they want to assassinate the president?" Despite his own suggestion that it should be done, Lloyd was shocked that there was someone out there actually planning to do it—not exactly displeased, merely shocked.

"Not necessarily, but yes, they intend to take what you might term drastic action, should it be necessary."

"And you want me to help them?"

"I shall explain. What these people I have mentioned

have in mind may require the assistance of certain attributes that they believe you possess and others, like me, for instance, do not."

"Whattaya mean? You mean because you're an Arab?"

If Jamil was insulted or put off at all by Lloyd's insensitivity, he did not show it. In fact, he seemed pleased that Lloyd had gotten the point the first time. "Exactly," he said. "They need the help of someone more like you, Mr. Kilpatrick. Someone who is similarly motivated, but who—who possesses other qualities."

"And you chose me just because of what I said the other day at the meeting?"

"Well, no, not exactly. Your remarks were noted, and they helped assure us that we had, indeed, found the person they were looking for."

"How'd you know who I was?"

Jamil laughed. "Oh, that was not difficult. Once we had identified you as a candidate, it was just a matter of doing some basic checking. It's amazing how much one can learn—and learn quickly—from the Internet these days, especially if one has, ah, certain contacts who can get into places on the Internet that the ordinary person cannot."

Lloyd digested this for a minute. "You mean you checked me out, like I was some kind of presidential appointment for the Supreme Court or something?"

"You might say that," Kahn replied with a smile. He seemed to smile a lot, no matter how serious the subject.

"And what'd you find out?"

"In addition to some basic information about your home, profession, and family, and the fact that you frequently travel to this area and to New York City and enjoy the services of, uh, female companions, we learned that you have very deep convictions when it comes to politics, and especially where the Second Amendment is concerned. Apparently, this is not the first time you have expressed your opinion that what we might call extreme measures should be taken to prevent the loss of your constitutional rights. Is that correct?"

Lloyd answered reluctantly, "Yeah, I guess so. So what?"

Kahn ignored the question. "We also found that you are the owner of several handguns, semi-automatic weapons, and other firearms. You have been arrested more than once for displaying such weapons in a threatening manner, although you have managed to stay out of jail. You also have given financial support to organizations that advocate the violent overthrow of the American government, or at least that advocated it during the administration of the former president."

"Yeah, well, that was an insult to every white man in America, and his policies—"

Kahn cut him off. "That is beside the point, Mr. Kilpatrick. The point is that we believe you are a man of action, and not just words. We believe you would be an excellent addition to the people of whom I spoke earlier and their mission."

He let that sink in for a while. Lloyd seemed deep in thought, although, in truth, his thought processes tended to run relatively shallow. But Lloyd was nothing if not a shrewd salesman, and his next question reflected that fact. "What's in it for me?"

Jamil Kahn's smile was now broader than ever. It was the smile of an angler who had hooked his fish, and the rest would be just a matter of reeling him in. "That would depend somewhat on how future plans evolve. That is, you may be asked to do a great deal, or very little. This is still a 'work in progress,' as they say. But we can guarantee what I'll call a retainer of, say, fifty thousand dollars, for your basic services."

Now it was Lloyd's turn to smile broadly. No one had ever offered him fifty thousand dollars for anything, much less for possibly doing very little. But again the sharp salesman in him took over before he could rashly accept the offer. "Now I ain't saying I would or wouldn't join this group you're talking about just yet. First I need to know what the deal is. Who's in this group? What do I have to do for that fifty thousand? And how do I know I'll get paid?"

"Fair questions, Mr. Kilpatrick. I'll take them one at a time. First, I am not at liberty to tell you exactly who it is you are…uh…assisting, but I can tell you that it is an organization with worldwide connections that is dedicated to freeing citizens in many nations from oppressive regimes. Second, as I already said, you don't necessarily have to do anything for that money. It's a retainer, like hiring a lawyer before you need one, just in case you do. Our plans are not yet fully formulated, but we are moving forward rapidly."

"What if they ask me to do something I don't want to? Like maybe it's too dangerous or something?"

"In that case, you'll be free to refuse; but of course, you'll have to sacrifice the retainer."

"You mean I don't get the money until I do whatever it is they want?"

"No, you get the money 'up front,' so to speak, which I suppose answers your third question. You know you'll get the money because you'll already have it."

Lloyd thought about that. "Wait. You said if I didn't want to do what they ask, I have to give the money back. How do they know I'll give it back? What if I've already spent it, say?"

Kahn's face became virtually expressionless as he responded. "Let us just say that would be a most unwise thing for you to do. I would suggest that you put the money away for safekeeping rather than spend it, just in case it becomes necessary to return it." There was no mistaking the implication behind Kahn's words, despite the dispassionate way in which they were delivered.

Again Lloyd was silent. This put things in a slightly different light. He needed to think about it before deciding, and he told Kahn as much.

"Of course," Kahn replied, "I would not expect you to decide this moment. I shall give you a call tomorrow for your answer. Will you still be at this hotel?"

"Yeah, I suppose so. I'm scheduled to go home tomorrow evening, so I check out here by noon."

"Then I shall call you before noon. That will give you a chance to sleep on it, as they say."

Lloyd considered this. He would have liked more time to think about it, perhaps to discuss it with…but whom could he really discuss it with? Maybe Mara, although she was always skittish about anything dangerous he might want to do. Certainly not his business associates. No, he'd have to figure this out for himself. Maybe there was some way to get that money without sticking his neck out. "Um, where can I get hold of you if I've got questions or anything?"

"I regret that that would not be possible. You will have to wait until we contact you."

"Well, okay. Call me, say, between eleven and noon,

and I'll let you know what I've decided."

Jamil Kahn rose from the sofa and turned toward the door. "Fine. I shall do just that." He walked to the door and began to open it, but paused with his hand on the knob and looked back at Lloyd. "Oh, by the way, just to mention that should you decide to pass our conversation along to…to the wrong people, they will find that I do not exist, this meeting never took place, and there is no such organization as I described. Oh, and possibly you also might soon not exist either."

And with those parting words, spoken with a warm smile, Mr. Jamil Kahn made his exit.

****

The following day, at eleven a.m. sharp, Lloyd Kilpatrick received a telephone call at his hotel room in Washington, DC. It was brief and to the point:

"Mr. Kilpatrick?"

"Yeah."

"Have you decided on Mr. Kahn's proposition?"

"Yeah. I'll do it."

"Very good. You'll be hearing from us in due course. It will be with the name 'Smith.' Meanwhile, please keep this strictly confidential."

"When do I get my money?"

"The money will be deposited to your account within the next week."

"And what—"

But the click at the other end of the line told him there was no longer anyone there.

Chapter 3

Smith

Lloyd Kilpatrick returned home as scheduled, saying nothing about his meeting with Jamil Kahn and its resulting agreement. The money was indeed deposited in his checking account the following week, and Lloyd quickly transferred it to a new savings account he opened for the purpose. If Mara were to discover the deposit—she usually did the bank statement each month—he would tell her the deposit was an error by the bank and was quickly rectified.

Lloyd was a little nervous about what might happen next, now that he had signed on with…with whom? He didn't know, but he had a strong feeling it was not the kind of people he would normally associate with, or for that matter normally come anywhere near. These were seriously dangerous people.

It was not until three weeks after he returned home that the call finally came, to his office in Knoxville.

"Mr. Kilpatrick?"

"Yeah. Who's this?"

"My name is Smith. I would like to meet with you to discuss a business proposition. Would tomorrow be convenient?"

At first, Lloyd did not understand, but then he remembered that Smith was the name Jamil Kahn told him his caller would use.

"Yeah, sure. Where and what time?"

"There's a Starbucks on the edge of town, on Route 70. Do you know where it is?"

"Yeah, I been there. What time?"

"Would ten a.m. be convenient?"

"Sure. How'll I know you?"

"That won't matter, Mr. Kilpatrick. I'll know you. I'll see you tomorrow."

And the caller hung up.

Lloyd held the receiver in front of him and stared at it for a few seconds before hanging it up. Now that he was to find out what he had sold for fifty thousand dollars, he was afraid he might not like the bargain. But he could always refuse whatever this person asked him to do—and return the money, of course. That'd be the hard part.

Still, no harm in listening.

At least he hoped not.

****

The next day, Lloyd showed up five minutes early at the appointed coffee shop. He looked around. When no one approached him, he stepped up to the counter, ordered an overpriced plain black coffee—he didn't "cotton to them fancy lattes and espressos," he was fond of saying. He waited to receive and pay for it then found a small table for two and sat down to wait.

He watched everyone who entered, trying to guess which one would be "Smith." If he was expecting another "Arab" or a rugged mountain man, he couldn't have been more wrong. The person who finally entered the café and, after looking around and spotting Lloyd, came over to his table and held out his hand was short, bespectacled, overweight, and almost bald. It was January and pretty cold outside, and he was wearing a very plain overcoat.

After they shook hands, Smith removed the coat and hung it on a nearby coat hook. His attire under the coat was just as plain, a somewhat rumpled gray suit, a white shirt, and a light gray tie. He obviously didn't need to ask "Are you Lloyd Kilpatrick?" because he already knew.

"Mr. Kilpatrick," he said, after settling himself in the chair opposite Lloyd, "thank you for meeting me today. My name's Smith. John Smith."

Lloyd doubted it, but he just said, "Nice meeting you. I take it Mr. Kahn sent you."

"I'm sorry, I don't know a Mr. Kahn, Lloyd. Okay if I call you Lloyd? You can call me John."

"Yeah, I guess so. You wanted to talk with me?"

"I did." He looked around, as if concerned someone might be near enough to listen. Apparently satisfied, he said, "I have a little business proposition for you. I think you know what I'm referring to. But it's a bit confidential, so I'd appreciate it if you would take your drink there and come out to my car, where we can talk business freely."

Lloyd didn't like the sound of that, but he also didn't want to make a fuss about it, so he nodded. "Well, okay, I guess."

"Good. I appreciate that. Can I get you something else before we leave? A muffin or something?"

"No thanks." Lloyd wasn't hungry.

"Okay, then I'll just get myself some hot tea and we'll be on our way."

Mr. Smith rose and retrieved his coat, put it on, made his way to the counter, and ordered his tea. When it was delivered and paid for, he indicated to Lloyd they should leave, and Lloyd followed him out the door. He approached an ordinary dark blue Chevy Malibu. About the only thing remotely unusual about the car—at least for Lloyd—was its license plate, RHH 1187, which reminded him of his favorite hunting rifle, a Remington 11-87. Was this a sign he was doing the right thing getting in this car?

Smith unlocked the doors and went around to the passenger side, where he opened the door for Lloyd. Lloyd slid in and put his coffee in a cup holder as Smith closed the door and went around to the driver's side. Once buckled in, he started the engine and began backing out of his parking place.

Lloyd was a bit alarmed. He had thought they would just sit in the parked car, not go for a ride to who knew where. He issued a weak protest. "Uh, why're we driving? Can't we talk here?"

Smith looked over at him and smiled. "No, it'd be pretty conspicuous if we sat there very long, especially if we ran the engine to run the heater, and it's too cold not to. No, we'll just take a short drive and talk on the way. I promise I'll get you back here in a half hour or less."

That satisfied Lloyd, and he nodded in agreement.

They made their way over to Interstate 40 and headed west, cruising in the right lane.

Smith then began the conversation. "The people who have retained you, Lloyd, have spent a lot of time considering the many ways in which our freedom might be assured, especially as it applies to Patrick McNeil, most likely our next president. They've decided on a plan, a plan that they feel has the best chance of succeeding and that retains a great deal of…of flexibility. They have also considered several, uh, possible additions to their group, looking for someone who would best fit their plan."

So far nothing new or unusual, thought Lloyd. *Hope he gets to the point soon.*

"So where do I fit into this here plan?" Lloyd asked.

"First, we just want some advice."

Lloyd was almost startled. "Advice? What kinda advice can I give you? I assume you don't need any advice about furniture." He chuckled at this little joke. "You mean about guns and stuff?"

Smith smiled. "No, not furniture or guns. Let me explain. It's been decided that our little plan requires the services of a very attractive, very…sexually active young woman. Other characteristics are important also, but we can discuss them later. When you first came to our attention, and we examined your background in some detail, we became aware that you've been a frequent user of a particular high-class escort service in New York. When we connected that fact with your…let's say…forthright attitude toward politics, we saw you as what you might call a 'natural' for our plan." He looked over and although he didn't actually wink at Lloyd, his expression was a close equivalent.

Lloyd was now thoroughly lost. "What the hell does my having sex with those ladies got to do with knocking off the president?"

"No one said anything about 'knocking off' anyone, Lloyd. Remember, that was just one of the so-called alternatives you yourself suggested. There are actually many ways, as they say, to skin this cat. Anyway, I'm afraid I can't go into detail now, but you can take my word for it."

"Okay, so where do I fit in?" Lloyd was beginning to wonder where this was all leading—certainly not in the direction he had expected.

"Right. We've done a background check on some of the…uh…ladies who are employed by this escort service, looking for certain characteristics, and we've narrowed it down to one young lady with whom you've had several…several encounters. Her name is Suzanne Dahlstrom. Do you recognize the name?"

Lloyd thought. "Not the last name—I don't think I ever knew it—but I sure recognize the first name."

"Good. Now given the, uh, experience you've had with young women of this…this type over the years, how would you rate Ms. Dahlstrom with regard to…to experience in handling a man?" Smith's serious expression indicated no pun was intended.

Hey, if I can earn fifty grand just for talking about some women I've slept with, Lloyd thought, *they can ask me anything they want!*

"Well, she's kinda young but she sure is good at…at what she does."

"So tell me about Suzanne."

Lloyd began to warm to his subject, as if he were down at the corner tavern bragging to his buddies. "Well, she's just something else. She's about the prettiest gal I've ever seen, with a body that just won't quit, I mean the boobs, the ass, the face—everything. And then she just seems to know exactly what a guy wants, how to treat him, know what I mean? And I never had sex with anyone who knew so many…well, so many things to do to a guy to satisfy him. Makes me sweat just thinking about it."

Smith didn't say anything for a while, then he asked, "Do you have any idea how she feels about men? I mean, in general. Does she worship them? Tolerate them? I realize you may not know—"

"Oh, I know about that," Lloyd interrupted. "While she doesn't say much, I don't think she particularly likes men all that much. Except to screw 'em, of course."

This caused Smith to raise his eyebrows. "You mean, she likes to have sex with men, but she doesn't really like them? I mean as a whole?"

"Something like that. Like once I told her about the time my daddy put a real whippin' on me when he caught me playing with myself in my bedroom. I forget how I got on that subject, but she came over real funny, like she was remembering something unpleasant. She seemed to catch her breath, like, and started to say something about men being bastards, then she sorta' caught herself and shut up."

"Hmm. I see. Interesting. And what about her politics? Has she any strong feelings about the president?"

Lloyd scratched his head. "I don't rightly know. I think when it comes to politics, I tend to do most of the talking and her the listening. But at least she never gave me any argument about it. I think she pretty much agreed with what I was saying, though that could be just 'cause I was paying her to listen."

Smith nodded but didn't say anything, concentrating for a few minutes on his driving. Then he asked, "It sounds like you have a good relationship with this woman, right, Lloyd? I mean, you two get along, and you can talk to each other, even about politics. When you're not having sex, that is. Am I right?"

Lloyd scratched the stubble on his face. "Yeah, I guess you could say that."

"Good," Smith said. Then he was silent again, seeming to be thinking things over. Meanwhile, Lloyd too was thinking, wondering whether his answers had been what Smith was looking for, whether he had passed the test, so to speak. He hated being kept in the dark like this.

Finally, Smith said, "I think we've covered most of what we had to, Lloyd. Let's get you back." He turned around at the first opportunity and drove back to the Starbucks in relative silence, only making occasional comments on the weather or the passing countryside.

When they were again parked in the parking lot, Smith indicated that he had to get back and that their interview was over.

"So when will I hear from you next?" Lloyd asked before leaving the car.

"It may not be from me," said Smith, or whatever his name was. "Or maybe it will be. But as soon as the people I report to have had a chance to digest what you've said and decide on our next step, someone'll be in touch. Meanwhile, remember what you've been told about keeping all of this quiet. Real quiet."

He looked over at Lloyd, and for the first time since they'd met, the expression on his face was not only serious, but close to threatening.

These bastards don't fool around, Lloyd thought. *As soon shoot you as look at you.* And not for the first time Lloyd wondered just what part of him he had sold for that fifty-thousand-dollar pot of gold.

Chapter 4

The Proposition

As it turned out, it was indeed Smith who next contacted Lloyd. "Same place, tomorrow morning at ten," the now-recognizable voice said. "Please be on time. We have a lot to talk about."

This is it, Lloyd said to himself. *Now I find out what I've gotten myself into.*

He didn't bother going into the coffee shop this time. He recognized Smith's car in the parking lot—same familiar license plate—and saw Smith inside it. He parked his car, walked over to Smith's, and climbed into the passenger seat.

"Howdy," he said to Smith, trying not to sound nervous.

"Hello, Lloyd. Glad you could make it so soon. Once our people decided on a course of action, they wanted to get started as soon as possible. Events are moving along, and we have to be moving with them."

"Events? What events?"

"The election, mostly."

"But that's not for another…another several months or so."

Smith nodded. "Right. And as you'll soon see, there's a lot to accomplish before that. Let's get going so we can talk."

Smith started the car and eased it out of the parking lot. Again they headed for I-40, where they fell into the same easy cruising pattern as the last time.

"Lloyd," Smith began, keeping his eyes on the road, "maybe it's best I give you the whole story first, so you know exactly what your role's gonna be."

"Suits me," Lloyd answered. Maybe he finally was going to find out what the hell was going on.

"You know the first part," Smith began. "There's a group of folks who believe, as you do, the current government is taking this great country of ours down the path of socialism and straight into the hands of our enemies." He didn't specify which enemies he had in mind, which allowed Lloyd to fill in the blanks any way he wished.

"Yes, sir," Lloyd answered.

"And you know that this group, of which you are now a part, of course—"

Lloyd didn't like how that sounded, but he knew it was technically correct.

"—our group is determined to turn things around, beginning with the presidency. We chose you to help in that effort, Lloyd, because you expressed a willingness to do whatever it took to accomplish that goal, even if that meant eliminating the current holder of that office."

"Now hold on. As I've told you, I didn't really mean—"

"Never mind that, Lloyd. We know what you meant. But combined with other…other important qualities, we decided you were the man for the job."

"For the job," Lloyd said. "What—"

"I'm getting to that. With an election coming up, it's really too late to deal with the current president effectively. He'll be out of office soon, anyway. It's the next president we have to worry about. Now, we have nothing against the democratic process and electing someone who shares our concept of America. We, which includes certain very wealthy individuals with similar views, have the financial resources to outspend the opposition by ten to one, maybe more. Unfortunately, however, it appears that the Republican Party has so bungled the nomination process as to saddle us with candidates who couldn't win the next election against a cocker spaniel, much less against a man as popular as Patrick McNeil. Even if they paid every voter in America one hundred dollars to vote for them. That means we'll have to resort to—to other means to see that McNeil does not become president, or at least remain in that office for long."

"Uh, could I ask a question?" Lloyd interjected meekly.

"Sure, go ahead."

"Well, just suppose we did eliminate this guy McNeil in some way after he was president. Wouldn't whoever was vice president just take over and be just as bad?"

Smith was clearly impressed by Lloyd's question, and he said so. "I'm glad you're thinking this through, Lloyd, and that's a great question. The answer is no, it wouldn't be just as bad. Victor Freeny, the man who is likely to be elected vice-president, is a weak and ineffectual party hack. They'll put him on the ticket only to repay some political debts they owe, but he won't be allowed to touch anything that could be dangerous, if you know what I mean. Once Freeny's in office, Patrick McNeil's whole program will fall apart from lack of leadership. And who knows? Freeny might just be…well, eliminated somehow also, leaving the government in the hands of the speaker of the house, who would be even less of a threat than Freeny. So not to worry. Now where was I?"

"You were saying we don't have much chance to win the next election."

"Right. We need to have a plan to address that probability. And that's where you come in."

Finally, Lloyd thought. *Here it comes.*

"There's more than one way to undermine a president's program," Smith began, "without having to resort to violence. In fact, we've decided just the opposite is what's called for in this case."

"The opposite? I don't follow you."

"You will. Now we all know that Patrick McNeil, in addition to being against true American values, is also a hypocrite. You know what a hypocrite is, don't you, Lloyd?"

"Of course I do. He says one thing and does another."

"Exactly. Well, McNeil likes to spout all these platitudes about the importance of being a good husband and father, making it sound like he invented family values."

"Yeah, I've heard him talk about that."

"And don't get me wrong—I'm all for family values. In fact, you'll recall we Republicans used to make it one of our major party planks, until too many senators and congressmen in both parties—and especially ours—got caught with their hands up the skirt of some dolly not their wife, or worse. Well, it turns out McNeil's no better than those bastards."

"You mean he screws around just like other guys?"

"Uh-huh, just like you, Lloyd. And me, if it comes to that. But my point is, we could prove McNeil screws around, as you put it, we even have pictures. But in the long run, it probably wouldn't sink either his election or his program once elected. The American public has become pretty well accustomed to their leaders being…to put it nicely…unfaithful. Kennedy, Clinton, rumors about others—it's just not a big deal anymore, so long as they keep it more or less discreet. A fling with Marilyn Monroe? Who could resist? A blow job from a young intern? Just another day at the office.

"But what do you think would happen if Mr. Family Values were discovered in bed not with some movie star or two-bit intern, but with his own brother's wife? What if he was screwing his sister-in-law?"

Lloyd gave a low whistle and shook his head. "I'd say he'd be pretty well screwed himself," he responded. "That's a whole 'nother kind of 'family values,' ain't it? But what's that got to do with me? Has McNeil even got a sister-in-law? Or a brother, for that matter?"

"A brother, yes. A sister-in-law, not yet. As I said before, that is where you come in."

Lloyd began to ask what he could possibly have to do with the president's non-existent sister-in-law, when Smith braked to avoid a drunk-or-stoned driver who swerved into the lane ahead, then back into the fast lane.

After a few well-chosen words describing the driver's parentage, Smith continued. "Actually, it's where your little dolly Suzanne comes in. Patrick McNeil has a brother, all right. His name is Adam and he's about twenty years younger than Patrick, in his late twenties. One of those late-in-life surprises for his parents. He isn't married. And in fact, left to his own devices, he probably never would be. He's extremely shy, hardly ever socializes, hates politics and politicians—except his brother, that is, whom he worships—and to the best of our knowledge, he's never had a serious girlfriend, much less a lover."

"Sounds like McNeil isn't likely to have a sister-in-law real soon," Lloyd ventured.

"So it would seem. But we have other plans. The way we figure it, if anyone can bring Adam McNeil out of his shell and get him interested in producing a sister-in-law for his brother Patrick, it's this Suzanne Dahlstrom, at least if she's all you say she is—and believe me we've checked up on her and we agree one hundred ten percent with your assessment."

Lloyd was having trouble getting his head around what Smith was saying. He needed some clarification. "Hold on now. Are you saying you want Suzanne to…to seduce this fella Adam and to marry him, become the president's sister-in-law?"

"Excellent, Lloyd. Got it in one. Yes, we want Suzanne Dahlstrom to become not only the next president's sister-in-law, but to thereby become our entrée into the White House."

"What do you mean, your entrée?"

"Just that. Think about it. Everywhere the president goes, he's surrounded by secret service agents, not to mention a platoon of staff people, reporters, and miscellaneous hangers-on. His only privacy, such as it is, is in the White House residential section. The White House is guarded like Fort Knox—well, maybe not that well, but pretty damn well—and no one gets in without a good reason. Certainly no one gets into the private living quarters except—except who, Lloyd?"

"Well, I guess just the president and maybe his family and—okay, I think I see where you're going with this. If Suzanne becomes the president's brother's wife, she becomes part of the family and has access to—to just about everything, right?"

"Right. And what is it we particularly want her to have access to?"

"To the president?"

"Right again. And finally, why do we want her to have access to the president?"

Lloyd had to think for only a moment to answer that question. "So she can end up in bed with him, like you said earlier?"

"Lloyd, I'm really proud of you! I wasn't sure, to be honest, how quickly you'd pick up on all of this, but I see you're right on top of it. We're all gonna get along just fine."

"But wait!" Lloyd said. "I still don't see where I come in. Was all you wanted me for was to tell you about Suzanne and kinda reassure you that she's as sexy as you thought she was, the kind of gal who could seduce McNeil and his brother?"

Smith laughed. "Now that would be an easy fifty grand, wouldn't it? No, your part is just beginning. Who do you think is going to recruit this Suzanne, explain what we want from her, and convince her to do it?"

Lloyd gulped. "Me?"

"Of course, you. Who else? We already know an awful lot about Suzanne Dahlstrom: where she's from, who brought her up, where she lives and works now, all that. For example, she lives with some black bitch who's a call girl like her—a damn good one, I'm told, but unfortunately, I couldn't say from personal experience—who probably could talk her into it if she wanted. But the chances of getting her on our side are about zero. She doesn't seem to need money, her political leanings are way too far to the left, and she knows way too many people in high places to take a chance telling her about our plans. You, on the other hand, already have a good working relationship with Miss Dahlstrom, she probably trusts you, and she's used to talking politics with you. No, you fit our needs much better. We're real pleased to have you aboard."

Lloyd was not sure he was as pleased as Smith and his bunch were, but he knew it was too late to turn back, so he asked the next logical question. "Okay, so how am I supposed to get this gal to go along with your plan? I mean, we have a sort of relationship, I guess, but hardly where she'd take any advice from me—"

"Of course," Smith said in a reassuring tone. "We understand all that. But she'll listen to what you have to say. What we want you to do is to present Suzanne with our proposition, which we think she'll find very attractive, and urge her to accept it."

"Just what is that proposition? Why would she want to do what you want her to do? Sounds like a tough job, and maybe a dangerous one."

"Ah, yes. The proposition. First, you say you've been sort of explaining the way the world works and she seems to have accepted your point of view. That's good, and if she has a political motivation, it's kind of a bonus. Because the real motivation will be the money. One million dollars. Cash."

That certainly got Lloyd's attention. He had signed on for a mere fifty thousand dollars. Granted, he wasn't being asked to marry the president's brother and seduce the president, but still…

Lloyd whistled. "That's a helluva lot of money. Can you folks actually come up with a million bucks?"

Smith chuckled. "You kidding? Like I told you, if the election weren't already lost because of screw-ups by the so-called Party regulars, our backers could buy every fuckin' presidential vote in America and have change left over for Congress. We're talking billionaires here, Lloyd, so a lousy million bucks, to essentially castrate the president? That's less than a few ads on TV cost. Just pin money."

"Right. I see. So I'm supposed to offer Suzanne a million bucks and talk her into joining your…your group."

"That's right, Lloyd. Hey, you've got the easy part."

"Yeah, I guess so."

But Lloyd wasn't at all sure of that. All he knew was he had no intention of giving back that fifty grand, and so he didn't have much choice in the matter.

And he didn't want to think about what might happen if he failed.

PART 2: SUZANNE

Chapter 5

Violation

Suzanne Dahlstrom sat on the edge of the bed, wearing only her panties and unhooking the flimsy bra she usually wore—when she wore any bra at all—over prominent breasts that needed no support. She reached for her nightie and then paused. She looked over at Marguerite Matson, her roommate. Marguerite didn't look like her usual cheerful self.

"Is something bothering you?" Suzanne asked. "You look like something's on your mind. Can I help?"

Marguerite, having paused naked between undressing and putting on her own nightie, looked up and smiled. "Well, to tell you the truth, honey, it sorta involves you, what I've been thinkin' about."

"Me? What do you mean?"

Marguerite slipped the nightie—a bright pink one—over her head and arranged it neatly on her breasts. Tall, black, and very well-proportioned, Marguerite Matson looked equally exotic in the sometimes outrageous clothes she wore and when she was wearing nothing at all. In her profession, this was a considerable asset.

"Well, this afternoon I had a new client, someone who'd asked 'specially for me. Now that's not so unusual, so I didn't think nothin' of it. I like new playthings, 'specially if they've got lots o' money."

Suzanne and Marguerite both worked for New York's Red Carnation Escort Service, whose clientele was both "exclusive" and, generally, wealthy. A new client should be a cause of satisfaction, not concern.

"And did this one have lots of money?"

Marguerite laughed. "Oh, absolutely. So that part was just fine. We had a good roll in the hay, and afterward, he says he wants to talk for a few minutes, that he's glad to pay for any extra time it takes. Well, folks sometimes need someone to tell their story to, or to complain to, or whatever, and so long as I'm gettin' well paid to listen, I'm all ears."

"Me too," Suzanne said. "What did he want to talk about, sports? Sex?"

"No, what this guy wanted to talk about was way different. He wanted to know about you."

"Me?" Suzanne was startled.

"Right. He said he'd heard you were really hot—that's how he put it—and he was interested in havin' a go at you next and wanted to know what you were like. But some of the questions he asked seemed to have nothin' to do with what kind of service he'd get from you."

"Really? What kind of questions?"

"Oh, stuff like did you have any close friends around here, were you much interested in politics, stuff like that."

"And what did you tell him?"

"Not a thing. Don't worry, honey, I know when to keep my mouth shut, and this seemed like one o' those times. It's just that I wonder why the heck he wanted to know."

Suzanne was concerned. "Do you think he was from

33

the police or something? I mean, I haven't done anything, but—but who else could he be?"

"I haven't any idea, and as I said he didn't get anythin' out of me, but I'll ask the boss about it. They screen every client, and I'd like to know a little more about this guy. It could be he really just wanted to know more about you before gettin' in bed with you, kind of makin' the experience more personal or somethin'. Who knows?"

Suzanne looked down. "Yeah. Who knows?"

She wished she did.

****

Suzanne didn't trust men, especially men whose character or motives were suspect, and with good reason.

At the age of ten, she had been raped by her father, Frank. A man who apparently loved his liquor and his guns more than his family, Frank had come home one evening drunk and in an ugly mood, having just been fired for drinking on the job. He slammed the front door and headed upstairs toward Suzanne's bedroom. Suzanne's mother, Mary Sue, who had had a few drinks herself but was mostly sober, met Frank at the top of the stairs and, seeing his condition, tried to calm him down. He shoved her roughly aside, so hard that she fell partway down the steps. He then burst into Suzanne's room, where she had just finished getting ready for bed. She was wearing her nightgown with nothing underneath. For a moment she and her father were frozen in time, staring at one another. Then Frank came toward her.

Her father had approached her many times in a drunken state, and usually she had been able to avoid him, either running to another room or hiding behind her mother's skirts. If he managed to corral her, the worst she suffered was some clumsy, unwelcome fondling. But she could sense that this time would be different. The look in his eyes and the way he moved told her that she was not likely to escape so easily.

And she had been right. Forced onto the floor of her bedroom, Suzanne screamed for help, she screamed in pain, she screamed and sobbed with the raw emotional shock of what her own father was doing to her. To stifle her screams, Frank roughly put his hand over her face so that now she couldn't breathe and was in danger of suffocating.

Upon this scene of horror entered Mary Sue. When she heard Suzanne's screams and had recovered her balance and composure enough to realize what was happening, she struggled back up the stairs and rushed into her bedroom, took her husband's Colt .45 pistol from his bedside drawer, and then ran next door to her daughter's bedroom. What she saw was beyond the worst nightmare she could imagine, and her partially inebriated state only made her less able to control what she did next. With fumbling fingers, she disengaged the safety mechanism and more staggered than walked toward the terrible scene of her child being raped by her husband.

Frank heard his wife enter. He looked around to see her advancing toward him. Lifting himself unsteadily away from his violated daughter and twisting around to face his enraged wife, he began to shout at her to go back and threatened what he would do to her when he was through with Suzanne. He never had a chance to finish his threat. As Suzanne watched in disbelief, Mary Sue stumbled forward, shoved the gun into Frank's ribs, and pulled the trigger. The sound was deafening, punctuated by Frank's agonized scream.

Suzanne fainted. The next thing she remembered—and she would remember it for the rest of her life—was being carried from her bedroom by a police officer as her father lay, covered with blood, at the foot of her bed and her mother sat on the bed, head in hands, sobbing.

Chapter 6

A Troubled Childhood

Frank's attack on Suzanne was not the first time he had made sexual advances toward his daughter, just the most heinous instance. Frank had been fondling and otherwise touching Suzanne inappropriately almost from the time she was born. By the age of seven, Suzanne had almost become afraid to complain about Frank's unwelcome attentions, not only for fear of physical reprisal, but also because she thought she might somehow be blamed for allowing it to happen. She was confused as to why her father acted as he did toward her, and she began to think it might have something to do with her as much as with him.

In a perverted way, she was not far from the truth.

Suzanne was an unusually pretty girl, clearly destined to grow up to be a "boy magnet." Almost from birth, she stood out among her peers. She had soft blonde hair and the most unusual eyes—one was brown and the other blue, a condition her doctor called *heterochromia iridis*, but that Suzanne just called her "two-toned eyes"—which gave her a somewhat exotic look. She also developed physically quite early. She was developing, in fact, what could fairly be called a perfect body.

Frank's inappropriate behavior toward Suzanne continued off and on during the first decade of her life.

It caused Suzanne a great deal of mental and emotional anguish, but it did her no physical harm, until that night when she was ten. Frank's drunken attack resulted not only in the loss of her virginity in the worst possible way, but in far-ranging consequences that Suzanne, even in her wildest dreams, could not have imagined.

That fateful night in March, when her mother literally saved her life, everything changed.

Everything.

Suzanne's father did not survive the gunshot wound inflicted by her mother. The days and weeks that followed were a living hell for Suzanne. The scene in her bedroom replayed itself over and over in her head, like a terrible nightmare from which she couldn't wake up. But it was not just the scene itself that reverberated in Suzanne's mind; it was also the utter confusion it created in her perception of herself and her family. Why had her father attacked her? Was it because of something she had done, or not done? If she had given in to him, would he still be alive? Where did her mother's reaction fit into the picture? Was she, Suzanne, ultimately responsible for that as well? They were questions to which Suzanne had no answer, questions to which she would never fully find an answer.

Mary Sue was not charged with a crime, it being very obvious what had happened and there being no doubt that she had killed her husband in defense of her daughter's life. But although there was widespread sympathy for her mother's plight and understanding of her actions, when all the investigations were concluded and all the details were known, the court concluded that Mary Sue, an emotionally unstable alcoholic, was not a fit mother for Suzanne. The pretty young girl with the mismatched eyes was taken away and placed in a foster home, "for her own protection and safety."

****

It was very hard for Suzanne to accept what looked like a permanent separation from her mother, having grown extremely close to her emotionally. But she knew she was, at least for a while, powerless to avoid it, so she determined to make the best of her new role as a foster child.

Suzanne's first foster home did not last for long. Here too, her unfortunate precocity brought out the very worst in the men she encountered, including her foster father. When he began to take liberties similar to what she had experienced with Frank, Suzanne saw the writing on the wall and ran away from home. She spent two miserable nights on the street before she was picked up by a police patrol and, once identified, kept in custody until a new foster home could be arranged for her.

Even in police custody, she was not entirely safe from unwanted attention. Although almost all of the male officers she encountered were friendly but restrained, treating her with respect, one older officer, finding himself alone with her, tried to put his hands where they didn't belong. By this time, and even at her young age, Suzanne had identified a definite pattern, one that told her men were not to be trusted, whether they were strangers or close relations, police officers or civilians.

So Suzanne turned and bit the officer's straying hand so hard she drew blood. He screamed, but when help came running, he declined to admit how and why he had been injured.

"Hit my finger on the edge of the chair," he told

them.

"Pretty nasty gash for a chair," a colleague responded, but no one pursued it, and Suzanne knew it was best to keep her mouth shut as well. She was beginning to understand how her adversaries' minds worked; and as far as she was concerned, everyone, especially every man, was potentially her adversary.

****

Suzanne's second foster home worked out better for her, probably because the man of the house was seldom at home when she was awake. He worked the night shift at a nearby auto parts factory. His wife was a well-educated woman who understood Suzanne's delicate situation and treated her accordingly. Suzanne's time there was her first chance in many months to let down her guard a bit and just be a child.

Meanwhile, Suzanne's mother had entered a rehabilitation program, intending eventually to reclaim her daughter. She had been so traumatized by what her husband had done to Suzanne, and what she had then done to him, that she willingly accepted the help of the psychologists and caseworkers attached to the program. She stopped drinking and joined Alcoholics Anonymous. She became more selective in the company she kept.

And so it was that, at age thirteen, Suzanne and her mother were reunited. In the years since they had last lived together, Suzanne had further matured both physically and emotionally, and she had gained a large measure of street smarts. Her mother had turned her life around in a different way. One thing they now had in common, however, was that both had come to mistrust, disrespect and, in their own ways, despise men. In the case of Mary Sue, this led to her keeping to herself and avoiding further entanglements with men whenever possible. In the case of Suzanne, however, it ultimately led to much greater entanglements with men.

On her own terms.

Chapter 7

Dave

Suzanne's life with her mother was relatively uneventful, at least by comparison with her life with both parents. Her fourteenth and fifteenth birthdays passed without further crises, as Suzanne settled into a somewhat normal routine.

Mary Sue was determined that Suzanne should get her high school diploma, and Suzanne was of the same mind. She was not interested in education per se, but she realized the importance of making it through high school. She had big plans for herself, and the people she knew or had heard about who had dropped out of school—including both her parents—were not the type who fitted into those plans.

Although Suzanne did not distinguish herself in class, she certainly did in the competition of life outside of class. Once again her stunning good looks, combined with a cynicism that somehow came across as sophistication, guaranteed her popularity, at least among the boys at school. To Suzanne, that meant she could manipulate them for her own ends, whether it was buying her lunch when she was short of money or lending her their homework when she had neglected to do her own. In return, they might receive anything from a sweet smile to a quick feel behind the gym, depending on the value or importance of the quid pro quo.

Even these almost-innocent encounters with boys had their emotional barbs that Suzanne had to overcome. By now, of course, she understood—at least intellectually—that she had been raped by her father, and that he had deserved the fate to which it had led. But she continued to harbor the suspicion that she somehow shared in the responsibility for what had happened, that if she had not allowed him the liberties he took during her earlier childhood—as if she could have prevented his taking them—or, contradictorily, if she had allowed him the ultimate liberty that fateful evening, it would not have led to the tragic end that it did. So even letting a boy touch her breasts or, especially, letting his hand roam under her skirt would cause her heart to pound and her body to tense, not with sexual excitement but with emotional stress. It was a heavy burden for a girl still in her early teens.

Nevertheless, Suzanne was quite clear about at least one aspect of her father's actions: They represented for her a paradigm for the male of the species on a grand scale. Men had a terrible weakness, one to be feared and, at the same time, one that could also be exploited, and in exploiting it she could regain a measure of what had been taken from her. Suzanne therefore gained more than help with her grades from her early sexual encounters with boys. They taught her further important lessons about human relationships—and how to manipulate those relationships—that would color her actions and, for the most part, stand her in good stead for the rest of her life.

****

Until she was fourteen, Suzanne had not had any sexual experiences with the opposite sex that might be called normal. True, she was already quite mature physically, but she had kept boys mostly at arms' length, except for those occasional liberties in return for favors. But at thirteen, she discovered the pleasures of sexual excitement the way most girls do, through masturbation. And, like most girls, her first self-induced orgasm took her quite by surprise.

Over time, she also taught herself to exercise some control over her body's reaction to sexual stimulation, which she instinctively knew would be important if she was to be in control of every sexual encounter. In effect, she was in early training for what would become her career of choice.

****

It was soon after Suzanne discovered the pleasures of an orgasm that she experienced her first real test of the psychological and physiological effects of being raped by her father.

She was walking home from Tyler Middle School with two girlfriends on a sunny Wednesday afternoon, carrying a binder and two textbooks. As they passed a local drugstore, Suzanne remembered that her mother had given her some extra money to buy a new tube of toothpaste. Her friends were in a hurry to get home, so Suzanne excused herself and entered the store alone.

Having picked up a tube of "Fresh Mint" flavored toothpaste, Suzanne got in line to pay. There was only one cashier working, and there were four shoppers ahead of her, so she resigned herself to spending several minutes with nothing to occupy herself, a difficult assignment for an energetic fourteen-year-old. She was looking vaguely around the store when a good-looking young man stepped into line behind her, holding a magazine. He was certainly something worth looking at, she thought, with his bright blue eyes and shock of blond hair combed neatly back. His red checked shirt was open at the collar and his sleeves were rolled up, revealing impressive biceps. She smiled in his direction and he returned the gesture. Suzanne might have negative feelings about the opposite sex in general, but as a normal teenage girl, she had normal teenage hormones and could appreciate a good-looking boy as well as the next girl.

As they moved a bit closer to the cashier, the young man, who appeared to Suzanne to be about sixteen—an "older man," probably in high school—asked, "Do you go to Tyler?"

"Uh-huh," Suzanne answered softly.

"I went there 'til last year," the boy replied with a broad smile. "Now I'm over at Adams." Adams was the neighborhood high school that Tyler students generally would attend after graduation. "Do you live around here?"

Suzanne had no problem at all talking, playing, even "fooling around" with boys she knew at school, but she seldom encountered boys she didn't know, especially one-on-one with no friends around to support her. Therefore she was uncertain whether to respond to this overture in kind. Finally, she decided there was no harm in a friendly conversation, and she replied, "Yes, over on Vine Street."

"I live over that way," the boy said as Suzanne finally reached the cashier and paid for her toothpaste.

Feeling that her conversation with the boy behind her had not quite ended, she dawdled on her way to the front door, so that as she reached it the boy, who had paid for his magazine quite hurriedly, came up behind her and, reaching out, opened the door for her. It was the first time a boy—or a man, for that matter—had ever opened a door for her, and it made her feel somehow special.

Outside, the boy said, "Okay if I walk with you? I'm headed in the same direction."

Suzanne just nodded. Could she refuse? Could she tell him he should walk ten paces behind her, or on the other side of the street? Wouldn't that be rude, especially after he had so politely opened the door for her? Or should she make an excuse to go back into the store to avoid his company? She didn't feel in control of the situation, and that made her both nervous and uncertain. In the end, she just shrugged her shoulders noncommittally and continued to walk.

The boy fell in next to her. "My name's Dave," he said. "What's yours?"

After a few seconds' pause, she answered, "Suzanne."

With the ice finally broken, a stilted but friendly conversation ensued, and by the time Dave peeled off onto a side street where he lived, he no longer seemed like a stranger to Suzanne. She didn't think of him as a boy, or even a male, but merely as a new friend.

In the weeks that followed, Suzanne encountered Dave several times on her way to or from school, meetings that appeared to be by chance but Suzanne suspected were carefully planned by Dave. For one thing, they never seemed to occur when she was with her girlfriends.

As they walked home one afternoon, Dave suggested they detour through the small park that bordered their neighborhood. Suzanne felt comfortable enough with Dave by now that she didn't object, and they strolled toward a stand of trees and bushes that formed a broad greenbelt between the park's grassy play area and the street beyond.

Later Suzanne was unsure how it happened that they walked off the path and into the little forest, but before she realized it they were in a small clearing, darkly shaded and private. They could not see the park or the street, and no one in either could see them. Dave sat down on the ground, carpeted with soft pine needles, and gestured for Suzanne to sit beside him. Not wanting to seem unfriendly, she gathered her skirt and sat, finding the ground comfortably warm despite the lack of direct sunlight.

Suzanne sat to Dave's left, her shoulder only inches from his. Dave put his left arm around Suzanne's shoulder and with his right hand began to massage her upper right arm. It felt quite nice, and Suzanne, ignoring the little voice in her ear that warned her against it, didn't object. When Dave's hand drifted from her upper arm to her shoulder, the little voice got louder, and Suzanne made a decision. She was quite aware of where Dave was headed, and she was not averse to heading there with him. Although she had let boys take liberties in many ways, she had never let a boy touch her intimately in a situation where she was not in control, and where there was not a quid pro quo. She was, therefore, curious to see how she—how her body, for that matter—would react when it was the boy who was calling the shots and she was in a strictly passive role. She had heard the stories a thousand times from her girlfriends.

This story would be hers.

Predictably, given Suzanne's lack of resistance,

Dave's right hand soon made its way down from her shoulder to her right breast, while his left hand began a similar course around Suzanne's left breast. It was all quite smooth and seamless. This was clearly, Suzanne thought, not Dave's first rodeo.

Suzanne lay back, feeling the soft ground beneath her back, and Dave correctly took this as a sign she was ready for further exploration. One thing led to another, and soon both were naked from the waist down.

Suzanne had fantasized often about the first time she would let a boy take her, when they would become joined as one in a rhythmic dance that would culminate in a glorious simultaneous orgasm for them both.

So what happened next surprised Suzanne almost more than it did Dave.

As soon as Dave touched the bare skin of Suzanne's thigh, alarm bells went off in her head, her legs involuntarily closing together, and when he tried to spread her legs farther apart, the alarm became a full-blown panic attack. Suddenly it was Frank again, it was Suzanne's father, not Dave, who was forcing her legs apart and climbing onto her. Suddenly the horrific rape scene through which she had barely lived, and through which Frank had not, was playing itself out again in Suzanne's mind.

She screamed. She beat her fists into Dave's face. She threw him off and struggled to her feet, crying. She looked down then and saw Dave, whose glorious conquest had just turned into a dreadful defeat, cowering on the ground and protesting his innocence. She sat down again, her face in her hands, and cried like she had not cried since that terrible night when she was ten. She cried for herself. She cried for Dave. She cried for her mother and her dead father.

****

Suzanne and Dave were fortunate—or perhaps it was mostly Dave who was fortunate, as the circumstances would not have been easily explained away—that there was no one passing within earshot at the time Suzanne screamed. No one rushed to her aid, no one called the police, and Dave did not find himself branded for life as a sexual predator. In fact, he had the presence of mind, despite the shock of Suzanne's breakdown, just to let her sit there and cry until, finally, her sobs subsided and he could ask her what had happened, what he had done to cause her distress.

It was difficult for Suzanne to find the words to explain. She hardly knew why Dave's foreplay and abortive attempt at intercourse had triggered such a violent reaction in her. But she knew she owed him an explanation of some kind, so she tried her best.

"I—I was raped by my dad when I was ten. I guess—I guess when I felt you there—when I felt the sensations I felt when my dad attacked me—it just all came rushing back and—and—"

Dave took her hand. "And you thought I was like him? That I was trying to rape you?"

Suzanne shook her head. "No, no, not exactly. It was more like—like he was trying to rape me again. Even though he's—he's dead."

And that was all she could say before the crying returned. Dave didn't press her for more. It was clear she was not blaming him.

A thoughtful young man, in time he could see that the crime of Suzanne's father probably would never cease to victimize Suzanne, and it would continue to claim new victims as time went on. He, Dave, was merely the first.

****

Suzanne and Dave still occasionally walked home together, but by unspoken mutual consent they did not stray again into the woods, or anywhere else. Dave might have learned something valuable about the unpredictability of the opposite sex. Suzanne definitely had learned something invaluable about herself. Although she had yet to test herself fully, she was sure that so long as she was in command, so long as she was initiating the action, she could both control her emotions and even enjoy the experience. It was only when it was the other way around, when the boy was the aggressor and in the dominant role, that she was in danger of suffering the kind of déjà vu, and the resulting panic attack, that had ended her brief sexual relationship with Dave. At least this is what Suzanne fervently hoped was true, because although she was not sure just how, she had a strong feeling that sex was going to play an important—and positive—role in her life.

And not just because she enjoyed it.

Chapter 8

Johnny

In truth, Suzanne's feeling that sex would somehow be her ticket to the good things in life, so long as it was sex on her terms, made its way gradually into her psyche, almost without her consciously recognizing it. The little benefits she had acquired in school in return for small sexual favors were the progenitor of bigger things to come.

Suzanne's first venture into serious "play for pay" occurred when she was sixteen and a junior in high school. Although she was technically no longer a virgin, thanks to Frank, she had never let boys go "all the way," especially since her encounter with Dave. It was not that she was prudish or reticent. It was just that, after her disastrous experience with Dave, she knew she had to choose her sexual encounters carefully and always be in control. Nor did she ever want to give a boy the satisfaction of a conquest. If she was going to have sex with someone, it would be for her benefit, and on her terms.

Suzanne had been to a movie with a senior named Johnny Byrnes. Mary Sue was struggling just to support herself and Suzanne, and she couldn't give her daughter extra money to pay for movies, much as she would have liked to. Therefore, Suzanne was not averse to letting a boy pay her way. On the way home in Johnny's car, he must have felt lucky, because he detoured by way of Mulholland Drive and pulled into one of the many overlooks, among Los Angeles' most popular places to park and make out. Suzanne didn't object, not being in a hurry to get home and feeling sufficiently in control of the situation to take a chance. The radio was on and for a while they just looked at the twinkling lights below in silence, Johnny's arm resting innocently on the seat back behind Suzanne.

After a few minutes, Johnny brought his arm down to Suzanne's shoulders, the first move in a familiar game. Suzanne was not there to make out, particularly with Johnny, who was a nice enough guy but short on sex appeal. Nevertheless, she decided Johnny had earned a little fooling around. It might be fun, so long as she kept it under control. She even let his hand wander a bit without protesting. But when Johnny suggested they might watch the view better from the backseat, Suzanne balked. It was time to go home, and she was about to tell him so, when Johnny's cell phone rang, or rather played a snippet of a heavy metal song. He apologized and quickly took it out—it was an expensive new iPhone— and turned it off. Suzanne was a bit jealous, as she couldn't afford luxuries like that, being one of the few girls in her class who didn't have even a basic cell phone. Again Suzanne began to tell Johnny to take her home, but suddenly she stopped herself.

She had an idea.

Suzanne put her hand on Johnny's wandering one and stopped it.

"Would you like to get inside me, Johnny?"

Totally taken by surprise—he had imagined a long

campaign with little or no chance of a successful conclusion—Johnny didn't answer immediately. But after he recovered from the shock, he responded weakly, "Yeah, I sure would."

"Then I'll tell you what. You give me that pretty phone you just took out, and I'll give you a really good time."

Suzanne didn't consider her proposition all that different from the bargains for homework; it was just on a grander scale. She was simply doing what most of the girls in school did, only she wasn't "giving it away free."

Again Johnny Barnes was taken aback, and he had to think about Suzanne's offer for a moment. His parents had given him the phone for his birthday, and they certainly wouldn't approve of his trading it for sex. On the other hand, he could just say he'd lost it, and, although they would scold him for his carelessness, he would apologize and, in the end, they would buy him another one, which they could well afford. But even were this not so, he was much too far gone to turn back now. Here he was, a relatively homely boy who had never had sex with anyone, with a chance to lay the hottest girl in school. He could no more turn down Suzanne's offer than a thirsty drunk could refuse a shot of whiskey.

Johnny took the phone out of his pocket and handed it to Suzanne, who slipped it into her purse. They then climbed into the backseat of the car. Fortunately, it wasn't a Beetle or a Mini, but Johnny's dad's Camry, a car with reasonable space in the back for three sitting adults or two outstretched teenagers. Even so, finding a comfortable position was awkward, especially as neither of them had any experience with backseat sex.

Johnny, being overeager, wanted to get right to it,

but he couldn't quite figure out the right position. Suzanne, however, took a more businesslike approach to the problem. She quickly decided that she could best control the proceedings, and her own reactions, if she were the dominant partner, on top of the situation, so to speak. She maneuvered Johnny, who was willing to do whatever she suggested, onto the center of the seat, quickly unbuttoned her blouse, undid her bra, then raised her skirt, pulled off her panties, and climbed aboard.

Uncomfortable and cramped as her body was in this confined space, Suzanne let herself absorb and enjoy this, the first time she had felt the sensations of intercourse since that awful day when she was ten. From now on, she did not have to forever associate that feeling with the horror of being raped.

Suzanne was trying to think of other positions they might try, but the ride didn't last long enough for that. Johnny, despite trying desperately to prolong this milestone in his manhood, could not. Suzanne didn't mind, as she had been well compensated for a half minute or so of fairly pleasant work. And perhaps most important, she had been in control all the way, and none of the adverse consequences she had suffered with Dave had arisen, just as she had hoped.

She had not only had her first real sexual experience, but she had begun to get a bit of her own back against the male of the species.

Johnny was both elated and exhausted, and it was another ten minutes before he felt up to driving home. He said little as he drove, savoring the memory of his "conquest." He hardly remembered the phone that he had traded for it. Suzanne too was silent. She was sorting out in her mind the new lessons she had learned that evening, not only about the logistics of backseat sex, but also about the awesome power of sex in any locale.

As a footnote to her first venture into the world of sex for sale, Suzanne's love affair with her new phone was short-lived. She had not been aware that the high cost of a fancy "smart phone" was not just in its acquisition, but in its maintenance. As soon as she learned the considerable cost of signing on to a cell phone network, she realized she could no more afford to own that phone than to buy it in the first place. She considered selling or pawning it, but, in the end, she decided to give it back to a very surprised Johnny Byrnes. It was the only refund for services performed she ever offered.

****

Following her generally successful arrangement with Johnny, Suzanne employed similar tactics to secure various small favors during her senior year in high school. By the end of that year, she had become quite proficient in using her body as an irresistible bargaining chip and to its best advantage. She was learning how to tantalize, arouse, excite, and ultimately either frustrate or satisfy a man as she wished.

At age seventeen, Suzanne received her high school diploma, scraping by with a C-minus average. What she had failed to learn in math or science class she more than made up for with what she had learned in the practical application of human relations. She left behind many disappointed boys who viewed her with admiration and desire, but whom she viewed mostly with contempt. Although she thought it might be an exaggeration to say, as the joke went, that a boy's—or a man's—brain was located in his sexual organ, she found it surprisingly easy to use the urgency of the latter to overrule the reasoning of the former. It served her purpose, but it did not engender her respect.

A man's sex drive, Suzanne decided, was both his most dangerous and his most vulnerable characteristic. In her father Suzanne had experienced the dangerous side, and at its worst. That side could lead to assault, rape, even death. In Johnny— and the many others who followed—she saw and learned the vulnerable side. By the time she graduated from high school, she had made great progress in understanding the power that that knowledge could yield.

Chapter 9

New York

Having successfully put her daughter through high school, Mary Sue Dahlstrom was justifiably proud of both herself and Suzanne. She had had to work two jobs to earn enough to support them, and she had deprived herself of even a limited social life in order to devote herself to her daughter's care and feeding. Suzanne, in turn, genuinely appreciated her mother's love and devotion, and she was determined to pay her back some day, both financially and by being there for her in her later years. This was the second time Mary Sue had come to Suzanne's rescue, the first time literally and the second figuratively. Suzanne would not forget.

But first Suzanne had a life to lead, and she knew that required her eventually to leave home and begin to make her own way in the world. She also realized that she needed to make a clean break with her past, with the memories both good and bad, with the people with whom she grew up—also both good and bad. In fact, she had plans for herself that could only be played out on the biggest of stages, where what she had learned about herself and about others could serve her best.

Although she would have preferred to make her break with her past immediately after graduating, Suzanne realized she needed more money and experience before tackling the big world outside of her small neighborhood. She got a job as a waitress at the local diner, which paid well when tips were included, and she made sure she received lots of those. It was amazing how a shy smile or a quick wink at the right time could stroke a working man's ego while loosening up his wallet.

Sometimes she agreed to go on a date with one of her customers—she had many more offers than she accepted—and that not only saved her the cost of entertainment and/or dinners, but also the occasional extracurricular activities that followed offered an opportunity to discover and practice some of the tricks and techniques that would serve her well in the future.

Finally, two years after graduating, Suzanne moved out of her mother's house. She did so with more than a tinge of regret, but also with an excitement she had never known. For the first time, she was truly on her own.

With the money she had saved up working and a small contribution from Mary Sue, she bought a ticket to New York City.

****

When she left for New York, Suzanne had a few nice clothes, $2,000 in cash left over from her savings, and the names of several "friends of friends" she had accumulated once she had decided where she wanted to start her working life. It wasn't much, but she knew it was much more than a lot of early refugees had had when they arrived in New York knowing no one and speaking a foreign language. Besides, she was well aware she had one prime asset at her disposal that would trump any other she might have brought with her from home, if it were used intelligently—and ruthlessly:

She had her body.

If Suzanne, indeed, had that one prime asset, she was determined to be in firm control of it at all times. Only she would determine when and how it would be put to use, whether for business or for pleasure.

Her first opportunity—and clear need—to apply this strict rule was not long in arriving. To save money, Suzanne was taking a red-eye flight with two stopovers. She had booked a window seat. The middle seat was empty. The aisle seat was occupied by a middle-aged man dressed in suit and tie, the tie loosened and his collar open. He smiled broadly as Suzanne reached over him to put her carry-on in the overhead compartment, and she could smell liquor on his breath. He offered to help her, but she declined politely. He then got up so she could pass, her back to him, to the window seat. As she brushed by him, he let his hand stray ever-so-lightly across her bottom. She was unsure whether it was deliberate, and she let it pass. She looked over at him with a neutral expression. He was still smiling.

Once they were airborne and the seat belt sign was off, a stewardess came around offering drinks—water and pop free, beer, wine, and liquor for a "small charge." The man on the aisle ordered whiskey, then asked Suzanne if he could order something for her.

"No thanks," she said.

She then asked for a Coke and began reading a magazine she had picked up at the front of the plane. After a while, the stewardess came back and asked whether they wanted to purchase any food. It was an early morning flight, and Suzanne had had only some cereal and milk before leaving home, but she was determined to keep as much of her savings as possible intact until she saw what she would need in New York, so she declined. The man on the aisle just ordered another whiskey, which Suzanne believed was at least his fourth.

Suzanne fell asleep shortly after, her coat draped over her. After perhaps fifteen minutes she half-awoke to an odd, not entirely unpleasant sensation she couldn't immediately identify. But when she did identify it with the agreeable feelings she experienced when masturbating, she sat bolt upright, wide awake. It was dark, but it only took her a few more seconds to discover two things. The man on the aisle was now in the middle seat, and the hand that had brushed her bottom was now between her legs, her skirt having crept up when she sank into the seat to sleep.

"What the hell do you think you're doing?" was all she could say at first, as she roughly shoved his hand away.

The man didn't seem deterred. He smiled ingratiatingly. "Aw, c'mon, honey," he said in a hoarse, slightly inebriated whisper. "We can have a good time and no one'll know. You look like a girl who likes a good time." And he returned his hand to her crotch, this time moving his fingers under her panties.

If this was an example of what she was going to be facing out in the Big World, Suzanne thought, she had better establish her boundaries right now. She looked over at the man, smiled sweetly, and moved her own hand over to rest on his crotch. Just as he began to think he was in for a terrific flight, Suzanne grabbed his privates and squeezed as hard as she could. The man screamed in pain while elevating at least a foot off the seat cushion.

Suzanne immediately removed her hand—his having removed itself from her as he rose—and turned toward the window, feigning sleep. By the time the stewardess and a passenger or two arrived in the aisle to find out what had happened, the man-who-would-grope was left, out of breath and with tears in his eyes, to explain he must have had a bad dream, one that apparently propelled him into the wrong seat as well. And of being in the wrong seat he was now quite convinced.

For the rest of the ride, nothing disturbed Suzanne's sleep. As unpleasant as the incident in the plane was to Suzanne, it did serve as an early warning, one that she took very seriously.

****

When she got off the plane from Los Angeles just before noon—three hours ahead of Los Angeles time—on that sunny Tuesday in June, Suzanne was tired but excited. She consulted her list of names and phone numbers. The first name on her list was Celia Gordon, the cousin of a friend of her mother, who lived in the Bronx. After claiming her luggage and finding a bench on which to alight, she got out her cell phone—she had by now acquired her own with money earned by conventional means—and dialed Celia's number. A woman answered.

"Celia Gordon?"

"Yes. Who's this?" The voice on the other end did not sound particularly friendly.

"My name is Suzanne Dahlstrom. I got your name from my mother, Mary Sue. She's a good friend of your cousin, Darlene."

"I see. What can I do for you?" The voice was a little

softer in tone, perhaps because Celia no longer suspected she was talking to a telemarketer.

"Well, I've just moved to New York, and I don't know anyone here. I need a place to stay until I find a job and get settled. Is there any chance you could put me up for a few days?"

There was a long silence on the line. Finally, Celia cleared her throat. "Gee, I'd like to help, but I really don't have any extra room. And—and I may have to be out of town this weekend. But I'm sure you'll find something."

Of course, Celia was lying. She had plenty of room in her flat, and she had no plans whatsoever to be out of town. But her response was not unexpected by Suzanne, who had been warned not to expect an open-armed reception from New Yorkers, so she simply thanked Celia and hung up.

The next two names gave her similar responses. They would love to accommodate Suzanne, but for various reasons they simply could not. Again, Suzanne crossed them off and moved on to the next—and now the last—name on her list. She had hoped at least one of the friends of friends would put her up for a few days, if not longer, and she really had no Plan B for where to go or what to do if none of them would. Therefore, it was with a little more anxiety that she punched in the last phone number.

A man answered.

"Hello?"

"Hi. Is Patricia Lee there?"

"Pat isn't home right now. Can I take a message?"

This wasn't sounding promising, but Suzanne soldiered on. "Sure. My name is Suzanne Dahlstrom. I was given Patricia's name by her cousin Lorraine McKnight, at school in Los Angeles. I've just arrived here in New York, and I don't yet have anywhere to stay and kind of limited funds. I was hoping she could put me up for a couple of days, until I can find a place to live and start looking for a job."

There was a pause at the other end of the line, but finally the man said, "Well, I'm Pat's husband Gene. She won't be home for a while, and I'd really have to discuss this with her. But why don't you come over anyway if you haven't got anything else going. I'm sure we could give you some lunch and at least some ideas where to stay."

Suzanne was less than encouraged by this offer, but having "nothing else going," as Gene had put it, she agreed.

"That would be very nice of you. Thanks. How do I get there?"

"Where are you now?"

"Well, I'm here in the airport."

"Which one? JFK?"

"No, I think it's LaGuardia. Is that a problem?"

Gene laughed. "No, not at all. In fact, it's very good. La Guardia is in Queens, and that's where we live. Look, I'm working at home, and we're only a short ride from the airport. Why don't I come and pick you up? It's no fun finding transportation, especially dragging luggage around. And expensive."

Despite the attractiveness of the offer, Suzanne hesitated. She had already had enough experience not to trust a man alone in a car—or a house, for that matter—unless she had good reason to do so. On the other hand, maybe she did have a good reason to take a chance with this seemingly well-intentioned man. She decided to risk it.

"That would be wonderful. I really appreciate it."

"No problem. Give me your name again?"

Suzanne did so, and Gene told her where he would meet her.

She hoped for the best, and also hoped she was prepared for the worst.

Chapter 10

Gene

Gene had told Suzanne to wait for him at the passenger pickup area nearest to where she had phoned from. He said he would be driving a red Honda sedan. Suzanne sat on her largest piece of luggage and looked expectantly for approaching red cars. It had taken her only five minutes to find the spot he had suggested, but it was another forty-five minutes before a bright red Honda, several years old and having seen better days, drove into sight and pulled up at the curb. The driver got out and came around the car to greet Suzanne. He was not exactly what she had expected.

Eugene Lee was a short, prematurely balding Asian man of between thirty and forty, slightly paunchy but otherwise well-proportioned. He had a broad grin on his face that looked as if it might be a permanent feature. He was dressed in new-looking blue jeans and a plaid short-sleeve shirt. White sneakers filled out the look of a man who dressed casually, probably because working at home, he didn't have to dress any better. The overall first impression was of a warm and friendly teddy bear. This put Suzanne's hard-wired wariness, so recently sharpened by the incident in the plane, at least on temporary hold.

Despite his teddy bear appearance, however, Gene

was, after all, a male. As such, he could not have encountered Suzanne for the first time without at least a momentary pause and double take. Even tired and hungry after a long plane ride and a short wrestling match with her luggage, Suzanne was a striking figure. The smile with which she greeted Gene only enhanced her appearance, and he stopped to look her up and down before putting out his hand in greeting.

Probably realizing that he had been staring at Suzanne, if only for a moment, Gene laughed. "Please excuse my saying so, but you are a very beautiful young lady, as I'm sure all the men you meet tell you."

Suzanne smiled. "Thank you. To be honest, what men say isn't always so polite. But I must be a mess after that long plane ride. Which reminds me: Would you mind waiting here while I run back to the rest room? I didn't want to leave my bags to use it while I waited and, well…"

"Sure. No problem," Gene said. "Go ahead, and meanwhile I'll get these things loaded into the trunk."

"Thanks. I'll be right back," Suzanne said. She hurried off to the restroom. While sitting on the toilet, she had the awful thought of Gene Lee driving off with her luggage and leaving her stranded there at the airport with nothing and no one.

She knew she was being silly, but she couldn't help worrying, and a silly worry quickly became an even sillier panic. She did her business just as fast as she could and had hardly pulled her panties up and her skirt down when she sprinted past a startled elderly woman who remarked to her companion, "Must be missing her plane."

Of course, as soon as she saw out the window that

Gene's red Honda was still parked where she had left it, she put on the brakes and, feeling quite foolish, walked slowly out to the car. On the way she told herself that, as important as it was going to be not to trust any man, at least until she was sure of his intentions, it was equally important to avoid irrational judgments based solely on a person's sex.

Kept in their place, men could be useful.

The drive to the Lee residence was not terribly long, and, during it, Suzanne said little as she watched the passing scenes out the window. She had never before been in New York, or any big city other than Los Angeles, and she wanted to learn all she could about her newly adopted home. The streets, the houses, even the people, looked different from their counterparts in Los Angeles. It was both inviting and intimidating, a brand new world to explore, and to conquer.

Gene stopped the car in front of a small, nondescript two-story house on a quiet side street. It was old, but obviously well kept, with a few neatly trimmed bushes in front and a fairly recent coat of white paint with blue trim. Gene got out of the car and opened the trunk. He reached in and extracted Suzanne's suitcase. Suzanne meanwhile got out of the car with her purse and carry-on bag and followed Gene up the few steps. Gene unlocked the front door, opened it, and let Suzanne pass into the entrance hall before following her in. He put down the suitcase in front of the staircase leading to the second floor, looked at Suzanne and smiled.

"Well, here we are. It isn't much, but Pat and I really like it. New houses don't have much character, compared to these older ones."

He made a sweeping gesture to indicate the

character-infused walls, ceiling, and staircase. And indeed the fancy crown moldings, the carved banister on the staircase, the leaded glass in the front door, and other such architectural touches did set this vintage home apart from the run-of-the-mill ticky-tack tract homes that made up so much of the modern housing supply.

Suzanne agreed it was lovely and waited to see what would happen next.

Gene took the carry-on from Suzanne and put it, together with her suitcase, by the staircase wall. He then invited her to take off her coat and have a seat in the living room.

"Pat should be home soon. Meanwhile, relax. You must be tired after that long flight. Can I get you something to eat or drink?"

"Sure. Thanks. To tell the truth, I'm starving." She entered the living room, just to the left of the entrance hall, and sat down on the sofa.

"Didn't you have anything to eat on the plane?"

Suzanne was a little embarrassed to say she hadn't. "I guess I just didn't want to spend six dollars for a cheese sandwich. I kinda have to watch my savings pretty carefully."

Gene turned to go to the kitchen. As he was leaving the room, he said, "I hope you aren't carrying your savings around with you. That could be pretty dangerous. You could lose it, or even be held up. New York can be a tough place, especially until you get used to it."

Suzanne didn't answer. She was indeed carrying her money with her. Her mother had warned her too, saying she should take only what she'd need immediately and leave the rest with her, to be sent when she needed it. Suzanne refused, thinking it would detract from the clean break she was trying to make with her prior life. Now she wasn't so sure.

When Gene returned, he was carrying a sandwich on a plate and a glass of milk. He put them down on the coffee table in front of Suzanne. In addition to the sandwich, Gene had put some carrots and potato chips on the plate.

Suzanne quickly said "Thanks" and began to eat. She hadn't realized just how hungry she was, and it took her only a few minutes to finish. Gene watched her with interest, his face impassive.

When she had drunk the milk and wiped her mouth on the napkin that Gene had also provided, she said, "I am carrying my money with me. What would you suggest I do with it? To be safe, that is?"

"Well," Gene said, "if I were you, I'd open a bank account just as soon as I found a place to live. Just where do you intend to live, now that you're here?"

"I don't know. I just assumed that, if I could stay with someone when I arrived, after a few days I'd find a job and maybe a little apartment. That's why I called Patricia. I was hoping she—that is, you and she—could put me up just until I get started."

"Well, I'll really have to talk with Pat about that," Gene said. He bent down and picked up the empty plate and glass and headed back to the kitchen. He called over his shoulder, "Would you like anything else?"

Suzanne was tempted to say, "Just a place to stay," but she just said, "No, thanks."

Chapter 11

Patricia

At about five-thirty, Patricia came home. Patricia Lee, nee McKnight, was as Caucasian as Gene was Asian, with a light complexion, red hair, freckles, and a very sweet smile. In her mid-thirties, she seemed to exude energy and good nature.

Patricia looked at the visitor and asked, "Who have we here?"

Gene explained about Suzanne's phone call, his offer to bring her to the house, and her desire to stay a few days. Suzanne said nothing, beyond shaking hands with Patricia and saying "Very nice to meet you" when introduced by Gene.

"So you're a friend of my cousin Lorraine?" Patricia asked once Gene had finished recounting the circumstances.

"Yes, ma'am. Lorraine and I were in the same class in high school. We both just graduated."

"Hmm. I haven't seen Lorraine in at least two years. I guess I didn't realize she was graduating already. I'll have to phone and congratulate her. Anyway, why don't you relax here, and Gene and I will talk this over. Shouldn't take long. Okay?"

She was smiling pleasantly, but of course, however she looked, Suzanne had no choice but to say, "Okay.

Thanks."

Gene and Patricia disappeared into the kitchen. Suzanne assumed they were not only discussing what to do with her, but probably phoning Lorraine to be sure she wasn't some kind of con artist or crook. That was fine with Suzanne, as Lorraine was one of her best friends and Suzanne knew she would give her a good reference.

That was apparently what had happened because when the couple returned from the kitchen, Patricia smiled and said, "Gene and I have talked it over, and I might add we also talked with Lorraine—mostly to congratulate her on her graduation, but also to ask about you—you understand—"

Suzanne nodded.

"—and we think it would be fine for you to stay with us for a few days while you look for work and a place to live."

A wave of relief swept over Suzanne. Had the Lees been unwilling to let her stay, she really had no idea what she would have done next.

"Thank you. I really appreciate it, and I'll try really hard to find a job and a place to live as soon as possible. And while I'm here I'd be glad to help out around the house. I'm actually not a bad cook. My mom taught me, 'cause she knew I'd be on my own for a while."

Patricia laughed. "Don't worry about that. You're our guest and you don't have to pay your way. You should spend your time finding a nice job. What are you looking for?

Suzanne shrugged. "I don't really know. I mean, I just assumed I would look for a job as a secretary or a receptionist or something, you know, where I don't need a lot of experience."

Patricia and Gene exchanged a glance, and Patricia said, "That's okay, but I think you should know right off that finding a first job is a lot harder than you might think. In fact, it's a lot harder than it should be. Most employers are looking for someone with experience. But of course you can't get that experience unless someone gives you your first job. It's kind of a 'Catch Twenty-Two' situation."

"A what?" It wasn't a reference Suzanne was familiar with.

"Never mind. I mean it's ironic—it's kind of backward. You can't get a job without experience, but you can't get experience without a job."

"But surely everyone eventually gets started somehow," Suzanne said, almost pleading for a positive answer.

"Oh sure," Patricia said, "it's just that it isn't quite as easy as it would seem. You just have to be persistent and not get discouraged if you get turned down."

"Or," Gene added, "you have to know someone."

Suzanne turned toward him. "But I don't know anyone in New York. I just got here."

She was becoming somewhat distressed. Had she made a terrible mistake coming here? She had grand plans for herself, using her wiles and her womanhood to get ahead in the "big city." But she had to get herself settled and employed before she could even begin to execute that plan.

Patricia turned to Gene. "Gene, don't they need another secretary at your office?" To Suzanne she explained, "Gene is an engineer with a pretty big firm, and they have a large secretarial pool. Gals are constantly coming and going—it's that kind of job, no one stays long, but it's an okay place to start."

"I see, that sounds good," Suzanne said.

Patricia turned back to Gene. "What do you think?"

Gene looked very uncomfortable and hesitated before finally answering, "I don't know. We'll see."

He didn't sound enthusiastic.

****

Later, when Suzanne had gone to bed and they were alone, Patricia asked Gene why he had hesitated regarding helping Suzanne to get the secretarial job at his office. "She seems like a good kid," Patricia said, "and without some kind of help, she's going to have a tough time finding anything."

Gene looked down and cleared his throat. "I know, and I'd like to help, but let's face it. We really don't know much about this kid. I mean, she seems like a nice person and all that, but I have no idea how well she can type, how reliable she'd be, or anything else I'd want to know before I recommend her to my company. It'd be pretty embarrassing if I pulled a few strings and got her hired, and she turned out to be a royal screw-up."

Patricia seemed about to object, but she apparently thought better of it because she just sighed and shook her head. "I suppose you're right," she said. "I kind of feel sorry for her, and she does seem really nice, but I see your point. Maybe if she doesn't find anything and we get to know her better…"

And that's how they left it.

****

In the morning, before leaving for work, Gene explained to Suzanne that he simply couldn't recommend her without knowing enough about her qualifications.

"Of course, you're welcome to come down and apply for the job," he assured her, "but I just can't try to influence the decision."

"Sure, I understand," Suzanne said. "Thanks anyway."

She understood, but she hadn't conceded.

Chapter 12

An Important Lesson

Gene had sounded pretty definite about being unable—or unwilling—to put his thumb on the scale in Suzanne's favor and help her land the secretarial position. But Suzanne merely considered this an early challenge to her ability to get what she wanted, at least from a man. And Gene, for all his good humor and lack of prepossessing appearance, was at his most fundamental level just that: a man.

By the next day, Suzanne had formulated a simple plan to bring Gene around. A frontal attack seemed best, in a literal as well as figurative sense.

Suzanne waited until Patricia was well on her way to work, and Gene, who was working from home that day, was padding around in his casual clothes. When Suzanne saw that he had taken a break and was getting himself a snack in the kitchen, she stripped down to her bra and panties, mussed her hair a bit, and wandered casually through the kitchen door.

Gene looked up from in front of the open refrigerator and saw Suzanne. He almost dropped the milk carton he was holding, but he managed to put it back down on the shelf and close the refrigerator door.

Suzanne appeared to be surprised at seeing Gene there. But she made no effort to cover herself up.

"Gee, I'm sorry Gene. I thought you'd gone out and I was the only one here."

"I don't know what made you think that, but in any case, you'd better go and get some clothes on. You shouldn't be wandering around the house undressed like that."

Suzanne came closer. "I'm not undressed. See? I've got clothes on. If I took this off, like this, then I'd be undressed." And she slid one bra strap and cup down and exposed her left breast. It could not have been more of an invitation if it had been engraved with Gene's name.

Gene was clearly uncomfortable and looked a bit uncertain how to respond. "I told you to get dressed," he said. "And cover that up. What're you trying to prove?"

Suzanne just smiled and came even closer, took his right hand and placed it gently on her still-naked breast. "Why don't we have a little fun before Patricia gets back?" she almost purred. It was an invitation that virtually every boy she had ever met, not to mention the man in the aisle seat, would have killed to receive, and accept. That was why what happened next was such a total surprise.

Gene, who had been too startled at first to resist, suddenly reacted. He pulled his right hand away from Suzanne's breast and struck her across the face with the back of his left. It was not a particularly hard blow, but it was sufficient to draw blood from a cut on Suzanne's lip. More painful was the psychological shock, so unexpected was this violent reaction. Suzanne fell back and just barely caught herself on the kitchen counter then sank to the floor holding her lip, blood seeping through her closed fingers. She had the look of a puppy that had just been struck by her master and couldn't understand why.

Suzanne didn't know what to expect next. Had it been her father who had struck her, some sort of sexual attack probably would have followed. But Gene only stood where he was, looking both astonished and angry. For several seconds he and Suzanne stared at one another. Then Gene shook his head, as if trying to clear it, and said in an almost-normal tone of voice, "Go upstairs and get dressed. And don't ever try anything like that again."

He walked out of the kitchen without looking back and, a few seconds later, Suzanne heard the sound of his office door closing.

****

Suzanne spent the rest of the day half-heartedly reading help-wanted ads and making phone inquiries, so far to no avail. When Patricia came home that evening, Suzanne was up in her room, brooding over the scene in the kitchen that had gone so wrong. When she heard the front door closing, she ran into the bathroom to see whether the cut on her lip was still visible. It was. Suzanne was uncertain what to do. If she went downstairs and acted as if nothing had happened, Patricia would see and ask about the cut on her lip, and Gene would tell her what had happened, and then…and then what? Would she be lectured? Warned to stay away from Gene? Or simply kicked out of the house?

She was frightened at what was to come, but she was also confused as to what had happened. Had it been a problem with her technique? With what she said? Was there something peculiar about Gene that she couldn't have known about?

Or was this another, more general lesson, perhaps to

be transformed into another rule? Was this, in fact, a lesson about both an unsuspected inconsistency in the male of the species, and an equally unsuspected limit—it was unsuspected even that there were limits—to her prime asset?

From upstairs, Suzanne heard raised voices. Apparently, Gene had already reported to Patricia what had happened and they were discussing it angrily. Perhaps Patricia blamed Gene for bringing Suzanne to their home in the first place.

Much as Suzanne would have preferred to stay in her room and hide from the consequences of her actions, she was no coward. If this was to be another lesson in life, she might as well get the full benefit of it and put it behind her.

She walked downstairs and in the direction of the voices.

Gene and Patricia were in the kitchen when Suzanne entered. Seeing them, she almost flinched, as if warding off a blow that had not yet been struck. She stopped a few feet into the room and waited.

Gene and Patricia stopped talking and turned in her direction. Suzanne braced herself.

Unexpectedly, Patricia smiled. "Gene tells me you've had a rough afternoon. Slipped on the floor here and cut your lip. I'm afraid I got a little upset for a moment, because I've told the woman who cleans the house—you know, Maria, who comes in every other week—if I've told her once I've told her a hundred times not to use wax on the floor, because it leaves slippery spots. But Gene assures me you slipped on some food you dropped while eating and not because of the wax. Just the same I'm going to remind Maria again. Now let me see where you were hurt."

Suzanne moved toward Patricia while looking over Patricia's shoulder at Gene. But she could read nothing in Gene's face. It was as if nothing had happened earlier in the day, at least nothing worse than a slip and fall.

Patricia examined the cut and declared it sufficiently benign so as not to warrant further attention, beyond being careful to avoid reopening it, and of course to be more careful where she stepped in the future.

Suzanne thanked her and added, in a meaningful tone that was meant more for Gene than for Patricia, "Don't worry. That's one mistake I absolutely won't make again."

Chapter 13

First Job

Suzanne accepted both her temporary defeat and her hosts' good advice. The next day she rode with Gene to his office and was first in line to apply for the vacant secretarial position.

Gene's company, East Coast Associates, was located on two floors of a large downtown office building. The secretarial pool was housed in a separate, large section of the eighth floor, with most of the secretaries in small cubicles. The head secretary had the only enclosed office, and it was on her door that Suzanne gently knocked.

"Come in," called out a strong, low voice, and Suzanne opened the door and stepped into the office. It was sparsely decorated with vintage photographs on three walls and a large calendar with spaces for writing notes on the wall behind the desk. And sitting behind the desk, according to the small name plate on the desktop, was Angelina Vasquez, a fortyish woman of substantial build with shiny black hair cut short and friendly brown eyes. She gestured for Suzanne to sit on one of the chairs facing the desk, which Suzanne promptly did, handing the woman a copy of her sparse resume. Ms. Vasquez was dressed very modestly in a plain long-sleeved dress and had no discernable makeup on, and Suzanne was glad she had worn a similarly modest, high-necked blouse and below-the-knee skirt. This was no time or place for emphasizing her physical attributes.

There followed a pleasant conversation, Angelina asking mostly non-threatening questions about Suzanne's education, interests, and the like.

Apparently pleased with Suzanne's responses, she moved on to more technical matters. She asked Suzanne questions about her computer skills and filing techniques. She had her type out some passages from a report on her desk. Fortunately, Suzanne had taken a very good computer course in high school, her mother having insisted it would be crucial to almost any job she might seek in today's world.

Angelina made some notes on a printed sheet and put them into a file folder. She then looked up smiling. "So far so good. I think you would fit in nicely here. There is, however, one more step before I can hire you. Every new hire has to be interviewed by one of the senior partners in the firm, since it's for the members of the firm you'll be working, not for me."

When Suzanne looked a bit downcast at having to jump one more hurdle before she had a job, Angelina said, "Don't worry. It's mostly a formality. They usually take my recommendation to hire someone. But it's no sure thing. Occasionally the interviewing partner won't take well to the candidate, so it's important you make a good impression." She smiled again and added, "Which I'm sure you will."

Suzanne smiled back modestly and thanked her.

"Whom do I see, then, and when?"

Angelina checked her calendar, made a quick phone call "upstairs," and told her, "You can see Mr.

Henderson tomorrow morning, if that works for you."

"That'll be fine," Suzanne said.

"Good. Nine sharp, ninth floor, office nine-oh-three. Just identify yourself to the receptionist on nine."

Angelina rose, indicating the interview was over, and Suzanne rose with her and headed for the door. There she turned back. "Thanks very much, Ms. Vasquez. I really hope I get the job."

"So do I, Suzanne. Good luck."

And so both elated at having—almost—gotten a job on her first try and nervous at the prospect of tomorrow's "final exam," Suzanne made her way back to her temporary home with the Lees.

****

When Gene and Patricia came home from work that evening, Suzanne told them about her interview with Angelina Vasquez and how well it had gone. Both of them seemed genuinely pleased at her success so far. She then mentioned the remaining part of the hiring process that still awaited her.

"Tomorrow morning I've got an interview with a Mr. Henderson, and if he okays me, I guess I'm in."

"I see," said Gene. "With Jim Henderson, eh?" And he exchanged an odd look with Patricia, eyebrows slightly arched.

Suzanne noticed the look. "Um, is there something I should know about this Henderson guy? Is he, like, really mean or something?"

Another look, and finally Patricia smiled. "No, nothing like that. It's just that…well, let's put it this way: He might be just a little *too* nice, if you know what I mean."

Suzanne was puzzled. "No, I'm not sure. What do

82

you mean 'too nice'?"

Patricia looked over at Gene for help. "Isn't he the one you once told me about? Maybe you'd better explain."

Gene sighed. "Some of the girls in the secretarial pool have complained that Jim gets a little too…too intimate with them."

"You mean he, like, gropes them and stuff?"

"Oh, I'm not sure it comes to that, but…well, maybe."

"Isn't that against the law these days? I've read in the paper about guys getting fired or even arrested for things like that. How come he can get away with it?"

"Oh, I'm sure it isn't that serious. And besides, whatever the law says, as a practical matter unless it's some kind of sexual assault or something, and no one has accused Jim of anything like that, the woman isn't likely to put her job on the line trying to get him fired."

Patricia added, smiling, "I guess Jim Henderson is just one of those guys who considers himself God's gift to womankind, and thinks womankind agrees. I'm quite sure he doesn't mean anyone any harm or insult. It's just his way. Just be aware of what you're doing, like with any strange man you're dealing with. Sitting across a desk in an interview, it shouldn't even be an issue.

"Now let's have dinner and celebrate your getting a job, or almost."

****

After dinner in her room, Suzanne considered what Gene and Patricia had said about Jim Henderson, as well as what Angelina Vasquez had said. She had Angelina's recommendation, but she had no experience and girls had been turned down before. This guy Henderson was apparently nice enough, but he had wandering hands and a big ego.

Perhaps the latter could be put to her advantage.

Perhaps this time she needed to have a Plan B.

Chapter 14

The Interview

Suzanne again rode downtown with Gene, feeling a little nervous, but confident that she had prepared as best she could for all eventualities. Gene dropped her off and went to park the car, wishing her luck. "If you're still here at noon," he said, "come by my office and I'll take you to lunch. I hope you'll be one of us by then." Suzanne gave him a wan smile. "Thanks very much. See you then, or tonight."

She rode the elevator to the ninth floor and easily found the receptionist, who told her to wait until Mr. Henderson was free. So Suzanne sat down on a metal-framed leather sofa and waited. She was wearing a very modest, very plain brown coat that she had borrowed from Patricia, and she pulled it down over her knees, which she kept tucked tightly together. All but the top button were fastened securely.

After about five minutes, the receptionist called over and told her Mr. Henderson would see her now. She rose, walked across to the office door, and knocked.

A deep male voice called out, "Come in."

Suzanne opened the door and entered.

Jim Henderson was sitting behind his desk, fingers steepled. A man of about forty with black hair combed back, he was more what would be called rugged in appearance than handsome. He had a deep tan and looked like he spent a lot of time outdoors. He was wearing a dark blue suit, or the pants of same, his jacket hanging on a coat tree by the door, and a white shirt with the sleeves partly rolled up.

He was not smiling, his facial expression being quite neutral. In front of him was a file folder with a few papers lying on it, probably Suzanne's file sent him by Angelina. He motioned Suzanne to sit with a nod of his head. The interview had hardly started and it did not appear to Suzanne to be going well. She sat, again pulling her coat down over her knees.

Henderson spoke for the first time. "Suzanne Dahlstrom?"

"Yes."

"Jim Henderson." He put out his hand and Suzanne shook it. "I understand you've applied for a job in the secretarial pool, and Ms. Vasquez has recommended you."

"Yes, sir."

"I've been looking at your file, and while I'm sure you have many good qualities, secretarial experience doesn't seem to be one of them."

"No, sir. I was hoping to get that experience here."

"Hmm. I understand that one has to start somewhere, and it isn't your fault that this would be your first job, but I believe in general that, for our best interests at the firm, it is better to hire someone already trained than to train them ourselves."

It was pretty clear to Suzanne where the interview was headed. She decided the only way to save it was to initiate Plan B.

Time to bring out the heavy artillery.

She slowly unbuttoned her coat and pulled it open. If the coat itself was modest, what was under it was anything but. All that Suzanne was wearing above the waist was a very tight white V-neck sweater, with no bra beneath it. It left very little to the imagination.

Suzanne rose, shedding the coat entirely and revealing a bright red skirt so short that it was hardly more than a very wide belt. It just covered her buttocks in back and her crotch in front. She had brought it with her to New York for any occasion that might call for her to advertise her wares, although of course she could not have anticipated the occasion would be her first real job interview.

She leaned over the desk and pointed to her resume.

"If you'll look closely at my resume, Mr. Henderson, you'll see that I did very well in my computer classes." Her voice was sweet enough to cause a sugar high.

Jim Henderson was indeed looking closely, but his eyes were nowhere near the place where Suzanne was pointing. In fact, they were fixed on a pair of the most shapely breasts he had ever had the privilege of seeing at such close quarters, or at any distance. Suzanne made sure she leaned and pointed long enough for him to get a good, long look.

The company's interviewer was having trouble concentrating on the oral part of the interview. "Yes, well, I suppose…I suppose that should be considered…"

Suzanne straightened up—slowly—and sashayed—slowly—around to Henderson's side of the desk, the better to point out her computer grade. As she turned her back on him to read from the paper on his desk, his hand wandered, as if it had a mind of its own, onto her right buttock.

Things were going more or less the way Suzanne had imagined them the night before. Suzanne wiggled her behind just a little to indicate she was not averse to a little friendly fondle. She bent farther over and turned slightly, so that Henderson could now see that, just as she was wearing nothing beneath her white sweater, she was wearing the very same beneath her red mini-skirt.

Having given him a peek at her wares, Suzanne quickly straightened up, turned toward her would-be interlocutor, and asked, "Isn't there some way I can prove to you that I'm worth taking a little risk?"

To emphasize her point, Suzanne bent her knees just enough to let her hand drift lightly onto Henderson's thigh.

"Well…yes, I suppose we could…" He was having difficulty stringing his words together. "…we could give you a…a trial period."

Suzanne, knowing she had made a purchase and now needed to pay for it, reached for the zipper of his fly. The rest of the payment followed naturally.

From that point, the interview did not last long. As it happened, God's gift to womankind came up pretty short in the endurance department. All the while, Suzanne assumed he was praying that no one would walk into his office at this extremely sensitive moment.

She knew she was.

Unfortunately for both of them, someone—in this case, Jannette, the receptionist who had been stationed outside Henderson's office—did choose this most inopportune time to enter. She knocked briefly, then opened the door, and stepped into the office. When Jannette, a reserved and virtuous woman in her late fifties, saw her boss and the shapely young applicant locked in carnal embrace, she gave an involuntary little scream, dropped her notepad, turned and fled, leaving the door ajar.

Before Henderson and Suzanne could completely rearrange themselves, three others had entered the office to see what had so frightened Jannette. The first looked shocked. The second was unable to stifle a laugh.

The third was Henderson's boss, Jeffrey Franklin.

Franklin, a stocky, sixtyish white-haired gentleman with a round, pink face and bushy eyebrows, who under other circumstances was quite a jolly sort, shooed the other onlookers out of the office and shut the door. He then turned and asked, in a tone indicative of barely-controlled anger, "What the hell's going on here, Henderson?"

While the unfortunate Jim Henderson searched for an answer that would not incriminate him, Suzanne took the opportunity to answer first.

"He told me that was the only way I'd get this job," she said in an injured tone. "I had to have sex with him. I didn't want to, but I really need the job." She managed to force out a few tears to add a note of authenticity to her tale.

Jim Henderson tried in vain to deny Suzanne's story and accuse her of initiating the coupling, but he had several things working against him: his reputation for inappropriate behavior toward women in the office; the fact that even if Suzanne had been the instigator, there was no excuse for accepting the invitation; and perhaps more important, the law.

Jeffrey Franklin was no doubt aware that the public had become very sensitive to charges of sexual harassment in the workplace, and that even the suggestion that East Coast Associates had required a female applicant to endure the humiliation of a casting couch would do his company irreparable harm. All he said in response to Henderson's attempted explanation was, "That's the last straw, Jim. You're fired." He then turned to Suzanne, who was hurriedly putting herself back together, "Miss…uh…"

"Dahlstrom. Suzanne Dahlstrom," Suzanne inserted.

"Miss Dahlstrom, when you're…uh, when you're decent, please come to my office so we can straighten out this unfortunate situation. Room three-eighty-one." And then he was gone.

Jim Henderson, of course, was now furious, and if Suzanne hadn't grabbed her coat and purse and fled the office before he could decide what to do with or to her, she might have suffered more harm than the loss of a job opportunity.

Suzanne hadn't planned to get Henderson fired, of course, and she wasn't proud of having done so, but as she hurriedly made her way to Franklin's office she rationalized that he was probably getting what he deserved, because of his past disrespect of women like her.

When she found Franklin's office, she put her modest coat back on, knocked, and entered.

Franklin asked her to be seated. "I'm terribly sorry, and embarrassed, by what just happened," he said. "Believe me, we've never had this kind of problem before and had absolutely no reason to believe—"

Suzanne put him out of his misery, interrupting in a magnanimous tone. "Yes, I understand. I guess I should have just left the office when he first suggested…you know…but like I said, I really need this job and…well, I guess I thought if this is how it works in New York, I'll have to do it. But I'm sure glad you…you got there when you did."

"Yes. Well. So here we are." A long pause as Franklin looked down and appeared to be considering his alternatives. Finally he said, "Again, I assure you this is in no way indicative of how this company treats its employees, male or female. And I want to prove that to you. How about if we consider you hired, at a small increase over the usual entry-level salary, and try to forget this most unfortunate incident? Of course, we'll want you to sign something absolving the company of responsibility for what happened. You understand."

That was fine with Suzanne. She briefly considered putting the squeeze on Franklin for an even better deal, but she decided it was best not to be greedy, especially as she had, in fact, initiated the entire incident and hadn't minded the sex at all.

So she just answered, "I think that would be more than fair, especially since it looks like that Mr. Henderson won't be here, so I won't have to worry about running into him again."

"Absolutely not. Well, I'm so glad we can resolve this amicably." He looked as relieved as Suzanne felt.

Suzanne's experience with Gene Lee notwithstanding, she was now convinced more than ever that most men—and especially those with a reputation for wandering hands and a big ego—shared the same fatal weakness. She had only to exploit that weakness for her own benefit, before it could ever again exploit her.

She had only one more question for Jeffrey Franklin,

the same one she had been ready to ask Jim Henderson had they not been so rudely interrupted: "When do I start?"

Chapter 15

The Blue Note

Suzanne found that she fitted nicely into the secretarial pool at East Coast Associates, despite her lack of experience. The skills of the twelve women in the pool—there were currently no men in the pool, although apparently there had been from time to time—varied. Some were better at one task, some at another. Suzanne was pleased to find that her computer skills—the ones she was attempting to point out to Jim Henderson when he understandably changed the subject— were actually better than most of the other women's, and her filing was no worse than average.

Suzanne was now self-supporting, if only barely. Gene and Patricia had congratulated Suzanne heartily, and it seemed quite sincerely, on her new position. They had then helped her to look for an apartment she could afford that was not too far from the subway that would take her to work.

After a week of searching the newspaper, Craigslist, and various bulletin boards, finding most apartments too expensive or in very bad neighborhoods far from transportation, Suzanne found an ad for a roommate in a decent location in the Bronx. She met Georgina Ginsberg, the woman who had placed the ad, at a coffee shop near the apartment. Georgina, twenty-six and of average height, weight, and appearance—and, therefore, difficult to describe or remember—told Suzanne she was looking for someone who would be easy to get along with, wouldn't be bringing a string of men friends back to sleep with them, and didn't mind pitching in on cooking and housework. Suzanne, who had no present interest in relationships and didn't mind hard work, seemed to fit that description quite well, and the two women hit it off immediately.

It was arranged that Suzanne would move in with Georgina as soon as was convenient, which Suzanne decided was the following weekend. Gene and Patricia helped her to move her belongings across town, and by the following Sunday, she was sharing Georgina's two-bedroom walk-up.

By the time she moved out of the Lees' home, they had grown quite fond of Suzanne. Gene seemed to have forgotten, or at least forgiven, Suzanne's attempt to gain his cooperation by seduction, and Suzanne appreciated his apparently having kept the incident just between the two of them. Patricia saw in Suzanne a young woman with spirit, ambition, and a winning personality, who also happened to be drop-dead gorgeous, something Patricia wished she herself were. Patricia was sufficiently well-adjusted and self-assured that she didn't resent Suzanne's good looks, but she did admire them.

Suzanne for her part admired the close and relaxed relationship Gene and Patricia seemed to have. Pat was an easy-going, comfortable woman in whom Suzanne could confide and of whom she could ask the many questions she had about her new surroundings. Gene served not only as one of the few men she had met whom she genuinely respected, but also as a constant and important reminder that, whatever she might believe— and however correct she might be—about men in general and how they could be manipulated, there would always be exceptions.

****

Suzanne's secretarial job at East Coast Associates was a satisfactory beginning and brought in a steady, if small, income, and she soon settled into a routine both at work and in the shared apartment. After several months, however, she became anxious to move beyond that routine. Her job and her roommate were not exactly boring, but they certainly were not exciting.

She also could use more money, as what she earned barely covered her share of the rent and food, transportation, her cell phone plan, and an occasional movie. She couldn't afford new clothes, except when she desperately needed them for work.

Suzanne was, therefore, very interested when one evening in December Georgina happened to mention that a friend of hers, who worked as a cocktail waitress at a well-known downtown lounge, was planning to leave her job and move to California.

"She says she can't take the weather anymore," Georgina said over a take-out dinner. "Too bad, 'cause that job pays really well, and they let her pretty much set her own hours."

"I can understand that," Suzanne replied. "Coming from California myself, I can see why she would say that."

"Have you found it hard to adjust to the weather since you've been here?" Georgina asked.

"Not too much, 'cept I don't really have the right

clothes for winter. I've been pretty cold walking to the subway these last few days." New York was experiencing one of its chillier winters, and Suzanne's walk was almost two blocks.

Suzanne thought for a moment about what Georgina had said about her friend, then asked, "Do you think I might be able to get a job like that?"

Georgina looked up, puzzled. "But you already have a good job in a nice office. Why would you want to take one where you have to stand around half-naked and serve drinks to a bunch of ogling men?"

Somehow Georgina's description of the job, intended to be disparaging, didn't strike Suzanne as all that negative. In fact, it sounded rather inviting.

"Oh, I don't know. I don't think I'd mind being stared at, as long as they aren't allowed to touch me. And you said it paid really well. Besides, I'd only be interested in something like that part-time, to earn extra money. I wouldn't leave my present job."

"Well, to each his own, I guess," Georgina said. "You're a lot prettier than me, or my friend for that matter, so you're probably used to men staring at you. I'll give you my friend's name, if you like, and you can talk to her about it."

"Thanks, I'd like to."

So Georgina wrote down on a piece of paper the name Gail Hanson and a phone number in Manhattan, and she gave it to Suzanne.

The next evening Suzanne called the number and spoke with Georgina's friend. Gail was indeed getting ready to move, and she had given her employer notice that very day. She gave Suzanne the name of the lounge, the Blue Note, and its manager, and she even said

Suzanne could tell him Gail recommended her.

"If you're Georgina's roomie, that's good enough for me. She's really particular about people, so you must be okay. Besides, once I'm gone how well you do there is their problem, not mine." A mixed endorsement, perhaps, but good enough for Suzanne. She thanked Gail and determined to phone early the next morning. On second thought, however, she decided she had better take an hour off of work and see the manager in person.

****

When Earl Ballard, the manager of the Blue Note, got a good look at the considerable attributes of the young woman who wanted Gail Hanson's job, he was duly impressed. There was no need for Suzanne to offer any of the inducement she had offered—and delivered—to Jim Henderson at East Coast Associates. When it came to this job, sexuality wasn't an added benefit, it was a basic requirement. A cocktail waitress at the quite respectable Blue Note was not supposed to offer sexual favors to the customers; she was just supposed to make them wish she would. In that respect, Suzanne passed the interview with flying colors.

"I have a day job," she told Ballard, "so I could only work here part-time in the evenings. Would that be okay?"

Ballard considered this. On the one hand, he had to replace a waitress who worked full time, although with flexible hours.

On the other hand, this new recruit would brighten up the place twice as much in half the time.

"Okay, I think we could arrange that. Maybe seven to ten, Monday, Wednesday, and Friday, and five to eleven Saturdays? Would that work?"

Suzanne considered this. She didn't want to get into a position where she had no time to eat dinner or get enough sleep.

"If I could eat dinner here during the week, so I could come directly from my office job and change here, that might work. Saturday wouldn't be any problem."

Ballard thought this over and nodded approval. "Okay, you've got a deal. We serve a nice bar menu, so you won't starve."

They went over the salary arrangements briefly. Suzanne's basic salary wouldn't be much more than she was making at the office, but she could keep any tips, and, if she was good at her job, they were likely to be sizeable, Ballard assured her.

Suzanne planned to be very good at it.

****

Suzanne knew that working as a cocktail waitress, although it paid well enough and put her considerable assets to at least limited use, was only a step toward her ultimate goal. She wasn't entirely sure what that ultimate goal was, but it would have to include money and power—especially power over men.

And when it came to men, her second job turned out to be a perfect classroom in which to increase her knowledge of what made them tick, or to be more precise, what made them angry, happy, boastful, careless, anxious, generous, or in many instances just plain obnoxious. Like a bartender, she "heard it all," from how his wife was cheating on him to with whose wife he was cheating on her, whom he'd really like to hug and whom he'd prefer to kill. But unlike the typical bartender, Suzanne could do much more than merely nod sagely or commiserate vaguely. She could offer her customers a shoulder—or breast—to cry on, an understanding smile, even some womanly advice. She could re-inflate a man's ego with just the merest hint that he was worthy of attaining the favors of a woman like her. It was a classroom where she got well-paid to study and learn.

And the homework was all good.

PART 3: MARGUERITE

Chapter 16

Jerry

It was at the Blue Note that Suzanne met Jerry Gannon. He was sitting alone at a table in the back of the club. Suzanne approached, trying to read his features for what mood he was in. She decided he was not there to drown his sorrows or celebrate a victory; he just wanted a drink and a chance to relax.

She turned out to be right on both counts. She congratulated herself. Her powers of observation were improving steadily.

"What can I get you?" Suzanne asked, flashing a smile that almost invited a crude response.

But Jerry was a gentleman. "Straight bourbon, please," he answered, smiling back at Suzanne. Then almost as an afterthought, he added, "Can I buy you a drink?"

Suzanne flashed her smile again and accepted. Her instructions, and those of the wait staff in general, were to persuade customers to buy drinks, whether for themselves or for the servers. But the latter were to sip lightly and slowly, while encouraging the former to order frequent refills of their own glasses. If after five minutes of conversation the customer was still nursing his first drink, the server was to move on.

Suzanne went to the bar, collected a bourbon for

Jerry and a vodka and tonic that was mostly tonic—all the servers' drinks were deliberately watered down to preserve both money and their sobriety—and returned to the table where Jerry was waiting. He watched her approach with an appreciative eye, of which Suzanne was well aware.

Suzanne sat down and, after they exchanged names, she asked Jerry what he did for a living.

"I'm an architect. I just got off work and need a bit of time to regroup and mellow out." He smiled, looking pretty mellow already.

Half an hour and several drinks later, Jerry rose to go. Suzanne had quite enjoyed their conversation, as Jerry seemed to be well educated, articulate, and above all could avoid leering, touching, or otherwise making her uncomfortable.

Suddenly Jerry sat back down and asked, "D'you have a minute, Suzanne? I just had an idea."

Coming from someone else, Suzanne might have assumed Jerry's "idea" involved their getting naked and the inevitable consequences that followed. But Jerry just didn't seem like the type, and she sat back down to listen.

"My company does a lot of business with one of the big banks in town," Jerry began, "you know, planning new buildings or remodeling old ones when they take over some smaller bank and want to wipe out any traces of the old regime."

Suzanne smiled and nodded.

"Well, the bank sometimes has these big parties for their best clients, fancy ballroom, champagne, the works, and they also invite people like us, companies they work with closely."

"Uh-huh," Suzanne said. She was waiting to see

where this was going.

"So sometimes I get to go to the party and represent the firm. It's fun and it's a free night out, with entertainment. I take my wife, Nancy, and we have a good time."

Suzanne was still smiling, but she wanted Jerry to get to the point so she could get back to her job.

"Well, there's one of these parties this Saturday evening, at the Palace Hotel, and Nancy and I are scheduled to go. In fact, our firm is kind of counting on us going, as it wouldn't be good form not to show up, if you know what I mean."

Suzanne nodded. She had heard of the New York Palace. It was supposed to be just as luxurious as its name implied, although she had never even seen the outside.

"To make a long story short," Jerry went on, and Suzanne wished he would do just that, "yesterday Nancy fell while running and broke her ankle. She won't be able to go to the party, and I was either going to have to go myself—and that's no fun—or cancel, which as I said wouldn't be good for the firm. I know it's a last minute thing, and you don't really know me or anything, but would you like to come along to the party with me? It'd be fun."

Suzanne wasn't prepared for such an invitation and wasn't sure how to respond. It did sound like fun—her evenings, when she was not at work, were not exactly filled with glitter and champagne, more like television and beer—but there were several red flags to consider.

"Won't your wife—Nancy—get mad if you take someone else to the party?"

"No, especially since she won't meet you." The look

on Suzanne's face caused Jerry to add hastily, "What I mean is, she won't know how pretty you are. No, wait, that doesn't sound right. Let me explain. Nancy told me this morning I should go ahead without her, and when I said I didn't want to go by myself, she suggested I take one of the girls from the office—one of the secretaries, or a woman architect we have on the staff. So I did ask them, but none of them was available. Well, I didn't ask them all—one of them is old enough to be my mother, and another one needs to lose about two hundred pounds before we'd make a reasonable-looking couple. But I did try."

Suzanne laughed. Jerry was fairly svelte and would indeed look strange with a woman twice his girth.

"So I'll just tell Nancy I took someone from the office, and she'll never know the difference. And besides," he added with a smile, "I doubt she really cares who I take, as long as I behave myself and come straight home afterward."

That, of course, was the other "red flag" Suzanne wanted to consider. She generally didn't trust a man she knew almost nothing about.

More important, she was wary of giving anything away for free, now that she knew how valuable her favors could prove to be.

And in any event, she wanted to be sure it was her decision whether to give it away or not.

From all she could tell about Jerry—which, granted, was not a great deal—he was looking for the kind of good time that involved the conversational type of intercourse, rather than the carnal variety. She decided to take a chance. After work, Suzanne asked Earl Ballard if she could come in and leave earlier this one Saturday, so she could "attend an important event with a friend." Ballard agreed, and Suzanne phoned Jerry to tell him she had taken care of her work schedule and would be pleased to go to the party with him.

Jerry sounded more than pleased himself.

****

Jerry said he would pick Suzanne up at eight on Saturday evening. Although it was not a formal affair, he asked her to wear "something like a cocktail dress, you know." While she did know what a cocktail dress was, she didn't have a clue where she would find one. It was not something for which she had had any need until then, but she realized that if she wanted to move up in the world, she would have to be able to dress the part. So she didn't tell Jerry she had no such dress, but instead decided that she would have one by Saturday.

She called Patricia, the only person she knew who might be able to help. She explained the situation and asked for advice.

"If I had a dress that would fit you, I'd be glad to lend it to you," Patricia said. "But let's face it, you and I are built very differently; you would be falling out of any of my dresses. Would you like me to come shopping with you to find something?"

"That's sweet of you, Pat, but I really don't have the money to buy a fancy dress. If I can't borrow one, I may just have to tell Jerry to find someone else."

There was a long pause before Patricia said, "Wait a minute. I recall that the daughter of a friend of mine needed a dress for the school prom, but they couldn't afford to buy her one. They went to one of those second-hand places where rich ladies bring the dresses they wore once and can't be seen in again. At least it seems that way, because apparently the dresses are very fancy, almost new, and cost next to nothing."

"That would be great, if we could find such a place. Do you know where one is?"

"No, but I'll phone my friend and find out where she went. I'll get back to you."

So on Saturday morning, Patricia picked up Suzanne and they drove to a small shop in Queens named Second Time Around that proclaimed in its window, "Nearly New Couture!" There Suzanne found an elegant dark red cocktail dress that was not only "nearly new," but nearly fit her. It was just a little tight in the bust, so that it revealed a bit more décolleté than Suzanne would have liked on this particular occasion, but at $45 it was too good to pass up.

Cinderella was ready for the ball.

Chapter 17

The Party

Patricia came to Suzanne's apartment Saturday afternoon to help her get ready. She was beginning to feel toward Suzanne almost as she would toward a younger sister who was just finding her way in the world, but needed some guidance from another woman who had a bit more experience. For her part, Suzanne reciprocated the feeling. She relied on Patricia for advice and confided in her as she might in an older sister, although she was careful not to share with her either what her father had done or how that horrific event had shaped her attitude toward men. Nor was Patricia aware of just how sexually experienced Suzanne already was, and to what end. To all appearances, Suzanne was a normal young woman learning typical lessons about life, about the outside world, and particularly about men. And in most ways, she was.

Jerry picked Suzanne up promptly at eight. Although he was well aware of Suzanne's physical attributes from seeing her in her scanty cocktail waitress attire, he seemed unprepared for how she would look in the stunning red dress she had found. It took him a moment to catch his breath, but then he complimented Suzanne on her appearance, and, after helping her on with her coat, offered his arm, and escorted her to his nearly new black Lexus. Since this was not a "date" but only a chance to see how the other half entertained themselves, Suzanne felt no pressure or need to be wary of her escort's motives. It was the first time she could recall that she could relax in the company of a man; even around Gene she had had to be careful how she acted, especially after the incident in the kitchen.

They arrived at the hotel and Jerry pulled up to the curb just as a long black stretch limousine pulled away. A liveried doorman helped Suzanne from the car as Jerry turned the keys over to a young man she assumed was a valet—either that or a car thief, because he promptly sped away, tires squealing as he rounded the corner.

The event was being held in the second-floor Reid Salon, an elegant, high-ceilinged space decorated in brown and beige tones. They entered to find the party was well under way, with over a hundred people eating, drinking, and talking in groups of two to ten. Buffet tables covered with brown cloths held heavy hors d'oeuvres, rich desserts, and a variety of wines and spirits. Suzanne had not had dinner, and she looked longingly at the food and drink around her.

"Would it be okay if I had something to eat?" she asked Jerry.

He laughed and assured her it would not only be permissible, but expected. He led her over to one of the tables and they both picked up a plastic plate and began to fill it with appetizers made from shrimp, smoked salmon, and several things neither of them recognized. As they drifted away from the buffet table, Jerry said, talking around a mouthful of an unidentifiable but delicious green substance, "I'd better find someone from the bank to talk to, just so they know I came."

Spotting a man he recognized as a bank officer, Jerry led Suzanne in his direction. The man, whose arm was occupied by a statuesque and very elegant black woman, immediately recognized Jerry and put out his hand in greeting. After they had shaken hands, Jerry said to Suzanne, "Bill here is the guy who really runs the bank, even if his bosses don't know it." He then introduced Suzanne as "one of our secretaries," being sure to add, "My wife hurt her ankle and couldn't make it. Suzanne here was good enough to fill in at the last minute."

Bill—no last name was offered—looked Suzanne up and down as if appraising her for later auction sale. He seemed to approve. He then introduced his own companion.

"This is Marguerite Matson. She's a…a friend." Somehow he didn't seem entirely comfortable with the introduction.

Marguerite smiled, showing very white teeth surrounded by extremely red lips. She said, "Pleased to meet you" in a smooth, almost Ivy League accent, shaking hands with each in turn. She was probably in her late twenties, with her wavy black hair falling below her shoulders and very little makeup other than the red lipstick. She was dressed conservatively, but the rings on her hands and the jewels on her neck and wrist told a different story. Either Marguerite was wealthy enough to afford some very expensive jewelry, or she had exceptionally good friends who could.

Jerry and Bill immediately fell into a discussion of some real estate deal the bank had recently financed and Jerry's firm had participated in as architects. Suzanne nibbled on her food, wondering whether there would be more to the evening than listening to "shop talk" in which she had no interest.

She looked around at the room's furnishings, the crystal chandeliers, the intricate carvings over the doors, and thought that although it was beautiful, and she was lucky even to be allowed into such a hoity-toity affair, it was not her idea of a good time.

But she had agreed to come, and she would try to be a good companion for the evening.

She noticed, as her eyes returned from sweeping the room, that Marguerite was looking at her in an appraising way, not Bill's almost leering fascination with her sexuality, but a woman's dispassionate appreciation of another woman's virtues.

The men were deep in conversation and virtually ignoring the women beside them. Marguerite, a resigned expression on her face, stepped closer to Suzanne. "C'mon, honey, let's you and me get better acquainted while these idiots have their 'business' meetin'. Can't even leave it at home for a party!" She took Suzanne's elbow and steered her to a fancy upholstered settee nearby, and they both sat. Suzanne noticed how long and shapely Marguerite's legs were. In fact, her entire body could be described as long and shapely. Her voice, which was just a bit husky in a way that men would probably call sexy, seemed to fit her perfectly. The Ivy League accent, if that's what it was, was gone.

"So tell me, honey, what d'you do at Jerry's office?"

Suzanne felt uneasy telling Marguerite the truth, but she hadn't prepared a backup story, so she simply said, "I don't actually work there. I met Jerry at the Blue Note where I'm a waitress and agreed to sorta' stand in for his wife, who hurt her ankle."

Marguerite looked closely at her to assess her story. "Hmmm. So you're just his date for tonight, huh? Then he goes home to Mama?"

Suzanne thought that was none of Marguerite's business, but she was afraid if she protested and insulted Marguerite, it might be bad for Jerry's business relationship with the bank, so she decided to change the subject rather than answer.

"I guess so. And what about you? Do you work for Bill?"

Marguerite laughed, and quite loudly. "No, honey, not exactly. Let's just say we're old friends."

Hoping to keep the conversation on Marguerite instead of her, Suzanne asked, "So what do you do? Do you work here in New York?"

Marguerite looked at Suzanne as if appraising her for several moments and deciding how, or whether, to answer. Having decided, she smiled and said, "Yeah, I work in town. I work for an escort service."

Suzanne wasn't quite sure what an escort service did. For some reason, that term had not come up in any context as she was growing up or since she had come to New York, so she asked in all innocence, "Who do you escort, and where?"

Marguerite laughed again. "I escort men, honey, mostly in hotel rooms, sometimes in their apartments."

Suzanne was beginning to get the picture, but she wanted to be sure she understood. "Uh, if you don't mind my asking, what exactly do you do for them? I mean as an 'escort'?"

"Whatever they want, honey, as long as they pay well."

Then she added, emphasizing it with a wink, "Only

more often'n not, it's what I want—they only think it was their idea."

Suzanne thought about this a moment, then asked, a bit timidly, "Um, I assume you mean having sex with them?" She hoped she hadn't misinterpreted what Marguerite had meant. If she had, it could lead to dreadful embarrassment.

"Usually, yeah. But you'd be surprised at what some men want a woman to do. One time I just read a book to a guy. O'course I was naked at the time, but all he wanted was for me to read this book. Kinda weird, but it was his nickel."

"So you're a prostitute—" It was not the most tactful thing to say, but Marguerite didn't seem offended, just surprised at Suzanne's lack of understanding.

"No, no. You got a lot t' learn, kid. A prostitute's one o' them gals who hang out on street corners pickin' up tricks. You know, a whore. I'm what's called an escort, or a call girl. I got clients who make a reservation for my services, and I'm *verrry* picky about who gets a reservation. Got some of the biggest shots in town on my list. Same kinda folks as you'd expect to be invited to the governor's mansion for dinner." She laughed. "In fact, those lists might look very similar." She was obviously quite proud of her list of clients.

"Is that how you met Bill?" As soon as she said it, Suzanne realized it was not the right question to ask.

But Marguerite only laughed. "Now, honey, you know I can't tell you that. If I start blabbin' to folks who my clients are, I'll be outta work faster'n a horny john'll shoot his wad. No, Bill'n me are just old friends, like I said."

Suzanne was fascinated. Here was a woman who

made her living with her body, taking advantage of men's greatest weakness on her own terms, and who was apparently very well paid to do it. She even held a certain amount of power over them, because only she knew that their names were on her list. That definitely resonated with Suzanne.

It was not that she had never before heard of prostitutes, of course, or even call girls, even if the term "escort service" was new to her. But she had never actually met one, much less one who was willing to share with her details about her profession. And Marguerite was clearly about as high up in the profession as one can get. This was an opportunity she needed to take advantage of, if possible. She decided to give it a try. But not now, as Bill and Jerry were headed their way, apparently having exhausted whatever topic had so occupied them for the past ten minutes.

"Uh, Marguerite, d'you think we could get together sometime and talk a little more about this? I'd kinda like to learn more about what you do. No, that's not what I meant. I mean, about your…your profession." She was feeling embarrassed and not sure why. It wasn't as if she were shy about her sexuality. Maybe it was just the presence of this brash, self-assured woman.

Marguerite cocked her head and gave Suzanne an even more appraising look than she had earlier. Finally, and just as the two men reached them, she said, "No problem. You and me might just have somethin' in common." She took a business card and a pen out of her purse. She stood up and said to Bill, who was now standing next to her, "Turn around, please" at the same time gently taking his shoulders and helping him do so. He looked puzzled. When his back was turned she used it to rest the card as she wrote on it. When she was finished she handed the card to Suzanne, saying softly in her ear, "There y' go, honey. Give me a call any time. As long as I'm not tied up," and she laughed at this little joke, "we'll have a drink and get better acquainted." She turned Bill back around, took his arm, and said to him, returning to her cultured persona, "Shall we go and find ourselves a drink? It's been very nice meeting you both." She looked over at Suzanne, winked, and was gone.

It was interesting, Suzanne thought, how Marguerite could turn the sophistication, including the language she used, on and off as the occasion required. She was no doubt comfortable in many different worlds.

"You two seemed to hit it off," Jerry remarked. "Did you have a nice chat?"

"Oh, yes. Turns out we have a lot in common."

"Really? What does she do?"

Suzanne thought for a second, then answered vaguely, "Oh, some kind of service business, I think."

But to herself, she answered without hesitation, *Whatever the hell she wants*!

****

After Bill and Marguerite left them, Jerry introduced Suzanne to a few more of the guests whom he happened to know and made sure she had a chance to sample all of the sumptuous snacks laid out around the room. An hour later, they left the party and Jerry drove Suzanne home. He escorted her to the apartment house's front door, and while she dug her key out of her purse he said, "Thanks so much, Suzanne, for coming along to the party. I really appreciate it, and I hope you had a good time."

"I did. At first I was kind of thinking it'd be boring, but I actually enjoyed meeting all those people, and especially Bill's friend Marguerite. We may get together sometime."

"I'm glad. I know everyone was real impressed with you. I just hope my wife doesn't find out what a gorgeous 'employee' I took there."

Suzanne blushed slightly, something she was not accustomed to doing. She opened the door, and once she was safely inside the apartment building, Jerry turned and left, waving through the glass door.

As she walked up to her shared apartment, she considered where Jerry fit in her growing mental catalog of types of men. He had treated her absolutely properly, had not even hinted at anything out of line, yet he had made it clear he found her very attractive.

By the time she had reached her door, Suzanne had decided that although her opinion of men in general had not changed, nor her determination to make them pay for their sins, Jerry belonged with Gene Lee as exceptions that proved the rule.

His wife, like Patricia, clearly had nothing to worry about.

Chapter 18

An Unexpected Lesson

A few days after Jerry's party, Suzanne came across the card that Marguerite had given her, which had worked its way to the bottom of her purse. Although she had every intention of getting in touch with Marguerite, she had been so busy with her two jobs that she had not really looked at the card since that fascinating woman had given it to her.

Until she met Marguerite, Suzanne had not fully formulated a plan for her immediate future. She knew what she wanted, but she had not decided just how she would or could go about getting it. She knew she wanted to use her feminine assets, her sexual strength, to take advantage of—and benefit from— men's sexual weakness; but she had not actually decided she would simply sell her favors for cash. She certainly had not decided she would become a prostitute. And yet prostitution, or some form of prostitution, was really the only logical way in which she could achieve all of her goals.

Then came her brief conversation with Marguerite Matson, and everything seemed to fall into place.

To Suzanne, Marguerite represented more than just someone "in the profession." She was not a common prostitute, not a street walker, not even an ordinary call girl. She was in the big leagues, obviously making a lot of money and servicing only the best clientele. That's where Suzanne wanted to be, and she wanted to be there as soon as possible.

The front of the card had the logo of the Red Carnation Escort Service, with a toll-free telephone number and the double entendre slogan, "Pleasure to serve you." On the back was written, in a very formal hand that suggested a good education, *Marguerite Matson,* followed by a phone number with a two-one-two area code.

No time like the present, thought Suzanne as she punched the numbers into her phone.

Marguerite didn't immediately recall who Suzanne was, until Suzanne reminded her about the party.

"You gave me your phone number and said I could call and arrange for us to meet sometime. Is that still okay?"

"Sure it is, honey. I'm kinda busy the next few days, but how about next Sunday?"

"That'd be great. Where should we meet?"

"Hmm. Why don't you come over to my apartment? It'll be a nice private place to talk."

Marguerite gave Suzanne her address and they arranged for Suzanne to drop in about three o'clock in the afternoon the following Sunday.

Suzanne was excited at this chance to get better acquainted with—and get reliable information from—someone who clearly knew the ropes in the kind of profession she had decided suited her talents, and her desires, very well.

It was not the kind of information one obtained from a high school counselor, or even a friend like Patricia.

Suzanne sat down and made a list of the questions she wanted to ask.

She could hardly wait for Sunday.

****

Promptly at three o'clock in the afternoon on Sunday, Suzanne pressed the button next to the name "Marguerite Matson" on the gilded directory of a fancy Manhattan apartment building. Half a minute later a voice Suzanne recognized said, "Suzanne?"

"Yes. Can I come up?"

"'Course, honey. Third floor, three-eighteen, turn right off the elevator. Just a second and I'll let you in."

A buzzer sounded, and Suzanne pushed open the glass door and entered the inner lobby, a deeply carpeted, conservatively decorated antechamber. The elevator door opened as soon as she pushed the "up" button, and she was taken swiftly and silently up to the third floor. She turned right as instructed and almost immediately arrived at Marguerite's door, number three-eighteen. She knocked lightly.

"C'mon in," called a voice from within. Suzanne went in.

The apartment was decorated like none Suzanne had ever seen. Whereas the apartment building itself exuded conservative taste and understatement in its façade, lobby, and hallways, Marguerite's apartment made a different statement entirely. Although most of the walls were painted off-white, there were accent walls in each room in deep shades of red, blue and gray. But it was not their color that made the walls so unusual, and interesting, but the paintings that adorned them.

Everywhere Suzanne looked, and she could see not only the foyer she was in but also into the living room ahead of her, she saw examples of erotic art. Some were clearly older works by European masters, in a style such as Suzanne had seen in museums on school field trips, except their subject matter was blatantly sexual. In one, for example, a lady dressed in fine silk and crinolines with a bouffant hair-do was bending over, exposing a bare bottom, and being spanked by a "gentleman" dressed in dark blue silk tailcoat, waistcoat, and breeches. And cheek-by-jowl with that painting was a smaller, cruder rendition of a pose from the Kama Sutra, examples of which Suzanne had seen when a girlfriend brought the book to school disguised in the jacket cover of a perfectly respectable math book. Other pictures were of various genres and eras, but the general subject matter was uniform.

Suzanne suddenly noticed that Marguerite was standing a few feet away and watching as she took in the apartment's décor. And she was smiling very broadly.

"Whattaya think, honey? Like the artwork?"

"It's…it's…uh, unusual."

Marguerite laughed loudly. She was wearing black short-shorts and a yellow halter top with a bare midriff, looking very relaxed but somehow very sexy. She, like Suzanne, was the kind of woman who sent out sexual vibrations no matter how she dressed.

"Yeah, it sure is that, I guess, though it's been described a lot more, shall we say, colorfully. Anyhow, c'mon into the living room and set yourself down. I'll get us a couple of drinks. Wine, liquor, or beer?"

"A beer'll be just fine, thanks."

"Comin' up. Make yourself t'home."

Suzanne entered the living room and sat down on a sofa covered in soft gray velvet. It was the kind one could sink into and easily fall asleep. She looked around and saw more examples of erotic art, some more explicit than others, from the past and present. *She has a regular museum of this stuff,* Suzanne thought. Some of the artwork she liked, and some she could live without—and might have trouble living with—just as anyone might react to a particular work of art. Her opinion was not, however, based on the subject matter, which she found at least a bit arousing. Although she had never cared much for the examples of graphic pornography—or what she would call "dirty pictures"—she had occasionally come across, these paintings didn't seem pornographic at all, just very graphic. And stimulating.

Marguerite emerged from the kitchen with two open bottles of beer and a bowl of pretzels. She put them down on the coffee table in front of Suzanne and took a seat next to her.

"So what would you like to talk about? You said you had some questions. 'Bout what-all I do."

"Yes, I did want to ask you about that. I hope you don't mind talking about it with me."

Marguerite laughed. "Look, honey, if I was ashamed of what I did, or afraid to talk about it to a friend, I'd stop doin' it." Her expression became more serious. "I mean, no one wants to be spendin' all their time doin' something they can't talk about." Then she smiled again and added, "Unless maybe if they're a secret agent or something."

Suzanne smiled at the joke, cleared her throat, and turned to face Marguerite. She had looked over her list of questions many times in the past few days, and now they just came pouring out.

"Okay, here's what I want to know. What does

someone like you working for an 'escort service' actually do? That is, do you sit around waiting for some guy to call you and then meet them somewhere? Where do you go on a...on an assignment? Do you have dinner or something, or go right to his apartment? Do you have sex with him right away and then leave? Or stay overnight? Does he pay you in advance? Do you feel safe doing that? What if he turns out to be some kind of weirdo and attacks you or something?" Nearly out of breath, if not out of questions, Suzanne stopped talking.

Marguerite said nothing but looked at Suzanne in amusement, or so Suzanne interpreted the expression.

After a minute, Marguerite laughed. "Honey, you've got more questions than a dog's got fleas. D'you mind if I ask why you want to know all this? I mean, I don't mind tellin' you, and I will. Like I said, I'm not ashamed of what I do, and in fact it's damned interesting work. But I'd like to know if your interest is what you'd call purely academic, or more...more practical, if you know what I mean."

Suzanne now had to consider how much she wanted to tell this woman, whom, after all, she still hardly knew. *But what the hell,* she decided, *what's the harm in her knowing everything about me?*

So in as brief a synopsis as she could manage, Suzanne told Marguerite about her childhood, her experiences with her father and at school, how she felt about men in general—conceding there were always exceptions like Jerry—and her desire to find a profession that both took advantage of her God-given physical attributes and satisfied her determination to redress her personal grievances by taking advantage of men's psychological and emotional weaknesses. Marguerite's profession, or at least that part of the "oldest profession" in which Marguerite worked, seemed to fill the bill nicely, especially since she, apparently like Marguerite, had always enjoyed the physical side of sex. She then waited tensely to see if Marguerite would still be willing to answer her questions.

Marguerite, who was now standing in front of the sofa and looking down at Suzanne, seemed to be studying her intently, perhaps to assess how seriously to take what Suzanne had told her. Her expression was sober, business-like.

Finally she nodded slowly. "Okay, honey, let's see what you've got."

Suzanne wasn't quite sure what Marguerite meant by "seeing what she'd got," but she soon found out.

"Take off those clothes and let's see what you look like. From here it looks like you've got all the right dimensions, but it's what's underneath that counts, 'cause that's what most men are payin' for."

Suzanne was somewhat taken aback by this request and didn't immediately know how to respond.

"You want me to—yeah, okay, I guess. Where should I…" She looked around for a place to undress.

"Right here, honey. If you're too shy to undress in front of someone you hardly know—and you know me a whole lot better than you'll know some john you've never met—you should forget about doin' what I do right now."

Suzanne could see the logic in that, even if Marguerite was a woman, which should have made it easier, not harder. Having nothing to lose and a lot to gain, she began to undress. As she did so, Marguerite watched her closely, perhaps looking for signs of shyness or reluctance, perhaps just enjoying the show.

Suzanne was wearing a fairly conservative outfit, having thought of this get-together as something of a business meeting. She had put on a pair of dark blue slacks and a red cotton blouse with blue embroidery that matched the color of the slacks. With her extra earnings at the club she had been able to expand her wardrobe considerably and now had several choices of "looks." Blue socks and black casual shoes finished off the outfit.

She began by kicking off her shoes and removing her socks. She then unbuttoned her slacks and let them fall to her ankles, then stepped out of them, picked them up, folded them and laid them on the arm of the sofa. This revealed a sexy, frilly thong that mostly covered her genital area and about half her buttocks. Next, she unbuttoned her blouse and slipped out of it, at which point her perfectly shaped breasts made their first appearance, restrained by a lacey black bra that supported them without adding any unneeded shape. Having laid the blouse on top of the slacks, she paused.

Marguerite was still watching intently as Suzanne posed in front of her, wearing only her bra and thong.

"Continue," she said when Suzanne appeared uncertain whether to do so.

Suzanne continued.

"Oh, and while you're at it," Marguerite added, "I assume you ain't got any kind of STDs or other nasty stuff goin'?"

Suzanne thought this a strange question to ask under the circumstances, but answered truthfully, "No, of course not."

"Just askin'," Marguerite said. "Can't be too careful these days."

When she was completely naked, Suzanne stood still as Marguerite continued to look her over, as if she were appraising a horse she intended to buy. But instead of opening Suzanne's mouth and examining her teeth, she moved closer and laid a hand on her breast. *Maybe,* thought Suzanne, *she's making sure they're real.* There was no question such perfectly shaped breasts raised a legitimate suspicion of artificial enhancement. At least on this score, Suzanne knew she had nothing to worry about.

Marguerite then ran her hand over the front of Suzanne's body, feeling the curves and textures, like a sculptor checking to be sure she has left no rough spots on the perfect surface of alabaster or marble.

Apparently satisfied with her inspection thus far, Marguerite stepped around Suzanne to her back and ran her other hand down Suzanne's shoulders and spine and then over her buttocks, stopping there to give them just a slight squeeze. This was clearly not some test for enhancement so much as a tactile sign of her appreciation for the near-perfect sculpture that was Suzanne's body.

"Very nice," Marguerite said slowly. "And no tats to mess up that beautiful skin. Very nice indeed. Honey, you got what it takes, as the song says. Now what can you do with it?"

Suzanne again was uncertain what Marguerite meant or what she was expected to do, as Marguerite could plainly see. She said, "Here, let me show you, honey," and she gently guided Suzanne back onto the sofa. Marguerite bent down in front of her, saying, "Honey, you never know who's going to want your services, and just occasionally it's another woman.

Here's what you can do then."

What followed was a surprising and totally unexpected lesson in girl-on-girl sex. At first, Suzanne didn't know how to react to Marguerite's unexpected attentions, and it was obvious both to her and to Marguerite that she was uncomfortable. No woman—or girl, for that matter—had ever come on to her, certainly none had ever gone down on her. For that matter, she had never had sex with a black person of any stripe or gender. She had absolutely no lesbian inclinations, and she had never associated with anyone who purported to be one. Her immediate reaction was therefore somewhat guarded, and her body tensed at this unwelcome and unexpected invasion of her most intimate regions. But when she realized that she had nothing to fear, and in fact everything to gain, by simply lying back and letting Marguerite explore, she began to relax and to enjoy sensations that she had never before experienced.

This was different. Very different.

It didn't take long for Marguerite, clearly using techniques she had long practiced, to bring Suzanne to sexual arousal and then a satisfying climax, just as satisfying as if Marguerite were a man—a very skillful and experienced man.

Then Marguerite did another unexpected thing. She stood up and quickly but expertly slipped out of her minimal wardrobe. She was wearing nothing underneath except a black string thong that covered little enough to be considered merely decorative.

Seeing this, it suddenly occurred to Suzanne that, except perhaps in pictures of African tribes in National Geographic, she had never really seen a black woman naked, certainly not up close and in the flesh. It was like walking in a garden and unexpectedly coming upon a black rose: beautiful, unusual, and exotic.

It also passed through Suzanne's mind to wonder whether this was how Marguerite always dressed around the house, or if she had dressed this way because she had planned to give Suzanne a sexual baptism to test her suitability as a call girl.

These thoughts quickly left Suzanne's head again as Marguerite changed positions with her and said softly, "Your turn, honey." This time at least Suzanne knew exactly what to do. Her first lesson in lesbian-style lovemaking having occurred such a short time before, and with her second already underway, Suzanne was determined to pass her first exam in escort proficiency with flying colors.

When at last both women lay exhausted on the sofa, they slowly disentangled themselves from their awkward positions and sat up together.

"Well, honey, if you can do a man the way you just did me, you shouldn't have no trouble at all in our profession."

"I've really never done—never been in that position before. With a woman, I mean."

"I gathered that. But you are one quick learner."

"Does that mean I passed the test?" Suzanne asked hopefully.

"Honey, you not only passed, you went right to—if you'll pardon the pun—the head of the class. With a gorgeous body like yours, an obvious talent, and me to show you the ropes, you're a natural. Any time you want to join our little band of merry makers, I'll be happy to vouch for you."

As the two women got up and re-dressed, Suzanne

said, "I really would like to give it a try. But I'm afraid to just quit my current jobs, which I like and which give me a decent income, in case…you know…it doesn't work out for some reason."

"That's okay, honey. I'm sure you can sort of come in on a part-time basis. Maybe just on the weekends, at first. If everything works out, you can drop one of your other jobs, or both. Take it slow-like."

"I'd like to do that," Suzanne said. "When do you think I can start?"

"Well, I gotta talk with the boss and get him to go along with the idea, but like I said, I don't think it'll be a problem. Just leave it to me. I'll give you a call after I've had a chance to set things up."

Suzanne and Marguerite sat and talked a while longer, but not about sex. There would be time for "business" later, Marguerite said. At present she was more interested in learning more about Suzanne the woman, pressing her for more details about the life she left in California and her new life in New York. Suzanne found Marguerite to be a good listener, who also was free with details about her own background.

After about half an hour, Marguerite rose and said she had to get ready for an "important client" that evening.

Suzanne thanked her and walked toward the door, her body still tingling from the workout it had received. Marguerite followed, and before ushering her out, she gave Suzanne's derriere a firm pat and a gentle squeeze.

"And honey, any time you want t' come by for another little lesson, just let me know. We all gotta keep our game sharp, y'know."

If Suzanne hadn't known before, she definitely knew now.

Chapter 19

Ron

A week after her encounter with Marguerite, Suzanne had not yet heard back from her. She had thought, after she left Marguerite's apartment, things had gone very well, if in an unexpected direction. But now she was beginning to wonder whether, on reflection, Marguerite had decided she might not fit in. Or maybe she had not shown enough proficiency, or enthusiasm. Should she call Marguerite? Should she ask for another "interview"?

She considered confiding in Patricia—straight-laced Georgina was out of the question—but she was unsure how her questions would be received. For that matter, she was unsure what Patricia would say about the whole idea of joining the escort service. Then, on second thought, she decided she was pretty certain what Patricia would say, and it would not be pretty. Patricia was far from prudish or judgmental, and she seemed to accept Suzanne for who she was, but she probably would draw the line at condoning her becoming, in effect, a prostitute, no matter what the reason or rationale. Still, she needed to talk to someone.

To Suzanne, having sex with men—she was still a little uncertain about women—for pay was not a question of morality. For her it fulfilled needs, one financial and one emotional. It was, she rationalized, her body, and what she did with it should be her decision. As for the men, if they were cheating on their wives or otherwise acting immorally, that was a matter for their conscience, not hers. For all she cared, they could all rot in Hell.

These were the thoughts that were swirling through Suzanne's head and keeping her awake at night when the matter finally resolved itself. It was a Tuesday and she was hurrying out the door, late for work. A muffled jingle from her purse brought her to a momentary stop. She fished out her cellphone and glanced at it to see who was calling at such an inconvenient time. When she saw it was Marguerite, she stepped back into the apartment, closed the door, and sat down as she touched the button to accept the call.

"Marguerite?"

"That you, honey? Did I catch you at a good time?"

Suzanne started to say "Not really," but quickly changed it to "Not at all. It's good to hear from you. I was kinda wondering—"

"Yeah, it took me a while to get to talk to the boss. He was outta town for a week, then stuff came up— anyway, I finally caught up to him."

Suzanne waited for Marguerite to continue, not wanting to come right out and ask what she had said to "the boss" and what he had replied.

"Anyhow, I told him I'd met this gorgeous blonde who, I had reason to believe, would be a real asset to his business."

Suzanne breathed a sigh of relief. At least she got a good recommendation.

Marguerite's tone changed a bit when she added, "He didn't ask me how I knew this, and of course I didn't tell him 'bout our little session on the sofa."

Another tinge of relief, although Suzanne wasn't quite sure why. Would the boss object to Marguerite's auditioning the prospects?

Marguerite was taking too long to get to the important part, so Suzanne spoke up: "And what did he say?"

"No problem. He knows I've got good taste. He said to bring you by so he can see for himself."

Suzanne relaxed for the first time since answering the phone. She was elated.

She was going to get her audition for the major league team.

Although she was pleased that she would be getting her chance, Suzanne was unsure just what she would be expected to do to qualify for a position such as Marguerite's. She assumed she would be expected to demonstrate, in some way, that she was "equipped" for the job and had the necessary experience and talent. But just how would that be carried out? Would she be asked to perform a sex act right then and there? Or would she be given some assignment and tested out "on the job"? Either way, it would be a strange and possibly scary situation. But this was the kind of job she wanted, so she would just have to accept whatever was necessary to get it.

Meanwhile, she tried not to think too much about it.

****

The interview occurred about a week later, on a Wednesday. "The boss" turned out to be named Ron Gillette. Gillette's office was in a Manhattan skyscraper, and when Suzanne met Marguerite there late on a Wednesday afternoon, she first thought she must have come to the wrong place. She wasn't sure what she had expected, but a sedate office suite that could as easily have been a lawyer's or accountant's office was not it. The wood paneling was dark, the artwork was understated, and the secretary/receptionist was as prim and proper as a librarian.

Well, I guess I shouldn't have expected red drapes and pornographic pictures, Suzanne thought to herself. *But still...*

Marguerite told Suzanne to wait while she spoke with Gillette. She sashayed past the secretary, who smiled and nodded, and waltzed into the boss' office without even knocking. No, it was definitely not an accountant's office.

A few minutes later she emerged, laughing at whatever had transpired within, and told Suzanne to "go on in." She gave her a little pat on the backside and took a seat on a nearby settee.

Suzanne hadn't been particularly nervous about the interview until now. In truth, she had tried not to think about it, and she had mostly succeeded. But as she approached Gillette's door and knocked softly—she certainly couldn't take the liberties Marguerite had—she almost lost her nerve. When she heard "Come in" from within, she took a deep breath, turned the knob, and stepped into the office.

The walls of Gillette's office were covered in the same dark wood paneling as the reception area. There was no artwork at all, other than a very interesting, very suggestive, bronze sculpture on a wooden pedestal in one corner. Two large windows on the far wall were covered by open wood-slat blinds. There was a large, leather-covered sofa against one wall, and Suzanne wondered whether it was the escort agency equivalent of a Hollywood casting couch.

Ron Gillette sat behind a fancy walnut desk, several neat stacks of papers in front of him. He was leaning back in his multi-adjustable executive chair, hands folded, watching Suzanne intently as she approached the desk.

Gillette was a man of about fifty, clean-shaven with wavy black hair combed neatly back. He was broad-shouldered and tall, at least judging by his appearance seated. He was wearing a lightweight gray suit and a white dress shirt and tie, although the suit coat was open, the tie loosened, and the shirt collar unbuttoned. The expression on his face was friendly, but Suzanne thought he looked a little like a fox welcoming a stray chicken into his parlor.

In a way, he was.

Suzanne reached the front of Gillette's desk, where there were two armless chairs, but he didn't ask her to be seated. He said, glancing at a sheet of paper on his desk, "Miss…Dahlstrom?"

"Yes."

"Ron Gillette. Marguerite tells me you want to join our company. Marguerite is one of our best employees, and her recommendation goes a long way with me. Nevertheless, I have to satisfy myself that you would meet the high standards that we set for ourselves. I take it you're well aware of what we do, the services we provide?"

"Yes, Marguerite told me about it."

"And that we have a very exclusive clientele."

"Yes." So far this could easily have been an interview for a position as receptionist or secretary in any of a thousand companies.

"And you think you're cut out to perform those services for us?"

"Yes, I think so. That is, I'm sure I can, and I can learn what I don't already know."

"Hmm. What do you already know?"

Suzanne didn't know how to answer that question, but it immediately became apparent that she was not expected to. At least not in so many words.

Gillette stood up, revealing that he was indeed tall, over six feet, and quite well built. His shoulders were broad and his waist slim. He walked around the desk, pushing a button on the edge of the desk that, to Suzanne's surprise, caused the blinds to close. And then, much like Marguerite in her apartment, he said to Suzanne, "So show me what you've got."

This time Suzanne did not ask whether he meant right then and there. He obviously did.

It suddenly struck Suzanne as ironic that, in order to get the job as secretary at Gene Lee's company, she had had to come on to—in fact, almost attacked—the interviewer. Now she was in the opposite position, with the interviewer taking the initiative, in the position of power. The sex act itself was not a problem—it was part of the job she was seeking, after all—but her position of vulnerability was. While this was contrary to her desire to always be in control of her body and her sexual gifts, she realized it was necessary to make compromises in order to achieve more important goals. This would be another step toward greater sexual freedom, freedom from the nightmare of her childhood.

So Suzanne took off her coat and laid it on one of the chairs. She undressed slowly, not exactly a striptease, but in what she hoped was a "sexy" manner.

"Very nice," Ron said when she had shed her last item of lingerie. "Marguerite said you were as pretty as anyone she'd ever met, and I see what she meant."

Ron then unzipped his fly and said, in a very friendly manner, "So pretend I'm a client."

One of the reasons Suzanne had tried not to think too much about this interview in advance was that she was anticipating just this kind of scenario: Performing under pressure.

Suzanne could only take a deep breath, tell herself this was what she had wanted so badly to do, and get it over with.

The rest of the proceedings, which consisted of pretty straightforward oral sex, took perhaps ten minutes, and when it was over, Suzanne looked intently at Ron's face and body language to see if she had passed the test.

Ron smiled and said only, "Be here tomorrow at five, and we'll continue the interview."

****

Marguerite was not in the outer office, nor was the receptionist, when Suzanne left Gillette's office. This she had expected, as Marguerite had told her she had a date that night—or maybe it was an assignment, she didn't specify—and would have to leave by five p.m. Suzanne looked at her watch, and it was five-oh-five. How long had she been in there with Gillette? Longer than she had thought.

She tried to get hold of Marguerite in the evening, but there was no answer on her home or cell phone. Obviously, she was tied up with her date, figuratively and perhaps also literally. Suzanne wanted to ask her what it might mean that Gillette wanted to "continue the interview" after closing time tomorrow. Was he just taking advantage of her? Or was this a legitimate attempt to assure himself that his posh clientele would be well taken care of by the newbie?

She would find out soon.

****

Suzanne arranged to come to work early the next day so she could leave in time to be at Gillette's office at five. She just made it in time, and she found him waiting with the door ajar. She knocked and entered.

This time Gillette was sitting on the big sofa she had seen the previous day. He was holding a folder and had his legs crossed—"male style," left ankle resting on the right knee. His jacket and tie were missing and his sleeves were partially rolled up. He was smiling.

"Come on in, Suzanne," he said as she peered around the door. He patted the seat cushion beside him and said, "Have a seat. We'll go over a few important details."

Suzanne smiled and walked over to the sofa. She noticed that the blinds had already been drawn, the only light being provided by a floor lamp in the corner and a small desk lamp. She sat, crossed her legs—"female style," right knee over left knee, keeping the features beneath her short skirt well hidden— and waited.

Gillette smiled. "I need to ask you a few questions. Just to be sure you're right for us, and we're right for you, if you understand."

Suzanne nodded that she understood.

"Good. Now, as an escort service, our clients will call us and request an escort. They'll tell us what type of services they need, and we'll try to match one of our employees to that service, and that client."

"Do you check the clients out before you send someone to them?" Suzanne asked.

"Oh, yes. We generally ask several questions intended to verify that the client is…is appropriate for the services in question. Sometimes we then do a little checking on the internet to be sure we have accurate information. If we're not sure, we may ask them to come into the office here to make an appointment."

Suzanne was impressed. "Do all the…uh…businesses like yours go to so much trouble?"

Gillette smiled. "I doubt it. But we have a very good reputation and a very exclusive clientele, and we can't afford to have any…any incidents. You understand."

"Oh, yes."

"Good. Anyway, most of our clients, though not all, are looking for some kind of intimate companionship. They're visiting from out of town, or they're local but just in need of someone to spend an evening, or the night, with."

"Sure."

"As you probably can guess, or Marguerite may have told you, some of the requests we receive, or our girls receive when they arrive, can get pretty, well, bizarre. As long as it's not actually dangerous, you're expected to go along with whatever the client wants."

Suzanne nodded. She wasn't thrilled with the idea, but she knew it was part of the job she was seeking. "What if…you know…it does get dangerous once a girl's there? I mean, I don't know much self-defense stuff, and—"

"Good question. Whenever you're sent out to a client we don't have complete confidence in, you'll go out with a male driver—an escort for an escort, you might say—who'll check out the situation and make sure it looks okay. If it gets really dicey, you'll have a device to call us. You just press it and it brings your driver back for you—you don't have to actually talk to him. That's gotten a few of our girls out of tricky situations. But the bottom line is, we can only do so much. We can't guarantee your safety in this business. Call it an occupational hazard."

"Okay, I understand. But can a girl refuse a job if she knows it's for something she…she doesn't want to do?"

"To some extent, yes. For example, if you're not into bondage, we'll try not to send you out to a client looking for it. Does that answer your question?"

Suzanne nodded.

"Good. Any other questions?"

Suzanne had a few, mostly related to payment arrangements, hours, and the like. She would be permitted to choose her hours of availability, and the financial side was more than adequate, especially combined with the possibility of substantial tips or expensive presents from particularly satisfied customers.

"Now let me ask you some things," Gillette continued. "First, just why do you want to get into this business? I understand you have a good job, or is it two? This one carries lots of risks, physical ones like we just talked about, but also legal and moral risks. The cops generally leave us alone, as long as we keep ourselves low-key and out of trouble. But your friends might not understand, and your family almost certainly won't."

"I know, and I've thought about it, and I still want the job. I guess I enjoy having sex with guys, and I don't mind getting paid to do it. I'll try to avoid letting my friends know about it, but if they do and they don't like it, well, I can handle that, I think."

"And your family?"

"It's only my mom, and she lives in LA. I'd hate it if she found out, but there's no reason she should."

Suzanne didn't mention, of course, the more complex motivation behind her choice of occupation. All those men, all needing something she had and willing to pay dearly to get it. All potentially at her mercy...

"So how much real experience have you had? I don't mean have you slept with a bunch of men—I assume you have—but with really different stuff? You know, positions, that sort of thing."

Suzanne had thought this might be a problem, but she answered truthfully. "I guess most of what I've done has been pretty ordinary. But I'm a fast learner."

"Hmm. I don't doubt it. I was pretty impressed with yesterday's little test. Let's see what else you can do."

He stood up and helped Suzanne to her feet. She was still wearing a light jacket, which Gillette helped her remove. Underneath she wore a tight sweater that fully emphasized her breasts. Her skirt was short and loose. Gillette reached over and lifted the sweater over Suzanne's head, laying it and her jacket on the broad arm on the end of the sofa. He unzipped her skirt, letting it fall to the floor. She was wearing only a bright red thong underneath, and he helped her step out of it.

Gillette removed his own clothing quickly and laid them with Suzanne's on the sofa's arm. He then placed his hand on her shoulder and lowered her onto the sofa. Suzanne had a pretty good idea this next test would involve more than oral sex.

She was right.

The intercourse was fairly conventional, although Ron was clearly accomplished at the fine nuances of the various positions he included in the curriculum. When at last he reached what seemed to be a very satisfying—and explosive— conclusion, he rose and helped Suzanne off the sofa.

No words were spoken as the boss of Red Carnation Escort Service and the new recruit dressed. The silence continued as Gillette walked back to his desk and sat behind it, motioning Suzanne to take a seat in front, which she did.

When both were seated, Gillette took a minute to gather himself, then he smiled. "So, do you still want the job?"

"Yes," she said nervously, "I think I can handle it okay."

Gillette smiled even more broadly. "So do I. In fact, I think you'll fit in quite nicely." After a second he laughed. "Sorry, no pun intended."

That broke the tension for Suzanne. She too laughed, and after a brief discussion of what papers she had to fill out—a lot of them—and when she could have her first client—the following Saturday would be fine— Suzanne left the office and headed home. She walked a bit gingerly, as might be expected given the workout her insides had taken, but she was thrilled.

She and Marguerite were now colleagues. She was only twenty-one and was already in the "big time," where she would be earning more money than she ever had, money to spend on herself and to send home to Mary Sue. And she would be earning it satisfyingly at the expense of that evil trait in men that had once ruined her childhood and indeed threatened her very life.

She had what they wanted, what they needed, and now she would be in a position to make them pay dearly for it.

She had once heard an expression that seemed in a way to fit how she now felt: When someone does you wrong, "don't get mad, get even."

Yes, she would get even, and along the way she would, she hoped, get rich and have some interesting experiences.

She couldn't know then just how right she was.

****

Suzanne phoned Marguerite when she returned home and told her she had the job.

"That's great, girl! I knew you would. You and I need to celebrate. And I mean sell-a-BRATE! You had dinner yet?"

"No. I hadn't even thought about it."

"Good. Let's you an' me hit one of them fancy-shmancy places. How about the Twenty-One Club, over on West Fifty-Second? Ever been there?"

"No, I haven't been anywhere fancier than Denny's since I've been here."

"Well, you'll like this place. Like an old-time speakeasy, which I think it once was. Kinda appropriate for what we're celebrating, huh?"

Suzanne laughed. "Yes, I think so. Sounds great. Should I meet you there?"

"Hell no. I'll get a cab and pick you up. We're doin' this in style." The last word was drawn out to add extra emphasis.

"Okay, if you say so. What should I wear?"

"Somethin' sexy. You never know who you might meet at one of these places. Hell, look where you met me!" Marguerite laughed loudly, and Suzanne joined in. "Be ready in a half hour," Marguerite concluded, and hung up.

The 21 Club turned out to be just as Marguerite had said, and the two women had an excellent dinner—complete with champagne—while Suzanne related, more or less, how the "interview" had gone.

"Worked you over pretty good, did he?" Marguerite asked.

"Yeah, I guess so. But I expect that'll be part of the job. I mean, I imagine some clients are more...more aggressive than others."

Marguerite laughed. "Yeah, or more kinky, or sometimes more abusive." She suddenly got serious. "You gotta watch out for the odd ones. The agency does a pretty good job of screening out the real nut cases, but occasionally one slips through. And it can be a fine line between kinky sex and plain old assault. That's why we're always a quick message away from help."

"Have you ever had to call for help?"

"Oh, yeah, maybe once a year or so. Mostly I can take care of myself. I took self-defense classes when I got into this gig, and I can handle almost anyone, 'cept maybe if they have a weapon. Fortunately, that hasn't happened yet."

Suzanne thought about this for a minute. "Do you think I should take one of those classes?"

"Absolutely. You never know when you might need it, not just 'on the job,' but just walkin' down the street. There's a good class over at the Y, in the evening."

"Good. I'll sign up for it. Any other suggestions?"

"Just keep your wits about you. Remember that the client is payin' for service, but you're still in charge. If he wants you to do something you don't want to, like it's dangerous or against the law—I once had a guy ask me to hide a wad of money he was carryin', probably stolen—you just say no. Even if you have to give him a refund." She laughed and continued in an exaggerated mock-Black accent, "But, honey, I ain't never given nobody no refund, nohow. Uhh uh."

With that she poured more champagne, and, with a click of glasses they toasted Suzanne's new job and Marguerite's new colleague.

Chapter 20

Learning the Ropes

Now Suzanne had three jobs—one full-time as a secretary and two part-time, as a cocktail waitress and as an "escort," or to put it more plainly, a "call girl." She had taken the waitress job only for extra money and to meet people who might advance her toward her ultimate goal. Now it had done just that and could be left behind, so she gave her notice and soon was again down to two jobs.

Earl Ballard at the Blue Note was not pleased to lose Suzanne, who had quickly become one of the club's most popular attractions, and he told her she was welcome to return any time. Suzanne was glad to hear that, because this new adventure of hers was, to some extent, a step into the unknown. Despite her satisfaction at having this opportunity and her conviction that it was just what she was looking for, she was far from certain how it would ultimately work out.

For one thing, Suzanne had not, in effect, worked her way up the ranks in the business of providing sexual favors to an exclusive clientele. When it came to prostitution—which, after all, it still was—she was a newbie. It was one thing to trade her favors for small benefits, or even a job offer, always to her advantage and at her instigation, with partners of her choice. It might turn out to be quite another to offer those favors to the highest bidder, with the buyer an unknown quantity and dictating the nature of the payoff. As she remarked to Marguerite in a candid moment, "I'm pretty sure my body can handle it, at least from the neck down. I'm less sure my head can."

****

Unlike when she had taken the cocktail waitress position, this time she didn't wish to advertise the nature of her second job, so she told everyone that she was still working at the Blue Note, but her hours had changed and were now quite variable. Since no one she knew, at least no one who counted, ever went to the Blue Note, she was confident her ruse was not likely to be discovered.

Ron Gillette had told Suzanne before she left his office that she would have "a few things to learn" before she was ready to take on their most important clients, and that he would ask Marguerite to act as mentor and "show you the ropes." That sounded good to Suzanne, who was sure there was quite a bit she could learn from her new friend.

Suzanne phoned Marguerite the next day and asked when they could get together for some instruction. Marguerite consulted her schedule and didn't find a lot of time available, at least not in the evenings, and Suzanne worked all day.

"That's okay, honey," Marguerite assured her. "I'll just tell the boss I need some time off to get you up to speed. Tell you what. C'mon over here for dinner tomorrow about six, and we'll spend the evening goin' over a few tricks o' the trade."

****

The next evening Suzanne rang the buzzer for

Marguerite's apartment at six-oh-two. She was a little nervous, not because she expected anything untoward to happen, but just because she really didn't know what to expect.

Marguerite appeared at the door wearing bright purple, tight-fitting capris with a matching top that left several inches of bare midriff. She smiled broadly and said, "C'mon in! Dinner's almost ready."

Suzanne entered what was becoming a familiar scene, having visited Marguerite there several times since that first, unexpectedly carnal, encounter. She was no longer surprised at the art work or other décor, which now she hardly noticed. Marguerite took Suzanne's coat, put an arm around her, and ushered her into the kitchen. Something aromatic and delicious was simmering on the stove, and against one wall a small table was set with two brightly-colored placemats and silverware.

"Sit yourself down, honey," Marguerite said, "while I finish the cookin'."

Suzanne did as she was told. The cozy atmosphere, delightful aromas, and generally warm ambience helped Suzanne to relax, so that within minutes any nervousness she had been experiencing was gone. Marguerite seemed to have a way of putting her at ease. She wondered whether Marguerite had the same effect on everyone, especially her clients.

The two women exchanged small talk while Marguerite stirred and tasted and finally served up what turned out to be a spicy, creole-inspired pasta dish. During dinner the conversation turned to cooking, which Marguerite apparently loved to do, and where she had learned to do it so well.

"My mama was a great cook," Marguerite said, "and

I guess that's why I developed an interest in it. But I didn't get really good at it until I met one of the chefs at a fancy restaurant uptown."

"Was he one of your clients?" Suzanne asked. "I mean, is that how you met him?"

"Actually, he was. We hit it off and he offered to come by and give me some cooking lessons, in exchange for another kind of lessons, if you know what I mean." She laughed and winked at Suzanne.

"Is that usual? I mean, becoming friends with a client outside of…of…well, business?"

"Not really. And I'm sure the boss would frown on it, for lots of reasons, including the company not gettin' any of the proceeds of those cooking lessons."

"So you just don't mention it to them, I assume."

"Hell no! It's none o' their business what I do on my own time."

They finished eating and together cleared the dishes and put them into the dishwasher. As they were drying their hands, Suzanne said, "I guess this evening's kinda company business, isn't it? Mr. Gillette wanted me to learn some of the ropes before I start. Do you know what he was referring to?"

"Yeah, he gave me kind of an idea. Let's go in here."

She led Suzanne into the living room and they both sat on the sofa.

"Want a drink while we talk?"

"No thanks. So what do we talk about?"

"Well, to begin with, he wants you to be sure to know the lingo, so you won't embarrass yourself—and also the agency— if a client asks for something and you don't know what it is. It'd be sorta like you ask a barista at a cafe for a 'vente Americano half-caf wet,' and she ain't got a clue what you're talkin' about. Not good for business."

"I guess not."

"So let's go over some of the things a client might ask for, or expect."

Marguerite proceeded to quiz Suzanne on the terminology of her new profession, such as "owo"—oral without protection.

"Do I have to do that—without a condom, I mean?" Suzanne asked.

"You'll make a lot more money if you do," Marguerite said. "Your choice. Most of the gals just do it."

"Do you?"

Marguerite hesitated before answering. "Only in what you'd call special circumstances. Let's put it this way: It's takin' a chance, but it depends on the money and the client. The businessman from Podunk who's gettin' laid for pay for the first time ain't likely to cause no problems—"

"And do you also sometimes have intercourse without a condom?"

Marguerite looked horrified. "Hell, no! That's where I draw the line, no matter who the client is. Well, almost, anyway. It's a sure way to a short career and a long recovery. I'm not sayin' some gals don't do it, 'cause they sure do. It's called goin' 'bareback,' among other things. But then, some people jump off cliffs for kicks, or snort coke. Like to live dangerously. While they live, that is, which usually ain't all that long. No, ma'am, with very few exceptions, if a client don't wanna wear a condom, he's stayin' outside this lady's body."

"That works for me," Suzanne said. "Anything

else?"

"Hmm. Let's see. Oh, yeah, how about if a client wants an 'a-level'?"

Suzanne thought about that, then said slowly, "I hope it doesn't mean what I think it does—anal sex?"

Marguerite clapped her hands. "Right the first time."

Suzanne cringed. "Do we have to do that? I've always avoided it."

"No, honey, you don't have to do anythin' at all. Like I said, the more you do, the more money you can make. The more bizarre the request, the more you can ask for doin' it. But if you refuse too many things, you won't last long in this business. Here, let me tell you what my approach is. If it's basic sex, even in some weird position, of course I'll do it. If it's strange or disgusting but safe, like involving costumes or whipped cream, I'll do it. But if it's simple but dangerous, like BDSM— you know what that is, right?"

"Yeah, isn't it bondage and stuff?"

"Yeah. Sado-masochism. I ain't lettin' some nut tie me up and start whippin' my butt, no matter how much he's willin' to pay. And if it's somewhere in between gettin' beat and just gettin' laid, I sorta play it by ear, takin' into account who the client is, how much money's involved, that sort of thing."

They talked for a little while longer, Marguerite explaining some further terminology, Suzanne asking more questions. When the subject was exhausted for the present, Marguerite suggested they adjourn to the bedroom for what she called "a little demonstration."

The demonstration turned out to be a lesson in the use of sex toys, which apparently came in almost as great an array of shapes, sizes, and colors as children's toys.

Marguerite demonstrated a few of them on Suzanne, just teasing her with some of the sensations they could produce.

Marguerite also explained that clients who "lasted longer" were more satisfied clients than those for whom the expensive experience covered only a few minutes. "So if we can help them last a little longer, it's all good."

"And how do we do that?"

"Well, one little trick is you apply pressure right here, like this," and she demonstrated on a dildo, "and it sorta calms things down for a while."

"Really! Wish I'd known that a long time ago."

"That is, of course, unless it's one of them real unpleasant types, and then the quicker it's over the better, an' don't come back."

"Unpleasant how?"

"Oh, lots of ways. Body odor, rough handling, racist remarks, you name it. Fortunately, it don't happen often. Next thing. Remember, we're always tryin' to make the clients happy, 'cause happy clients are generous clients, not to mention repeat business. And what would you say makes a guy happiest in bed?"

"Like you just said, the session not ending too soon, I guess."

"Well, yeah, but next to that."

Suzanne thought for a minute, then shook her head. "Okay, what?"

"Next best thing to him comin' at the right time is you comin' at all. Makes a guy feel real macho, like he's God's gift to women."

"Do you usually come when you have sex with a client?"

Marguerite laughed. "Hell no! This is work, honey,

not pleasure."

"I thought you enjoyed what you do?"

"Oh, I do, I do. And sometimes I really get into it and come right along with the client. But most of the clients just don't have what it takes to give a lady an orgasm. They're in a hurry, or they're clumsy, or nervous, or whatever. Anyway, they're real disappointed if it seems like they're the only one havin' a good time. So you make sure they think you are too."

"You mean you fake an orgasm?"

"You got it. Can you do it?"

"I suppose so. I've done it a few times, I guess, but I don't know how convincing I've been."

"Hmm. Well, let's just find out how good your actin' skills are."

It seemed to Suzanne there was no end of tests she was having to take. *I guess it's just like any acting job,* Suzanne thought. *Here goes what I hope is an academy award performance!*

A bit embarrassed, even before her friend, she made the proper noises and gyrations that she thought simulated being in the throes of a glorious orgasm. She ended the performance with cries of "Yes, yes," and a final thrust that almost knocked Marguerite over.

Suzanne thought her performance was worth, if not an award, at least honorable mention. "Well, how'd I do?" she asked Marguerite after her instructor had regained her balance.

Marguerite just shook her head. "Girl, you've got a ways to go. I mean it was pretty good for a start, but it kinda lacked that abandon that makes it look real authentic."

Suzanne was a bit disappointed in Marguerite's

review of her performance, but she supposed one could always improve on an acting job.

"Now you keep in mind exactly what you did there, girl," Marguerite continued, "and compare it to the real thing." What followed was, in essence, a reprise of the performance that occurred on Suzanne's first visit to Marguerite's apartment, only using one of the sex toys she had produced, an odd-shaped vibrator. Expertly placing it in just the right spots on, and in, Suzanne's body, she was quickly able to bring Suzanne to a peak of sexual arousal. When it was over and Suzanne had experienced a genuine, uninhibited orgasm, she was forced to admit that Marguerite was right.

"Okay," she said, "I see what you mean. But I'm sure I can improve." She laughed, and Marguerite gave her a strong hug.

"I'm sure you can," Marguerite said. "I just wanted you to see the difference."

Suzanne saw the difference.

****

Over glasses of Cointreau, Suzanne and Marguerite wound up the educational evening on a relaxed note. Suzanne still had a few questions, such as: what Marguerite's average client was like—"well educated, businessman, politician, lawyer, or CEO, neat and well-dressed"; whether they tended to be single or married— "about half and half: single and too busy for a real affair, or married and lookin' for a safer lay than his secretary"; what she usually charged—"anywhere from twelve hundred to two thousand dollars an hour, maybe ten thousand for the whole night"; and whether she had ever fallen in love with a client—"it's happened a few times, never came to much, given the circumstances." On this latter issue, Suzanne suspected, but didn't think she should ask, that Bill was one of those few, and she wondered whether it might just "come to something" this time.

"Speaking of what we charge," Suzanne said, "suppose a client pays for an hour, but he lasts, say, half an hour?"

"Means you did a helluva job, honey," Marguerite said, laughing.

"Right. But he's paying for an hour. Assuming he can manage it, do I give him another go at it? Surely I don't give him a refund."

Marguerite looked shocked. "Hell no, girl! Not your fault his timing's bad. But as to whether he gets another go-round, it's really up to you. Personally, I like to give a client their full money's worth. If he can get it up two or three times in an hour, I'm good to go. In fact, there's a great expression for that: MSOG."

"Which means?"

"Which means 'Multiple Shots on Goal.'"

They both laughed at the image this conjured up and finished their Cointreau.

When the evening finally ended, Marguerite showed Suzanne to the door and gave her a big hug.

"Don't worry, honey, you're gonna do just fine. And I'll do whatever I can to help. Something comes along you don't understand or can't handle, just let me know. I've been in this business long enough to have seen almost everything, good and bad."

Suzanne thanked her and hugged her back.

"Let's get together," Marguerite said, "after you have your first client or two, and compare notes, so to speak. Okay?"

"I'd like that," Suzanne said. "I'll give you a call."

And that's how they left it. Suzanne went home a little less nervous and a lot more prepared.

Her preparation was to be tested sooner than she thought.

Chapter 21

First Date

The very next evening was Suzanne's first on her new job. She got a call from the escort agency telling her to be ready to be picked up at eight p.m. sharp. She would get any further instructions on the way to her client's hotel.

Suzanne couldn't help but be nervous. She was unsure of so many things. What would the client be like? Would he demand one of the simple, straightforward sex acts Suzanne was quite comfortable with providing, or one of the more dangerous ones even Marguerite shied away from? She assumed the agency would not set her up with the latter on her first job, if they could control such details. She and Marguerite had decided that, since she was really a newbie in the business, she should charge about $600 an hour for ordinary sex, something more for anything out of the ordinary. How would that go over with this first client?

Suzanne slid into some sexy underwear from Victoria's Secret and stuffed a few "spares"—just in case…of what she wasn't sure—into a tote, together with some cosmetic and cleaning items, an assortment of condoms, and just for good measure, a small can of Mace. She also carried a cell phone and a "panic button," which only had to be pressed to bring her driver back, how quickly depending on how many times she pressed it. One press was for "We're through here, please come and pick me up"; two was for "Get me out of here ASAP"; and three, which she fervently hoped she never had to use, was for "…and bring reinforcements!"

She carried no cash, except an emergency five dollars. She expected to come home with plenty, however.

She dressed in a tight dress with a very high hemline and a very low neckline—if it had been any more so, it would have resembled a sash more than a dress—and spike heels. She didn't like walking in them, but she knew they showed off her calves and her derriere, and besides, she didn't plan to do much walking, or anything else vertical, that evening. She went easy on the makeup, on Marguerite's advice, but that was her usual practice anyway. She had soft, unblemished skin with a fresh, natural sheen that makeup could only lessen.

She double-checked herself and her wardrobe and found everything in order.

She was ready for battle.

****

Promptly at eight p.m., there was a knock on her door. Fortunately, Georgina was out for the evening, so Suzanne didn't have to come up with an explanation for the man picking her up, or where he was taking her.

She opened the door to find a very imposing gentleman waiting patiently, hands folded in front of him. He was well over six feet tall, broad shoulders and thick neck of a football lineman, buzz cut of an ex-soldier, but friendly smiling face of the "boy next door."

He was wearing a well-cut gray suit with a conservative red tie and highly polished shoes. He also had a bright red carnation in his lapel, both for identification—a girl can't open her door to just any man who knocks—and to add a bit of zest to an otherwise ultra-conservative ensemble. He spoke first.

"Hi. I'm Mike. I'm here to take you to your…uh…assignment." He looked almost embarrassed. Perhaps Mike was as new at this as Suzanne was.

"Hi. I'm ready." She put on her coat, turned off the lights, and stepped out the door, locking it behind her. Mike took her tote and followed her out to the street, where a black Mercedes limousine—not a stretch, but as long as they come without adding the extra doors and windows—waited by the curb. Mike opened the back door for her, and as gracefully as she could, considering the awkward spike heels, Suzanne stepped in and settled into the plush seat for her first ride to her first client.

Mike took the driver's seat and started the engine. Before driving off, he showed Suzanne the address he had written on a notepad, a small boutique hotel downtown, to be sure it matched the one she had been given. It did.

The name of the client was Walter Jenkins. He was, she had been told, in his fifties, an in-house lawyer for a multi-national corporation. That was all she knew about Walter Jenkins. She expected she would know a lot more about him soon.

They arrived at the hotel, and Mike pulled the limo into the passenger drop-off zone. As the doorman came out and opened her door, he looked back and said, "I assume you've got that gizmo for calling me, and they told you how to use it?"

"Yes, thanks. I hope I'll just be giving you one ring."

"Me too. Don't worry, we almost never get even two." No, apparently this wasn't Mike's first date.

As Mike drove off, perhaps to deliver another escort to another client, Suzanne stepped into the lobby through the door being held open by the liveried doorman. As she passed him, he gave her an appreciative once-over. Even in her plain coat, Suzanne turned heads.

Suzanne had been told to call Mr. Jenkins from the lobby, and he would come down for her. The elevators required a room key card to operate, and it was easier—and less embarrassing—to fetch her himself than to make some arrangement with the desk to send her up. She called, and within a minute a plain-looking man of medium height and weight appeared from the elevator bank and approached Suzanne. He was wearing a white dress shirt and blue tie, but no jacket. He looked like he had just come back from a board meeting and had just had time to take his coat off.

"Are you Suzanne?" he asked, a bit tentatively, but since she was the only woman in the lobby—and even had she been one of several, it would have made no difference—it was impossible to mistake who had made the call.

"Yes. I take it you're Walter?" They shook hands. Hers was warm; his was damp. That was interesting, Suzanne thought: She was understandably nervous, but apparently Walter was as well.

Walter gestured that she should precede him to the elevator, which she did. He pushed the "UP" button and they waited in silence for a few seconds until a door opened, a male passenger exited (there was the appreciative scan again), and they entered. Walter inserted his key card into the reader and pressed a button for the top floor, twelve. *Probably a nice suite,* Suzanne thought.

She was right. Walter ushered her into a large, high-ceilinged ante room with soft lighting, a plush carpet, and light beige walls.

Through a doorway, she could see a fancy four-post bed, turned down and ready for action.

Walter took Suzanne's coat from her and laid it over a carved wood armchair near the door. Then he just stood there, obviously uncertain what to do next.

Suzanne was equally uncertain, but she knew she was on the clock and expected to do more than stand there looking delicious.

"So, shall we?" she said, gesturing toward the bedroom.

"Uh, yes, sure. I'm sorry, I've never—never done this before. That is, I've had sex before and all that, but never with a…a…"

Suzanne put him out of his misery. "Person you've hired?"

"Yes. Right. So I'm a little nervous."

You aren't the only one, Suzanne thought, but she said, "No problem. It works the same way whether it's me or your girlfriend or your wife."

That was meant as a joke of sorts, but Walter took it seriously.

"Not *my* wife," he said with feeling. "Not only does she not look like you—and I mean you look great—but she hates having—having sex. I mean, she'll do it if I insist, but she doesn't seem to enjoy it, and so I don't enjoy it. And we can't do anything—anything different, if you know what I mean. Just a quick one and get it over with."

Suzanne was thinking that "a quick one and get it over with" was more or less what she had in mind too, but she refrained from saying so. Besides, she at least had to give this poor guy a better time than his wife apparently did. She was just concerned that he might be so nervous that he wouldn't be able to perform.

She needn't have worried.

"Well," she said, "let's see if we can improve on that." She put her hands on Walter's shoulders and steered him in the direction of the bedroom. Once there, she proceeded to remove his clothes, until he was standing before her in his underwear, looking a little forlorn, probably uncertain whether he should be doing this. Fortunately, the suite was pleasantly warm, so his lack of clothing was not a comfort problem.

Suzanne, however, was determined to make this first job a success, and for both of them. She finished undressing him, and he seemed to be enjoying, or at least appreciating, her assistance, standing there docilely, like a small boy being undressed for bed by his mother.

Once Walter was comfortably in bed, Suzanne decided it was time for her to do what she had come to do. She had practiced a strip-tease routine at home, wanting to undress in a way that added to a client's enjoyment, and ultimately a client's largesse, which was always the main object. This was her debut.

Once undressed, Suzanne joined Walter in bed and gave him an experience far different than any he had had with his wife, or anyone else. The so-called "cowgirl" position she chose had the benefit of putting her in the dominant role, controlling the sex act on her terms. In fact, in more than appearance it was very much like the true cowgirl relationship between a horse and rider, in that she was able to take control over a much larger and stronger animal and subject it to her will. There would be no flashbacks to her childhood rape when she was the partner on top, physically and psychologically.

Suzanne found that she was enjoying the experience almost as much as was Walter. By the time they were finished, Walter had clearly gotten his money's worth; and Suzanne had gotten Walter's money's worth as well. It was hard to beat that result.

****

When Suzanne had dressed and Walter had put on a hotel robe, Suzanne wondered whether she would have to ask for her fee or he would simply hand it to her. As it turned out, it was a little of both: Suzanne started to ask, somewhat tentatively, "Uh, Walter…" but got no farther, as he got the hint immediately.

He put his hand up. "I know. I've got it right here." He handed her an envelope that, upon quick inspection, contained six one-hundred-dollar bills, crisp new ones, obviously just obtained that day from the bank. As Suzanne tucked her very first fee-for-service into her tote bag, Walter produced, almost like a magician, a seventh hundred-dollar bill and handed it to Suzanne.

"And this is for being such a fantastic 'first date,'" he said. "I hope you'll be available next time I'm in town."

Suzanne accepted the tip, which she tucked into her cleavage, and smiled. "I hope so too," she said.

She now also had her first "regular."

She was on her way.

****

A press of the pager button—one time only!—soon brought Mike to the hotel. Walter accompanied Suzanne

160

to the elevator, but due to his lack of clothing he left her there to descend to the lobby alone. Mike was waiting patiently for her and followed her out to the limo.

"How did it go?" he asked as they drove away. "Any problems?"

"It went fine," Suzanne said. "I hope all my clients are as nice as this one was."

"Hope so," Mike said, "but as I understand it, they tend to vary. But then, people tend to vary in lots of ways, so why should this sort of thing be different?"

That seemed like a pretty sound philosophical position, especially coming from the driver for an escort agency. Suzanne accepted it as pretty much laying out the landscape of her new job. She was dealing with people engaging in the most intimate, most emotional, most pleasurable, and sometimes most risky activity in their lives. She could expect their behavior, their reactions, and their satisfaction quotients would, as Mike put it, "vary in lots of ways."

Lots of good ways, she hoped.

****

The next day, after sleeping soundly and late, Suzanne could hardly wait to tell Marguerite about her first experience as an escort. She dialed Marguerite's cell number.

"So how'd it go?" Marguerite asked as soon as she had answered. "Any problems?"

"I think it went real well. The client seemed satisfied—no pun intended—and I even had a good time."

Suzanne described the evening in some detail.

"And did he pay you without no fuss?"

"Not only that, he gave me a hundred dollar tip and

said he hoped he could have me again. So he must have been happy with the service."

Marguerite whistled softly. "That's great, honey. I knew you could do it. Hell, with that body you can make a real splash around here. I've done real well myself, and I ain't got nearly the figure and looks you have."

Suzanne blushed at the compliment, even though she knew it was a vast exaggeration. Marguerite had raw sex appeal written all over her voluptuous figure, and she didn't hide it. In fact, this was the first time Suzanne had heard Marguerite say anything even slightly negative about her own appearance, which she usually was not shy about promoting, so she clearly was just trying to pay Suzanne a compliment.

"You're just saying that to be nice, Marguerite, but I appreciate it all the same. Let's just say between the two of us, men don't stand a chance."

Marguerite laughed loudly. "You said it, honey." Then she was silent for a moment before continuing. "You know, that sorta gives me an idea. Or rather it brings up an idea I've already been thinkin' about. What would you say to movin' in with me? We could kinda compare notes, I could teach you a whole lot of new techniques, and when we weren't otherwise occupied, we could have our own fun, if you know what I mean."

Now Suzanne was silent a while, thinking it over.

"Hmm. That sounds really tempting. But wouldn't I be interfering with…you know…your entertaining there?"

Marguerite laughed. "Honey, I seldom have a man over to my place. I just don't like to mix business with my personal life, you know? And besides, there's a small second bedroom one of us can use if it's necessary to be scarce for a night. Otherwise, you've seen that big king-size bed of mine has plenty of room for us both."

After another brief pause, Suzanne said, "Actually, in addition to the things you were saying, it might also fix a real problem I was going to have living here."

"Oh? What's that?"

"Well, the girl I'm living with, Georgette, is really nice and all that, but she's kind of straight-laced, if you know what I mean."

"You mean she doesn't approve of your choice of profession?"

"Oh, I haven't told her about that! Hell, she didn't even like my being a cocktail waitress. Anyway, I had to kind of sneak out last night—fortunately, she wasn't home when I left—and I just hoped she wouldn't ask too many questions about where I'd been or what I was doing. I hate telling lies, and I'm not very good at it, or making them up to tell. If I was living with you, I wouldn't have to worry about any of that."

"I should say not. Just the opposite, honey. Whattaya say?"

"That'd be great, Marguerite. I'll give Georgette notice for the end of the month, to give her time to find another roommate."

"Works for me. Just let me know when you're ready to move in and I'll get everything ready."

"Okay, I will. And thanks for offering. I think it'll be great living together."

"I'm sure it will be, honey. You and me are gonna make a great combo."

And with that the conversation ended, with Suzanne left holding onto the phone, daydreaming about an exciting future.

She had no idea just how exciting it would be.

PART 4: OFFER AND ACCEPTANCE

Chapter 22

A New Client

Over the next several months, Suzanne became more comfortable with her new role. Some of her clients were as easy to deal with as Walter, her first, had been, and some were, as she put it to Marguerite, "a literal pain in the ass." She gained confidence in her ability to satisfy virtually any man's fantasy, and if she occasionally failed to fully live up to a client's expectations, she assumed—correctly, in most instances—the fault was not inadequate performance, but unrealistic expectations.

Gradually Suzanne became one of the most requested, and highest paid, escorts in the agency. This was due to a combination of factors: her remarkable good looks; her ability to learn quickly, remember what a particular client wanted, and perform flawlessly and enthusiastically; and her relationship with Marguerite. Marguerite not only taught Suzanne tricks of the trade that it would have taken her years to discover for herself, but she provided a stabilizing influence, whether as a cheering section when things went particularly well, or as a confidant and comfort when things went poorly. And, with time, Suzanne was able to offer something of the same benefits to Marguerite in return.

About eighteen months into her new profession,

Suzanne was assigned to provide services to a long-time agency client, one she had yet to meet. His name was Lloyd Kilpatrick, and Marguerite knew all about him.

"Oh, yeah, Lloyd. He's a good ol' boy from Tennessee. Not a bad fella, at least if you don't talk politics with him. He's somewhere to the right of Henry the Eighth." She laughed.

Suzanne knew virtually nothing about politics, seldom read the newspaper or watched television news, and could not be described as leaning either left or right. But she understood what Marguerite's description meant, and it didn't compute.

"Doesn't sound like the kind of client you'd be interested in, or who'd be interested in you, for that matter," Suzanne said.

Marguerite chuckled. "No, I'll grant you that. Funny, though—we got along just fine. From my point of view, I couldn't care less about a john's politics or prejudices, so long as he's got his equipment in the right place, acts like a gentleman, and pays up without a fuss."

"Is he rich?"

"I guess so, if he could afford me. No, actually he's been a client of the agency from about the time it started, before I got here. He's got money, of course. Buys himself some expensive sex every time he's in town, I think. But he's not one of those 'special' clients. That's why he's not on my list anymore."

"Okay, but why would he want a black woman in the first place? If he's a Southern redneck, I'd think he'd only want to have sex with 'his own kind,' with white women."

"Probably 'cause of the kind of sex he likes. Wants to start with spankin' before gettin' it on. In fact, that's probably how he gets it up so he can get it on at all. And maybe when he's slappin' my black ass he's picturin' himself disciplining some poor slave girl back on the plantation, somethin' like that." She chuckled again at the thought.

"Wait. He wanted to spank you? And you were okay with that?"

"Oh, yeah. It wasn't violent or nothin', though I guess it did sting some. Got him all aroused for the good part, and truth be known, it kinda got me a little excited too. Some gals really get turned on by it. All I know is we had some pretty wild humpin' after that."

Suzanne was thoughtful. This was a complication she hadn't yet had to deal with. She had made it pretty clear that she was not interested in being the victim of any sadistic bondage freak. And up to then, her wishes had been respected, as there were always clients with more normal demands who wanted her services. But apparently she had now been assigned to this Lloyd Kilpatrick, who liked to inflict pain on his women. She asked Marguerite if she knew why.

"No, and to tell you the truth, I'm kinda surprised they've given him to you, both because of what he wants and because you've moved up to more exclusive clients already. But I guess you're still considered new here, or maybe they just didn't have anyone else available just now."

Suzanne was silent, unsure what to do. She didn't want to make a fuss and refuse to take an assignment unless it was absolutely necessary. But she also didn't want to have the kind of bad experience she was afraid this could turn out to be. She asked Marguerite for advice.

"Well, honey, if it were me, and it ain't, but if it were, I'd give it a try. Like I said, Lloyd's a gentleman, and if things get too bad, you can put a stop to it. He won't insist or get violent or anythin' like that, I'm pretty sure. And, hey, you might like it."

Somehow Suzanne doubted it.

****

The next evening, Mike drove Suzanne to the Esquire Hotel, a good middle-of-the-road hostelry favored by traveling businessmen who wanted a practical, rather than elegant, place to stay while in town. It was furnished with good taste in low-key accents and comfortable furniture, and it featured a wide array of business amenities, from printers and fax machines to conference rooms with special conference phone hookups, and, of course, Wi-Fi in all areas.

The elevator didn't require a key card, and Mike accompanied Suzanne to Lloyd's door before wishing her a good evening and returning to the limousine. Suzanne knocked gently.

"C'mon in," boomed a voice that seemed to be straight out of the Beverly Hillbillies, only a bit more refined. Suzanne entered.

As she stepped inside, Lloyd was standing at the other end of the foyer, hands on hips. He stared at her as if a twelve-point buck had just walked through the door. Suzanne saw a stocky man of medium build, in his fifties, with a paunch that spoke of a lot of good Southern cooking washed down with liberal amounts of beer, and a round, almost cherubic face. His hair was thin and combed to the side. He was smiling broadly.

"My, oh my," he said in a strong Tennessee accent, shaking his head slowly. Then he whistled—just a soft whistle, of admiration. "You are one bee-you-tee-ful lady. I think I'm gonna really enjoy myself tonight."

Suzanne, taken a little aback by Lloyd's greeting, just gave him a little smile and started to remove her coat. Lloyd, the consummate Southern gentleman, quickly stepped forward to help her, carefully hanging the coat in the closet next to the entrance door. As he was doing this, he introduced himself with a casual "I'm Lloyd. Lloyd Kilpatrick. They said your name's Suzanne, that right?"

"Yes, that's right. Nice to meet you, Lloyd."

Lloyd turned to face Suzanne and smiled even more broadly than before. "And it's very nice to meet you, Suzanne. Can I get you a drink? Whiskey? Wine? Beer? Coke? They got it all in the minibar."

"No, no thanks. I'm fine. But you go ahead."

"Don't mind if I do." Lloyd opened a mini-bottle of whiskey and poured it into a hotel glass. He took a sip, sighed with satisfaction, drank the rest down, then said, "Well, let's get down to business. I know the meter's running."

Suzanne nodded. She kicked off her shoes and began to unbutton her blouse. She was not wearing a bra.

Lloyd held up a hand. "Uh, no, don't do that just yet. I have a particular little, shall we say, routine I like to go through. Did they tell you?"

Since "they" had not, and most of her information was obtained quite informally from Marguerite, Suzanne decided to play it innocent.

"Tell me what?"

"Well, what I like to do in these little, uh, sessions. It's nothin' special, but maybe a little different than you're used to."

"It's your nickel. What would you like me to do?"

What he wanted her to do was to undress from the waist down and assume a position over his knees from which he could slap her on the behind in much the same way a father might punish a naughty child, only with far different intentions. The slaps stung, but it was more the humiliation than the pain that bothered Suzanne, who was having a serious conversation with herself. This was just the kind of sex play she had tried to avoid, not just because of the obvious discomfort, but because it did not fit into the course she had so adamantly determined for herself.

Perhaps even more troubling, however, was her simple fear of finding herself in a helpless, submissive position, subjected to the will and the physical abuse of a man for his sexual gratification. Would she have a panic attack, as she had when she almost had intercourse with the unfortunate Dave, way back in middle school? It seemed like such a long time ago, but she had never since been tested in that way, not until now. Would she imagine her aggressor was her father, feel the agony of being raped again, and lose control? Or had she finally gotten to the point that she could accept a more submissive role, even to the point of being physically struck and sexually humiliated, at least briefly and in a relatively safe setting?

These, of course, were questions that had gone through her mind ever since Marguerite had told her about Lloyd's preference for spanking his women before bedding them. She had not discussed her fears even with Marguerite, not wanting to open up a subject she not only found painful even to think about, but one that might undermine her credibility as a first-class call girl.

Suzanne knew the only way she could be certain was to take a chance. Here was a man whom Marguerite had assured her was not a real threat, just one who liked a slightly kinky, if not uncommon, form of sex. If she was going to try it with anyone, it might as well be with Lloyd Kilpatrick.

And now the test was for real. Lloyd was not hitting her hard, but it was not a gentle caress either. Suzanne bit her lip and determined not to cry out. Marguerite had said it would just "sting" a little, but then she knew Marguerite, with the typical body type of an African-American female, had a lot more padding in her nether region than she did.

At first, she could feel her body tense, as Lloyd's open hand landed on her bare bottom with a loud slap, while her mind flirted with the memory of her father spanking her, and then with those horrific images of the rape scene and its aftermath.

But she didn't panic.

She hurt, but she didn't panic. She fought off those images of the past, reminding herself over and over that this was not an attack by the man, this was something she had chosen to do.

She was the one in control. This was really on her terms, not his, and he would be paying a substantial price for her acquiescence.

At last, Lloyd was through with the preliminaries and ready for the more conventional part of the package he had purchased. Although his preferred arrangement put him in the top, dominant position, Suzanne had become used to it and no longer needed to be physically on top to feel she was in control. And despite the pain in her behind and the somewhat humiliating scenario to which she had been subjected, Suzanne was surprised to find that, all in all, she was almost enjoying the experience.

Sensing that this session was over, and well within the allotted hour's time limit, Suzanne stood up and began to dress. From the bed, Lloyd, who was now propped on his elbows, watched in wonder.

"You are just the prettiest little thing I have ever seen," he said, and he sounded as if he meant it. "And that was the best fifteen hundred dollars I have ever spent." He sounded like he meant that as well.

Rubbing her still-tender bottom gingerly, Suzanne smiled and thanked him. She was still unsure what she thought of the experience. The spanking, while unquestionably a symbol of male domination, had actually turned her on. More importantly, it had not caused her to panic or lose her ability to complete her mission. Was she finally free of her father's sexual curse?

Time would tell.

****

Lloyd put on a robe and extracted his wallet from the slacks he had shed at the bedside. He took out fifteen hundred-dollar bills and handed them to Suzanne. It was more than her usual twelve hundred dollar fee, but she had taken Marguerite's advice and charged extra for the "extra service." Lloyd didn't seem to mind.

"Little lady," Lloyd said as Suzanne was tucking the money into her tote bag—it was too thick a wad of bills to fit into even her substantial cleavage—"I'd be pleased to see y'all again next time I'm in town. That okay with you?"

"Sure. Just let the agency know and they'll fix it up."

"I'll do that. I had a real good time."

And so began a business relationship that would prove to be far more complicated, and far more dangerous, than either of them could then imagine.

****

Following their initial liaison, Lloyd became a regular customer of Suzanne's. He came to New York on business frequently, and he always made sure to reserve an evening for a visit from Suzanne. Even as Suzanne increased her fees with more experience and greater demand, Lloyd continued to ask for her and made no protest. For her part, Suzanne made sure she continually introduced Lloyd to new and ever more satisfying variations on the theme of copulation. As Suzanne perfected her techniques, Lloyd was often the client on whom she perfected them.

Occasionally Lloyd purchased more than one hour of Suzanne's time, and in those instances he might ask her to dress in a certain way—such as in a scanty maid's uniform—or otherwise vary the routine. But during these extended sessions, with extra time between bouts of sex play, Lloyd also wanted to talk politics. To talk, not to discuss, as it was a one-way conversation. Never mind that Suzanne hardly knew the difference between Republicans and Democrats, much less who were the leaders of either party. She knew the name of the president, but that was about as far as it went. Sometimes she wished she had paid more attention in Civics class, but it was too late for that, and all she could do was listen to Lloyd's litany of complaints against the evil forces of darkness, otherwise known as "them damn Commie Liberals," and nod at appropriate intervals. If Lloyd was not plowing a virgin field when it came to sex with

173

Suzanne, he most definitely was when it came to politics.

Occasionally, Suzanne would tell Lloyd a little about herself; not enough to reveal any important personal details, but just a glimpse into her life outside the bedroom. But apparently she said enough so that Lloyd, not a fool despite his paranoia when it came to politics, could detect something of her attitude toward men.

He couldn't care less, of course, so long as Suzanne continued to satisfy his many carnal desires in such an expert way.

Over time, Suzanne began to understand and to sympathize with Lloyd's multitude of grievances. It was, after all, like a prizefighter with an extensive repertoire of punches and long experience at using them pitted against a pacifist with no defenses, a verbal punching bag. After a while the punches begin to make an impression. Lloyd's grievances were extensive, but they mostly boiled down to the urgent need to get the current president, a Democrat, out of office and a "red-blooded American" of the opposite persuasion in. Suzanne listened, because she was being well paid to listen, but she much preferred sex to politics.

Lloyd, on the other hand, found that both sex and railing against the government gave him welcome relief. Getting off was a great relief to his body; sounding off was an equal relief to his troubled mind.

It was the latter form of orgasm that was to get Lloyd in trouble.

Chapter 23

Setting the Bait

A few weeks after he accepted the assignment from Smith, Lloyd was back in New York and made his usual reservation with Suzanne, an extended one with an extra half hour. The evening went about as usual—Lloyd had asked for black underwear and net stockings this time—except Suzanne detected that there was something on Lloyd's mind besides spanking and intercourse, two things that generally seemed to occupy him fully, as it would most men. Suzanne assumed he had become agitated by some political issue or other, and she no doubt would soon be hearing all about it.

Sure enough, when the sex play was over and Suzanne and Lloyd were getting dressed, Lloyd said casually he had something important to talk to her about. This wasn't unusual— Suzanne had come to expect some kind of post-intercourse conversation from Lloyd—except that Lloyd didn't usually specifically ask, he just began his usually-political lectures without ceremony. So she finished dressing and sat down to listen.

What Suzanne heard, while it had definite political aspects, was far from what she had expected to hear. First Lloyd swore her to secrecy, telling her that both she and he would be "in big trouble" if either of them told the wrong people what he was about to tell her. At that point, Suzanne wasn't at all sure she wanted to hear whatever it was Lloyd had to say, but after a bit of cajoling by Lloyd, who insisted it was definitely in her interest to listen, her curiosity got the better of her doubts.

Lloyd explained how he had been recruited to find the right person—the right woman, to be exact—to seduce and marry the younger brother of the probable next President of the United States. He further told her what that woman would be expected to do once she had become part of the White House family: seduce the president himself!

Suzanne guessed, at that point, that Lloyd was not telling her this just as an interesting story, but because she was the woman he had chosen to carry out this bizarre plan. She was about to tell him in no uncertain terms that she had "no intention in the world" of doing any such thing, and "if he thought for a second—"

But then Lloyd mentioned the one million dollars.

Suzanne assumed she had misunderstood. "Did you say one million dollars?"

"I did. I couldn't believe it myself when they told me, but that's what they said. You sleep with the president, you get a million bucks."

Suzanne was silent for a long time before asking, "What makes you—them—think I could get this guy to marry me, much less get into bed with the president?"

Lloyd scratched his head. "Let me put it this way: I'm not too sure you could do it either, but I am sure of one thing. If anyone can do it, you can. You are the prettiest, sexiest little thing I have ever come across, and you really know the ropes. Yes, ma'am, if anyone can, you can."

Suzanne thought about this for a minute, then asked, "Okay, let's skip that for now. How do I know they'll pay me? How do I know I can trust them?"

"Hey, I had the same question when they offered to pay me for helping them out. No million bucks, of course, but still a lot of money. They said they'd give me the money in advance, in my own bank account. Long as I didn't spend it until I'd earned it. And that's exactly what they did. Got the money in my account right now."

Suzanne was torn. She was doing quite well financially in her new profession, and she was happy in her work. But a million dollars, she thought. *What could I do with a million dollars? What could I buy for my mother, as well as myself?*

The temptation was strong, but not strong enough to elicit an immediate answer.

"Can I—can I let you know in a few days? I've gotta think this over."

"They told me I can give you up to a week, if you need it. That okay?"

"Yeah, sure. I'll let you know."

Lloyd took a business card out of his wallet, together with the cash for the evening's services.

"Here, take this. I'll be home day after tomorrow. Just call me with your answer. That's my business number there— wouldn't want you getting' hold of my wife!" He laughed at the thought. Suzanne smiled.

"I hope you'll decide to do it," Lloyd said as he ushered Suzanne out the door. "I'd like to see that sonofabitch McNeil get his comeuppance, and this way I get to be partly responsible for it."

He also would be assured of keeping his fifty thousand dollars.

Chapter 24

Advice

Suzanne's head was swimming by the time she got home. All during the limousine ride, and even as she walked down the hallway to her and Marguerite's apartment, all she could think about was that million dollars. Would she be a fool to take it? Or a fool not to? Was there any risk involved, other than being made the object of public scorn, like that poor girl who had sex—or whatever they had—with President Clinton? She didn't have any concern over the political aspects of the plan, as she had pretty much absorbed Lloyd's point of view from his constant repetition of it, and to be honest she was no more interested in who was President of the United States than who was president of the local Rotary or Kiwanis clubs, for several of whose members she had performed services.

A more immediate issue, however, was should she tell Marguerite. She had promised not to mention to anyone what Lloyd had said, and he had hinted that it would be very dangerous for her to do so. But she really needed advice and to talk the offer over with a trusted friend. Could that friend be trusted enough to keep her mouth shut?

Marguerite was home when Suzanne entered the apartment. As soon as she saw Suzanne, she guessed that something was on her mind. Suzanne was not the type to have serious issues on her mind, so the worried look on her face was a matter of immediate concern.

"What's the matter, honey? You look like you got the world's troubles on your shoulders. Somethin' happen with Lloyd? Problems back home?"

"Uh, no, nothing really. Just tired, I guess."

"Hmm. Okay, but if you want t' talk later, just let me know." And that was how Marguerite left it, not wanting to pry.

Suzanne slept poorly that night, unable to get Lloyd's offer out of her head for even a few minutes. Should she tell Marguerite? Or even Patricia? What could she do with all that money? But was it worth being branded a slut in every newspaper and news program in the world? And a new worry: What would be the effect on Mary Sue's life if her daughter were at the center of a major political scandal?

One mitigating factor in the latter regard was that Lloyd had told her "the group"—he didn't know what else to call them— had said they would give her a whole new identity for the operation. It was not just for her protection, but to make the scheme work at all. If Adam McNeil, or Patrick for that matter, were to discover her real identity and therefore her profession, not only would that likely torpedo any hope of a marriage, but even if not it would make the marriage such a sensation—in the negative sense—and Suzanne so notorious that an eventual liaison with the president would be highly unlikely. Thus she would be given a new identity, complete with employment history, social security number, and family history—an orphan, of course. These days such identities were quite easily created, if one had enough money and the right connections in high places. And these folks had plenty of both.

Another powerful factor in Suzanne's thinking was the unbelievable opportunity this would give her to reach what had to be the greatest possible achievement in the quest she had set herself from the time she was a young girl: taking advantage of men's inherent weakness, their insatiable sexual appetite, for her financial and psychological benefit. It was one thing to make ordinary men pay thousands of dollars for an hour's worth of her sexual services. It would be quite another to count as her ultimate victim the President of the United States. Mitigating this factor, however, just to make things more complicated, in the last few months Suzanne's feelings toward men had in fact mellowed somewhat. Yes, she still had the scars and the need for revenge. But now that, for quite a while, she had easily and successfully sold her services for a high price, to men who didn't seem to be bad so much as needy, she had begun to feel part of the debt they owed her had been repaid.

By morning, Suzanne had decided she would go crazy if she didn't tell someone she trusted about the proposal and get some advice. She determined to tell Marguerite, although she had a good idea what that advice would be.

****

"Can I talk to you about something? Something really important?"

They had just finished breakfast and Suzanne decided there was no time like the present to broach the subject of Lloyd's proposal. Marguerite, of course, was hardly surprised to find out Suzanne had something she needed to get off her mind, considering how Suzanne had looked and acted when she got home the previous evening.

"But you have to promise not to tell anyone about what I tell you, no matter what."

"Hmm. If it's that secret…but okay, I'll keep it to myself. Go ahead."

Suzanne decided not to start with the million dollars, but, like Lloyd, to leave that little wrinkle to the end.

"I'll cut right to the chase," she told Marguerite as they sat on the sofa in the living room, coffee cups in hand. "Lloyd apparently got in with some group that opposes this guy Patrick McNeil as the next president. They came up with a scheme to have a woman get McNeil's brother to marry her, get into the White House that way, as part of the family, and then to get the president himself into bed, where he can be discovered having sex with his own brother's wife. And he wants me to be that woman."

By this point, Marguerite's jaw had dropped several inches. She hardly knew what to say.

"Are you serious, girl? Is this some kinda joke Lloyd's pullin'? 'Cause it has to be the craziest idea I've ever heard. And I've heard plenty of crazy things in my time."

"I know it sounds crazy, and now that I'm repeating it to you, it sounds even more stupid than when I first heard it. And that's what I was thinking at the time. But I need to tell you the last part."

"There's more? Does he want you to have sex with the president while balancing on a high wire between the White House and the Capitol?"

Suzanne smiled. "No, but almost as unbelievable. They're offering me a million dollars for doing this."

Again Marguerite's mouth hung open, and this time she really was speechless, until she finally managed, "Honey, did you say one million dollars? As in one with six zeros after it? In cash?"

"That's what Lloyd said. And it would be paid in advance, although I couldn't spend it until I'd done the job. That's how Lloyd was paid."

"He got a million bucks just to ask you?"

"No, not that much, but whatever they promised him. Apparently these guys have all the money they could ever need. They think it would be wasted trying to defeat McNeil in the election, so they want to spend it to discredit him after he wins."

Marguerite was quiet, obviously thinking through this bizarre situation. Suzanne waited patiently for her response.

After a few minutes, Marguerite said, "Okay, let's back up and examine it piece by piece. I assume you're supposed to quit your job at the agency—I doubt a practicing call girl would get very far with people like Patrick McNeil and his brother, whoever he is."

"Yeah, they would give me a whole new identity, with a different family and job history and everything. And I guess I'd have to live somewhere by myself."

"Kinda like the witness protection program, huh? Okay, so you become Miss Shirley Smith, fashion model, or somethin' like that. How do you feel about quittin'?"

"Not good. I like my job. And I like living here with you. I don't want to become someone else."

"Don't blame you. But let's go on. What are the chances you could actually get this—what's the brother's name?"

"Adam."

"What's the chance of getting this Adam to marry you?"

"Well, Lloyd says he's very young and innocent, not good looking, probably a virgin, not comfortable around women. I guess the idea is that they'll set up a meeting somehow and expect me to be real nice to him, get him to trust me, then get him in bed and let him find out what he's been missing. Make it clear if he marries me, he can have it all the time. You know, that kind of thing."

"You think you can do that? Convince him?"

"I don't know. I could try. If I can't, I guess I just don't get the million dollars. Lloyd said I get twenty-five thousand at the beginning that I can keep whether the plan works or not."

"They've thought of everything, haven't they? Okay, so let's assume you get as far as marrying Adam McNeil. What next?"

"Well, I guess next is the election, and they assume his brother will win."

"Right. That's likely, all right. I've got clients in high places who've said the same thing. So that makes you part of the 'first family,' as they call it. You get to be right there in the White House, and no one can keep you out. No muss, no fuss. Pretty damn clever."

"And once I'm on the inside, I'm supposed to find a way to seduce the president."

"Which I take it you also think you can handle?"

"I-I think so, yeah."

"Well, I guess he's just another man, even if he is the president. Same basic equipment."

Yeah, and same basic weaknesses, Suzanne thought.

****

Now that the proposition was on the table, so to speak, and before she had heard Marguerite's response, Suzanne felt better. Marguerite definitely did not.

"You want me to advise you what to do? Join some far right gang of…of criminals who want to undermine the president, or turn down a million bucks?"

"But would you do it if Lloyd had asked you?"

"Geez, Suzanne, how do I know? I mean, to begin with, I like Patrick McNeil and what he stands for. I'm not big on politics, but I know which side is which, and those right-wing nut cases ain't on my side. Never have been, never will be."

"I guess I'm not so concerned about that. Lloyd says—"

"Lloyd is a nice man, but he's also a good ol' boy from the South who thinks the fuckin' world is flat and his worst enemy is the US Government. And it sounds like whoever's behind him is just as crazy, but a helluva lot more dangerous. Not only that, but what they got planned is pretty close to treason, if you ask me. Honey, I wouldn't get mixed up with a gang like that for all the gold in Fort Knox." By this time, Marguerite was getting pretty worked up and her tone was sharp.

Suzanne wasn't surprised by Marguerite's reaction—by now she knew quite a bit about her political leanings and her ethics. In fact, she would have been shocked if Marguerite had come out in favor of her taking the money. But she still was glad to have unburdened herself by telling her best friend.

"You're right, of course, about who these people are," Suzanne said. "And I have to take that into account. But it's really hard to pass up that money and what I could do with it, especially for my mom. I owe her everything. She'd never have to work again." Suzanne had been sending money back home to Mary Sue ever since she began her present, more lucrative job, but the amounts were relatively small. "Besides, I wouldn't really be doing anything wrong, just giving this guy who happens to be president the chance to do something wrong. Not my fault if he takes advantage of it."

Suzanne didn't really believe that last rationale, but she threw it in for good measure and to help assuage her conscience, which she knew would rebel if she took the money and joined the "gang."

Marguerite softened her tone. "Look, honey, you'll do what you gotta do, and if you decide to take the money, I won't hold it against you. I admit I'd miss havin' you as a roomie—I've really enjoyed our talks and our other...other activities. And just bein' together here. But if you leave and take the money, I'll understand, and I'll always be here for you if you need me. I just hope you'll think really hard before deciding. It could be the biggest decision of your life."

Suzanne was pretty sure it would be.

Chapter 25

Craig

Suzanne phoned Lloyd the next day to say she was uncertain whether to accept his offer, and she would need at least until the end of the week. "I'm pretty happy doing what I'm doing," she said, "but of course the money is tempting. I'm having a hard time deciding. You understand."

"Like I told you," Lloyd said, "you can have up to a week to decide, but that's all. Meanwhile, I'll let the fella I'm in contact with know he'll have to wait till then."

"Thanks. I'll be sure to let you know my answer by then."

The decision proved much harder to make than Suzanne would have thought. She wasn't quite sure what the problem was. Yes, she agreed with Marguerite these were dangerous people she would be getting mixed up with. But they needed her as much as she needed them, so they were unlikely to treat her badly. The political aspect didn't bother her as it obviously did Marguerite. And it would be an unbelievable adventure, thrusting her into the very highest political and social circles and testing to the extreme what she always had considered her most important asset and her ability to use it to her advantage.

A million dollars' worth of advantage.

Still unsure two days later, Suzanne arrived at her latest client's hotel room determined not to let her preoccupation with making a decision interfere with the quality of her services.

The client was a new one, apparently new to the agency as well. He was in town on business and had been checked out as usual by the agency: No criminal record, honorable discharge from the military, referred by a respectable former client. He had asked specifically for Suzanne, saying he had been told that she was by far the best "escort" the agency had. He offered to pay extra for her. Suzanne was flattered and wanted to live up to his expectations.

The client's name was Craig Johnson. He said he was an attorney living in Washington, DC. He was a big, athletic man well over six feet tall, with a Marine-like buzz cut and a scar on his left cheek that spoke of some kind of violence, possibly in combat.

Craig Johnson greeted Suzanne with a wide smile and a soft voice. He was the stereotypical "tall, dark, and handsome" dude right out of a men's underwear ad. Or more likely a jeans ad, since he was wearing a tight pair that showed off his better features, especially behind his fly. More often than not Suzanne's clients were older businessmen like Lloyd or needy husbands whose wives had lost their attractiveness, or just as likely they had lost their attractiveness to their wives. From the agency they could buy all the sex they wanted and be treated as if they were Greek gods.

Johnson was different. It didn't seem he would need to pay for sex. He just had to walk into a singles bar and the ladies would line up to go home with him. Suzanne was sure this would be a memorable evening.

"When he knew I was gonna be in town," Craig said, "a friend of mine told me he'd found this great little piece of—oh, sorry, this great girl at an escort service, and would I like to be set up with her when I get here. Well, naturally I said sure. And here I am." And indeed there he was, naked, ripped, and ready.

Although Craig's little macho slip of the tongue did nothing to endear him to Suzanne, she had a job to do, and it could still be a glorious evening.

They began with Craig sitting on the edge of the bed. He said he wanted oral sex before intercourse, and that was fine with Suzanne. She extracted, as usual, a condom from her bag and slipped it on him, then began what should have been a routine part of her job. Craig seemed to be enjoying the experience immensely when he gently pulled away. He lifted Suzanne's head and then her entire body, as if she were a rag doll, and laid her onto the bed. Suzanne was impressed with his strength, but what he did next made a much different kind of impression.

As Suzanne lay on the bed waiting for Craig's next move, he suddenly tore off the condom, saying "I don't need any of this shit." His features took on a much less friendly look, almost as if a different person had stepped into the room, mild-mannered Dr. Jekyll being replaced by bloodthirsty Mr. Hyde. He lowered himself onto the bed and began to mount Suzanne missionary style. She held her legs closed and protested she would not have unprotected sex with him or anyone else.

Craig slapped her across the face, raising a welt, saying, "You sure as hell will, you little slut. You fancy whores-by-appointment think you can tell a man how to screw you, real finicky. Well, I'm payin' for the real thing, and that means with no damn piece of rubber in the way." As he talked he grabbed her legs below the knees and forced them apart.

Suzanne had never been in this position since that terrible day when she was ten. The nightmare of being raped by her father flooded back, really for the first time since she had been in New York.

Although she'd been warned there were such dangers in her profession, it had always been just a theoretical possibility to her. Now it was a dead-serious reality. Suzanne tried to think of something she could do to stop Craig's assault.

The panic button that would bring help was in her tote bag, too far away for her to reach, and clearly she was no match for Craig in strength. She could kick and scratch, but she would ultimately be the loser. She started to scream, but Craig quickly clamped a hand over her mouth, saying, "If you scream, I'll shut you up for good. If you stay quiet, you'll be just fine." His smile was more menacing than reassuring.

Suzanne decided to stop fighting and let Craig have his way. It was really the only sane alternative, she thought. She would find a way to get back at him later. When all else fails, "relax and enjoy it," she'd been told. While she considered that pretty stupid advice, she did try to relax, so as to make the experience less painful.

Craig took Suzanne with no regard for her comfort. Likely because of the skillful service Suzanne had earlier given him, however, he lasted only short time. He then lay catching his breath, and Suzanne thought to herself she was lucky all he wanted was to take her "naked." It could have been much worse.

Unfortunately, she was wrong.

After a few minutes, Craig lifted himself to his knees. But instead of standing, he just stared down at Suzanne and said, "Now we're gonna have some real fun. Turn over." And Suzanne was astonished at how quickly Craig had regained an erection.

Again Suzanne didn't know what to do. If she didn't do as Craig said, she knew he could and would use force, but she was reluctant to even appear to acquiesce to whatever Craig had in mind. Suzanne decided to just take whatever Craig gave her and get it over with, determined to minimize any harm and hoping to have a chance to avenge herself later. But she apparently deliberated too long, because before she could respond one way or the other, Craig lifted her at the hips as if she were a mail-order inflatable sex doll and flipped her onto her stomach. She waited nervously for what he would do next. She soon found out.

Suzanne struggled, but to no avail. "You might as well relax," Craig said, "'cause I'm doin' this one way or the other, and it'll be a lot easier if you ain't so tight."

Although "relaxing" was out of the question, Suzanne tried to bring down the level of her anxiety and to relax the lower part of her body as best she could. What followed was a rough and painful introduction to anal sex, one of the few "services" Suzanne had never been willing to offer. Even worse, it was unprotected. She involuntarily screamed, but Craig quickly leaned over and shoved a pillow over her face, the force of his movement only increasing the pain. The pillow was suffocating her.

"Keep your mouth shut if you want to walk outta here," he growled, releasing the pillow.

Suzanne began to cry, but she bit her lip and held

back the screams forming in her throat.

When Craig had achieved his objective, he withdrew slowly, as if he now wanted to be careful not to hurt Suzanne, as if this had been a mutually agreed-upon experiment in unconventional sexual pleasure. He eased his way off the bed, as Suzanne lay shaking with silent sobs, and made his way over to the little pile of Suzanne's clothes. He picked them up and tossed them to her on the bed. He then pulled on his jeans and went over to where she had left her tote bag. Suzanne's immediate thought was that Craig was going to rob her as well as rape her, but there she was wrong. He reached in and took out Suzanne's calling device, putting it in his front pocket. From his back pocket he withdrew a wad of bills and stuffed them into the tote bag.

"Get dressed," he said. "Your money's there, with an extra fifty for a cab, since you won't be able to call your driver tonight." He obviously was familiar with the agency's routine.

Gradually Suzanne controlled her sobs and gathered her strength. Knowing when to keep her mouth shut and do as she was told, she slowly got dressed and picked up her tote bag as Craig watched.

When at last she was dressed and on her feet, if shakily, Craig, once again polite and soft-spoken, ushered her to the door. On the way, he laughed. "You know, that was just like it was advertised. I've had to really mess up a few whores who gave me a hard time, but you were smart. And you've got a great body. I know some politicians in DC in very high places. I'll be sure to recommend you to them."

Another laugh, a gentle push out the door, and the evening was over.

But the repercussions were just beginning.

Chapter 26

Decision

If Suzanne had been undecided about Lloyd's offer before her encounter with Craig, she was no longer undecided after it. While the arguments against accepting the offer were still good ones, and she had been leaning toward that decision, the attack by Craig—if it wasn't technically rape, in her mind it was pretty damn close to it—strongly reinforced one of the two main reasons in favor: her quest for payback and revenge against men, all of whom Craig now represented in her mind. All the hatred and resentment that had slowly been eased by meeting good men like Jerry and her success in taking advantage of men's sexual weaknesses now rushed back and created an ever-greater need to get her own back. There was no Mary Sue with a pistol to save Suzanne from a man like Craig. She had only herself.

Suzanne had begun, she reasoned, with small rewards for small sexual favors in school, graduated first to job security for larger favors and then to substantial sums for near-total sexual gratification. There was not much more of her body she could surrender, at least willingly; but there was still the prospect of even greater conquests with it. And none could be greater than a well-publicized sexual conquest of the President of the United

States, one that would likely result not only in his public humiliation, but also in his political downfall. Sweet revenge and a million dollars to boot.

It would, of course, have been more gratifying to get revenge over Craig Johnson himself, after he had assaulted and humiliated her that night. But that kind of revenge turned out to be impossible. Suzanne had arrived home in a cab, in tears of anger and frustration. She had told her tale of the evening with Craig to Marguerite, whose anger and disgust at Craig's actions almost matched Suzanne's. Suzanne declined a morning-after pill, since she was already taking birth-control pills, so at least pregnancy was not an issue.

"D'you think the cops would do anything about it?" she asked Marguerite.

Her friend laughed loudly. "You kidding? Can you imagine how they'd react? First of all, ladies like us need to keep our ass far away from the police—"

Which for the occasion she pronounced "Poe-lease."

"—at all times. Unless you been mugged and robbed in a dark alley—and even then, it better be real dark and a lot of money—just keep it to yourself. You're a professional call girl—just a prostitute in their eyes; you went to this SOB's room voluntarily; you happily gave him a BJ and then invited him to screw you, which he did. Both ways. You accepted a substantial amount of money for your services, and far from resisting your 'escape,' he opened the door for you and paid for a cab so you could get home. You think the fact that he refused to wear a condom, or that he took you from the back as well as the front without your permission, is gonna turn that into some kinda crime in their eyes?"

Suzanne looked down and said slowly, "N—no, I

guess not. But what about the fact he hit me? You can still see the mark."

"Yeah, I c'n see it. But it's your word against his how you got it, and besides, the cops ain't about to make a big case out of a john gettin' a little rough with a prostitute. I'm sorry to say it, but that kinda goes with the territory."

"Yeah, I guess you're right. That's really what I figured. But don't you think I should at least tell the agency, so they can warn the next girl who goes to this guy's room?"

"Absolutely. And don't worry—there won't be a next girl, not at our agency. In fact, I wouldn't be surprised if they didn't send a little welcome party around to pay the bastard a visit.

"They don't take kindly to havin' their girls mistreated."

Suzanne dutifully reported her encounter to Ron Gillette, in person. He took the information with a grave expression.

"Thanks for letting me know, Suzanne," he said. "Your driver had wondered why you hadn't called for a ride home, although occasionally a girl stays overnight or takes a ride back with the client. But first, I want to apologize on behalf of the agency for sending you there. We do our best to screen our clients, but sometimes we fall down on the job. Although this guy Johnson was referred by a former client, I recall we weren't able to get a very good line on him from our usual sources. We did check some references he gave us, and, well, I guess we got a little lax in how thoroughly we investigated, in light of the reference. I'm just glad nothing…nothing irreparable happened to you. Naturally, you can keep whatever he paid you—we could hardly take a commission for sending you there."

Suzanne thought Gillette's apology, as well as the extra money, was more than generous, and she considered the matter closed. There was just one more wrinkle to come: The next day, Marguerite reported she had heard that Gillette had indeed sent a couple of the "drivers" to see Johnson at his hotel. They were not surprised he was not there. What was surprising was what the manager told them, after a small monetary inducement: Johnson came with no luggage except a briefcase, and he checked out that same night. Just a few minutes after Suzanne had left.

****

Having made her decision, Suzanne telephoned Lloyd to tell him. He was, of course, very pleased. He had completed his job successfully and would be assured of keeping his money. Or so he thought.

"So what do I do now?" Suzanne wanted to know. "How do I meet this guy Adam?"

"They haven't told me everything yet," Lloyd said. "Let me get back to you after I've had a chat with them."

Lloyd immediately called the number he had been given. He reached Smith and gave him the good news.

"That's great," Smith said. "We're real proud of you, Lloyd."

"Thanks. You know, like I told you, when she first phoned me, it sounded like she was leaning toward turning you folks down. I was a bit surprised she agreed to do it."

There was a slight pause before Smith said, "Well, you never know, Lloyd. Sometimes something happens that just sorta…tips the scale one way or the other.

Maybe that's what happened here."

"Yeah, I suppose so. So what do I do next?"

"You get back in touch with Missy Dahlstrom and give her some details." Smith gave Lloyd a number Suzanne should call to set up an appointment with the people who would "alter her identity."

"Once that's done, and we have her living at a new address under her new name, we'll get in touch with her about her meeting Adam."

"How're you going to do that? I mean, arrange a meeting?"

"Don't concern yourself with that, Lloyd. Trust me, we have all the necessary connections."

"I guess so. And after I give her the phone number, am I through with my part? I mean, can I start spending the money?"

"Hell no, Lloyd," Smith said brightly. "You're just starting. Once the plan is put into action, we'll still need someone Miss Dahlstrom trusts to, shall we say, handle her. You'll still be the middleman between her and us. No, you're a part of the whole picture."

That was something of a shock to Lloyd. He had wanted to spend that money, or at least some of it. Even more important, he wanted out of the trickier parts of the scheme. He didn't think it had much chance of succeeding, and if it failed, he could go down with the rest of this bunch. If he had it to do again, he'd turn down the money; but it was too late for that now.

He wondered whether Suzanne would eventually regret taking the money as well.

Chapter 27

New Identity, New Address

Suzanne told Marguerite she had decided to take the money. She didn't elaborate, didn't want to be talked out of it. Although she was far from confident she had made the right decision, she knew that would have been true no matter which way she had chosen. Marguerite for her part didn't try to argue with her, sensing it would do no good. She just hoped Suzanne's choice would not turn into the disaster she was sure it could be.

A few days later, Suzanne met with a man who called himself "Ginger," no other name given, the nickname clearly referring to the color of his hair. He explained that Suzanne would soon have a new identity, complete with a family history that, for apparently legitimate reasons, could not be traced. She would keep her first name, which would avoid the embarrassment of failing to answer to an unfamiliar one, but change her last name. Her appearance would also be altered, but not drastically, just enough so the few people who knew her would not readily recognize her picture should one appear in the news. Suzanne knew that her looks were her major asset, together with her carnal talents, of course, and the idea of changing them made her nervous. But Ginger assured her it was just a matter of changing such things as hair and eye color, hair style, and the like.

Unusual glasses also changed one's appearance.

"But what if those 'few people' do recognize me? What then?" she asked.

"Best you become real camera shy, avoid having your picture taken as much as possible. Wear dark glasses in public. From what I understand, Adam is the reclusive type anyway, avoiding publicity and all that. You should be fine."

Another week passed before Suzanne again heard from Lloyd.

"They want you to give notice to your boss and be prepared to move on Friday."

"But that's in just three days," Suzanne protested. "I can't be ready by then."

"I'm afraid you'll have to," Lloyd said. "They apparently want to get this here plan of theirs underway." He told Suzanne a relocation company had been hired to find her a nice apartment in San Francisco, and to move all of her belongings there.

"San Francisco? I thought I'd be staying here in New York, or at least Washington, DC, where all the politicians are."

"No, Washington's maybe where the politicians are, but Frisco's where Adam lives. Remember, he's the one you'll be, uh, dealing with first."

This was not starting out as Suzanne had pictured it. She wouldn't just be across town from Marguerite, and for that matter from Patricia, her lifelines should things go south, but across the country. It was the first of many times she would regret her decision to take the money.

****

The money arrived in her bank account promptly after she had agreed to the group's proposition. Or rather it arrived in several bank accounts, each less than one hundred thousand dollars and each opened in a different name, but all accessible by Suzanne. She had received the same warning as had Lloyd about spending it before performing her part of the plan. She had asked Lloyd whether she could keep the money if she did her part but for some reason the plan did not work. He in turn had checked with "Smith," who answered in the affirmative.

"All she has to do is what we tell her. If, say, McNeil suddenly gets religion and becomes celibate, or some other unexpected shit happens that isn't her fault, the money's hers."

Lloyd reported this back to Suzanne. But, somehow, he didn't believe it.

****

Suzanne wrote to her mother that she had been offered a new job in San Francisco, so she would be moving there. She would be much closer to Los Angeles and could visit Mary Sue from time to time.

It was just the opposite with Marguerite. She would be too far away to visit, and besides, it was best she make a clean break with her former world, at least until this weird assignment was finished.

"I don't know, honey. I wish I could change your mind, could talk you outta this. We were both doin' so well, havin' a good time and makin' a pretty good living. Is the money really worth it?"

Suzanne had no ready answer for that, because she really didn't know. Although she had wanted not to discuss her decision further with Marguerite, she had to say what was on her mind, and in her heart. And she said it through tears.

"You know I'll miss you terribly," Suzanne said.

"I've never had a friend like you, probably never will again. What I really want is for this to be just one chapter in my life, and not the last one. Whether this stupid scheme works or not, whether I end up rejected by the president, or by his brother, or whether it all works as planned, in a year or less it'll be over. And when it's over I promise to come back, to pick up where I—where we left off. If you'll still want me to be your friend by then."

Marguerite put an arm around Suzanne's shoulder and spoke soothingly. "Why shouldn't I want you, honey? Why would I change?"

"No, I'm the one who'll change," Suzanne said. "At least if I end up in bed with the president."

"Well, you won't've committed any crimes. You'll just be famous."

"More like notorious, like Monica Lewinsky. Picture in all the papers, on the internet…you know. And while seducing the president may not be a crime—it isn't treason or anything, is it?—it's hardly considered good behavior, is it?"

Marguerite smiled. "No, I guess not. But neither is what we do now. Don't worry, you'll be welcome back."

And that was how they left it.

Before she moved out, Suzanne reminded Marguerite that she was not even supposed to have told her about the plan. "So whenever we talk or write, we'll have to be real careful what we say." The last thing Suzanne wanted was to somehow get Marguerite in trouble because of her. They decided the safest way to communicate was the old-fashioned way, by writing letters. It was safer than e-mail, safer than talking on the phone. To be extra careful, Suzanne would rent a post

office box for her "private" mail, just in case anyone was
watching what arrived at her apartment.

Chapter 28

Betsy Green

As Lloyd promised, the Gang, which—for want of a better term—was what Suzanne and Lloyd had agreed to call the mysterious group behind the sister-in-law scheme, arranged not only for Suzanne's belongings to be moved, but for her accommodations in San Francisco. Her furnished apartment was in a fashionable new building South of Market Street—or SoMa in the vernacular—a recently-redeveloped neighborhood that used to be referred to as Skid Row. Now rundown warehouses and flop houses were replaced by modern skyscrapers and toney bistros. If one ignored the pervasive aroma of urine from the equally pervasive street people, it was a very pleasant place to live.

Suzanne liked the location and the apartment. She had a nice view, modern appliances, even a doorman in front. In fact, it was similar to some of the better apartments she had visited in the line of duty, when she was engaged by a local client rather than one from out of town.

Waiting for her in the apartment was a complete new identity, everything from a birth certificate and social security card to a driver's license, all in a new name.

Apparently, she was now Suzanne Donohue.

Suzanne's hair was now a light shade of auburn and

she had a very short, chic new hairstyle, much different than she had ever worn her hair when it was long and blond. It took her a while to get used to seeing her new self in the mirror.

Colored contact lenses changed her distinctive two-tone eyes into baby blue.

Suzanne had already arranged for a transfer of her bank account—the one she had been using, not the ones containing the million dollars. She was to be given a monthly stipend for expenses, so she would not be tempted—or need—to spend the other money before she had completed her tasks.

The Gang gave her a few days to settle in before she was contacted by a woman calling herself Betsy Green. Lloyd had said his contact was named Smith. They were not very original with their names, Suzanne thought.

"Suzanne?" Betsy Green said. "Could we get together tomorrow morning? It's time to put our little plan into action." Betsy had a distinct Southern accent, not commonly encountered in the accent-neutral Bay Area.

"Yeah, sure. Where would you like to meet?"

"I'd prefer we talk at your place. More private than a coffee shop or the like. Ten o'clock okay?"

"Sure. Do you know where I live?"

"Sweetie, I'm the one who found it." And she hung up.

****

Promptly at ten a.m., the newly-minted Suzanne Donohue opened the door to a matronly woman of about fifty-five wearing a very plain wool skirt and a yellow sweater, loosely fitting over sagging breasts and generous midriff. She looked more like a refugee from a church social than a conspirator against the president.

Betsy Green, if that was her name, stuck out her hand and, when Suzanne reciprocated with hers, shook it soundly.

"I'm Betsy. Pleased t' meet you." She walked in without the formality of an invitation and sat on the sofa that she had probably selected. She patted the other cushion, saying, "Have a seat."

Suzanne sat.

"Would you like some coffee?" Suzanne asked, feeling she should make it clear who was hosting whom.

"No thanks," Betsy responded, not unkindly. "Let's get right down to business, if that's okay."

"Sure. What do you want to discuss?"

"Adam McNeil, naturally. How you're gonna get close enough to him to make your move. I assume you have the moves to make?"

Suzanne couldn't help laughing. "If you mean can I get a man interested in me, I suppose so. I'm sure you know what I was doing before I came here. Although I heard this guy is shy and not very social, so it'll be a challenge."

"That it'll be," Betsy said. Her eyes scanned Suzanne's face and figure. "But just looking at you, I can see you're up to it. If I was inclined that way, I'd be drooling over gettin' you in bed already."

Suzanne was very glad Betsy was not inclined that way.

"So how do I get to meet this Adam guy? If he isn't social, and being kind of a celebrity—"

"It's his brother Patrick who's the celebrity, but you're right, it does make him harder to approach, because there are always news people around looking for a storyline about Patrick or anything connected to him. But I think we've got that figured out."

"How to approach him?"

"Right. This is the plan. Adam McNeil is real big on good works. Supports lots of charitable organizations, that sort of thing. As it happens, he and I are both on the board of the local Red Cross chapter, and in fact I'm presently the president of the chapter, so I know him a little. He's a biologist by profession, spends most of his time in a lab over in Berkeley. Has a special interest in biomedicine. Well, I invited him to give a little talk to our chapter on recent breakthroughs in medical science, one of his specialties, and he agreed."

Suzanne shifted uneasily. "I hope you aren't expecting me to talk to him about biology. I was terrible at it in school—"

"Hush. I'm getting to that. So next week on Wednesday we have a special luncheon meeting where he'll give this little talk.

"We've invited some of our biggest donors, as well as chapter members. As the one organizing the shindig, I get to set up the seating arrangements. Want to guess where you and I'll be sitting?"

"Uh, next to Adam?"

"Got it. I'll bring you along as a friend who just moved here from New York. I'll say you're still finding your way around the Bay Area, looking for work, all that. I'm bringing you along to meet a few people, including Adam, of course. Also because you're interested in biology."

"But like I said—"

"Because you're *interested* in biology," Betsy repeated, more slowly. "I'll be giving you a bunch of reading materials to go over before next Wednesday. Sort of Biology for Dummies stuff. You don't have to be a biologist, just a layman who's interested and has read a little about it. Maybe seen a few specials on Public Television, that sort of thing. Just so you can talk— and listen—intelligently. It flatters a man that a woman is interested in what he does, but I don't have to tell you that, do I?"

Suzanne shook her head. That was pretty basic information. "But how will we get from sitting next to each other to, well, to something more intimate? I can't exactly come on to him there at the meeting, can I?"

"Of course not. All you can do is meet him there. But then you have to leave the meeting with him."

"And how do I do that?"

"Just listen. I'll tell him I was supposed to take you back home—you don't have a car and it's a long ride on the bus, and you don't know your way around yet, etcetera—but I just got a call that I have to rush home, as my husband fell and needs a ride to the emergency room, or something like that. I have to polish my story. Anyway, I'll ask him to please run you home in his car. He's a real nice guy and I'm sure he won't refuse and leave you stranded. So you'll have him to yourself for as long as it takes to get home."

"That sounds good, but I can't exactly propose marriage on the way home."

"Of course not. It's gonna be a long process. The idea is just to get acquainted. Tell him you're new around here, don't know anyone except me, would he maybe meet you for lunch, that sort of thing. I'm sure you'll come up with a way to get together with him again. If not, I'll call him and say something like you told me you'd really like to get to know him better, why doesn't he give you a call, etcetera. But I doubt that'll be necessary if you play your cards right."

Suzanne doubted it too.

After Betsy gave Suzanne the details of the meeting, Suzanne asked, "What should I wear?"

"Hmm. Do you have something that kinda emphasizes your curves and cleavage without seeming cheap or immodest? You know, muted colors, reasonable length skirt, not too tight on top, but open enough to give him an idea of what's underneath?"

Suzanne thought for a moment and said, "Yeah, I think I can handle that. I might have to go out and buy something."

"Good. We'll reimburse you if necessary. Any other questions?"

"Well, maybe you'd better tell me something about yourself, and how we're supposed to have met and such, in case he asks."

"Of course. How stupid of me. This is my first time doing anything like this too. I'm married. My husband's name is George. We live in the Richmond District. George is an architect, and I'm retired from teaching first grade." Suzanne thought she fit the school teacher image quite well. She also wondered how much she was being paid for her part of the scheme. Probably the same as Lloyd.

"Is Betsy Green your real name?" Suzanne asked.

Betsy looked a bit puzzled by the question. "Why, yes. Why do you ask?"

"Oh, nothing. I just thought the people behind this might not want to use their real names."

"Maybe not, but I'm just someone getting paid to be

your contact here. I mean, I believe in what they're doing and all that and am glad to be part of it, but I'm not one of the people organizing everything. Besides, they needed someone already established in the community with the right contacts, not some fictitious person."

"Yes, I see what you mean." But who were these mysterious people—the Gang—behind the plan? Suzanne wondered whether she would ever find out.

"How long have you lived in San Francisco, and where did you live before that?"

"Been here about fifteen years. Before that Dallas. Born and raised there, though I lived in New York for a few years. As for how we met, it was in New York a couple of years ago when you were a cocktail waitress at the Blue Note."

"How did you know I worked at the Blue Note?"

Betsy laughed. "Kid, I know more about you than your mama does at this point. And I'm sure the people who gave me that information have a lot more they didn't tell me."

Suzanne knew the Gang had a lot of information about her, but she hadn't realized just how detailed their information was. It sent a chill down her spine. Meanwhile, Betsy continued:

"My husband and I were visiting my relatives in the city and were there at the Blue Note for drinks after the theater. You were our waitress, you and I got to talking, and we sorta hit it off. We invited you to go out to dinner with us the next week, on a Friday."

"Where did we go to eat?"

Betsy thought. "Good question. How about the Gramercy Tavern? That's a really good place. After that we went to a few shows together, that kind of thing, and when you moved out here you didn't know anyone else, so you called us and, well, here you are. Can you remember all that?"

Suzanne smiled. "Probably not, but I'll make some notes after you leave while it's still fresh in my mind."

"Which is a cue for me to scram. Here's my contact information," Betsy said, handing Suzanne a piece of paper with some writing in a careful, school teacher's hand, "and I'll be back with that study material on biology tomorrow. Okay?"

Suzanne nodded. "I guess so. I sure hope I can bring this off."

Betsy patted her hand. "I'm sure you can, dear. You strike me as having all the necessary qualities: smarts and looks."

Betsy Green let herself out, leaving Suzanne to ponder once again what she had gotten herself into.

If nothing else, it was going to be an interesting next few weeks.

PART 5: ADAM

Chapter 29

The Luncheon

The following Wednesday morning, Betsy Green picked up Suzanne at her apartment to take her to the Red Cross luncheon at which Adam McNeil would speak on the subject of "Recent Advances in Biomedicine." She was wearing a light gray skirt that came down to her knees and a frilly, dusty rose blouse that, with the top two buttons open, just hid the décolletage separating her prominent ivory breasts behind a thicket of lace. It seemed to say "No Trespassing without an Invitation." Her lightweight coat, which was newly acquired at Macy's, was charcoal-colored and plain, revealing nothing more than her calves and a general outline of her body. Her makeup was light to non-existent, but that was usual for her, as her complexion had never required added color or softened lines.

For several days, Suzanne had been studying the materials on biology and biomedicine that Betsy had brought her. She had never lacked intelligence in school, just motivation. She had worked only as hard as she had to, and with ready access to her male classmates' work, she did not have to work overly hard. But now she had no one to do the work for her, and she knew the success of her mission—and the security of her million dollars—depended on her buckling down and learning what she could of Adam McNeil's profession and passion.

Suzanne assumed she would find the materials both deadly dull and too arcane to understand, but to her surprise, she found them quite interesting. They were sufficiently simplified as not to require any prior knowledge of the subjects, and they were written in a style closer to a magazine article than a textbook.

Prepared as she was, she was nervous. Like a young actor taking the stage for the first time in a starring role, she was uncertain how well she would remember her lines, or in this case her moves. *Not too aggressive,* she kept telling herself, *friendly but not fawning, interested in his opinions.* She wanted to achieve an air of positive but understated sexuality, just hinting at possible pleasure below the surface. Could she pull it off?

She would know soon.

****

They arrived in due course at a modern-looking building that declared itself to be the Knights of Columbus Hall. They entered a large foyer, off of which were three wide corridors. Betsy led the way, taking the right-hand corridor. At the end of the corridor were double doors. Betsy opened the right-hand door and indicated Suzanne should precede her in. Suzanne did and found herself in a wood-paneled banquet room containing about a dozen tables, each with four chairs. Most of the tables were already occupied by three or four guests. At the front was a lectern holding a microphone, next to which was a small table with a pitcher of water and a glass.

Suzanne turned to Betsy inquiringly. "Go on down to the front, dear," Betsy said. "We're at the head table, the one nearest the lectern." Suzanne wended her way to the head table as directed. One seat was already occupied by a youngish man who was glancing at some notes in his hand. He was not good-looking by any means, although he probably would not be considered homely. He was just very plain, with the type of face one forgets as soon as it is out of one's sight.

The man was wearing a slightly-rumpled blue suit, a white dress shirt, and a red tie, all just as plain as his visage. He also wore thick, dark-rimmed glasses that gave him a professorial appearance but did not flatter his face. *If that's the guy*, Suzanne thought, *it's no wonder he doesn't get out and about much. Probably spends all his time reading books.*

As soon as the two women arrived at the table and the man looked up and saw them, he smiled and rose to his feet. He looked from Suzanne to Betsy. "Hello, Adam," Betsy said, shaking the hand the man had extended to her. "Thanks so much for agreeing to speak to us. I want you to meet my friend Suzanne Donohue. She just moved here from New York and I'm the only one in the Bay Area she knows, so I invited her along to give her a chance to meet some people, and I guess you're the first one." Stepping back to allow Suzanne and Adam to face each other, she made the formal introduction: "Adam McNeil, Suzanne Donohue. Suzanne, Adam." The two shook hands, after which Adam pulled out a chair for Betsy on his right side, and when she was seated one for Suzanne on Betsy's right.

Seeing this, Betsy rose quickly, putting her hand on Suzanne's arm before she could sit in the proffered chair. "No, Suzanne dear, why don't you sit over there next to Adam? You'll see a lot better from there. We're the only ones at this table, so there's lots of room."

Suzanne did as she was told, and Adam didn't object. *This lady knows what she's doing,* Suzanne thought. *At least when it comes to arranging things.*

Once they were all seated, Betsy made sure there were no awkward silences that might be inappropriately filled.

She turned to Adam. "Suzanne was pleased when I told her the subject of your talk, Adam. She's very interested in the subject."

"Well, I don't know any of the technical stuff, of course. Just what I've read in magazines or seen on TV. But I find it fascinating. You must really enjoy your work."

Betsy looked pleased with Suzanne's contribution. She was taking the initiative and saying just enough to get a conversation started. With her lead-in, Adam happily explained what it was like to do research in biomedicine, the new challenges of microbiology, and other topics. He and Suzanne talked through lunch, until it was time for Adam's speech.

When dessert had been served, Betsy got up and went to the lectern. After asking for quiet, she introduced Adam with a list of his degrees and accomplishments and said how fortunate they were to have him as a speaker, as well as a member of their board. She then stepped back as Adam rose to polite applause. "I hope you enjoy it," he said to Suzanne before making his way to the lectern. Water poured and throat cleared, Adam began what turned out to be a half-hour speech, followed by fifteen minutes of questions and answers. During the speech, Betsy received a text message on her cell phone. She glanced at it, looked alarmed, then put away her phone and sat quietly. At the end of the question period,

Betsy again rose and went to the lectern. She thanked Adam, the audience applauded, and both returned to the table.

Immediately as they sat down, Betsy turned to Adam with a look of concern on her face.

"Is something wrong, Betsy?" Adam said, looking concerned himself.

"Well, yes there is. I just got a message from my husband, George. He's been in a little accident with his car, and—"

Now Adam really looked concerned. "I hope he wasn't hurt," he said.

"No, thank goodness. But his car is a mess and had to be towed and he needs me to come get him as soon as possible, 'cause he has to be at a conference in about an hour, and— well—"

"Do you need a ride out there to pick him up? If so, I could…"

Betsy saw that Adam had taken the bait but was tugging on the wrong pole. She moved quickly to straighten him out.

"No, dear, I have my car and can take care of George. But if you possibly could take Suzanne home, I'd really appreciate it. I drove her here, but her apartment is in the opposite direction I'll be going. It's kind of a long way by public transportation, especially for someone who doesn't know the city." She waited hopefully for a gallant response.

Adam wasn't just gallant, he was eager. Suzanne had that effect on even the most blasé of men. He turned toward Suzanne and smiled. "I'd be pleased to drive you home," he said, "if that's all right with you, of course."

Suzanne gave him her sweetest, most innocent

smile, and assured him it was just fine with her.

Betsy immediately got up to go, gathering her coat and purse. "Thank you so much, Adam. George and I really appreciate it. And I'm sure Suzanne does too. I'll be on my way, then." She took Adam's hand. "Thank you again for being our speaker. Your talk was most interesting."

Adam assured her it was his pleasure, and a few seconds later Betsy was gone and Adam and Suzanne were left by themselves.

"Well, I guess we'd better get going too," Adam said. He rose and helped Suzanne into her coat.

She smiled. "It's awfully nice of you to do this. I hope it won't be too far out of your way."

"Not at all," Adam said. "I'm glad I can help."

He led the way to the parking lot, where he opened the passenger door of a dark green SUV of indeterminate make and vintage.

They all looked alike to Suzanne. She got in, making sure Adam could get a peek at her thighs as she swung her legs around.

Suzanne gave Adam the address of her apartment, and they drove away from the hall in that direction. Adam didn't seem to be the talkative type; at least he didn't offer any conversation starters, concentrating on his driving. So Suzanne put into play the dialogue she had been rehearsing.

"I really enjoyed your talk, Adam. Biology is a subject that's always interested me, but I never had a chance to study it in school. I had to go to work after high school and didn't get to college. Did you always know you wanted to study biology and be a scientist?"

Adam laughed. "No, nothing like that. In fact, when

I was a kid, I wanted to be a fireman or astronaut, like most boys. Then when I was a teenager, I wanted to be in politics like my older brother. But when I understood what it was really like…well, that's another story. Let's just say I decided to wait until I was in college and explore whatever seemed interesting. I'd always liked the science experiments we did in high school, and when I took chemistry and biology at university, I knew that was the path I wanted to follow. And here I am. What about you? What do you do?"

Suzanne knew she would have to deal with that question early on, and she was prepared.

"I'm afraid I'm still looking for the right path to follow, as you put it. I went to New York thinking I'd find more opportunities there, maybe as a fashion model, but the only work I'd been able to find after a couple of years was as a secretary and as a cocktail waitress. That's how I met Betsy, waiting on her table."

"Yes, that's what she said. So why did you come out here?"

"I didn't like it in New York. Too big, too noisy, and I didn't like the weather. I grew up near LA and wanted to get back to the West Coast, sort of start over. I never liked LA much—too big and noisy, like New York—so I came here to the Bay Area."

Suzanne hoped she had been just forthcoming enough to avert suspicion, and just vague enough to avoid being caught in an inconsistency. She knew she had better direct the conversation to the most crucial subject of the day.

"Adam, I really do appreciate your taking me home like this, and I kind of hesitate to ask, but…well, as you know I'm new here and don't know anyone except Betsy

217

and George…and well, and you now. Betsy's a real nice lady and all that, but she's way older than me and we don't have—don't have the same interests, you might say. Would it be possible for us to meet sometime, maybe for lunch, so I can talk to you about the city and what there is to do here, and where I might look for work, that kind of thing?"

Adam laughed. "I'm afraid you've got the wrong man for that. I don't really get out much, and even though I've lived here quite a while, I'm almost as much a tourist as you when it comes to what a young person might do to have fun."

Suzanne persisted. She had to. "I understand. But I'm sure I'd still learn a lot from talking with you, and I'd feel like I had a friend here closer to my own age. Besides, I'd really love to talk a bit more about what you do in your work. It's still my ambition to go to college someday, and biology is what I'd like to study." She got this speech out just in time, as Adam was stopping in front of her apartment building.

Adam gave in. "Okay, you've talked me into it. I'd be pleased to have lunch with you and talk about whatever you like." He paused as if trying to decide what to say next, or whether to say anything at all, then added with a smile, "At the very least I'll enjoy looking across the table at you. You're a very pretty woman."

It was likely, Suzanne thought, Adam McNeil had never said anything quite so forward to a woman before, and certainly not so soon after meeting her. Suzanne appreciated the extra compliment in that circumstance and actually blushed, something that had seldom resulted from the myriad compliments on her face and body she had received from clients over the past two years. It was an interesting sensation.

They agreed to meet for lunch the following Friday. Adam said he would pick Suzanne up in front of her apartment building, where he was now dropping her off. He came around and opened her door and offered his hand to help her out. She politely declined the assistance and climbed out on her own, thinking it best to wait until their next meeting for even this minor level of hand-holding. She smiled and thanked him again, said she was looking forward to seeing him again, and walked into the building lobby without looking back.

Interest aroused. Intimacy avoided.

Further contact assured.

Chapter 30

Developing the Relationship

Dear Marguerite:
I sure miss you. It's pretty lonesome living here by myself. I can't even go out in the evening to find some action, in case someone who knows Adam McNeil might see me and ruin my chances with him. At least Adam isn't some kind of oddball like people seemed to think. He's just kind of shy and doesn't seem that comfortable with other people. He doesn't look like much, but he sure is intelligent.

Adam took me to lunch—remember I told you in my last letter how I practically had to beg him. He seemed real nervous and ill at ease at first, like I was the first woman he'd ever taken to lunch, though I doubt that. Maybe I'm the first woman like me he's ever taken to lunch, if you know what I mean. So after we talked a little about San Francisco and where I might look for work, I got him talking about his favorite subject, biology and what he calls biomedicine.

That's where you apply biology to medical problems. I'd have thought it would be really boring, but he's pretty good at explaining things at a level where someone like me can understand, so it was pretty interesting. And talking about his work he seemed much more relaxed, like he was in his element.

Anyway, it was a beautiful day and after lunch I said it sure would be nice to take a walk in Golden Gate Park, could he maybe drop me off there and I'd take a cab home. I was hoping he'd offer to go with me, at least for a half hour or so, and sure enough he did. We walked around Stow Lake, which is really pretty. No, we didn't hold hands. I'm taking this real slow. When he took me home, I was going to ask him if we could meet again sometime soon, but he beat me to it! He asked if we could have lunch next Wednesday. I said yes, of course.

When he dropped me off, I let him help me out of the car this time and gave his hand a little squeeze before letting go. He seemed kind of awkward, like he maybe wanted to show some affection but didn't know how or what was acceptable, so I gave him a little hug, just a friendly one, and thanked him for lunch and the walk. I think he wasn't expecting it, but he sure seemed to like it. I think we're still a long way from a kiss.

So far so good. I'll write again when there are any new developments.

Boy, this sure is different from my last job. I haven't had sex with anyone since I've been here. Another reason I wish you were here.

Love,
Suzanne

****

At their second lunch date, Adam seemed much more relaxed with Suzanne, even when he was not talking about his work. She took this as a good sign and decided to turn the heat up just a notch.

"I hope you don't mind my asking," she said when there was a lull in the conversation, "but do you have someone...you know...someone you're going out

221

with?"

Adam turned quite red in the face, and Suzanne was afraid she had made a false step, rushing him too fast.

"No, not really," he said, sounding quite embarrassed. "To tell the truth, you're—you're the first girl—sorry, I mean the first woman—I've been out with more than once in a long time. I mean with my work and all, I just don't get out socially very much. And besides, there aren't many what you'd call 'eligible women' where I work." He paused as if gathering his thoughts, or his courage, before saying, "I sure haven't been out with anyone as…as nice as you. Ever."

"Thank you for the compliment," Suzanne said, trying to look and sound demure. To Suzanne, Adam sounded more like one of the boys she had left behind in high school than a mature man in his late twenties. Here was someone who, probably because of a combination of his unprepossessing appearance and his introverted nature, had had almost no social life, at least little or none with the opposite sex. And speaking of sex, she guessed that was something else of which he'd had little or no experience.

Her goal, of course, was to change that. Radically.

****

Having established that Adam was available, which was no surprise, Suzanne thought it was time to get more serious.

"I was thinking," she said over dessert, "maybe we might take in a movie or something sometime. Would you like to do that?"

This was, in fact, exactly what Adam himself had been thinking, but he had not yet reached the stage of self-assuredness to ask the question. Much relieved that

Suzanne had made it unnecessary, he replied he would like very much to do that.

"How about Saturday?" he offered. "What would you like to see?"

"Saturday's fine," Suzanne said. "And I like just about any movie, so just surprise me." She assumed Adam did not follow the movies very closely and would need a day or so to get up to speed, an assumption that was largely correct.

On Friday evening, Adam telephoned Suzanne to say he would pick her up at seven-thirty. They would be seeing a Russian movie at the local art theater. "But they have subtitles, so you don't have to speak Russian," he assured her. "All the other movies I found seemed to be nothing but violence or sex or they were cartoons, and I didn't feel right taking you to one of those." Suzanne refrained from saying the ones with sex and violence were her favorites. This date was not for purposes of her entertainment, even if Adam thought it was.

On Saturday, Suzanne spent considerable time choosing her wardrobe for the evening. Should she wear something just a bit daring, thus turning up the heat a notch farther in their relationship? Or should she dress modestly and keep Adam's blood pressure normal for at least another week? Finally she decided they were sufficiently far along in their relationship—if it was yet a real relationship—to take a chance. To be honest, she was becoming anxious to get to what she was sure would prove to be the most difficult, the trickiest, and in a way the riskiest part of her assignment—maneuvering Adam, a seemingly contented bachelor, from the sunny fields of newfound sexual delight into the dark and possibly dangerous forest of marriage.

The movie Adam had chosen, *Endurance*—at least that was the subtitled translation of the Russian *Vinausleevast*, which was written in the Cyrillic alphabet and so unintelligible to them both—was what would be called a historical drama, if one could follow the subtitles. Suzanne did her best, but she lost the thread of the story before it was half over and spent the remainder of the movie worrying how she would discuss it intelligently with Adam afterward.

She needn't have worried. One of the first things Adam said when they were seated in his car was, "I don't know about you, but I didn't follow half of that movie. Next time I'll let you choose." This was, of course, good news on two fronts: Adam wasn't an intellectual snob who wouldn't admit to not understanding something; and there would definitely be a "next time."

****

The next time, a week later, Suzanne chose a romantic comedy, a "rom-com," thinking it would be safe and inoffensive, and possibly it would also give Adam some ideas. As before, at the end of the evening Adam stopped the car in front of Suzanne's apartment building and started to open his door so he could come around and help Suzanne out. But this time Suzanne put her hand on his arm and said, "Just a minute." When Adam turned back toward her, Suzanne leaned over, put her hand gently on his cheek, whispered "I had a really nice time," and gave him a light but meaningful kiss. Nothing dramatic. Just enough to say, "I like you, and maybe there's more where that came from."

Adam looked a bit stunned for a second or two, then recovered his composure, cleared his throat, and said in a slightly hoarse whisper, "So did I." He then got out, came around and helped Suzanne out, and saw her to the door.

"I'd invite you in for a drink," she said, "but I have an early engagement, so I'd better get right to bed. Maybe next time?"

Adam, who looked more relieved than disappointed, nodded. "Sure. That's fine. I'll call you during the week." Suzanne squeezed his hand, turned, and entered the building. She didn't look back, but she was pretty sure Adam was still standing there, wondering what it would be like if she did invite him in.

He would soon find out.

Chapter 31

Closing the Sale

Dear Marguerite:

Thanks for your letter. Yes, my little campaign seems to be going well so far. Betsy Green—she insists it's her real name—came over and asked for an update. She seemed pleased when I told her what had happened so far. She said our "relationship" had apparently gone unnoticed so far by the press, which was a very good thing. Apparently it would be okay if there were some mention in the local papers, but if it became national news, and if there were any pictures, someone back in New York was bound to see Suzanne Donohue's resemblance to Suzanne Dahlstrom. She said we would cross that bridge when we came to it, and the later we came to it the better.

It's still pretty lonesome here in my apartment, but I'm expecting things to get much more "social" next Saturday. That's when I make my first move on Adam. It will either seal the deal or scare him off. Keep your fingers crossed.

Miss you too. Maybe we can find a way to get together sometime. You're clever—try to think of something. Meanwhile, write soon. And wish me luck.

Love,
Suzanne

****

Filling in the time between meetings with Adam proved to be a little more difficult than Suzanne would have thought. After all, in a city as tourist-friendly as San Francisco, there should be no problem finding interesting places to go and things to see. And indeed she did go and see where every tourist went and what every tourist saw. That used up about two weeks. Suzanne was limited in where she could explore, because she didn't have a car. Betsy Green had not provided her with one, and she didn't want to spend the money to buy one. She was considering leasing one until she checked with Betsy, who told her the less her new identity was tested, as it would be for a credit check by the leasing company, the safer she was. So anywhere not easily reachable by public transportation was not reachable by Suzanne.

What Suzanne could do was make frequent trips by bus to Golden Gate Park. There she loved to wander along the miles of trails around and through the park, skirting ponds and lakes, winding among gardens and dells. She spent hours in the park's museums—the DeYoung, the Academy of Sciences, the Planetarium—and at the San Francisco Zoo.

One place Suzanne loved to sit on a sunny day was at the park's children's playground. She didn't know why she liked watching the kids play on the swings and slides, but somehow it seemed to help her forget for a while the less-than-honest role she was playing with Adam McNeil.

One day as she was finishing her sandwich on a bench near the sandbox, watching as several boys and girls played together, a woman of about her age sat down on the bench next to her. When their eyes met the woman smiled. "Okay if I sit here?"

"Of course," Suzanne answered.

After a few moments, the woman said, "My name is Fran. My son is the one there in the green outfit. It's his favorite color." She indicated one of the two boys in the sandbox, who looked to be about two years old. "Is one of them yours?"

"Oh, I'm not married," Suzanne replied. Realizing this did not necessarily answer the question, she added, "And I don't have any children. I just like to watch them play."

Fran laughed. "Yes, well, they're certainly fun to watch when they're playing nicely. Not so much when they're not." As if on cue, one of the children tried to take a plastic pail away from Fran's son, who responded with a loud shriek. Fran went over to the sandbox and quickly sorted out the property rights issues, settled her son down, and returned to the bench, rolling her eyes to indicate "see what I mean?"

The two women talked a while, mostly about children, until Fran left to take her son home for his nap. After she left, Suzanne sat and stared for several minutes at the remaining children in the sandbox, as well as others playing on the swings and slides. Something stirred inside her she did not recognize. For the first time she could remember, she wondered whether she would ever have a child.

She knew she did not want to be an unwed mother—she had seen more than her share of the tribulations of single parenthood. No, first she would need to have a husband—a real husband, not a temporary husband of convenience, as she hoped Adam would be—and given her history, her line of work, and her opinion of men, that seemed highly unlikely. What if her husband turned out to be like her own father, like her first foster father, like that policeman, like…like all men? How could she take that chance?

It was clear to her she could not.

****

Saturday evening. Another movie, another rom-com aimed at giving Adam ideas. Suzanne and Adam were settling into a comfortable routine, slowly getting to know each other better as they talked and shared.

As they pulled up in front of her apartment building, Suzanne said, "Would you like to come in for coffee?" When Adam's face seemed noncommittal, she added hopefully, "I've baked some yummy cookies for the occasion. Please?"

He could hardly refuse, and didn't. Looking a bit nervous, Adam accompanied Suzanne to her apartment door. When she opened it and waited for him to enter, he seemed to hesitate just a moment before crossing the threshold.

"Have a seat on the sofa," Suzanne said as she headed for the kitchen. "I'll put the coffee on and get out the cookies." She was no stranger to baking, having been taught by Mary Sue early in life. And although her cooking talents would not be tested on this occasion, she had learned the basics from her mother and plenty of exotic embellishments from Marguerite. Everything Marguerite did, it seemed, was exotic and embellished.

When she returned to the living room carrying a tray holding a coffee pot and cups and a plate of cookies, Adam was leafing through some of the magazines on the coffee table in front of him. Suzanne had taken pains to lay out an assortment that spoke of an interested, eclectic mind with just a touch of humor and adventure. *Discovery* and *National Geographic*, for example, were there. *People* and *Cosmo* were not.

Suzanne laid the tray on the coffee table.

"How do you like your coffee?" she asked.

"Black is fine."

She poured him a cup of black coffee and one for herself. She then seated herself next to Adam on the sofa.

"Cookie?" She held out the plate of large chocolate-chip cookies. Adam took one.

For a few minutes, they nibbled and sipped in silence. Then for several minutes they discussed the movie they had seen. Suzanne glanced at the clock. Eleven-thirty. Time to warm things up.

"Would it be okay if I put on some music?" she asked. "I just got a wonderful new album I'd like you to hear."

"Oh, sure." He looked at his watch, but said nothing about the time.

Suzanne got up and fiddled for a few seconds with her MP3 player. Immediately Frank Sinatra could be heard singing in the background as she returned to the sofa.

"Do you like Sinatra?" she asked Adam.

"Sure do. He's my favorite singer." This was no surprise to Suzanne, since Adam's fondness for Sinatra was one of the many things she had been told about Adam by Betsy Green. It still amazed her how much of a person's life was "out there" to be found and, in this case, put to good use.

"I'm glad to see you like him too," Adam said. "I guess we have similar tastes, in movies and music at least."

"And I hope in people," Suzanne said. She snuggled a little closer to Adam so their thighs were touching, although in a most casual way.

For a few minutes, the two Sinatra devotees listened in silence. Then Suzanne asked softly, "Would it be all right if I kissed you?" This was a most unusual thing for Suzanne to say, because no one she had ever gone out with had ever objected to kissing or being kissed by her. Eugene Lee's rejection of her advances didn't count, of course. But she wasn't taking any chances on seeming too forward with Adam.

He turned to her. "Absolutely. If I can kiss you back."

It sounded casual, as if he said it to all the girls, but Suzanne could easily see how nervous he was, could feel it in the slight tremor in his body.

She put her lips lightly on Adam's and gave him a gentle but meaningful kiss. He reciprocated. This was the easy part. What came next would be the real test of where this train was headed and how fast.

As they kissed, Adam clearly being in no hurry to end the experience, Suzanne took his left hand, which he had placed lightly on her right shoulder, and slid it over and onto her right breast. If he seemed nervous before, he seemed to shift into momentary panic now, but he didn't resist. Would he let it stay there? If so, would he explore farther? She would know in a moment.

For this date, Suzanne was wearing a loose, above-the-knee skirt and a simple cotton blouse covering a light bra. She had considered a tight sweater and going braless, but she was afraid that would send the wrong message. So although Adam's hand was definitely atop her breast, it would still take a bit of effort for him to get to the actual item beneath.

Suzanne made a start by casually unbuttoning the top button of the blouse. Would Adam follow through and unbutton the rest?

Yes. And it was all downhill from there.

****

Suzanne allowed Adam to explore to his heart's content, glad to see that he was definitely enjoying the experience. She could tell he was still somewhat nervous by the slight shaking of his hand, but that was to be expected. If he had ever been invited to fondle a woman's breasts before—and she doubted it—it was unlikely it was a woman quite like Suzanne. Rather than aggressively squeezing the merchandise, like most of her clients—and, for that matter, most of the boys in school—who had the opportunity, he was treating it with the kind of gentle care and respect one would use in petting a kitten.

Suzanne then took the next bold step, again one that could make or break the evening. She slid her hand casually onto Adam's crotch to gauge the activity beneath. It was immediately apparent Adam was well and truly aroused, as might of course be expected under the circumstances. *Here goes nothing,* Suzanne thought, then took the plunge. She pulled down Adam's zipper and, after checking to be sure he was not showing alarm or displeasure, knelt down in front of him and proceeded to administer a most skillful example of oral sex. By necessity, it was performed without a condom, something she was generally loathe to do, as her unfortunate experience with Craig demonstrated. But she had already decided that in Adam's case she would have to make an exception. The benefits outweighed the risks, she thought. If she had a condom at the ready, it would look as if she had planned the whole series of events, which of course she had. It would be much better to make everything look spontaneous, as if they began with an innocent kiss and just couldn't contain the passion that resulted. As for the risk, she was quite confident, from what she'd been told and what she'd observed, that Adam had not been sleeping around with prostitutes, or anyone else likely to have infected him.

The experiment didn't last very long, and when Suzanne looked up to see what expression was on Adam's face, she was pleased to see it was one of pure pleasure and contentment.

Now Suzanne could relax as well. If Adam had ever had this experience before—and she doubted it—it was unlikely to have been as well delivered, with as much practice as she had had.

"Did you enjoy that?" Suzanne asked unnecessarily.

Adam just nodded his head. Obviously he was still enjoying it.

Suzanne stood up and sat back down on the sofa next to Adam. She whispered, "I guess I got a little carried away. I hope you aren't upset."

Adam looked at her and said, "Upset? Jeez, no. I mean, I guess I started it anyway." Suzanne didn't disabuse him of this misconception.

"And I'm sure glad I did. I've never—that is, no woman has ever done that to me before." Again, no surprise there.

Suzanne chanced the next step. "Maybe next time we can…you know…do it properly. I mean—" And, here, she glanced downward. "—put that where it belongs."

She took his hand and guided it briefly under her skirt, then quickly took it away. Just a little sample to keep him interested.

"I'm sure I'd like that," Adam said, sounding extremely interested.

They made an arrangement to watch a movie together the following Saturday evening, only this time it would be a DVD they'd watch on Suzanne's TV. Suzanne doubted they would get very far into the movie before they became distracted by more urgent business.

This fish was well and truly hooked.

Chapter 32

Further Progress

Dear Marguerite:
Are you really coming to visit soon? That's great!
I've missed you so much. And I like your idea of meeting
only away from my apartment, in case it's being watched
or is bugged. I wouldn't put it past these people.

You wanted to know if I was still making progress
with Adam McNeil. I absolutely am! Last Saturday I gave
him the first, and certainly the best, BJ he's ever had. I
took a chance and suggested next week we might take
things all the way. I've actually been having a good time
going out with Adam. I know I'm just doing a job, but no
harm enjoying it, I guess.

Let me know when you have a definite date of
arrival. It's not as if I have much to do when I'm not
"working on" Adam, but I'd still like to know. I'm going
to look for some part-time work, so Adam doesn't get
suspicious about why I haven't found a job or think I'm
on welfare or something.

Can't wait to see you. (And not just see, if you know
what I mean.)
XXXX,
Suzanne

****

On Monday Suzanne received a visit from Betsy

Green. It wasn't unexpected, and in fact Suzanne was surprised Betsy hadn't visited much earlier.

"So, how's it going with Adam, dear?" Betsy asked after seating herself on the sofa.

"Oh, fine, I guess," Suzanne said. Her tone was noncommittal. She wasn't sure why.

"Just fine? That's not the way I've heard it," Betsy said. "Our sources say you've had two dates, and on Saturday Adam ended up here. Sounds like pretty good progress to me. Am I right?"

"I suppose so. That is, we didn't—didn't get very far the other evening. I don't know how long it might take before we—we get to the point I can begin to suggest marriage." Again Suzanne was not sure why she didn't come right out and say how quickly things were heating up. Was she really that unsure of herself? Or of Betsy and the others? Perhaps she was simply in no hurry to get to the next stage.

"Well," Betsy said with a hearty laugh, "I'm sure you'll have the guy roped and tied pretty soon." Her tone changed slightly when she added, "You'd better. That election is only a few months away, and if you two aren't hitched well before it, the whole plan could fall apart. And none of us wants that, do we?"

"No, of course not. Don't worry. I can handle Adam." *No pun intended,* Suzanne thought, but didn't dare add aloud. Wrong audience. Changing the subject, Suzanne said, "I was wondering, Betsy, if I shouldn't look for a job. At least a part-time one, anyway. I don't want Adam to get the idea I'm just lying around and being lazy, or that I have some other source of income I'm not telling him about. I'm supposed to be out here looking for work—"

"I get it," Betsy said, interrupting. "You're right. But I don't think you'll have t' go pound the pavement for work. I'm sure one of the bigshots we work for can find you something in their company."

Yeah, and keep an eye on me at the same time, Suzanne thought. But she knew better than to argue.

"That'd be great, Betsy. I'll wait to hear from you about it."

Betsy stood up and put her arm around Suzanne. "You're doin' fine, dear. I'll check back soon and hope to hear about lots more progress."

She gave Suzanne a little pat on the bottom, a pat that lingered just a little longer than was necessary, or so it seemed, and let herself out.

Even more than the implied threat in Betsy's earlier words, that last gesture gave Suzanne the shivers. *Let's not go there, Betsy,* she thought. *Let's not even think about it.*

****

Suzanne decided she needed to speed up the pace of her relationship with Adam, given Betsy's—and therefore her handlers'—apparent impatience. She thought it best not to confine their "dates" to sexual encounters, lest he consider her more of a recreational partner than a soul mate.

"Why don't we have a picnic in Golden Gate Park on Saturday," she asked him on the phone. "It's supposed to be sunny, and it'll give us a chance to talk."

"That sounds like a great idea," Adam said. "I'll pick you up at noon. Should I stop at a deli for some sandwiches?"

"No, no. I'll make sandwiches. I love packing a picnic lunch."

This was true, to an extent. As a young girl, Suzanne had always enjoyed the occasional picnics with her parents, when they were both sober and in a parenting mood. Since then she had had few opportunities to picnic, but when she did it brought back some of the few pleasant memories she had of her childhood, at least that part involving her father. Although she had never packed a picnic basket, she did love a picnic.

Suzanne went shopping for a proper picnic hamper. At William Sonoma she found a perfect one, wicker with a gaily printed lining and fitted out with all the necessary implements, including a ground cloth, plastic plates and cutlery, and even plastic wine glasses. It was expensive, but the cost was justified in her mind by the knowledge that this was to be an important battle in her campaign for Adam's hand.

Suzanne hummed to herself as she made sandwiches and tucked them into the basket, together with potato salad and a bottle of Napa Valley red wine. She added a half-dozen chocolate chip cookies she had baked. She was enjoying her work—if seducing an inexperienced male could be called work—more than she thought she would.

Adam appeared at Suzanne's door at five past twelve on Saturday. He was wearing much more casual clothes than she had yet seen him in, and he seemed more relaxed. Suzanne was dressed modestly, in not-too-tight jeans and a cotton blouse showing very little cleavage. This was to be a session for getting better acquainted socially, not sexually.

"Hi. You're right on time," Suzanne said as she handed Adam the picnic basket and closed the door behind her.

Adam lifted the lid of the basket slightly and peeked inside. "Looks delicious," he said. "Where should we go to eat?"

"There's a little lake in the park that has some quiet grassy areas around it. I thought we could eat there without a lot of other people crowded around."

Suzanne had spent several hours during the week scouting Golden Gate Park for just the right spot—quiet and romantic—for their picnic. Fortunately, unlike some city parks, Golden Gate Park had lots of beautiful trails off the beaten path, emerging at hidden ponds or quiet gardens. She directed Adam to the one she had chosen, just off a narrow pathway, next to a small lake, and far enough from the road that what little traffic noise there might be was muffled by the surrounding trees.

They spread the ground cloth, decorated to match the picnic basket lining and utensils, and Suzanne set out their lunch. Although there were occasionally people strolling by on the path, no one was within earshot, giving them all the privacy they needed.

Adam had told Suzanne, during their previous dates, a little about himself, most of which she already knew from her briefing before meeting him—although of course she purported to be learning it for the first time. But almost everything he told her was about his current circumstances—his job, what he did in his spare time, and so forth—and not his earlier years or his family. Now she asked for more details.

"Tell me about growing up with an older brother," she said between bites of a tuna salad sandwich. "I was an only child, for better or worse."

Adam laughed. "Well, it was mostly better, I guess. That is, better to have an older brother. Pat kind of looked after me, stood up for me if other kids teased me, that sort of thing. I wasn't much of an athlete or anything—still not—so I didn't do well in baseball or football, or fights, for that matter."

"Did you get into a lot of fights?" Suzanne sounded slightly alarmed.

"Not really, but I would get teased by the other kids sometimes because I was overweight and, like I said, not very athletic, and sometimes I would get mad and try to hit someone." He laughed again. "I usually lost, unless Pat was around and helped me out. He was a lot older, and in great shape, so it was like having King Kong on your side."

Suzanne laughed too. "Did you want to be just like your brother when you grew up?"

"Well, at first I did. I wanted to look like him too, but that didn't work out. He had lots of girlfriends; I'm sure he was having sex at an early age. I couldn't match him there any more than in a fight." He did not laugh at this reflection.

"So why aren't you in politics also?"

Adam became more serious yet. "That's a little…difficult to explain. I mean, I love my brother. He's a wonderful guy. But I think politics has…has somehow corrupted him. I think it corrupts everyone it touches."

"How so?"

"Oh, in lots of ways. It makes you beholden to the people who supply the money so you can get elected, whether you like those people or not. And without the money, you just don't get elected. Or reelected. Not president, not dogcatcher. Not that there aren't politics around a laboratory or a faculty, but it's not quite as pervasive—and destructive—in that setting. Did you know that from the day they take office, elected officials have to spend more time courting lobbyists and raising money for their next election than they do on the people's business? Whether they want to or not, if they expect to be reelected.

"You also have to compromise your principles in order to get anything accomplished, that or accept that you won't accomplish much, unless your party is strong enough you can ignore the other side. And then having too much power, like when the other party is real weak, often leads to the opposite result, doing whatever you like regardless of what the minority might want, or the people for that matter."

Adam stopped talking to chew on his sandwich and Suzanne thought about his words. She understood why Adam was so disillusioned about politics, and they could have an interesting discussion about it, but she could see it was a subject Adam became quite emotional over, which was not the kind of feelings she wanted this picnic to bring out. So she tried to steer the discussion toward more neutral territory.

"Well," she said, "I'm sure whatever it is politicians have to do to get by, your brother is doing the best he can, and if he does become president like people say he will, he'll be good for the country."

"Oh, I think he will," Adam said, his tone more upbeat. "As you can see, I'm not fond of politics, but as politicians go, my brother is one of the best. I just hope he can stay true to his principles once he gets elected. As for me, I'm happy having a profession that's pretty far from politics and lets me do what I think best—in my field, that is—without having to answer to anyone but myself, and my employers, of course.

"So now that I've bared my soul, what about you? You said you're an only child. What was it like growing up that way?"

Suzanne knew her early years were likely to be a topic of discussion, and the whole idea of the picnic was to get to know each other better, so she was prepared for the question. She had decided the best course was honesty, but not total honesty. She told Adam about her childhood and school years, the classes she most enjoyed, some of the friends she had, some of the lighter moments. But when it came to matters that might not sit well with this highly principled man, she became much more vague.

"I loved my dad," she said, which was the truth if she were referring to some of the years before he attacked her, then she added in monumental understatement, "but unfortunately he had a drinking problem, so there were times it was not so pleasant to have him around."

Adam nodded his understanding. It was not that she thought Adam, who seemed more than fair-minded, would think poorly of her for having been raped by her father, but he might pity her, and that was not the emotion that she wanted to elicit.

"I had a few boyfriends in school," she went on, "but I tried to keep them in their place, if you know what I mean."

That their "place" was serving her interests for minor sexual favors she omitted to add. Adam nodded again.

Having skipped lightly over the more dangerous aspects of her childhood story, she described briefly her move to New York. Of course, she omitted the part about the profession she ultimately chose, although she did admit to having been a part-time cocktail waitress. She didn't want to seem overly dull and unexciting.

From political and autobiographical, their discussion turned to more general topics, such as sports—neither of them was much interested—and some of the latest scientific discoveries—Adam thrived on these, and Suzanne was still finding the topic interesting, to her surprise.

After about two hours of eating, talking, and just relaxing in the sun, they packed up the picnic paraphernalia and Adam drove Suzanne home. If he was expecting her to invite him in or anything more intimate than a thank-you kiss at the door, he was disappointed. Suzanne knew the value of making her subject wait, giving him time to fantasize, to dream, to want to spend more time with this beautiful and—apparently—well-bred and down-to-earth woman. With this extremely sexy woman. The kiss having been delivered, Adam's hand squeezed for reassurance, Suzanne let herself in and closed the door.

She leaned back against the door and closed her eyes. Her goal was in sight. One more step to go.

The one big step.

Chapter 33

The Ultimate Weapon

It was time to bring out what Suzanne knew to be her best weapon. If, as she had told herself since she was a teenager, their sexual appetite was men's great weakness, and if, as she had demonstrated time and again since then, she possessed the means to take advantage of that trait, then Suzanne's next step was obvious.

The picnic in the park had been fun, more enjoyable than Suzanne had thought it would be, and she was sure it had accomplished its purpose of making Adam feel he now knew her more as a person, not just someone he took to the movies or who had given him his first oral sex experience. Having satisfied his brain, the next and, she hoped, final step was to satisfy the more important part of his anatomy.

Suzanne suggested that, for what was now their regular Saturday evening at the movies, they watch a DVD at her apartment. Adam was agreeable, doubtless anticipating that the entertainment would go well beyond that provided by the DVD player.

Promptly at five-thirty p.m. the following Saturday, Adam arrived again at Suzanne's door. He was dressed casually in gabardine slacks and a bright short-sleeve sport shirt, with matching socks and deck shoes. Suzanne, for her part, was wearing a tight black sweater over a short, loose yellow skirt. She was wearing soft ballet-type shoes with no stockings, and although she had on a bra, it was a very light one that in no way deterred her breasts from making a strong showing under her sweater. Adam couldn't help looking her up and down, but he quickly seemed to realize gawking was bad form and lifted his gaze to her eyes.

"It's great to see you again," he said. "I'm really looking forward to this evening."

So was Suzanne, for a similar but different reason.

Suzanne again had made dinner, subtly demonstrating her homemaking skills and inclinations. Adam's favorite dishes from his childhood had been included in the bio that Betsy had supplied—Suzanne had no idea where or how they were getting this kind of information, and she didn't think she really wanted to know—so it was easy to prepare something that made him feel relaxed and comfortable with this woman whose skills fitted so well with his needs and desires.

After dinner, Suzanne demonstrated the skill that best fitted Adam's most immediate desire. Suzanne had rented an R-rated movie that was just suggestive enough to arouse one's interest, without the explicit details that might lessen the live-action excitement to come. They watched snuggled together on the sofa, neither saying more than ten words throughout. When it was over and the TV tuned to a cable station of soft music, Suzanne snuggled a little closer, lightly stroked Adam's crotch, and said in her sexiest voice—which she usually reserved for her best clients—"I think I promised you some dessert. I'll show you where it's at."

Adam said nothing, but he looked more than willing to follow. Suzanne stood and took Adam's hand, waiting for him to get up from the sofa before leading him into the bedroom. There her king-size bed was open and waiting. Rose-colored silk sheets glistened in the soft lighting from two ceramic table lamps. Rose and white were the dominant colors of the walls and trim; the carpets were off-white. The furnishings—dresser, vanity with upholstered stool, full-length mirror, night stands— were also stained off-white. The entire package had a very sensuous, feminine quality that enhanced what was to come next.

Suzanne stopped and turned to face Adam. She smiled up at him.

"Is it okay if I take the lead here? After all, it is my apartment."

"Go right ahead," Adam said. "You're serving the dessert."

And that was the right answer, Suzanne thought. She reached up and began to unbutton Adam's shirt. Suzanne could tell that Adam was quite nervous, which she had expected. She had dealt with many first-time clients—first time with a call girl, and/or first time with any woman—and was used to it. It was no problem—he would be relaxed soon enough.

Once Suzanne had relieved Adam of his clothes, she led him over to the bed and gently guided him down, propping him up in back with two soft down pillows. This gave him a front-row loge seat for the next act.

Stepping back a bit, Suzanne stepped out of her shoes and began to undress.

****

Suzanne's aim was to increase Adam's desire for her body—as if he required much encouragement in that direction—without seeming coarse or cheap, and without giving him the impression she had practiced this act numerous times, as in fact she had. So when she had taken off her skirt and was wearing only a skimpy thong, she put her hands in front of the V of her crotch, gave a little giggle, and said in her sweetest, most innocent voice, "I hope you're enjoying this—I've never done it for anyone before." Well, she hadn't done it for free before, so she was being partly honest.

Adam, who clearly did not want Suzanne to stop at this crucial time, assured her he was thoroughly enjoying the show, and he was honored to be the first to see it.

Reassured, Suzanne continued by wriggling out of her thong and walked slowly to the bed.

****

When it was clear the session was over and Adam's body had relaxed, Suzanne, who had assumed the dominant upper position, rolled over onto her back, snuggling up against Adam's body.

"What do you think?" she whispered in his ear.

"I think you're terrific," he answered, and gave her a long kiss on the lips.

"You're actually not so bad yourself," Suzanne said.

Mission accomplished.

Chapter 34

Adam's Turn

After that first experience, Suzanne and Adam began dating regularly, often twice a week, sometimes going to movies, sometimes watching them at home, and on the weekends enjoying more picnics, as the weather continued to be perfect for lunch on a lawn. They didn't always end up in bed, although there was often a good bit of fondling on Adam's part. Suzanne didn't mind. In fact, she considered it both stimulating and flattering. Her body was, after all, Suzanne's finest asset, and it would be a shame for such perfection to go unappreciated.

Suzanne didn't think she was ready, despite the success of her seduction thus far, to make any suggestion of marriage to Adam. For one thing, she still had no idea how she would approach it. Unlike arousing—and satisfying—a man's sexual appetite, she had had no experience whatsoever stimulating a man's desire to marry, and she was unsure what would drive him toward the alter and what would drive him toward another state. Meanwhile, she telephoned Adam the following Tuesday and suggested to him that they reconvene at her place on Saturday evening, thinking at least one more session like the last one would be a good idea. To her surprise, he had a different idea.

"No, let's meet at my place," he said. "I'm actually a pretty good cook myself, and I'd like you to see where I live."

This was fine with Suzanne, as it seemed to indicate progress in their relationship: Not exactly bringing her home to meet the family, but a close second.

****

Adam picked Suzanne up on Saturday afternoon and brought her to his home, a beautifully restored Victorian with a grand view of the Golden Gate Bridge. The walls were hung with artwork quite different from either that in Suzanne's apartment, which was mostly colorful prints rented together with the furniture, or, of course, that in Marguerite's. Adam seemed to favor majestic landscapes in oil and interesting watercolors with meticulous attention to detail. Suzanne quite liked it and assumed it reflected Adam's personality and interests, just as Marguerite's did hers.

Adam had prepared a three-course dinner of lentil soup, beef bourguignon, and, for dessert, pecan pie. He clearly was being modest when he said he was a "pretty good cook." Dinner was preceded by some simple hors d'oeuvres served with dry sherry and was accompanied by a fine pinot noir. This man obviously loved to cook, and he was damn good at it.

All through dinner Adam and Suzanne chatted easily, covering Adam's favorite recipes, places Suzanne would like to visit, and other widely varied topics. After dinner, with the table cleared and the dishes in the dishwasher, Adam invited Suzanne to sit next to him on the sofa. He put his arm around her shoulder and said, "I really enjoyed what we did last week. This time it's your turn."

"My turn for what?" Suzanne said, a bit puzzled.

"Your turn to relax and enjoy yourself. You've kind of taken the initiative when we've been…been together, if you know what I mean. Which has been great, don't get me wrong. You probably can tell I'm not too experienced in these things and you seem to know…well, just what to do. But I want to make you as…as happy as you make me. It's only fair, right? So I've been doing some…some reading up on how to make a woman happy. In bed, that is."

Throughout his speech, Adam's face was turning progressively redder, as this clearly was not a subject he was used to talking about, especially to the person with whom he wanted to be in bed.

Suzanne was impressed. Most men, in her experience, were interested only in their own gratification. If they made any effort to satisfy the woman they were with, it was usually because bringing her to an orgasm heightened their own sexual pleasure. But it seemed as if Adam simply wanted to return what he had received, to make Suzanne feel as good as she had made him feel. This was definitely a good sign for the progress of their relationship, not to mention a point in Adam's favor as a man.

"That sounds…great," Suzanne said, putting her arms around Adam. "I sure wouldn't want to interfere with your studies." She kissed him lightly on the lips.

"Then step this way," he said, sounding relieved. He led her by the hand into his bedroom. The contrast with Suzanne's bedroom was striking, but hardly unexpected. Not that the room was as determinedly masculine as Suzanne's was feminine. There were no hunting scenes, no sports memorabilia, not a single mounted animal head. The walls were not paneled in walnut and the bed frame was not cut from lodge poles. But the medium-blue walls, the cherry-finished furniture, the light blue carpet, and the crisp white sheets on the open bed spoke of a gentleman who was comfortable keeping to the center and avoiding the extremes. That certainly seemed to fit the Adam Suzanne had thus far gotten to know.

Adam turned toward Suzanne, as she had toward him when they entered her bedroom. "Let me help you get ready for bed," he said, unbuttoning her white cotton blouse. He helped her out of her clothes, as slowly and carefully as she had helped him out of his. He clearly was determined to return the favor.

Throughout this undressing, Suzanne found herself becoming more and more aroused. She was not used to this kind of treatment from a man—the closest she had come was the way Marguerite had treated her before a girl-on-girl sexual encounter. The feeling increased as Adam touched her gently in some very sensitive places, sending a thrill up and down her body.

Geez, Suzanne thought, *whatever Adam was reading since the last time, I hope he gets a lifetime subscription.*

Adam now led Suzanne over to the bed, just as she had led him, and helped her lie back as he quickly undressed himself. He didn't try to make a show of it, and Suzanne was very glad. As stimulating as a woman's striptease might be for a man, she didn't think it worked well the other way, despite the popularity of beef-cake parlors. Hairy legs and curve-less bodies did not, in her opinion, equal sensuality.

This time Adam took the dominant position, and although he was not an accomplished player, he was more than competent, she thought. She let herself relax and enjoy the experience.

When they had both caught their breath and were lying next to each other on the bed, Suzanne turned toward Adam and whispered, "I don't know what subject you studied, but you get an A-plus on your final exam."

Adam laughed. "You probably could tell tonight— heck, you probably could tell when you first met me— this is all new to me. Can you imagine? At my age, you're the first woman I've really made love to. And I didn't want to screw it up." They both laughed at the unintended pun.

"You did just fine," Suzanne said. "I won't pretend I've never done something like this before, but I've never enjoyed it as much as tonight." Oddly, although this was true in part because it meant further progress, even perhaps sealing the deal, on her campaign to marry him and get access to his brother, she found it was also true on a purely physical and emotional level. It occurred to Suzanne with sudden force that she had almost never had sex with a man for any reason other than some kind of quid pro quo, whether it was copying his homework in school, being hired after a job "interview," or a cash payment. And although she was hoping for marriage as an eventual outcome of this evening's activities, she had a strong feeling that she would do it again with Adam even were marriage not an issue.

For perhaps the first time in her life, she was enjoying sex with a man merely for its own sake, merely to give him and herself pleasure.

Surely she couldn't be in love.

Chapter 35

Patrick's Men

Four days after Adam's successful reciprocation of Suzanne's lovemaking, on the following Wednesday, Suzanne received an unannounced visit. Late in the afternoon, she opened her apartment door to two men. As soon as she saw them, she wished she had looked out through the peephole in the door before opening it, but it was too late for that. It wasn't that they looked particularly threatening, just that they did not look particularly friendly, either.

"Suzanne Donohue?" the man closest to the doorway said.

His voice was deep and the tone businesslike, and Suzanne immediately thought, *cops!* This was not because she felt she had done anything to bring the police to her door, but more because the man sounded just like the policemen who come to the door of suspects or witnesses in the crime dramas she was fond of watching on TV. She decided to find out who these guys were before giving out any information.

"Who wants to know?" she said, trying to sound like the people who answered the door in those same crime dramas.

"My name is Fuller. John Fuller. This is George Barber," he said, indicating the other man. "We'd appreciate it if we could come in and talk with you for a few minutes." His tone was slightly friendlier than it had started out, but still serious and businesslike.

"What is it you want to talk about? If you're selling something—"

Fuller smiled. A businesslike smile. "No, nothing like that. It's about Adam McNeil."

Suzanne thought about this for a moment. "Okay, come in, I guess. But I'm busy so this better not take long."

"It won't," Fuller said as he stepped through the doorway, followed closely by Barber.

Suzanne invited the two men to sit on the sofa, and she sat opposite in the matching upholstered chair.

"I'm listening," she said, folding her hands on her lap. She realized she sounded less than friendly herself and wasn't quite sure why. But something about these men told her to be cautious.

Fuller was clearly the spokesman for the pair. "I'll get right to the point," he said. "You're dating Adam McNeil, are you not?"

Suzanne's first inclination was to deny it, but that seemed useless since they clearly knew she was dating Adam. She and Adam were frequently together in public, and it also would make it look as if she had something to hide. She did, of course, but not the fact of dating Adam. She decided to play it straight. She smiled what she hoped was a disarming smile. "I sure am. What has that to do with you?"

"Well," Fuller replied, "not us personally. We work for Adam's brother, Patrick. I'm sure you know that Patrick McNeil is very likely to become the next President of the United States. That is, so long as nothing…gets in the way."

"Gets in the way?"

"Yes, like something that might…might embarrass the man. Make people wonder if there's something not quite…not quite presidential about him. You know."

"I'm not sure I do. I'm dating Adam, not his brother, so what's—"

Fuller put his hand up to stop her. He flashed a thin smile. "We realize that, of course. But in politics, especially national politics, a scandal concerning a close relative, like a brother, can tend to rub off on the candidate himself. Divert attention from the real issues."

Suzanne was becoming both concerned and angry. "What do you mean scandal? What kind of scandal? We've just been going to the movies, for Christ's sake."

The other man, Barber, spoke up for the first time. "Yes, we know that, Miss Donohue. Or at least we don't know anything to the contrary. But, you see, Mr. McNeil, and the people behind him, don't want to take any chances. We've checked you out, and—"

Suzanne was quickly passing from angry to thoroughly pissed off. "What the hell business do you have 'checking me out,' or sticking your nose into my business?" She added a few choice observations on the bloody nerve of political hacks and such.

Fuller waited until she had finished her tirade before responding. "I'm sorry, Miss Donohue, but that's just the way it works these days. The opposition, and their friends in the media, of course, are constantly looking for anything at all that will discredit our candidate, including, and I have to say it again, a scandal in the family." He again held up his hand to head off Suzanne's attempt to reply. "Yes, I know there's no scandal, at least at this time. But we know very little about you, and what we know doesn't give us…doesn't give us confidence. All we know is that you're a very attractive young woman, unemployed, just arrived from New York, with a somewhat blank history."

"Blank? What's that mean?"

"It means that, while we can't find anything negative about you in your past, we can't find anything particularly positive either. Kind of a blank slate. It worries us."

"What? You think I'm out to get Adam's money or something? I don't even know if he's got any—"

"No, we don't think you're a gold digger or anything like that—although again, you might be—we don't really know. But it's possible you're some kind of plant by the opposition, planning to cause some kind of embarrassment to the family before the election. And even if you're not, the fact is you're not the kind of woman a man like Adam McNeil, the brother of the president-to-be, should be associating with to make the best impression on the public."

Suzanne had heard enough insults. And the fact that these men had come pretty close to guessing her real motive—except the embarrassment was supposed to happen after the election, not before it—only increased her anger. "Look, you bastards, I resent the implication that I'm some kind of political spy, or worse, and I don't give a damn whether or not you think I'm worthy of dating the next president's brother! That's up to him, and I'm sure he'll let me know when he decides we shouldn't do it. Meanwhile, you can get the hell out—"

"We're not quite through, Miss Donohue," Fuller said, remaining unperturbed and seated on the sofa. "We understand your feelings, and we don't blame you. As I said, we haven't found anything negative about you. You may be perfectly respectable and dating Adam McNeil may cause no problems at all. But we can't take that chance. So we are prepared to make you a...an offer."

An offer? Were they competing for her services with her present employers? *This is becoming bizarre,* Suzanne thought. She waited for an explanation.

"We are willing to offer you a sum of money to terminate your relationship with Adam McNeil."

Suzanne was speechless for several seconds, her temperature rising rapidly. "Let me get this straight. You want to pay me off to break up with Adam because you're afraid I'll either do something to embarrass his brother, or my just being a nobody dating a president's—"

"Future president's," Barber corrected.

"—*future* president's brother might be embarrassing enough to screw up his chances. Is that it?"

"In a nutshell," Fuller said, nodding. He handed her a card with just his name and a phone number on it. "If you're interested, give me a call and we can discuss details. And I might add that if you decline the...uh...offer, you could be putting yourself in a somewhat dangerous position."

It took Suzanne a few seconds to absorb this. When she had, she had trouble keeping herself under control. Both fear and anger were roiling her insides. She told herself to stay calm and stood up. "Is that a threat?" she asked very quietly.

Fuller also stood, followed by Barber, and headed for the door. "Take it any way you like. Politics can get very messy. We'll let ourselves out."

They walked to the door and left the apartment as

Suzanne stood and stared after them. She was angry. She was scared.

Mostly, she was confused.

****

Suzanne badly needed to tell someone about the two men, their offer, and their threat. And she needed advice on how to respond. Whether to respond. But whom should she tell?

Betsy would be interested to know, and at some point probably had to know, that Patrick McNeil's camp knew about Suzanne and were watching her closely. But Betsy was not the person from whom she wanted advice. There was really only one such person, someone who knew her situation, could be trusted with the information, and whose advice she would want to have: Marguerite.

Unfortunately, while their system of writing to each other discreetly was fine for other purposes, it was totally useless when Suzanne needed to communicate with Marguerite immediately. The only way was to phone her, on a phone that could not be tapped or intercepted. Suzanne wasn't sure whether her cell phone was vulnerable to the seemingly unlimited reach of her employers' intelligence network, but she didn't intend to take any chances.

There were very few pay phones left in San Francisco, but Suzanne had noticed two of them at the Ferry Building the last time she was there, so that is where she headed as soon as the men had left and she had composed herself.

She had remembered correctly.

****

"Marguerite?"

"That you, Suzanne?"

"Yeah. Sorry to bother you, but I've got to talk with someone, and you're the only person who can help me."

"Hey, no bother. It's great to hear from you. And judging from the fact you couldn't wait to write, this must be important."

"It is. I need some advice." And Suzanne described the distressing visit from the "friends" of Patrick McNeil.

As she concluded her story, Marguerite whistled softly. "My, oh my. This so-called job of yours is a lot deeper in shit than you or I suspected, ain't it?"

"I guess it is. So what do you think I should do? Should I take whatever they offer me and get the hell out before I end up lying in some back alley? A million dollars won't do me much good then."

Marguerite was silent for a moment, thinking. "From what you describe, honey, it doesn't sound so much like your life's in danger," she said finally. "I've been around a lot of politicians—real close around, know what I'm sayin'?—and most of 'em try to avoid even a whiff of scandal touchin' them. Murder would be about the worst kinda scandal."

"Yeah, they sure seemed to want to avoid scandal. So what could happen?"

"You could end up in the middle of a real messy war between these political factions. They'll put pressure on this dummy you're dating, he'll back off to please his brother, and suddenly you're out a marriage, out a million bucks, and out on the street to boot. They also could really screw up your reputation, once you're on your own."

"Actually, Adam's no dummy," Suzanne said, somehow feeling compelled to set that straight before continuing. "But he is very close to his brother. Wouldn't want to do anything to hurt him, I'm sure. So how do I avoid all that happening?"

"Seems to me it ain't you who can avoid it. Only this Adam fella can do that. If it were me, I'd do what you'd probably do automatically if this were a real romance. I'd tell Adam exactly what happened, and real soon. If he's really fallin' for you, he'll at least be prepared to fend these guys off somehow. And if he's gonna be loyal to his brother, or just plain scared, and back off to avoid any trouble, well, at least you can get out gracefully, take whatever they pay you, and come on home. Your bed is keepin' warm."

****

After hanging up the phone, Suzanne sat before it for several minutes mulling over what Marguerite had said.

What, after all, were her choices? Marguerite was right that, if her affair with Adam—although "affair" somehow had the wrong connotation—were genuine, she most likely would—and he would expect her to—tell him all as soon as possible, so he could be prepared to fight for their future together. At least that's how the movie plot would go. Never having been in a real affair, Suzanne could only guess at such things. Since her seduction of Adam had to at least appear to be genuine, she had to act as if it were and turn to him in this time of crisis.

Besides, he would know soon enough, if he didn't already, when he was told by his brother, or his brother's handlers, the facts of political life and political families that she had just been told.

Of two things Suzanne was certain. She wanted that

million dollars, and she did not want the affair with Adam to end just yet. Of course, these were two sides of the same coin, the first being dependent on the second, but somehow Suzanne didn't think of them quite that way.

****

Suzanne telephoned Adam that afternoon. "I apologize for phoning you at work," she said, "but it's really important."

"That's okay. I take it you're not just calling about the weekend," he said. "Of course, I hope we can get together on Saturday as usual."

"Well," Suzanne said, "actually I was hoping we could get together sooner, like this evening."

"This evening? I mean, I'd like to see you any time, but I usually get home kinda late and pretty tired—"

"I'm sorry, but there's something terribly important I have to tell you about, and it really can't wait. Could we get together for just a few minutes?"

There was a pause. Then Adam said, "Sure, Suzanne. I'll be home by about eight. Why don't you come by, say, eight-thirty? Will that be okay?" He sounded worried, but not as worried as Suzanne sounded, and was.

"I'll be there. Thanks."

She hung up and stared at the phone for a while. What would Adam say when she told him? What could he say? He was very close to his brother, and she couldn't see him doing anything to jeopardize Patrick's presidential bid. Adam would have to break off their relationship in order to protect his brother. All that tied Suzanne to him was their physical relationship—sex, that is—and while Adam might regret losing his first real sexual partner, sexual partners—even those as accomplished as Suzanne—were more easily replaced than older brothers.

Maybe it's just as well, Suzanne thought. *He never would've married me anyway. It's a long way from a roll in the hay to a place in the family!*

Therefore, it was with little hope of retaining either Adam or her million dollars that Suzanne knocked on Adam's door at eight thirty-five that evening.

****

Adam opened the door and ushered Suzanne in. He took one look at her and said, "You look pretty upset. What's this all about? Is it something I did?"

"No, not at all," Suzanne said, taking both his hands. "Let's sit down and I'll explain."

They sat, and Suzanne described the visit from Patrick McNeil's associates. Adam listened intently, interrupting only to clarify some details, until Suzanne had finished. Then he sat silently, putting his face in his hands, elbows on his knees.

Suzanne waited.

At last Adam looked up. It was he now who looked upset, but Suzanne could not tell whether it was with distress, anger, or some mixture of both. She continued to wait until Adam spoke.

"I—I need some time to think this thing through. I'm really sorry you've gotten mixed up in such an unpleasant situation. I wouldn't have had this happen for the world, and I bet right now you wish you'd never met me."

Suzanne hugged him and put her head on his shoulder. "No, that's wrong!" she said. "I'm very glad I met you, that we've had such a good time together. I was hoping it would continue—for—forever." She wasn't sure she should have added that last word, or just why she did it under these circumstances, but it was too late to retract it.

Adam held her, saying nothing. She couldn't see his face, so she had no idea what he might be thinking now.

Finally, he said, "Look, I really need to think about all this. Right now my head is spinning. Could I call you tomorrow, maybe come by your place? I'll have some answers by then. At least I hope so."

Suzanne hoped so too. She said as much and kissed Adam lightly on the cheek before leaving.

It was going to be a long wait until tomorrow.

Chapter 36

Adam's Decision

Suzanne didn't sleep well that night. She knew what Adam would have to do. She couldn't blame him. *Family comes first.* Suzanne had no family, at least none of which she was aware, other than her mother, and she knew she would never do anything that might harm Mary Sue.

The next morning, Suzanne had a job interview, one that had been arranged by Betsy Green following their conversation on the subject. It was for a standard secretarial position, intended only to add credibility to Suzanne's job-hunting story.

It was not good timing, and, under the circumstances, Suzanne considered it a waste of time, as she would soon be heading back to New York, but she felt obligated to continue with the charade, as long as the game was still in play.

The potential employer she was sent to was the Charles Ventnor Supply Company, located in a large warehouse building in the Mission District. It turned out to be one of those prewar brick and iron stalwarts, built to last a thousand years or until urban renewal caught up with it. The brown paint that had probably been applied around 1965 was peeling, and the large, relatively new wooden sign over the third-floor windows just covered an older one painted on the brick, faded with time, of a prior tenant, the Kendall Iron Foundry. All in all, it was not the most inviting of potential places of employment.

She had an appointment to see a William Tracy, who, she was told by a receptionist, could be found on the second floor. "Please take the steps," a sign said. There was only a freight elevator. The receptionist, a middle-aged woman of little beauty and less charm, looked Suzanne over as if she were wearing a clown suit; clearly attractive, sexy ladies seldom crossed the company's threshold.

Mr. Tracy turned out to be a youngish, decent-looking man ensconced in a small office and surrounded by stacks of papers that looked like bills of lading or similar documents, your choice of white, yellow, and pink. When Suzanne first saw him, and before he saw Suzanne, he seemed to be concentrating intently on one of those documents, scribbling notes in its margin. When he looked up, however, his expression and his area of concentration changed markedly and immediately.

Suzanne had not felt motivated, much less compelled, to wear anything even remotely daring to this unwanted interview. Nevertheless, a face and figure like hers did not hide easily and needed no assistance from clothing or makeup to work their magic on men. And magic is just what seemed to be working on William Tracy. The expression on his face, the look in his eyes, was one Suzanne had seen a thousand times, and it always meant the same thing.

Tracy stood and almost scooted around from behind his desk, dragging a wooden chair over from the corner and offering it to Suzanne. She thanked him and sat. He lingered in back of her, obviously taking in what small amount of cleavage her relatively modest blouse revealed, plus the balance of her bosom that, although covered, was hardly hidden. Finally he tore himself away, returned to his side of the desk, and began the interview.

This was a now-familiar scenario. Suzanne would answer the obligatory questions about her experience, background, and ambitions, then be hired either on her fair-to-good secretarial merits, which was possible, or on her excellent carnal merits, which was far more certain. A few minutes practicing an art at which she was now a skilled professional—and which she always enjoyed for its own sake anyway—and she would be the Charles Ventnor Supply Company's newest secretary, if not a vice president.

But strangely Suzanne had no desire to do any such thing. It was not that she didn't really want the job, as she had decided she would take it if offered, on the off chance she stayed in the Bay Area a while. And it was not that anything about William Tracy revolted her. He was no better or worse looking than her usual clients, had an athletic build, and seemed to be polite and well-spoken. Yet the idea of having sex with this young man merely to gain employment had no appeal whatsoever. In fact, it was the last thing she wished to do, job or no job. This confused her, because she could not remember a time in her life—other than the attacks by her father and Craig Johnson—she did not enjoy sex, whether with a friend or a stranger, or a time in recent years she did not enjoy using sex to gain an advantage, monetary or otherwise. Yes, it definitely confused her.

And it scared her.

****

The interview went quickly, consisting of the usual questions and a demonstration of Suzanne's skill at the computer, and she was told she would receive a decision in a few days. Suzanne did not encourage Mr. Tracy to come on to her, and although she had to shove his hand twice to remove it from areas it didn't belong as he escorted her out the door, it was a case of no harm, no foul. Suzanne went straight home, took a shower, and lay on her bed, trying to make sense of her emotions during the interview.

She was interrupted by the phone.

"Is it okay if I come over in an hour?" Adam said. "We need to talk."

He sounded stressed, not at all like the laid-back research chemist she had been dating, to Suzanne an ominous sign.

"Sure, that'd be fine. I'll see you then."

And she lay there, still thinking, and waited.

****

Just under an hour later, there was a knock on the door. Suzanne had drifted into a light sleep, and she was startled awake by the sound.

"Be right there," she shouted toward the door then darted into the bathroom to splash cold water on her face, glance at the mirror, and guide some stray strands of hair back into place. Satisfied she didn't look like she had just woken up, she opened the door.

Adam was standing patiently, looking like he would rather be somewhere else.

Suzanne just said, "Hi." Adam responded similarly and stepped through the doorway. Suzanne helped him out of his jacket, which she hung in the foyer closet. "Would you like some coffee, or maybe a Coke?" she asked.

"No, thanks. I've got something important to say, and I'd like to go ahead and say it before I lose my nerve."

Suzanne suddenly felt weak. She had anticipated what Adam would have to say, and she wasn't surprised he was finding it difficult, but now that he was about to say, it she found she wasn't really prepared to hear it.

Adam took Suzanne's hand and led her to the sofa, where they both sat and faced each other. Adam leaned over and kissed her on the forehead, then began what was no doubt a speech he had rehearsed in his head many times before this performance:

"Needless to say, what you told me about my brother and his…his friends, or supporters…came as a real shock. That's probably because I'm so politically naïve it never even occurred to me that who my friends were, who I went out with, who I…well, slept with…would have any effect on Pat's chances to become president. Maybe I just don't think past my own needs and desires, don't take others' feelings and needs into consideration. They say we science types can be that way—too wrapped up in our own little worlds to notice such things."

Suzanne was listening intently and didn't want to interrupt, but she wished Adam would come to the point and get it over with. However, he was clearly in no hurry.

"Anyway," he continued, "once you told me what they said—and especially what they threatened to do if we continued to see each other—it forced me to give a lot of thought to these matters. That's what I've been doing since then: thinking. And once I considered the whole matter from all sides—yours, mine, Pat's, everyone's—it became clear what I had to do."

Suzanne took Adam's hand. He was struggling with his speech, and she wanted to make it easier for him. "I think I know what you have to do," she said. "And I understand."

"You do? Are you sure? Because I thought—"

Suzanne squeezed the hand she was holding. "I'm sorry. I should let you tell this in your own way. Go ahead. I won't interrupt." She let go of his hand and sat back.

It took Adam a moment to get back on track, but eventually he continued where he had left off. "Like I said, Suzanne, I know what I have to do. First, I have to make sure that my brother is protected from any scandal, and I guess in some people's minds my running around with a woman not my wife and, as they say, beneath my class, would be scandalous." His smile told Suzanne he didn't share that somewhat dated point of view, but they both knew many people in the country still did. "Second," he went on, "I have to make sure you're protected from any kind of harm, either to your reputation or especially to your person, which isn't likely, but you never know what these political hacks and their ilk might be up to."

That sent a shiver down Suzanne's spine.

"Lastly, I have to think about myself. And that's proven to be the hardest part. How can I do what's right for me, while still protecting the people who're most important to me? But when I really thought about it, and I asked myself what's really important in my life, the answer became crystal clear."

He took both of Suzanne's hands in his and in a most solemn tone he said the absolute last thing she had expected him to say, "Suzanne, will you marry me?"

Chapter 37

Adam Explains

Suzanne had never been as dumbfounded as she was at that moment. She literally was speechless. Her mouth hung open but no sounds came out.

Having gotten no response from Suzanne, positive or negative, Adam felt compelled to press his case. "I know it's sudden, and I know we've only known each other for a few weeks—well, it's a couple of months now, but not very long—but…well, I've fallen in love with you. And I don't want to lose you. Ever. And that's what I realized when I thought about the possibility that this business with my brother and the election might drive us apart."

Suzanne started to say something, but Adam rolled right on. "And in case you're wondering, it's not just the sex I'm in love with, because it's been terrific and I'm sure no one would blame me for wanting it to continue. But I just love being with you. Like when we had that picnic in the park. I love talking to you, the way you seem to enjoy listening to what most women would probably consider just a lot of boring science stuff. And I love listening to you, telling me about a world you came from that's so foreign to any I've known. I love sitting in the movies with you, holding your hand. And just to top it all off, you're the most beautiful woman I've ever met.

And that's why I want you to marry me."

Adam finally had run out of reasons, and out of breath. He stopped and waited.

He waited while Suzanne tried to assemble in her mind the pieces of her preconceptions that had fallen so completely apart. First she had been uncertain how she could broach the subject of marriage with Adam, and how he would react to it. Then, after "the visit," she had been quite certain Adam would want to—no, have to, whether he wanted to or not—break off their relationship completely. Instead, not only had he not broken it off, he had saved her the trouble of raising the subject of marriage by raising it himself. And now, when she could complete the first part of her mission simply by saying "yes," for some reason, she simply couldn't do it. Not without thinking everything through again in light of this new development.

"I'm pleased and flattered by your proposal," she finally said. "But what about the other considerations you mentioned? I mean, what about your brother's reputation and his running for the presidency?" She didn't think it right to add, "And what about the possible harm to me?"

Adam let go of Suzanne's hands and sat back, a serious look on his face. "Yes, I've considered my responsibility to Pat and, of course, to you. In fact, that's part of the reason I'm so sure our getting married is the right thing to do. If you'll have me, of course. I can see where rumors about my having an affair with some gorgeous, mysterious—well, unknown, anyway— woman could get in Pat's way. And if, for example, the opposition found something in your background—I'm not saying there is, of course, but then I don't know everything about you, and they can dig up all kinds of things and make them look bad even if they aren't—if they did, it could hurt you, and hurt Pat's chances. But if we were married, it'd be a fait accompli. Perfectly respectable. It's strictly my business whom I marry, not my brother's, not the press's, not the opposition's."

Suzanne was a bit dubious about this. "Are you sure—"

"Absolutely. And as for those people who came here and threatened you, they might've tried to break us up, make you leave town, or make me end our relationship while it was still just a relationship. But once we're married, they can hardly try to force us to get a divorce!" He laughed at this. "Can you imagine the headlines? 'Candidate's Backers Insist Brother Get a Divorce.'"

Suzanne laughed too, a little. "Yeah, I see what you mean. Maybe you're right."

"Sure, I am. I mean, you say they offered to pay you to go away or something. They can hardly offer to pay you to leave your husband, without taking a chance on totally blowing the election if it got out."

Suzanne shook her head. "No, they really couldn't do that, could they?"

"And most of all," Adam continued, "it would protect you. You couldn't be painted as some kind of interloper, maybe even suspected of being a spy for the opposition, who knows what? You'd be my wife, all legal and aboveboard. And if they ever had any idea of harming you physically…well, they wouldn't dare."

Suzanne nodded. She was thinking as fast as she could, but rapid thinking had never been her strong suit. She still needed time to sort everything out. She was either elated at how well things were turning out, or scared at how muddled they'd become—or both.

"So, now," Adam said softly, "it's up to you. Just because I've fallen in love with you, I know that doesn't necessarily mean you're in love with me. Or that you have any desire to marry me, or anyone else for that matter. I confess I have no idea what a wonderful, gorgeous, intelligent, sexy woman like you sees in a plain, dull guy like me, or why you'd even consider going out with me, much less marrying me, but whatever the reason, I'm not going to analyze it too closely. It wasn't easy to get up the nerve to ask you to marry me— in a way, this business of your visitors made it necessary. Now I'll wait for your answer." And that was all he had to say.

"Give me a couple of days to think this over," Suzanne said. "It's been quite a surprise—a good one, really, but a surprise, for sure, and I want to make the right decision."

Adam almost beamed. "Hey, I'm just glad—no, make that elated—that you didn't immediately say no, or even laugh at the idea. Take as much time as you need. But I guess the sooner you decide, one way or the other, the sooner we can get those bastards off your neck."

"Yeah, you're right. I'll give you an answer as soon as I can."

"Then I'll get out of here. I've said everything I had to say, and you need time to think. I'll just keep my fingers crossed about your answer. And my toes."

Suzanne smiled and accompanied Adam to the door. When he was gone, she sat down on the sofa. And she began to cry. She didn't know why, or even whether she was crying because she was sad or happy.

Why did life have to get so complicated?

Chapter 38

Step One Concluded

For the second time that week, Suzanne took a streetcar to the Ferry Building and used the pay phone to call Marguerite.

When she explained everything that had occurred since their last conversation, ending with Adam's proposal, Suzanne asked almost pleadingly, "So what do I do now?"

"Hey, girl, I'm as surprised as you were the way that all turned out. You know I never liked that you agreed to this fuckin' charade in the first place, million bucks or no million bucks. But since you did, and now he's fallen for it, I'm not sure why you don't just get right on the phone to the preacher man. Wasn't gettin' this sucker to marry you the whole reason you've been hustlin' him?"

"Yeah, yeah, it was. I mean it is. That's why I'm so confused. He's just handed me a ticket to a million dollars, and now I'm not sure I want to take it."

"Why the hell not? You got cold feet, scared about the next thing you gotta do, seduce the president?"

"No, I'm sure it's not that. I'd been looking forward to the challenge, you might say. In fact, it's a lot scarier thinking about what those people who hired me might do if I try to back out now."

"Then if it ain't that you're scared, it can only be one

other thing. You've fallen for the guy and don't want t' hurt him by bonkin' his brother. That it?"

"No! Absolutely not. This is strictly business. I don't know why I'm hesitating, but it isn't that. I mean, he's a real nice guy and everything, but…but…"

"Hmm. Okay, then if it ain't that, and you ain't scared, there's only one thing you can do. Say 'yes' and get yourself married to the guy before he wakes up an' changes his mind. You seem to have him mesmerized, honey. You did your job real good. Now finish it an' move on."

Suzanne frowned into the phone and accepted the inevitable. "You're right. There's really no reason not to. I'm just being stupid about it."

"Yeah, you are. But listen, honey, even if it's a hustle, it's a big step for a girl gettin' married. Who knows? It may be the only time in your life you get to do it. If I was you, I'd treat it like the real thing, be happy about it, make the guy happy, and when the time comes to…well, to end it, at least you'll have had a good time, and he'll have gotten somethin' for his money, so to speak. Know what I'm sayin'?

"Yeah, I know. And that's what I'm gonna do. Thanks for helping clear things up. I don't know what I'd do without you to talk to."

"Oh, you'd find someone else. But since you got me, can I come to the wedding?"

Marguerite's laugh assured Suzanne she was just kidding. But Suzanne wished she could have a real wedding and invite her mother and Marguerite and Patricia and Gene, and—

But of course that was impossible.

Maybe someday.

****

The next day, Suzanne telephoned Adam and told him her decision. Once she had made up her mind, with Marguerite's help, she determined to follow Marguerite's advice and to treat her wedding and marriage to Adam as the real thing. She didn't want him to have any reason to doubt that she loved him as much as he loved her, that she was thrilled and excited to be marrying him, and that they would be living "happily ever after." So it was with joy and enthusiasm in her voice that she said over the phone, "I don't know why I even hesitated last night when you asked me. I just wasn't expecting it, and it's such a big step and everything…well, I just had to let it sink in. But now I'm so thrilled, I just want to put my arms around you and kiss you and…and do other nice things to you. When can you come over so we can make plans?"

"I'm sure I'm more thrilled than you are," Adam said. "I'll come over this evening and we can work out the details."

"I'll run out and get things for a nice dinner. Be here about six, okay?"

"Six it is. This is wonderful, Suzanne. I'm the happiest guy in the world right now."

Suzanne didn't respond immediately.

Suddenly she had a sharp pain in her stomach. And it wasn't indigestion.

****

"I hope you won't be disappointed," Adam said as they relaxed after dinner, "but, under the circumstances, I don't think we should plan on a big ceremony of any kind. Too much opportunity for someone to try to mess it up. If we just go down to city hall and make it official, it'll be done and no one can undo it. Will that be okay?"

Although it was true Suzanne had once dreamed of getting married in a fancy wedding dress surrounded by friends and family, that was when she was a young child. Since her father had changed the course of her life and her attitude toward men, a wedding of any kind was the farthest thing from her mind or her expectation. So she had no difficulty saying honestly in reply to Adam, "Absolutely. That's exactly what I would have suggested. The only important thing is that we'll be together. I don't care if we do it in a church or a closet."

Adam laughed, then put his arms around Suzanne, and gave her a long kiss on the lips. Their tongues became involved, and then their hands, and before very long they were in the bedroom. Adam's technique seemed to be improving with every time they made love—he was obviously a quick study—and Suzanne was certain, and very happy, that the physical part of their marriage would require no pretense or deception, no false moans or fake orgasms. Adam might not look like a great lover, but he was turning out to be one.

****

The following Monday, dressed in sedate, business-like attire, Suzanne Donohue—nee Dahlstrom—late of New York City, and Adam McNeil, resident of San Francisco and younger brother of the presumed next President of the United States, became husband and wife in a brief civil ceremony. No bells rang, no confetti was thrown. But for the couple it was just as momentous an occasion as if it had been celebrated at Westminster Abbey with an audience of thousands.

For him, it was the culmination of a brief and unexpected but wonderful chapter in his life.

For her, it was the beginning of phase two.

Chapter 39

Family and Friends

Suzanne moved into Adam's home, giving up the apartment Betsy had rented for her. Betsy was, of course, thrilled to hear of the marriage. She had been hired primarily to shepherd The Plan this far, and she had succeeded. Now it was just a matter of everyone waiting for the election and the near-foregone conclusion of Patrick McNeil's ascendance to the presidency.

For her part, Suzanne was both relieved to have completed the first important phase of her assignment and excitedly anticipating the beginning of the next phase. Meanwhile, in the interim between becoming Patrick McNeil's sister-in-law and becoming the president's, all she had to do was become an ordinary housewife, making sure this marriage lasted—and was seen as quite normal by both Adam and the outside world—until such time as she carried out phase two, the seduction of her husband's brother.

The housewife part Suzanne found to be amazingly easy, and even satisfying. It certainly beat working as a secretary, or even a cocktail waitress. And the "perks" were excellent. Adam was reasonably well off, and although he didn't have a lot of close friends, he attended many interesting social functions in connection with his work, and he loved to show off his new—and strikingly beautiful—bride. For her part, Suzanne didn't mind at all being shown off.

As for Messrs. Fuller and Barber, she never saw them again. She assumed Adam had been right in saying that once they were married, paying off Suzanne—or worse—was no longer an option.

She did, however, finally meet Adam's brother Patrick, The Candidate. The day after their marriage, Adam announced it to his family, as was only proper. A reception was hastily arranged by Patrick's wife, Anne, for the following Saturday in Washington, DC, where Patrick was currently living. The McNeils and whatever aunts, uncles, or cousins could be scared up on short notice, together with some of their best friends, gathered to see what kind of woman bachelor Adam, the least attractive and most socially inept member of the family, had married. They all imagined a plain, studious type drawn to Adam's strongest asset, his intellect. Certainly she would not have been attracted by his sex appeal, or lack thereof.

When the newlyweds arrived at the party, reality turned out to be as far from that image as their wildest fantasy might have conjured up. One look at Suzanne and the men were impressed to the point of envy, the women to the point of head-shaking disbelief. If they were suspicious that Suzanne was either a gold digger or a spy for the enemy, they were careful not to show it.

For his part, Adam beamed.

New brother-in-law Pat, the consummate politician, was as gracious as could be wished, revealing no signs he had either contemplated discouraging her or even been aware that his associates had attempted to do so.

And it was impossible for Suzanne to tell whether

Patrick's welcome to the family was genuine or contrived. She decided it didn't really matter. When the time came, she would make sure his attitude toward her was…well, appropriate to the circumstances.

Meanwhile, she gave him just enough of a sidelong look to pique his interest, without in any way compromising her virtue.

Yet.

****

As the presidential election drew closer, the newlyweds fell into a pleasant routine of work, play, and sex. Adam, who had missed out on the latter most of his adolescent and adult life, was clearly making up for lost time, while Suzanne was keeping her professional skills sharp, making for a mutually beneficial, and mutually enjoyable, arrangement.

But as election day approached, perhaps in part because of the pleasantness of their marriage routine, Suzanne began to get just a little less enthusiastic about phase two of The Plan. She still wanted that million dollars, of course, but she was less happy about how she was going to earn it. Nevertheless, she dismissed these feelings as just a natural nervousness and of no ultimate consequence.

About a month after the marriage, Suzanne received a letter from Marguerite saying she would be able to come out to visit any time in the next two weeks, if it was convenient for Suzanne. She was anxious to see her erstwhile protégé and, of course, to meet Suzanne's new husband. Suzanne was just as anxious to see Marguerite, and it was arranged that she would come for a three-day visit the following week.

Suzanne had never mentioned Marguerite to

Adam, of course, as she represented a part of Suzanne's life Adam was not to know had ever existed. But she could not very well entertain Marguerite in secret. She needed a cover story of some kind, and she and Marguerite worked one out: Marguerite was an old friend she had met while working as a secretary at East Coast Associates, and they had kept in touch since. It was simple, believable, and required very little fabrication.

Adam was quite pleased that he would be meeting one of Suzanne's old friends from New York. He still knew very little about her earlier life, and spending a few days with one of her close friends would give him a chance to fill in some of those blank spaces in his knowledge of his new wife.

Marguerite arrived on Friday afternoon and Suzanne met her at the Arrivals gate at SFO. Until she saw her friend, she didn't realize how much she had missed her, and Marguerite clearly felt the same. They embraced for a long while, then Suzanne took one of the two carry-ons Marguerite had brought and together they found a taxi and gave the driver the McNeils' address.

During the long ride from the airport, Suzanne and Marguerite caught up on a bit of what each had been doing since they last talked or wrote, but because of the nature of Suzanne's activities—and Marguerite's profession, for that matter—they saved any detailed discussion for later, in private.

They arrived at the house at about four-thirty in the afternoon. Adam was not due home for another hour, which gave the friends an hour to talk about what really had been happening in their respective worlds.

Suzanne described her marriage. "I wish you could've been there as my maid of honor. And the reception, meeting Patrick McNeil and the rest of the family." Marguerite, in turn, told Suzanne about some of the more "interesting" clients she had recently encountered. "Girl, this job of ours gets stranger all the time. I mean, some of these folks wanna go high-tech. Did you know that when it comes to quirky ways to get it on, there's an app for that? Yes, ma'am, they think just because some jerk has described a new way to put the meat in the ol' sandwich, they gotta be the first to try it out. Whatever happened to plain 'just lie there, honey, and spread your legs'? I could deal with that."

They both laughed and hugged and just enjoyed each other's company, until Suzanne saw out the window that Adam had arrived. Marguerite stood up, patted down her hair and straightened her blouse. Then she turned to Suzanne. "Quick, I forgot to ask. Which version of me do you want on display here, the sophisticated lady or the street-smart badass? Your choice, honey."

The question hadn't even occurred to Suzanne, and now she had only a few seconds to decide. But of course the answer was obvious: Adam would expect her best friend to be the woman she first met at that party now so long ago, not the one who emerged once they had gotten better acquainted. In any event, he was in no way prepared to deal with the real Marguerite, as her kind simply did not show up on his radar, either at work or socially.

"The first one, please. I'm not sure Adam could handle the other one too well."

"You got it." Marguerite smiled and, although she said nothing further, there was a remarkable change in her demeanor that Suzanne could not explain, but was almost palpable. Suddenly that mysterious woman she had first seen on Bill's arm reappeared. It was as if her friend had stepped into a new body that looked the same on the surface, but was totally different underneath.

And of course, in a way that's what she had done. Like a consummate actress, she had assumed a role she was very experienced at playing, and also like a fine actress, she made her audience believe she was the character whom she was playing. Thus when Adam opened the door and stepped into the room, he was immediately charmed by the elegant, statuesque black woman who stepped forward and offered her hand.

"Adam, this is my friend Marguerite Matson," Suzanne said.

Adam, who had, of course, never before his marriage come home to be greeted by even one beautiful woman, was almost overwhelmed at being greeted by two.

He froze for a split second but recovered quickly and took Marguerite's proffered hand in both of his. "I'm very pleased to meet you," he said. "Suzanne has told me what good friends you were back in New York."

"We certainly were," Marguerite said with her upmarket accent, "and still are. We can't let a few thousand miles and a body search by TSA come between us, now can we?"

They all laughed, that broke the ice, and the evening progressed easily from there.

****

Marguerite had never been to San Francisco, so Suzanne and Adam took her to Golden Gate Park, where they strolled and talked and dropped in on the DeYoung Museum and the planetarium. They dined in restaurants for which the City is justifiably famous, and they even rode the cable car. Suzanne had not done some of these things yet herself, and Adam admitted that even he hadn't ridden a cable car in years. "It always takes showing a visitor around for you to see what's in your own backyard," he said. Suzanne was pleased to see that Adam and Marguerite were getting along famously. "Your friend is quite a gal," he remarked to Suzanne at one point, and she couldn't resist answering, "You don't know the half of it."

The weekend passed quickly, and soon Marguerite was on her way back to New York. Although Suzanne missed her almost as soon as her plane took off, having Adam by her side, holding his hand, seemed to make her friend's departure much less traumatic than had she been alone.

And alone is what she had been for so long, even when she was among friends.

Chapter 40

Revelation

The election went as expected. Patrick McNeil won in a landslide, garnering over sixty percent of the vote; his opponent captured only two states, Texas and Arkansas.

There was a big celebration at McNeil headquarters, and no one was more excited about the victory than Adam. The next day, the party regulars began planning for the inauguration and the Inaugural Ball, which would mark the beginning of the McNeil presidency. Of course, unofficially those plans had begun many months before.

"It should be really exciting," Adam told Suzanne. "Of course, we'll be there."

Suzanne, too, was excited, mostly because she could see how much Adam was enjoying his brother's success.

But inauguration was still almost two months away. Two months until Suzanne officially became the sister-in-law of the president. Two months until Suzanne was expected to begin her seduction of the president in earnest.

And as those two months passed, Suzanne became less and less enthusiastic about completing her assignment. Many factors entered into her change of attitude. For one thing, her recent experience with men had been much less traumatic than her earlier experience had been, Craig Johnson being the most glaring exception. For another, the million-dollar motivation had become less urgent now that she was married to a man who had plenty of money—how much she didn't really know—and was more than happy to spend it on Suzanne.

But the primary reason for Suzanne's lessening enthusiasm was Adam himself. It was partly that she had come to really like and admire him—dare she think she had fallen in love with him?—and to appreciate how much he clearly loved her, so that she did not want to break up their relationship. She often lately recalled her conversation with Fran, the woman at the playground, and her feeling that she could not trust any man to be the father of her children. Suzanne was sure she could trust Adam.

More important than her own feelings, however, was the effect her seduction of his brother would have on Adam himself. It was one thing to be disappointed in love for some reason such as failure to attract the object of your desire. It was quite another to learn that the person you loved and had married, and who professed her love in return, was not only cheating on you, but was doing it with the married brother you loved in a very different way.

How can I do that to Adam, she asked herself. *How can I do something that not only will hurt him, but will ruin his relationship with the brother he loves?* She tried her best to put these thoughts aside and remember all the reasons she had accepted The Gang's proposition. She willed herself to suppress them. No, she was still determined to carry out her mission.

****

Suzanne decided that, if she was to make progress

toward the soon-to-be president's bed, there was no time to begin the operation like the present. Although she and Adam were still nominally living in San Francisco, they had already rented an apartment in Washington, DC, as Adam wanted to be close to his brother where he could help with all the difficult transitions involved in becoming the president, of which moving physically into the White House was only one.

As Patrick was also living in DC, the two families saw a lot of each other. On several of these occasions, Suzanne made sure she just happened to find herself and Patrick alone in some room or patio, where, as a good sister-in-law, she could get to know him better and, of course, let him get to know her even better than that. An accidental brush up against him here, an incidental contact there, combined with a very friendly (but never improper) demeanor, suggested, if only fleetingly, that in time this just might be a relationship worth exploring.

What Suzanne didn't know, of course, and what the success of her mission necessarily depended upon, was whether Patrick, despite his reputation as a womanizer, would stoop so low as to bed is brother's wife, no matter how strongly she came on to him and how insistently his ego and his sexual appetite inclined that way. She had to take it slowly and build up his desire for her to the point that it overcame whatever personal ethics might stand in the way.

****

Once the inauguration and Inaugural Ball had passed and the Patrick McNeils had moved (or, more precisely, had been moved by their staff) into the White House, it became time for Suzanne to shift her plans into a higher gear. Her opportunity came only a few days after the inauguration. Both families were together in the White House, Adam and Suzanne staying over for a weekend visit. It was a Sunday afternoon, and everyone except the president had adjourned to either the White House swimming pool or its movie theater. Patrick wanted to finish looking over a speech he was to deliver on Monday, so he told the rest of the guests and family to go on without him.

Suzanne saw her opening.

"I have a terrible headache," she told Adam. "I'm going to lie down for a while. I'll join you and the others later."

Adam gave her a kiss on the nose and said he hoped she felt better soon.

As soon as he and the others were safely gone, Suzanne made her way back toward the Treaty Room, where she knew Patrick would be working by himself. She knocked on the door, entered, and closed the door.

Patrick looked up and smiled when he saw Suzanne. Her preliminary campaign had had its intended effect, making Patrick acutely aware of what might be available should he wish to pursue it. He was, after all, the president. Suzanne, who was used to men undressing her with their eyes, knew that since the first day he met her, Patrick had been visualizing what that marvelous body would look like without all the pesky clothing in the way. Most likely he was also visualizing what that body would feel like next to his in bed. Nevertheless, it was a long way from undressing her with his eyes to doing so with his hands.

Suzanne leaned over the desk at which Patrick was working, as if to read what was on the page before him, meanwhile letting him have an excellent view of her décolletage and a whiff of her expensive perfume.

"It's too bad you have to be stuck here while everyone else is having fun," she said. She was too smart to add, "Maybe we could have some fun here, too," but the implication was obvious, even palpable. She held her breath to see whether he would take the bait or tell her to straighten up, as she was in his light.

To her great relief, he took the bait.

Patrick turned toward Suzanne, who was still leaning over, so that his face was almost enveloped in her breasts. Looking up at her, he smiled. "It is too bad, isn't it?" His hands moved slowly around to her buttocks, where they began a slow, circular massage. Things were progressing quite well, and the president's bed, while not quite an immediate prospect, would soon be within reach, and, with it, Suzanne's million dollars.

And then a strange thing happened.

Suzanne suddenly realized that she actually had no desire to get into bed with Patrick McNeil. Even if he was the president. Even if it would be the ultimate conquest over men and the final payback for the violations of her childhood.

Even for a million dollars.

This was now the second time in recent months that such a thing had happened, the first being her lack of desire to seduce William Tracy at the Kendall job interview. And she was even more confused and scared by the feeling now than she had been then.

She slowly straightened up, smoothed down her sweater. "I'm sorry for disturbing you. I'll let you get back to work."

She turned around and let herself out of his office.

She made her way to her bedroom and lay down on

the bedspread.

Now she really did have a headache.

****

As Suzanne lay there, all the thoughts of what her actions would do to Adam came swirling back in her mind. Once again, she asked herself how she could commit this act that would destroy Adam's relationship both with her and, perhaps more importantly, with his brother? How could she be the cause of ruining his, as well as his brother's, life?

The simple answer was, she couldn't.

Chapter 41

Change of Plans

Once Suzanne realized she could not and would not put an emotional dagger through Adam's heart, her next task was to decide how to avoid doing so. She reasoned that, as it was Lloyd who had made her the original proposition, or had at least been commissioned by The Gang to do so, it was Lloyd she had to tell that she was no longer a part of The Plan. She would contact him as soon as possible and tell him her decision. She realized The Gang, whoever they were, would not be pleased, and might even threaten to expose her to Adam for who she really was. But that was a chance she had to take. Better Adam should be disappointed in her, maybe even divorce her, than he should be devastated—even horrified—by her actions.

She was planning to contact Lloyd the next day, but doing so became unnecessary when she received a call from Betsy.

"I've got a message for you, dear. I think the shit is about to hit the fan."

"Meaning?"

"Meanin' Lloyd'll be comin' to see you next weekend with real important information. He'll meet you in the lobby of the Fairmont Hotel at noon on Saturday. Be there."

"I'll be there," Suzanne said, and the conversation ended.

Just as well, she told herself after putting down the phone. *He's probably coming with further instructions for the next phase of The Plan. I can save him the trouble,* she thought with satisfaction.

****

Saturday at twelve noon, having told Adam she was having lunch with a woman she had met while shopping that week, Suzanne waited for Lloyd on a sofa in the lobby of the Fairmont, San Francisco's fanciest hotel. Five minutes later she was alone with him in the elevator, rising slowly to the fifth floor.

"Y' know, Suzanne, I wish I was takin' you to my room for a real different reason, but unfortunately this is strictly business. Maybe next time."

"Sure, Lloyd. We always had a good time."

"Sure did." He smiled, obviously recalling some of those good times.

This was not going to be one of them.

They entered Lloyd's room, he closed the door, and he immediately went over to the minibar and poured himself a whiskey from one of the small, single-serve bottles.

"Want something?" he asked Suzanne.

"No thanks." Suzanne was nervous about what she was going to tell Lloyd and needed her wits about her. Liquor did not tend to help.

They sat opposite one another, Suzanne on the sofa and Lloyd on an overstuffed chair. Lloyd too looked somewhat overstuffed, having gained weight since Suzanne last saw him. He also looked nervous, even though it was Suzanne who had reason to be. Or so she thought.

Lloyd took a sip of his whiskey, put it down on a lamp table, and began the discussion. "You're probably wondering why I've come all the way out here to talk to you. It's 'cause I have something important to say that the fellers who're employing us wanted me to say in person."

"I have something pretty important to tell you also," Suzanne said.

"Well, little lady, why don't you go first? What do you want to tell me?"

Now that the time had come to tell Lloyd she was backing out of the agreement, she almost lost her nerve. It would have been so much easier to do it over the phone, or by letter or e-mail. Facing him made it scary, but she swallowed hard and began:

"Lloyd, I know I promised to do this thing with the president, to get his brother to marry me and then to—to make him sleep with me so we could get caught and he'd be in trouble and…well, you know. And I did come out here and got his brother to marry me."

"I know you did," Lloyd said, "and everybody's real pleased with how well it's all gone."

"Yes, I'm sure they are. But now—now I don't want to do the—the next thing. I just want to stay married to Adam."

Having gotten the worst part out, she took a deep breath and looked at Lloyd for his reaction. He was slowly shaking his head. He began to speak, and his tone was almost sorrowful:

"I—I don't think you can—"

Suzanne interrupted, her emotions overcoming her sense of caution. "I just can't do it," she said, almost pleading with Lloyd to understand. "I know I agreed, and I know I always wanted to get the better of men and all that, but things have changed. I've changed. I mean, even when I agreed to do it, I'd been starting to feel less…less bitter about men, and it was only because I'd just been roughed up by some asshole named Craig that got me looking for revenge again—"

As soon as she mentioned Craig, Suzanne saw Lloyd wince. Something about what she'd said had hit him like a physical blow.

"What? Why are you looking like that?"

Lloyd put his head in his hands for a moment then looked up and said softly, apologetically, "This guy, Craig. He wasn't just some guy. They set you up. I'd told them you were kinda on the fence about agreeing to their offer, so they made sure you had—you had sufficient motivation."

Suzanne was stunned. Set up. Set up to be raped by that animal. She had trouble processing this new information and felt physically weak.

Lloyd, seeing her distress, wondered whether he should have withheld that information, but it was too late to un-ring that bell now. He handed her his whiskey glass, and this time she didn't decline. He then cleared his throat and spoke, again almost reluctantly. "Now I'd better say what I came to tell you. Because it probably'll change your mind about quitting. And I truly wish I didn't have to say it. Last week, those fellas who are paying us got in touch with me and told me there's been a change in plans."

"A change? What kind of change?"

Lloyd swallowed hard. "They don't want you to sleep with the president—they want you to kill him."

Chapter 42

Persuasion

At first Suzanne thought she had misunderstood. But from the look on Lloyd's face, she knew she had not. She stared at Lloyd for a long moment before she could speak. "Did you say they want me to—to—to assassinate the president? To shoot him or something?" She couldn't believe she was actually saying this.

Lloyd nodded slowly. "Yeah, that's what I came to tell you. And to tell you how you're supposed to do it."

"And they really think I'll agree to this? They must be crazy!"

Lloyd nodded. "Yep, they're crazy all right. But they're also cold-blooded sonofabitches. They knew you wouldn't so easily agree to their little change in plans. So they told me to tell you one other thing that they think will convince you."

"And what's that? They're gonna send another goon to beat me up?"

Lloyd looked even more distressed now than he had when telling Suzanne the change in plans. He seemed reluctant to say what he had to say next. Finally, he said, "No, it ain't you they're gonna mess up if you refuse. It's your mom."

****

It took Suzanne at least a minute to absorb the

implications of what Lloyd had said. When she had, she leaped up and threw herself at Lloyd, crying and scratching his face, trying to get her hands around his neck. It wasn't Lloyd's threat he had passed along, of course; it was a classic case of shooting the messenger.

Lloyd managed to pin Suzanne's arms to her sides. He couldn't blame her for reacting as she did, and he just tried to protect himself from her fury.

A minute later Suzanne had calmed down enough to stop struggling. In fact, she sagged like a rag doll in Lloyd's grasp. He leaned her back against the sofa cushions as she sobbed quietly.

"How—what—what did they say they'd do to Mary Sue?"

Sadly, Lloyd laid out the details he had been instructed to pass along. "They of course know all about you, where you come from, about your parents. They know you were—are very close to your mom. They said to tell you if you don't cooperate with the—the new plan, they'll…well, they said they'll kill her. And not in a pretty way. So she would suffer."

Silence.

"Listen, kid, I'm really sorry it's come to this. I'm kinda in the same position, because I first refused to come out here and tell you this. I told them I didn't want any part of killing the president. Despite what I may've said at some time. I got a big mouth. I told them I wouldn't pass along a threat to kill your mom. They didn't threaten my mom—she's already dead—or nothing complicated like that. They just said if I didn't come out here and convince you to do it, they'd kill me. And I believe it. These folks are crazy as a shithouse rat!"

Suzanne still said nothing, still sobbed quietly, so

Lloyd continued softly, "I'm supposed to give you 'til tomorrow to decide. I'll be here 'til then, leaving Monday morning. Just give me a call when you have an answer for them."

Suzanne nodded slowly to indicate she understood. She rose from the sofa and walked slowly to the door.

"Can I give you a lift home? I got a rental car," Lloyd asked.

Suzanne shook her head. "No, I'll take a cab. Thanks. Not your fault. Gotta think."

Lloyd opened the door for her. Suzanne stepped out into the corridor feeling like she was walking the Last Mile to the electric chair.

She almost wished she were.

****

Suzanne tried her best to compose herself before returning home, but she couldn't completely hide the devastation in her mind, her emotions, and her soul.

Adam was home when she came in. He took one look at her and came over to take her in his arms.

"What's happened? You look terrible."

Suzanne gave Adam the response she had thought up in the cab, the only one that occurred to her in her current muddled state of mind. "I'm sorry, Adam. I just learned that a real close relative of mine back home was killed in a car accident. It's got me awfully upset." She sat down on the sofa.

Adam sat next to her, looking concerned. "I'm sorry," he said. "I can imagine it was a real shock." He squeezed her hand, then got up and poured her a shot of bourbon and brought it to her. "Here, this might help a little."

Suzanne, who seldom drank anything stronger than

beer, took the whiskey and gulped it down, making a face as it seared her throat.

I've got to pull myself together so I can decide what to do, she thought. *And I've got to keep Adam from asking me too many questions, or he'll figure out I'm lying to him.*

"I think I'll go lie down," she said at last, "maybe try to sleep."

"Sure, sure. Let me help you." Adam took her by the arm and led her to the bedroom, where she kicked off her shoes, slipped out of her skirt and blouse, and lay on the bed in her underwear. Adam covered her with a knitted afghan that usually was draped over a nearby chair, bent down and kissed her on the forehead, and left the room. "I'll wake you for dinner," he said as he left. "I'm sure you'll feel better by then."

Suzanne didn't want to sleep, however. She just wanted to think, or at least try to. She had only until the next day to make a decision.

****

By the time Adam returned to the bedroom to wake her, Suzanne had made up her mind and then, with the help of a sleeping pill, fallen asleep.

At dinner, Suzanne was no longer distraught. She did not feel nervous or scared. In fact, she did not feel much at all. She was emotionally numb, having realized that she really had only one choice: She could not put her mother's life in jeopardy by refusing to carry out this new version of The Plan, even if it cost her own life in the process. While she couldn't be certain, of course, that the threat to her mother would be carried out if she refused, she had no doubt the fanatics who were paying her would do whatever was necessary to achieve their ends. Her greed and her hatred of men had led her to make a terrible decision, and now she had to carry it through, or it would be Mary Sue who would pay for her stupidity and weakness. No, she would do it, no matter what the cost to herself.

And to the country.

****

Sunday morning, Suzanne rose early and dressed while Adam was still asleep. He would awaken expecting a warm embrace and, if Suzanne was feeling better, a playful romp under the covers, culminating in some new and exciting sexual discovery. Instead, he would discover a note from Suzanne saying she had gone for a walk, would be back before breakfast.

Once out of the house, Suzanne telephoned Lloyd at the Fairmont. She told him she had decided to carry out her new assignment, and she would be there sometime in the afternoon for instructions.

Back home, Suzanne tried her best to appear normal, but it was all she could do just to carry out normal activities, such as making Sunday brunch for herself and Adam. Adam's attempts to find out what had happened to his happy, vivacious bride were unsuccessful, and after several attempts he gave up. Even a near relative's death—except perhaps a parent's or spouse's—should not cause this much of a change. Perhaps, he thought, it was the time of the month—he had heard this could be a problem for married couples—or just a temporary mood swing.

After brunch was eaten and the dishes were done, Suzanne told Adam she had some shopping to do downtown, and no, there was no need for him to come along. As her tone made it clear that by "no need" she really meant "no desire" for his company, Adam just kissed her on the forehead and told her to hurry back.

Suzanne took a cab to the Fairmont, phoned Lloyd from the lobby, and soon they were back in his room on the fifth floor. Lloyd looked as if he too had been wrestling with Suzanne's dilemma and it had cost him a night's sleep.

"Okay," Suzanne said when they were again seated across from one another, "so tell me how I'm supposed to do this. You know, I've never assassinated a president before."

Lloyd didn't laugh at the black humor; in fact, he seemed to cringe. But he soldiered on: "Well, they tell me it's like this: You'll, of course, have the run of the White House living quarters, on the second and third floors. At least you and the president's brother—Adam, right?—will become pretty familiar guests up there. I understand there are at least a couple of places the president will be by himself, no secret service or anything, working or reading or whatever." He consulted a piece of paper where he had written down some notes. "Like what they call the Treaty Room, which is used as an office. All you gotta do—" He paused for a rueful smile. "'All.' That makes it sound pretty easy, don't it? Let me start again. What you gotta do is find the president alone in one of them rooms—don't matter where—make sure no one sees you go in, and, well, shoot him."

Suzanne was incredulous. "Shoot him? What do they mean shoot him? Where am I going to get a gun? How am I going to get it inside the White House? And I've never even held a gun before, much less fired one."

"They've thought of all that. First, you'll be taking

some lessons. You'll tell Adam you don't feel safe alone at night when he's at some meeting or whatever, so you've decided to buy a pistol and are learning how to handle it safely. There are lots of places giving lessons to women like you, afraid to be home alone. As for getting the thing into the White House, they've got a guy who can make a pistol totally out of plastic, even the firing mechanism. Uses one of them printers, I think they call 'em three-D printers."

"I thought I read there always had to be some metal in a gun so it could be detected at airport security and such."

"Yeah, I think that's what the law says. I recall the NRA lobbied against the legislation requiring it. Wish now we hadn't. But that's just what the law says. It don't stop people like these from making whatever they want. And it used to be too dangerous to make them all plastic. Liable to blow up in the shooter's face. But the technology's changed, and now they apparently work just fine."

"So I'm supposed to stroll right through security with this plastic gun and no one will know?"

"Sorta. They think they have it figured out where you shouldn't have too much trouble—at least if everything goes according to plan. To begin with, you'll be part of the family, so they may not check you at all, but we can't be sure of that. In any case, someone will bring you the gun, outside the White House. Before you take it through security, you'll go in and out several times, at the same time of day, past the same security guard, to get him used to seeing you. The day you bring in the gun, you'll be real friendly with him, maybe wear something low-cut to distract him, know what I mean?

The gun'll be strapped to your chest, just under your...under there." He pointed but didn't touch. "And you'll be wearing a kinda loose blouse, so there should be plenty of room under there without the gun showing."

Suzanne looked down and agreed there should indeed be room for a small gun, if not an army rifle, under her breasts.

"I see," she said. "And I suppose once I've got this gun inside, I just hide it somewhere until I need it, right?"

"Yeah, that's the idea. Sounds crazy to me, but it ain't my plan, and these folks seem to have it all figured out."

"Hmm. I bet. And so I take the gun and find the president alone and shoot him, and then what? Wait 'til the cavalry arrives to shoot me?"

Lloyd shook his head sadly. "God, I hope not. No, they say they've got that figured out too."

"What? They've got a way to make me invisible?"

Lloyd smiled, but ruefully. "Not exactly. The gun will make almost no noise. Got a silencer on it. So the president's been shot, but no one knows it yet. You wipe off your fingerprints and drop the gun and get the hell out. There's some secret passageways in the White House that family members have used, 'specially a president's kids, to avoid security and get out on their own—it's apparently pretty hard to be a kid when there's always some secret service fella watching everything you do. Anyway, you'll become familiar with these passages and use one of them to get away. By the time they find the president, you'll be outside the White House, or at least nowhere near where it happened."

Lloyd didn't add that he was highly skeptical of this part of the plan, and he very much doubted that if

Suzanne was successful in killing the president, she would escape as easily as the conspirators made it sound. In fact, he assumed one way or the other, she would end up dead, either shot by the Secret Service or executed by the government. He wanted to tell her this, and he hated himself for holding it back, but he didn't have the courage to tell her the truth and thus jeopardize his own life should she refuse to carry out The Plan. So he remained silent.

It didn't really matter. Suzanne was under no illusion that one could assassinate the president right under the noses of the Secret Service and somehow get away with it. Oh, she would try, but she knew she had about as much chance of escaping through some passageway as of levitating and escaping through the roof.

By doing what she was told, she could protect her mother. Even protect Lloyd, although that was a matter of indifference. She could not protect herself.

Lloyd explained a few more of the details he'd been given, a silent Suzanne taking them in without expression. When he was through, he took her down to the lobby and saw her out to the taxi stand.

"I really wish I'd never gotten you into this," he said as a cab pulled up. "I wish I'd never gotten myself into it either. I'm sorry. Really, I am."

Suzanne just nodded, indicating she understood, and got into the cab. Lloyd turned and walked sadly back into the hotel.

Suzanne watched him go as the cab pulled away. It was the last time she would ever see Lloyd Kilpatrick.

PART 6: ENDGAME

Chapter 43

Preparations

Dear Marguerite:

I'm afraid things aren't going too well here. I can't explain, except I guess I'm going ahead with this stupid plan, even if I wish I weren't. Lloyd Kilpatrick flew out here to give me instructions, and I was going to tell him I'd changed my mind and I wanted to stay married to Adam. I really like him, he's different than any other man I've met, and I think we could be real happy together. But for reasons I can't go into, I have to go ahead with the plan.

I'm trying real hard to be a good wife and pretend everything's okay between me and Adam, but it's not easy, and I'm sure he knows something's wrong. I just hope I can keep going until this is all over.

I've enclosed a sealed envelope with this letter. Please do not open it, not now. There will be a time when you will know you should open it. You'll just know. Until then, you must promise to just put it away unopened.

That's about all. I wish I could tell you more, but I can't.

I love you and hope you'll always love me, no matter what.

Suzanne

****

Marguerite read the letter, which had arrived in a large, nine-by-eleven-inch manila envelope, with mounting apprehension. She held the enclosed smaller manila envelope, which was quite heavy, and stared at it for a full minute. It was obvious that something had convinced Suzanne to go ahead with the crazy scheme to seduce the president, even after she had found what seemed like a happy marriage with Adam. That something probably was contained in the sealed envelope that had accompanied Suzanne's letter, the envelope she was not to open until…until what?

Whatever it was, it would apparently be so…so dramatic, or so horrific, that Marguerite would have no doubt it was the triggering event.

Marguerite was not an overly curious person, and just the fact that she had to put away the envelope without opening it did not concern her. It was the implications of the mere existence of the envelope that worried her, that made it so difficult for her to lock it in her dresser drawer where she kept her most private objects.

But lock it away she did.

****

Meanwhile, Suzanne had managed to shore up her courage and regain her composure sufficiently to satisfy Adam that she was simply going through some temporary funk and would soon snap out of it. There was, after all, the newness of married life, excitement of the election and its aftermath, and of course the tragic death of a close relative—apparently it was an aunt, who had practically brought her up—to explain her recent moodiness. He would wait and try not to exacerbate her condition by nagging her about it.

As she got more closely involved with the presidential transition, as the wife of the president's younger brother had to be, Suzanne found herself forgetting for a time the terrible thing she had to do now that Patrick McNeil's term as president had begun. She even found she could smile, even laugh when the occasion demanded it. If she was somewhat distracted in bed with Adam, she hoped she was enough of a professional to keep him from noticing, just as she was able to keep clients in whom she had no interest whatsoever thinking they were giving her the best sex she had ever had.

As predicted, she and Adam were frequent visitors in the White House, especially as Adam, who had taken a leave from work, had rented an apartment in Washington, DC so he could help his brother and his brother's family with some of the many adjustments required of a new tenant of the White House.

Suzanne soon became familiar with the White House itself, its large staff—five chefs for three kitchens!—and all of its rooms, secret and otherwise. She told Adam she wanted to see all of the hidden places she had read about, and he was able to arrange it quite easily with his brother. She thus found and tried out the tunnel once known as the "Marilyn entrance" that led from the ground floor, under the East Wing, to the Treasury Building next door. She investigated the hidden door next to the Queens' Bedroom that led to the floor above and the solarium, as well as the tunnel between the Oval Office and the residence. It seemed that perhaps there were indeed ways to disappear, once the deed had been done, although it was probably only wishful thinking. After all, the Secret Service knew about those tunnels too.

One thing about which Suzanne was certain was that, had she been planning to carry out the original plan of finding her way into Patrick McNeil's bed, it would not have been a difficult assignment. As she had found when she made her aborted attempt to pique Patrick's interest in her wares, she had the same effect on President McNeil that she did on most men. The president's reputation as a womanizer had preceded him, and it seemed to be fairly justified. The friendly hugs between a man and his sister-in-law were a little longer, a little more intimate, a little more exploratory, than was absolutely necessary. Oh yes, she thought, this would not have been difficult at all.

It also was obvious that, while Patrick was pleased for his brother's good fortune in marrying such a sexy, voluptuous woman, he was puzzled at how Adam, who he had always thought would be lucky to get any woman at all to marry him, had landed such a prize. None of the stereotypes for the man who would attract a woman like Suzanne seemed to fit. Not that he was jealous.

Well, maybe just a little.

****

On Tuesday, February sixth, just about a month after the Patrick McNeils moved into their grand new, if temporary, home, and while the Adam McNeils were visiting and staying in the Lincoln Bedroom—much handier than commuting from their apartment a mile away—Suzanne was contacted by Lloyd once again. He called her cellphone and gave her instructions as to when and where she would be given the plastic pistol to be used in carrying out her mission.

"Go out and buy yourself a roll of that tape they use

to attach bandages, you know. You get it at a drugstore, I guess. Then next Tuesday, the thirteenth, stand outside the Visitors Center at two in the afternoon. Have the tape with you and wear a loose kinda blouse. A blonde woman wearing a beige suit with a red scarf and carrying a small tote bag with an American flag on it will walk into the Visitors Center and go directly to the ladies' rest room. You follow her in. She'll go into one of the stalls, stay a minute or so, then leave. You're to go into the same stall immediately after she comes out—don't let anyone else get in there ahead of you—and look for a small package about the size of a juice box like the kids take to school."

"Where'll this package be?"

"Don't know exactly. I guess it depends on where there is to put it. Never been in a ladies' toilet myself. I assume you'll see it. There should also be a couple of bullets attached somehow to the package."

"Okay. Then what?"

"Then you use the tape to strap the package under your boo—under your bosom."

"What about the bullets? Strap them there too?"

"No, they're metal, and if they use a metal detector at security it could pick them up. D'you have one of them things ladies use to powder their noses?"

"You mean a compact?"

"Yeah. You'll need a metal one. Just put the bullets in there. A metal detector will just pick up the compact, which I assume you'll have had with you every time you went through before."

"A metal compact. That I don't have. They're mostly plastic these days. But I guess I can find one. And then?"

"And then you waltz right through security, take off the package when you're alone an' hide it somewhere 'til you need it. Somewhere no one else'll find it."

"No, I'll put it out on the president's desk where everyone can admire it."

"Okay, no need to get snippy. I don't like this any more than you do."

"On the contrary, I'm sure I don't like it much more than you don't like it, since I'm the one who has to do the dirty work." Then Suzanne's tone softened a little. "I'm sorry, I know you're just doing what you have to do. Anything else?"

"No, nothing I've been told, anyway. Did you find those secret passages and such, so you can get away?"

"Yeah, I found them. Not that they'll do me a helluva lot of good, but I guess it's better than having to stand there until somebody rushes in and shoots me."

Lloyd's wince at the other end was apparent even over the phone.

"Gosh, I hope it don't come to that. Really, I do. You're a good kid, Suzanne. I feel terrible I got you into this mess—"

"Never mind. It's too late for that. Gotta go."

And she hung up.

So Tuesday the thirteenth was to be the day. Suzanne decided she would get the deed over with as soon as possible, preferably the same day. The longer she waited, the more chance she would lose her nerve, and the longer the agony she was feeling inside would last.

Next week.

She had a compact and some tape to buy and a blouse to select.

Chapter 44

The Drop

The "drop" of the gun to Suzanne had been set, as Lloyd had told her, for two-thirty the afternoon of Tuesday the thirteenth. *It feels more like Friday the thirteenth,* Suzanne thought when she got up that morning.

"I'm going for a walk," Suzanne said to Adam after lunch, which they had shared with the president and the first lady in the second-floor dining room. "I'll probably wander around a bit. Be back later in the afternoon."

"I'll come with you," Adam said. "I could use a break from this place. My brother and I've been working pretty hard on that biogenetics speech." The president had been planning a series of speeches outlining his science program, and Adam was helping to educate him on some of the issues and talking points.

"No, no, that won't be necessary," Suzanne replied quickly, trying not to sound as panicky as she was feeling. "I—I'll probably take a bus downtown afterward and do some shopping or something. You'd just be bored."

"Well—"

And then Suzanne had an idea. "Tell you what: Why don't you meet me at that little coffee shop we like near the National Mall around five o'clock? We can have an early dinner there." This would keep him away from the White House, and the president, when she intended to use the gun she'd be picking up. If for some reason she couldn't find the president alone, she could postpone the act and meet Adam. And if she did find the president alone and killed him, the farther away Adam was from that terrible scene, the better.

"Sounds good. I'll see you at five."

They kissed and Suzanne, wearing a loose cotton blouse and carrying a roll of surgical tape in her purse, walked a bit unsteadily out of the White House and onto the path circling the South Lawn. She still had plenty of time and made her way by a circuitous route to the Visitors Center. She looked at her watch. It was almost two-fifteen.

Fifteen minutes. Suzanne would have to wait fifteen minutes before the woman with the American-flag tote bag was scheduled to show up.

Suzanne paced nervously back and forth, keeping an eye peeled for the woman just in case she arrived early. She just wanted to get this over with, not to have to think about it or agonize over it any longer.

She checked her watch again. Ten minutes to go. She thought of Adam, expecting to meet his new wife, his new love, for dinner that afternoon. She shook her head as if to drive the thought away. She tried not to think of anything at all.

Five minutes to go. Pacing. Still looking for the woman with the gun. She turned around and there was a woman coming straight toward her. Only it was not the woman with the American flag tote. It was Sarah Benson, wife of one of the president's close advisers, whom she had met on her and Adam's first visit to the

White House. Sarah had since become a friend with whom she enjoyed talking. But not now. Any time but now!

"Suzanne!" Sarah called out. "What're you doing here?" She held out her arms preparing to give Suzanne a friendly hug.

Suzanne glanced around to see if the woman she awaited was in sight, but saw no beige suit or flag tote. She forced a smile and greeted Sarah, accepting the hug and returning a halfhearted one.

"Oh, hi, Sarah. I was just out for a walk and—and wandered over this way. Nice—nice to see you."

Sarah, who was the chatty type and seldom picked up on the nuances of others' body language, didn't notice that Suzanne was looking past her. She launched immediately into telling Suzanne why she was there—to find some souvenirs for a niece she'd be visiting soon; where she had been—at the dentist, but it was only for cleaning; and where she was going next—to a late lunch, and why didn't Suzanne join her?

Suzanne was desperate to get away from Sarah, but she couldn't think of a polite, or even less than polite, way to extricate herself. She continued to look around as Sarah prattled on. Suddenly she spotted, over Sarah's shoulder, a plumpish woman with blonde hair, wearing a beige suit and sporting a bright red scarf around her neck. And yes, she was carrying a small white tote bag with a large American flag embroidered on its side.

"I have to run, Sarah," she said as the blonde woman reached for the door under the Center's blue and white awning. But Sarah, not sensing the note of urgency in Suzanne's voice, put her hand on her friend's shoulder and said, "Just let me tell you what happened—"

That was as far as she got. Suzanne pushed Sarah aside and rushed to fall in behind the blonde before she lost her in the crowd. Sarah stared after her, her mouth hanging open.

Suzanne hated having been so rude, but then, by the next day rudeness would have become almost an endearing trait, compared with the crime she would have committed.

Once inside the Visitors Center, Suzanne looked around frantically for the blonde woman with the tote. She finally spotted her, heading toward the sign marked Ladies. With more rude pushes and shoves, Suzanne reached the woman just as she was entering the restroom. The woman glanced casually over her shoulder to see if Suzanne was following her, then entered a stall and closed the door behind her, leaving Suzanne to linger on the other side, trying not to look conspicuous. That wasn't easy, because there were empty stalls available and it looked odd that Suzanne chose not to enter one. She couldn't move to a wash basin or anywhere but in front of that door and take a chance someone else would enter before her and find the package. On the other hand, she couldn't stand right in front of the stall door like an anxious mother prompting her three-year-old to "do her business." Not only would that look suspicious and call attention to her, but it would defeat the only possible reason—at least the only reason Suzanne had been able to come up with—for such an elaborate method of transferring the gun to her, which was to avoid anyone seeing an exchange between Suzanne and the courier. Clearly, The Gang did not want there to be any possible way a witness could, after the president was killed, connect one of their members with Suzanne just before it occurred.

So she backed off just enough to make it less obvious she was waiting for that particular stall and tried to look inconspicuous. She ignored the stares from other patrons and waited, sweating, at her station, praying the blonde woman would hurry.

Finally, Suzanne heard the click of the stall's lock. She stepped farther back, noticing with relief that she was now the only other occupant of the rest room. The blonde woman, whose face Suzanne had not yet seen, emerged. She appeared to be about sixty—*she probably has her hair dyed,* Suzanne thought, surprised that it would even occur to her at a time like this—and as hard as nails. She looked straight at Suzanne, scowled as if Suzanne had insulted her, and, turning on her heel, left the restroom as the spring-hinged stall door quietly closed with a light tap of metal to metal.

Suzanne had relaxed a bit once the competition for the stall had left, but before she could put her legs in motion and walk the few feet to reach the stall door, she heard another, louder and more ominous sound. A tour bus must have just discharged its load of world travelers, because to Suzanne's dismay, a noisy band of middle-aged Asian women burst into the rest room, all apparently with full bladders and a single-minded intention to empty them at the earliest possible moment.

Suzanne reached the stall in a photo-finish with a short, stocky woman wearing a bright turquoise blouse and an expression somewhere between grim determination and emotional distress. The woman shoved Suzanne aside with surprising ease, given her size, entered the stall, and locked the door. The next sounds that emerged were water on water and a loud sigh of relief.

Suzanne began to panic. What if the woman found the gun? Had the courier put it in plain sight? Should Suzanne stay around to find out and possibly be caught up in an investigation of how a plastic pistol found its way into the women's rest room at the Visitors Center? Or should she flee and live to fight—and in this case perhaps die—another day?

Now it was Suzanne who was about to pee her pants.

****

Suzanne decided to take a chance. She didn't know if she could go through all this again, or even how she would explain to The Gang her failure to secure the gun. So all she could do was wait and hope the woman inside the stall was too busy enjoying blessed relief to notice the contents of her surroundings.

After what seemed like an hour, even if it was only a few minutes, Suzanne again heard the click of the lock and she saw the stall door open.

The Asian woman emerged, and, to Suzanne's horror, she was carrying a small juice-box size package that she had not been carrying when she entered. Suzanne almost fainted, but she managed to keep her wits about her. The woman was holding the box in the air and saying something in Chinese, or perhaps Japanese or Korean—Suzanne didn't speak any language other than English—to the other women in the room, who were either washing their hands or touching up their hair or makeup in the mirror. Suzanne, seeing her chance, stepped forward and grabbed the box out of the woman's hands. She then began determinedly gesturing, pointing to herself and then to the stall, what she hoped would be interpreted as, "This is mine. I left it in that stall. Thank you for retrieving it for me." She shoved past the little woman and entered the stall with her package, locking the door behind her.

Suzanne didn't know whether the ladies would accept her attempted "explanation" and go away quietly, or perhaps the entire band would pound on the door demanding the box back. She never found out, because just then a new voice called out loudly in that same foreign language. From its authoritative tone, Suzanne guessed it was a call for the ladies to get back on the bus. The potty break was over. Apparently she was correct, because the entire group immediately began filing out of the rest room, chattering loudly. Suzanne could hear their voices fading away as the door closed behind the last of the ladies.

Suzanne put down the box, relieved herself on the toilet, then just sat there until she had collected her wits sufficiently to carry on. She sincerely hoped this was not an example of how the rest of The Plan was going to unfold.

****

Taking a deep breath, Suzanne reached down and picked up the small box she had snatched from the Asian lady. *Just my luck it'll be her lunch,* Suzanne told herself.

But it wasn't.

The box was wrapped in brown paper, with string holding it together. Suzanne slipped off the string, ripped off the paper, and opened the box. The first thing she noticed was that there were four bullets inside, instead of the two Lloyd had mentioned.

I guess they figure I'll be a lousy shot and need four tries. Or maybe the other two are for when I'm making my getaway, she thought with the blackest of humor.

Or for me.

Suzanne took from her purse the empty metal compact she was carrying and dropped in the bullets. Two would have fit nicely. Four were a tight squeeze, but she managed to close the compact lid over them. Next she had to take off her blouse, hang it up (*thank goodness there's a coat hook on the door*), and again reach into her purse for the roll of tape. Strapping the package under her bosom wasn't easy, especially in the confines of the tiny room in which she was working. She really needed a second person to wind the tape while she held the package in place. No doubt the people formulating this part of the plan were men, and they had never actually tried it out.

It took several tries, but eventually she managed to secure the package in a spot usually reserved for more intimate purposes.

She threw the remaining tape back into her purse, put her blouse back on, and left the stall, hoping she appeared as nonchalant as a normal woman who had just left something behind, rather than picking something up.

On her way out of the restroom, Suzanne stopped to wash her hands and glanced into the mirror to see if the package showed under her loose blouse.

It did a little, at least when she stood quite straight. *Another slight miscalculation by the geniuses who thought up this delivery system, she thought. I'll just have to be sure to bend over slightly when I'm going through security. Oh well, it'll give the guy a better look at the top of my boobs, so he'll be too busy to worry about what's under them.*

Fifteen minutes after she entered the stall—and a half hour after she had entered the rest room—Suzanne emerged and quickly left the Visitors Center. It was almost three o'clock.

She still had work to do.

Chapter 45

Seeking Her Quarry

During the two weeks before receiving the gun, Suzanne had made several trips into and out of the White House at approximately two-thirty in the afternoon, as she had been instructed to do. She had found that security was quite light, if not nonexistent, for family members like her, with only a cursory wave of the Magic Wand of Detection over her and her packages. Nevertheless, she made a point of befriending the two or three young men who worked the security detail, one of whom was always on duty when she re-entered the White House. Suzanne had never had trouble interesting a man in her wares—if, once again, one ignored the unfortunate incident with Eugene Lee, which she considered the exception that proved the rule—and the security detail was no different. Their eyes tended to focus much more on her body than on her belongings.

So when Suzanne prepared to pass through security, gun firmly taped under her breasts, bullets inside her metal compact, décolletage prominently displayed inside her loose-fitting blouse, she assumed she could be carrying a fully-armed grenade launcher and the officer on duty would not notice.

But when she approached the entrance to the White House, what she noticed made her catch her breath.

Instead of one of the usual security detail with whom she was familiar, and who were all familiar with her, she saw a new person on duty.

And that new person was a woman.

Even apart from the fact that this woman would not be familiar with her and, more important, would not be distracted by her décolletage, in her experience with security officers generally, Suzanne had always found women to be much more thorough, more businesslike, than men. Perhaps it was her appearance—turning the men on and the women off, so to speak—but she always preferred to face a male screener. This time, this crucial time, she seemed to have no choice. She modestly buttoned the top of her blouse and waited.

There was another woman ahead of her in the security line. The screener, whose badge introduced her as "Geraldine," eyed the woman up and down, then instead of simply X-raying her purse, asked her to empty its contents onto the counter. Suzanne swallowed hard, her knees feeling rubbery, as Geraldine examined the woman's copious inventory of lipsticks, pills, keys, and assorted detritus, finally nodding and sending her on her way.

Suzanne stepped forward.

Geraldine was not looking at Suzanne. When she did look up and into Suzanne's face, Suzanne was prepared for the worst. Much to her surprise and relief, however, Geraldine smiled. "You're Mrs. McNeil, aren't you? I mean the other Mrs. McNeil." She chuckled. "I've seen you around. Nice day for a walk, isn't it?" After a cursory look at—but not in—her purse and sweep of her wand, Suzanne was waved through.

Once past security, Suzanne had to stop and catch

her breath. She was nervous enough without that kind of added anxiety. She just wasn't cut out for this sort of work.

But it was too late for that. The plan laid out for Suzanne was to conceal the gun in an appropriate place, such as the bedroom in which they were staying, and retrieve it in the next day or two when the right opportunity arose. She had to find President McNeil alone and unguarded, an easy target for someone who would likely be nervous and shaking a bit when she pulled the trigger.

That was the plan. But Suzanne couldn't wait that long. She had to get this over with sooner.

She had to do it now.

****

Suzanne strolled as casually as she could down the hallway and past the Oval Office. She passed one of the president's aides, who nodded and smiled, and although he was in no way acting in a threatening manner, her knowledge of what she was about made her shiver with fear. She nodded back and hoped she looked normal, even if she felt anything but normal.

Suzanne reached the Lincoln bedroom without further encounters and shut the door. She sat on the bed and unbuttoned her blouse. As she began removing the tape that held the gun under her breasts, she looked up at the massive rosewood headboard with its intricate carvings and huge golden crown. Lincoln himself had never slept in it, she had been told, but it was part of the White House furnishings when he was president, so it had seen a great deal of American history and a great many distinguished occupants. She wondered whether an assassin had ever slept in it, or would this be the first time.

Her gaze then fell to the other Victorian furnishings in the room. It was an impressive display, and every time Suzanne saw it, every time she slept in that bed, she realized that now she too was a part of that history. In fact, when she had first entered the Lincoln bedroom, and really when she had first entered the White House as a close relative of the president, Suzanne had been awestruck by the sense of dignity and history that her surroundings exuded. She had found it difficult to comprehend how she, Suzanne Dahlstrom, who had begun life as an unwanted "accident," had been raped by her father, and been driven to a life of selling her body and its sexual favors, was now an honored guest in perhaps the most distinguished edifice in America.

Looking at those surroundings now, her heart ached for what could have been...

Shaking her head and taking a deep breath, Suzanne willed herself to concentrate on the task at hand. She finished removing the tape that held the pistol. It stung a bit when she pulled the tape away, but her mind was occupied with far too important matters to worry about a little discomfort. Next, she retrieved two of the bullets from her compact and loaded the gun.

It was now four-oh-five. Where was the president now? Was he alone?

Suzanne put the pistol into her purse and left the bedroom.

Where was Patrick McNeil?

****

Given the time of day, Suzanne was unsure just where the president might be, but there was a chance he was alone in some part of the residence. She walked down the hallway feeling nervous and afraid, clutching the purse that held the loaded gun so hard it would probably have permanent creases where her fingers gripped it. With a myriad of conflicting thoughts running through her head, she failed to notice the young man, obviously in a hurry, coming around the corner of the hallway in the opposite direction. His arm hit hers, not hard but enough to throw her off balance. She fell, and as she put out her hands to break her fall, she lost her grip on her purse—the purse containing the gun. It skidded out in front of her, just out of her grasp. As it landed, the catch came open and some of its contents spilled out.

The young man, probably some kind of messenger, had kept his balance. Now he turned, looking stricken, as might anyone who has just collided with and knocked down a person who was likely a member of the president's inner circle. He began to apologize and reached out to help Suzanne up. But Suzanne was focused on only one thing: her purse, lying on the hallway floor two feet in front of her. Had the gun been among the items that had spilled? She couldn't tell. She also couldn't take a chance on this guy finding it there. She shook off his offer of assistance and crawled forward to where the purse lay.

Although the pistol had not fully emerged, a part of the barrel was sticking out. Suzanne quickly grabbed the purse, shoved the gun and the other spilled contents back into its interior, closed the catch, and then just lay there, crying, in a combination of frustration, anger, and despair.

Looking thoroughly confused, the young man just stood there, apparently uncertain what to do. He again tried to apologize. But Suzanne, finally taking control of herself, sat up, holding her purse tightly, and said, "No, it was my fault. I wasn't looking where I was going. I'm okay now." This time she let him help her up, thanked him, and walked away, still a bit shaky.

She could only hope the young man had not noticed the gun barrel, or if he had that he hadn't guessed what it was.

As for her task, she knew she was in no condition now to do anything except call it a day.

The last act in this drama would have to be postponed until at least tomorrow, Wednesday.

Chapter 46

The Envelope

From the moment Marguerite read Suzanne's cryptic letter, with its accompanying secrets, she'd had a very bad feeling about its implications. Although she had put the sealed envelope that Suzanne had enclosed away without opening it, as the days passed she could not get her mind off of it and its possible contents. Was it some kind of directions? A confession? A will?

Whatever it was, if she followed Suzanne's directive, when she finally did open it, it would be too late to do anything except deal with it as instructed. Whatever was going to happen so that Marguerite would "just know" it was time to open it, would already have happened.

It wasn't until late in the morning of Wednesday, February fourteenth, that Marguerite finally made a decision. Suzanne probably would never know if she opened it now, unless perhaps if she changed her mind and asked for it back. That would cause Marguerite a lot of embarrassment, and it might even cost her Suzanne's friendship. But the alternative might be much worse, if Suzanne was in some kind of trouble that Marguerite could help her with. It had to be something other than seducing the president, because Marguerite already knew all about that, so there would be no need to keep those facts away from her. No, it had to concern something very different.

And if she was wrong, if the envelope contained nothing more sinister than…well, than what she already knew, again there would be no harm done. Marguerite would reseal the envelope and put it back in her dresser drawer.

Yes, she would open it now.

****

The sealed envelope that Suzanne had enclosed contained another letter addressed to Marguerite and three more sealed envelopes. One was addressed to Adam McNeil, another to Patricia Lee, and the third to Mary Sue Dahlstrom, Suzanne's mother.

The contents of Suzanne's letter made Marguerite catch her breath. It began:

Dear Marguerite:

As you have opened this envelope, by now you know why I sent it to you. President McNeil has been shot and presumably killed, and I have been identified as the one who killed him. I am either dead or in police custody, and the world knows who I am.

Suzanne then went on to describe in detail how this tragedy came about: Her meeting with Lloyd where he told her of the change in plans; the threat to kill Mary Sue if Suzanne did not carry out the new plan; her agonizing over what to do and final decision that, convinced the conspirators would not hesitate to carry out their threat, she could not jeopardize her mother's life to save the president's—and likely her own.

Now you know why I did this horrible thing, and I can only hope you will understand and not judge me too harshly when you think of me. The three letters I have enclosed are to the only three people I care enough about to ~~want~~ need to explain this to them also. They have to know I'm not an evil person, or a crazy person. I used terrible judgment getting involved in this insane plot to embarrass the president, but I stupidly thought no one would get really hurt, it was just politics, and I didn't care who was the president. And of course I was greedy for that million dollars. I'm not making excuses, just saying I never would have gotten involved had I known where this was going.

Maybe you could go and see my mom sometime and tell her about me and what I've been doing these past few years. I never told her, but I think she'd understand, and maybe it would help explain how this all happened.

Marguerite, I'm so sorry for everything. The happiest time of my life was when you and I were living together and I was in a profession that fulfilled so many of my needs, whatever other people might think about it. Or maybe the happiest time was the short time I've spent as Adam's wife. Either way, it's over now, much as I wish it weren't.

Thank you for your friendship—for your love—and for carrying out this last request of mine.

All my love,
Suzanne

****

For a long while, Marguerite, who had been standing when she opened the envelope but had had to sit down to steady herself as she began to read, just stared at the letter in her hands, not really seeing it. She felt faint. What she was seeing was the face of Suzanne, a beautiful, vivacious, caring person she had grown to love like a sister. Suzanne, a girl who had been terribly abused when she was young and who now wanted only to be happy and to even the score a bit against the opposite sex that had so injured her growing up. Suzanne, gone now in the most terrible way—

Wait a minute. Suzanne wasn't gone. The president hadn't been shot. Not yet.

There had to be something Marguerite could do to stop it from happening, without endangering Suzanne or her mother.

But what?

Marguerite thought harder then she had ever thought about anything before. But there was so much she still didn't know.

How was this assassination to be carried out? And more importantly, when? It could be a month before it was supposed to happen. Or an hour.

Was there still time to stop it?

She couldn't go to Suzanne for the answers. It was clear that Suzanne had made up her mind, having decided going through with the plan was the only way to protect her mother. Marguerite was unlikely to persuade her otherwise, mostly because there was no way she could assure her that Mary Sue's death would not be the result. And by revealing she had opened the envelope with which she had been entrusted, she might lose whatever faith in their friendship Suzanne would have had. And worse yet, Suzanne might be forced into acting sooner than she had intended, now that her intentions were known.

But she could get the information she needed from someone else: from Lloyd.

That fucker is gonna tell me what I want t' know, or he'll regret the day he ever laid eyes on me, Marguerite told herself.

****

Marguerite knew that Lloyd lived in Tennessee, but she also knew he frequently visited New York, and when he did, he used the services of the Red Carnation Escort Service. More to the point, he had used the sensuous services of Marguerite until she unloaded him onto other ladies, and eventually Suzanne, something she now regretted terribly. If she was lucky, he would be in town that day. Otherwise she would have to make a fast trip to Tennessee. She telephoned the Red Carnation office to find out whether Lloyd Kilpatrick was a scheduled client that day.

She was lucky; Lloyd had called in two days earlier to say he'd be in town on business for a few days and to line up a "partner" for Tuesday and Wednesday afternoons. They had scheduled one of their newer girls for that assignment, as Lloyd was still not considered an important client, even if he was a regular one. Marguerite said she wanted the assignment for that afternoon, and when the woman setting the schedules protested, she said simply, "Listen, honey, I ain'taskin' you, I'm tellin' you, I'm taking this turn with Lloyd Kilpatrick. You can go check with Mr. Gillette; tell him if he gives me any trouble about it, he can get himself another girl, 'cause I'll quit. Know what I'm sayin'?"

Apparently the woman on the other end of the phone didn't particularly want to deliver that message to Ron Gillette. "Okay, okay, I don't know why you want to service this old guy, but if it's that important, I'll put you down. This afternoon at one-thirty, Esquire Hotel as usual, Room 218."

"Thank you, ma'am," Marguerite said in her most

syrupy sweet tones and most sophisticated accent. "I appreciate your understanding and assistance."

She hung up and began the long wait until she could get her hands—or whatever body parts were necessary—on Lloyd Kilpatrick.

****

When Marguerite knocked on the door of Room 218 early that afternoon, she was not yet certain how she was going to get the information she needed, mostly because she didn't know how closely Lloyd would try to guard it. She hoped she was ready for any eventuality.

Lloyd opened the door and almost fell backwards. Marguerite, the woman with whom he had had so many wonderful encounters in the past, but who had been denied to him for more than two years, was again standing in front of him, just as sexy looking, as sassy looking, as ever. What had he done to deserve this?

He would soon find out.

"Hello, Lloyd," Marguerite said in a soft, almost whispered greeting. "Been a long time."

Lloyd, who looked like he hadn't been sleeping well lately, gulped. "Yes, yes it has. Why are—that is, I didn't—didn't expect you. But I'm right glad to see you."

"I'm glad t' see you too, Lloyd. And I think we should get right down to business, don't you? Time's awastin'."

"Yeah, sure. Sure. This is great, Marguerite." And he immediately closed the door, patted Marguerite on the ass, and headed for the suite's bedroom.

Marguerite followed him in. "Y'know, I think we'll skip the spankin' part this time and get right to the main event." She began to undress.

332

From her tone, Lloyd could tell Marguerite was not asking him, she was telling him, and he decided he didn't really want to argue with her. If she wanted to get right to screwing, with all the wonderful tricks of the trade she knew and had introduced him to, he was not about to complain. He took off his clothes.

Marguerite maneuvered Lloyd onto his back on the bed, then climbed aboard as if she were going to assume the cowgirl position for sex. But instead, once she was straddling Lloyd, leaning with her hands on his shoulders, her demeanor became serious and she said, very softly, "Okay, Lloyd, I know all about what you told Suzanne. About the so-called change in plans. Killin' the president. All that. Now I want you to tell me. Everything."

The menace in her voice was unmistakable, but Lloyd, clearly shocked by what Marguerite had said, protested. "Geez, I don't know how you found out about that, but I can't tell you anything. They'd kill me!" He started to get up.

Marguerite immediately put her knee in Lloyd's crotch, just hard enough to cause some pain and his eyes to water. Her fingernails, which she had been sure to sharpen that afternoon, dug into his shoulders. Her tone became even more menacing.

"Lloyd, honey, if you don't tell me what I want to know, they won't have to kill you, 'cause I'll do it first. You get my meaning?"

Although Lloyd was fairly strong, he was in no position to argue. Marguerite was no lightweight herself, and she was clearly determined to have her way. Besides, Lloyd had long since regretted his part in the plot against the president. He had simply lacked the fortitude to stand up to the conspirators. At first, he had been afraid of losing his fifty thousand dollars, later he became afraid of losing his life. Nevertheless, Marguerite was now making surrender much more palatable: He might die later if he talked. He probably would die sooner if he didn't.

He talked.

Lloyd told Marguerite everything he knew about the conspiracy, up to and including his latest instructions to Suzanne. While he talked, Marguerite kept her knee in his crotch and her hands tight on his naked shoulders, just in case. He ended by saying, "And honest, I'm glad I got this off my mind. I was having trouble living with myself because of what I knew."

"When is Suzanne gettin' that gun?"

"She got it yesterday, I think. At least she was supposed to."

"Holy shit, then she could maybe even use it today."

Lloyd nodded. "I assume she'll wait for the right moment and all, but—but yeah, I guess it could be any time."

When Lloyd had said all he had to say, and Marguerite had no more questions, she relaxed her grip and eased back her knee from his privates.

She began to climb off the bed, trying to think what, if anything, she could do now. Then she paused. "And just to show you my appreciation for the information, honey," she said sweetly as Lloyd cringed, preparing for another onslaught, "if I can put a stop to this shit, I'll see that you get treated real nice next time you're in town." Her tone and expression changed ominously: "If I can't…"

While Lloyd lay on the bed sorting out in his mind

what had just happened, Marguerite quickly dressed and let herself out.

She had a lot of thinking to do, and she had to do it fast.

As she was closing the door behind her, she had parting words for Lloyd. "No charge."

Chapter 47

Concealment

The previous afternoon, after her near-disastrous encounter with the young man in the hallway, Suzanne had made her way back to the Lincoln Bedroom feeling sore from her fall and exhausted from the stress she was under. Now that she had not completed her task the same day she acquired the gun, she would have to conceal it, together with the bullets in her compact, for at least another day.

Where could she hide the gun so that there was no chance Adam, or anyone else, would find it?

Sitting on the bed, she took it out of her purse and held it out in front of her, thinking. Would it be safe in a dresser drawer? On a closet shelf? Or should she just keep it in her purse until the time came to use it? She had already seen how risky carrying it with her could be. And what if, when she wasn't actually carrying it, Adam decided to open her purse, perhaps looking for the breath mints she always carried, as he sometimes did?

Just then the door of the bedroom opened and Adam entered. In a panic, Suzanne quickly shoved the gun back into her purse and closed the catch, praying that Adam hadn't noticed what it was.

If he had, he didn't say so, although the puzzled look on his face left the question open.

"Did I startle you?" he asked, walking toward the bed.

"What? No, no. I just wasn't expecting you, was kinda lost in thought."

"Oh. Well, I just thought I'd take a short nap before dinner. Didn't sleep well last night." He smiled and added, "Maybe it was Lincoln's ghost or something keeping me awake."

Suzanne tried to smile too, but couldn't. What should she do now? She didn't dare leave the purse with the gun lying around where Adam might open it, but she couldn't sit there holding it either.

"I...I was just going out for a while," she said. "I should be back...soon."

She stood up, and on her way out of the room she gave Adam a kiss on the cheek. Then she stepped out into the hallway and wondered what to do, and where to go, next.

****

Suzanne felt like someone carrying around a time bomb. She could almost hear it ticking. She had to conceal it somewhere other than in her purse, and now the bedroom was out. Besides, putting it there would connect it to her if it were found. Better to hide it in some neutral place.

But where?

It had to be somewhere accessible, yet out of sight and not frequented by members of the household or the staff.

The women's rest room? No, she'd had enough of that. Behind a potted plant? No, not secret enough.

Then she had an idea.

Suzanne turned and marched toward the Queens'

Bedroom. She knew it was not being used at present; she and Adam were the only guests currently in residence. When she reached the bedroom door, she didn't actually enter, but she opened the secret door just outside it and slipped into the passageway that led up to the solarium. She looked around for somewhere to conceal the pistol and finally found a niche in the wall near the floor just big enough to fit the small weapon.

Before leaving the passageway, Suzanne listened carefully at the door to be sure no one was coming down the hallway.

She was about to open the door and slip out when a thought occurred to her. She quickly ran back, retrieved the pistol, and wiped it on her blouse to remove any fingerprints.

She was, more to her chagrin than her satisfaction, becoming a more accomplished criminal.

****

Back in the Lincoln Bedroom, Adam was snoring softly on one side of the bed. Finally able to relieve herself of her purse, Suzanne kicked off her shoes and lay down next to Adam.

Tomorrow she would try again.

Chapter 48

A Valentine

Wednesday, February fourteenth. Valentine's Day.
Suzanne awoke, disoriented at first but then
remembering she was in the Lincoln Bedroom and she
had a terrible task to complete. Adam was sleeping
peacefully beside her. She had not slept well, as one
might expect of a young woman about to commit her first
crime—if one doesn't count prostitution—and her first
crime was to be the assassination of the President of the
United States.

Although Patrick McNeil had been away at some
conference the day before—and therefore Suzanne
would not have found him even had she not fallen in the
hallway—she knew he would be back in the White
House this day. Would Valentine's Day be a propitious
time to commit an act so divorced from that of love?

At first, Suzanne thought she would slip quietly out
of bed and let Adam, who had been up late talking with
his brother, sleep a while longer. But then she considered
that this might well be the last time she would ever wake
up in bed with Adam, perhaps the last time she would
ever wake up at all. If so, she would make the most of it.
And besides, it was Valentine's Day. How could she not
show her love for him on Valentine's Day?

She snuggled up close to Adam and stroked his

forehead until he awoke enough to realize where he was, and who was there with him.

"Happy Valentine's Day," Suzanne said softly, forcing a smile despite her feeling of desperation. She gave him a long and meaningful kiss, he reciprocated, and a few minutes later they were making love.

"Happy Valentine's Day," Adam said as they came up for air. "I only hope I can always wake up to such a wonderful woman and equally wonderful sensations."

He could not have understood why this simple sentiment brought tears to her eyes.

****

Suzanne knew that between four and six p.m., on those occasions when he had no pressing matters of state to attend to, the president liked to work alone in his office in the Treaty Room. That would be the only time she could be sure to find him and finally get this terrible thing over with.

That meant she would have to wait for over six hours, wait and worry, deal with the stress and anxiety, and not let Adam notice her torture.

She decided to tell him she had a luncheon engagement with a friend and would be away for several hours. When she did, he was surprised she had not mentioned it before, but he said he had a lot of work to do anyway and would see her later in the afternoon.

After breakfast, Suzanne's first task was to retrieve the gun she had concealed in the secret passage. She headed for the Queens' Bedroom.

Outside the secret door, Suzanne had to linger, trying not to look suspicious, until there was no one within sight. Then she opened the door and darted into the passageway as quickly as she could. She didn't know what she would do if the gun was no longer in the niche where she had left it—probably faint, among other things—but fortunately when she stooped down and looked, it was still there.

Greatly relieved, Suzanne lifted it up and put it back into her purse. But first she checked that it was still loaded. It was.

Once again, Suzanne was carrying that time bomb in her purse. She didn't want to leave the building with it and have to pass it through security again, so she made her way to the ground floor and the White House library. There she spent over five hours in considerable distress, at times reading but mostly immersed in dark thoughts about her upcoming task. Fortunately, no one else seemed interested in using the library that afternoon, so she could at least brood in privacy.

Finally, at four p.m., Suzanne left the library and headed for the Treaty Room, which was next door to the Lincoln Bedroom where she and Adam had slept. This time she made sure she kept her wits about her, as well as her purse. This time there could be no slip-ups.

Suzanne had one hand on the door knob of the Treaty Room and the other on the gun in her purse when a deep voice behind her said, "Suzanne! Good morning."

Suzanne turned to see Bob Harrison, the president's press secretary, smiling at her. She stepped back.

"Oh, hi, Bob. I…I was just going to…to ask Patrick something…" It was all she could think of to say. *So much for no one seeing me go in*, she thought.

"Sure," Bob said. "I was just coming to get some papers from the president. Do you mind if I dart in before you for a second? I really won't be long and I have to have the information for a press release this morning."

"No, no. Please go ahead. I'll wait out here."

"Thanks. Won't be a minute." And Harrison opened the door and stepped into the Treaty Room, closing the door behind him.

Suzanne waited nervously for the press secretary to return, both hands now grasping her purse in front of her. She hoped she didn't look nervous, but she was pretty sure she did. What she felt was well beyond nerves.

Finally, after several minutes, the door opened and Bob Harrison emerged from the Treaty Room, papers in hand and smiling.

"He's all yours," Harrison said as he turned and walked down the hall at a quick pace.

I guess he is, was all Suzanne could think.

****

Suzanne waited for several minutes to give her target a chance to get back to whatever he was doing. She wanted to surprise him, giving herself the best possible chance to carry out her assignment.

She entered the room as quietly as possible, her hand shaking as she turned the doorknob. Patrick McNeil was indeed alone, reading a document on the heavy Resolute Desk—so-called because it was made from the timbers of the British ship HMS Resolute, one of the many fascinating details Suzanne had learned since coming to the White House. He apparently didn't see or hear Suzanne enter, as he did not look up from his reading. Suzanne crept softly to one side, where she had a better angle for a shot. Just after she did, the president turned around to consult other documents that were spread out on the credenza behind him, so that now his back was to Suzanne.

As soon as the president's back was turned, Suzanne

reached into her purse and retrieved the pistol. Her hand was shaking quite badly as she raised the pistol and took aim with both hands, as she had learned in the gun safety class she had taken. Class or no class, she still doubted she could hit anything smaller than the wall beyond, but she knew she had to try.

For several seconds Suzanne seemed unable either to pull the trigger or to lower the gun, becoming more and more agitated as the seconds passed. Suddenly the door behind her opened and Adam entered the room, breathing hard as if he had been running. When he saw the scene before him, he froze.

Now the president did turn around, saying, "What the hell is—" As soon as he saw Adam and Suzanne, posed as for a tableau, his voice failed.

Adam, in a voice filled with anguish, said quietly, "Suzanne, please. Don't."

Suzanne looked around, first at Adam, then at the president, both of whom were staring at her. She looked again at Adam, directly into his eyes, as hers welled with tears.

Then she turned the gun toward her chest and pulled the trigger. There was a deafening report, as if a firecracker had gone off in the room.

Suzanne slumped to the floor, dropping the gun, blood spreading over the front of her clean white blouse.

The two-toned eyes were closed.

The perfect body was perfect no more.

Chapter 49

Reaction

They had lied, of course. The gun had no silencer, and the shot echoed around the Treaty Room and up and down the corridor, past the Oval Office. In less than a minute, three Secret Service officers were in the Treaty Room with guns drawn.

They found Adam bent over the bleeding body of his wife as the president, standing but supported by the Resolute Desk, looked on, looking resolute.

"Get someone from the MU here," he said to one of the men. "Now!"

"But what—" the man started to say, but the president cut him off.

"I said *now!*" Then he addressed all three men, "And put those guns away. Call an ambulance." Before they left, he seemed to think of something else: "And don't say a word about this to anyone. That's an order."

The secret service agent to whom the president had first spoken holstered his gun and ran from the room. He had only to run to the physician's office a few doors away to find help, which was on call twenty-four hours a day. No more than a minute later, a thirty-ish woman entered the Treaty Room carrying a doctor's bag and headed straight for the fallen Suzanne. She was an Air Force nurse, trained in emergency care, only recently assigned to the White House Medical Unit. This was her first case since arriving.

As the nurse shoved Adam aside and bent over her patient's body, Adam looked over at his brother. "She couldn't help it. Pat, she couldn't help it." His voice cracked and he was on the verge of tears. He looked back at the scene on the floor and said to the nurse, "Is she—is she—alive?"

Without taking her eyes off of her patient, who was lying unconscious in a pool of blood, the nurse said, "Barely. I don't think she'll make it, but we'll do what we can. We have to get her to a trauma unit immediately." A minute later, two men arrived with a gurney, and they carefully lifted Suzanne's limp body onto the wheeled stretcher and headed down the hall.

Adam started to follow, but he turned back to speak to his brother, who was still standing.

"She couldn't help it," he said again.

"It's a good thing—at least for me—you showed up when you did," the president said to Adam. "You looked like you knew what was happening here."

Adam looked down, as if sorting out things in his mind, then faced his brother. "I did. At least I knew it was going to happen sometime soon, and when I couldn't find Suzanne and—"

"How did you know?"

Adam talked slowly, trying to make sense of what he was saying. "I got a call a few minutes ago. From a woman who was Suzanne's best friend back in New York. I'd met her when she came to visit. Quite an extraordinary woman. She sounded frantic, apparently having been trying for hours to get hold of me—or you. Finally found my cell number through one of her 'clients,' whatever that means. She told me about some bizarre plot against you that Suzanne got caught up in. Said these people ordered her to—to kill you." The president abruptly sat down but didn't take his eyes off of Adam, who continued. "She refused to go along with it, so they threatened to kill her mother, if she didn't—if she didn't—didn't do it. Suzanne was—is—very close to her mother. Apparently her mother saved her life when she was a kid. The friend said Suzanne agonized over it but finally gave in. She was going to be getting a gun somewhere as soon as yesterday, and she could be using it at any time. I tried to find her, and when I couldn't, I ran up here to find—to find you."

"So why didn't she kill me? She had plenty of time."

"I think—I think she just couldn't. I'm not sure why, but probably it just wasn't in her nature, despite how much she loved her mother."

The president thought about this, and his features softened a bit before he said quietly to his brother, "Maybe, in the end, she loved you more." There was silence as both men were lost in thought. Then Pat McNeil looked up. "You'd better get going to the hospital," he told his brother. "I hope for your sake, and for mine, she survives."

Adam wasn't quite sure what his brother meant by "for mine," but he had no time to seek an explanation. He ran from the room. He was not a particularly religious man, but he prayed harder than he ever had before, all the way to the hospital.

Chapter 50

Gathering Family

Mary Sue Dahlstrom was folding the laundry, using the little time she had between jobs, when the man knocked on her door.

She looked through the peephole in the door and saw what appeared to be a tall man dressed in a dark suit. Suspicious even of men she knew, and perhaps with good reason, Mary Sue put the door on its chain and opened it only enough to speak to this unexpected visitor.

"Mary Sue Dahlstrom?" the man asked as soon as it opened.

"Who wants to know?"

"My name is Brady. Charles Brady. I'm a federal officer." He flashed a silver badge, but Mary Sue could not read what it said in the dim light of the hallway.

"What do you want with me?" she asked. "I haven't done anything."

"No, of course not," Brady said. "Can I come in? I need to talk to you about your daughter, Suzanne."

Suzanne? What could they want with Suzanne? The last she had heard, Suzanne was living in San Francisco, working as a secretary.

"What's this about? Is Suzanne in some kind of trouble?"

"Please, ma'am, I need to explain the situation. May

I come in?"

Against her better judgment, but anxious to know what this man had to say about Suzanne, Mary Sue reluctantly unhooked the chain and opened the door.

The man entered the small, sparsely furnished apartment. His coat was open and Mary Sue could now see the gun he was carrying in a shoulder holster. She backed away so she would have time to scream if the man attacked her. "Okay, you're in. What do you want? What about my daughter?"

"I'm afraid your daughter has suffered a—a serious injury. She is in a hospital in Washington, DC."

Mary Sue felt faint, started to collapse, when the man calling himself Brady stepped forward and caught her, lowering her into one of the two stuffed chairs in the room.

"What—what happened? Is she going to be all right?" Her tone was almost pleading.

Brady sat down in the other chair, facing Mary Sue. He looked grave, as if reluctant to be the bearer of bad news, even if it was his job. "I'm afraid I can't say if she is, ma'am. All I know is she suffered a gunshot wound, she's in the hospital, on life support and in a coma, and they don't know how much longer she will live. I've been told to bring you to DC and to the hospital. Your being there just might help her to survive, and if she doesn't...well, you'd want to be there, wouldn't you?"

Mary Sue had begun to cry, but with an effort she pulled herself together. "Go to the hospital? Yes, I have to go there, but—I can't—I have no money—and my job..." She was barely coherent.

Brady put a hand on her arm. "Yes, ma'am, we know about that. It's all been arranged. There's a plane waiting for us at the airport, and we've spoken with both your employers and explained this is a special request from the president."

Mary Sue looked up. "The president? Of the United States? Why the president?"

"I think it will all be explained to you when we arrive. To be honest, I don't know the answer myself. I've just been told to bring you."

Mary Sue nodded. Almost in a daze, she went into the bedroom and gathered up some underwear and clean clothes, took a few more items from the pile she had been folding, and stuffed them into an old suitcase rescued from the back of her closet. She put on her good coat, put her prescription medicines into her purse, checked that she had her keys, and walked out through the door held open by Charles Brady.

She wondered just what other surprises were in store for her.

She could never have guessed.

****

Patricia Lee, in New York, did not receive a visit from a federal agent. She did receive a telephone call from Marguerite. As tactfully as she could, Marguerite explained Suzanne's circumstances to a dumbfounded Patricia, who of course knew nothing of the real life Suzanne had led since she last saw her. A call girl? Married the president's brother? Shot herself in the White House? It was almost too much for her to take in, and she had to sit down and take a deep breath. At least Marguerite didn't consider it necessary to mention why Suzanne had married Adam, and what she had intended to do with that gun. That might have finished Patricia off.

Marguerite promised to let Patricia know when—

and if—Suzanne regained consciousness, and Patricia promised to come to DC to see her when—and if—she did.

Meanwhile, Patricia was uncertain how to tell Gene what she had learned. Although he had liked Suzanne well enough while she stayed with them, he was much less open-minded about things like sexual conduct than she was. In fact, at times he had a tendency to be a bit judgmental, and this could be one of those times.

Finally she decided she really had to tell him, especially if she were to take off for DC on short notice to see Suzanne. As she had feared, Gene did not take the news with equanimity. Of course, Patricia did not know of the additional bit of information that Gene had never revealed to her, Suzanne's abortive attempt to gain his favor by offering him her body. Nor had he ever told Patricia that Jim Henderson had been fired after having sex with one of the applicants for a secretarial position. Although Gene never knew for sure, he had no doubt it was Suzanne.

Gene Lee was, therefore, not as surprised as Patricia had been to learn the direction Suzanne's career had taken after leaving their home, although the part about marrying into the president's family was as much a shock to him as to Patricia, perhaps more. He was also understandably less sympathetic to Suzanne's plight than was Patricia, despite believing that Suzanne was, at heart, a good person who just needed direction. But whatever his feelings, Gene loved his wife and was not about to dispel her illusions about Suzanne, which would do neither of them any harm. Let Patricia continue to love Suzanne, as she seemingly did. She could only be a positive factor in Suzanne's life. *And God knows she seems to need one,* Gene thought.

Chapter 51

Explanations

The plane carrying Mary Sue, a military aircraft, landed several hours later at Andrews Air Force Base in Virginia, a short distance by helicopter from Walter Reed Medical Center, to which Suzanne had been transferred. Mary Sue had never flown in an airplane, much less a helicopter, so the trip was exciting, terrifying, and nerve-wracking all at one time.

Charles Brady had escorted Mary Sue to the lobby of the hospital, where they were met by Adam McNeil and a tall, exotic-looking black woman, neither of whom Mary Sue—or Brady, for that matter—knew. Both looked as if they had not slept in many hours. Adam thanked Brady and dismissed him to return to Los Angeles. Then he introduced himself as the president's brother, and the woman as Marguerite Matson, a friend of Suzanne's.

Other than a polite acknowledgment of the introductions, "Where is my daughter?" was all that Mary Sue could manage.

"She's upstairs in a hospital bed," Adam said. "She's in a coma, fighting for her life."

Mary Sue willed herself not to cry. "Will she—what are her—her chances?"

"I'm not a doctor, and I really don't know," Adam

said. "We're all waiting and praying."

"Then why are you here? Why is the president's brother here?"

"I'm sorry. Didn't I say? I'm Suzanne's husband."

****

It took Mary Sue a few minutes to recover from the shock of learning that her daughter, Suzanne, who had left home at nineteen to make her way in the world with only a high school education and a few dollars, apparently had made her way as far as becoming a member of the president's family. She was at the same time confused, proud, and, of course, still nervous and frightened.

Adam and Marguerite escorted Mary Sue to a small conference room the hospital had set aside for them. There, over the next hour, Adam and Marguerite explained the long, tortuous, and somewhat bizarre path that had led Suzanne from Los Angeles to New York to San Francisco and, finally, to Washington, DC. They had decided it was best to tell her the whole story, rather than a sanitized version that excluded either Suzanne's life as a call girl or her involvement in a plot against the president. The only thing they omitted was the fact that Suzanne had shot herself in the climactic moment of an attempt to assassinate the president. As far as she was to know, Suzanne had tried to commit suicide in her guilt and anxiety over her part in the original plot to seduce Adam's brother. It was almost an overwhelming revelation for a mother to receive about her only child, but Mary Sue accepted it with surprising grace and fortitude. Her life and Suzanne's had been so unstable, so chaotic during those first nineteen years, that almost anything she learned about her daughter's later life paled in comparison.

Almost.

****

Adam himself, of course, had only learned most of these extraordinary facts a day earlier. As soon as it was clear that Suzanne's condition was stable and the doctors said they could only watch and wait, Adam telephoned Marguerite and asked her to come to DC to be with Suzanne, and to give him more details about his wife's real background.

Marguerite told the escort agency she would be taking an indefinite leave of absence, effective immediately. They didn't like it, of course, but Marguerite was not really a replaceable member of their organization, and they preferred the prospect of having her back at some later time to that of losing her services altogether.

Marguerite arrived in DC the next day. She was met at the airport by one of the president's interns and brought to the hospital, where Adam awaited her. For a while she and Adam talked about Suzanne's life both before and after her move to San Francisco. Marguerite then gave Adam the letter, still sealed, that Suzanne had written to him and included in the packet sent to Marguerite. He read it slowly, then read it again, and finally, without a word spoken, he handed it to Marguerite. She read:

Dearest Adam,

When you receive this, I will likely be dead. I will have killed your brother Pat. I don't ask for your forgiveness, because what I've done cannot ever be forgiven. I do ask that you consider the reason I have committed such a terrible act.

The letter continued with a recounting of what had brought Suzanne to this point. She told Adam she was not proud of having become a call girl, but neither was she ashamed of it, having hurt no one and given pleasure to many, including herself. Suzanne explained about the offer of a million dollars to seduce the president, which she finally decided she could not turn down, especially as it seemed to represent the ultimate payback for the way men had abused her as a child.

Now comes the hard part to tell you, it continued. Their plan was that I would meet you, Adam, and convince you to marry me. Once your brother was elected and I was part of the president's close family, I would have the freedom and opportunity to seduce him, which I was confident I could do. The idea was that we would be caught in bed together, the newspapers and TV would tell the world that the president had been sleeping with his own brother's wife, and, well, the rest is obvious.

I freely admit that when I first set out to seduce you, I was doing it just as my part of the plan, and you were just one step on my road to a million dollars. But once I got to know you, and especially once we were married and living together, I came to see you very differently. To put it simply, I fell in love with you. For real. I had never been in love with anyone, except my mother, in my life. The closest thing to it was my love for my wonderful friend, Marguerite; but that was a different kind of love, like that for a sister. I had no idea what it would feel like, or how it would change my life, to be in love with a man, until I met you.

I knew I couldn't carry out the plan to seduce your brother, not for his sake, but for yours. I couldn't do this to you. I told the men who hired me they could have the money back, I was not going through with it. I wanted to stay married to you, to live the rest of my life with you.

They told me I couldn't back out. Not only that, they said the plan had changed, and I was to kill your brother. Of course, I refused. That's when they said they would kill my mother, torture her and kill her, if I refused.

Adam, please understand that the only person in the world who is as important to me as you is my mother, Mary Sue. She gave me life, then she saved my life, and then she sacrificed herself for me so I could have a chance to make a life for myself. How could I let them do such a horrible thing to my mother?

Maybe I'm just weak, I don't know, but I finally agreed to do what you now know I've done. And I have paid the price for it.

Please do not think of me as a terrible person. Please remember me as someone who, although I deceived you and although I committed an unforgivable sin, was unable to help myself. Please believe that I truly loved you and only wish I could be with you now, to tell you so myself.

I said I would not ask your forgiveness. But I cannot go to my death without asking.

Please forgive me.
Your loving wife,
Suzanne

****

Marguerite stared at the letter for a long time, tears in her eyes. Adam came up behind her and gently took the letter back, folded it, and put it in his pocket.

Marguerite looked closely at Adam for clues as to how the revelations in Suzanne's letter had affected him. Would he stalk off in disgust? Would he try to distance himself as much as possible from Suzanne's plight?

After a few minutes of silence, eyes closed, as he digested the letter's contents, Adam opened his eyes and looked at Marguerite. "Okay, what can we do to give Suzanne the best chance of pulling through?"

Marguerite smiled, put her hands on either side of Adam's face and gave him a very appreciative kiss.

Then they decided on a plan of action.

****

The first thing to do, they decided, was to fill the president in on all the pertinent details. He didn't have to know everything, of course, but he had to understand what drove Suzanne to do what she did.

Adam went to see his brother alone.

"How is Suzanne doing? Any change?" the president asked.

"No, no change. The doctors say it's touch and go. Apparently, she was extremely fortunate that she'd been holding the pistol in both hands, so when she turned it toward herself it was aimed more or less at the center-right section of her chest. Had she aimed at her left side, as a right-handed person holding a gun in that hand ordinarily would do, she would have shot herself in the heart and died instantly. As it was, the bullet didn't penetrate any vital organs, but it caused a great deal of damage nonetheless, and of course she lost a lot of blood. They give her about a twenty percent chance of coming out of this."

"I see. I'm sorry, Adam."

"Yeah, thanks. Not much we can do, or the doctors for that matter. But if she does regain consciousness, I'm told it could be very beneficial if the people she's closest to are with her. Her friend Marguerite, who got hold of me and told me what Suzanne was planning to do, is here from New York, and of course I'm here. But we thought the best person to be here would be her mother."

Adam then explained to the president the gist of Suzanne's letter. He listened quietly and was clearly moved by it.

"Pat," Adam said, "I'm sure what happened is this: Suzanne came in here feeling like she had to commit murder, to kill you, to save her mother from a terrible death. But when it came to doing it, and especially when she saw me, she couldn't. I think she thought, during those few agonizing seconds, if she killed herself, there would be no reason for those bastards to kill her mother. They had nothing to gain by it at that point. And she would save me from seeing my brother shot in front of me."

The president smiled. "You don't think it was to save me? To save the president?"

"No—no, I don't, much as I hate to say it."

"That's okay, it's what I thought all along. Remember what I said: she loved you more. Certainly more than me or my office."

They both were silent for a minute, thinking their own thoughts, and then the president said, "But I guess it's actually a little more problematic than that, what with her having deceived you and married you under false pretenses. I imagine this creates quite a…a complication in your feelings for Suzanne."

Adam nodded. "You could say that. Right now I don't know how I feel, or whether I could ever feel the same about being married to Suzanne as I once did. But I know I'll do anything to help her recover. I still love her."

The president nodded.

Then Adam seemed to think of something else. "You said earlier you wanted Suzanne to survive for your sake as well as mine. What did you mean? And why have you ordered everyone involved to keep quiet about this?"

His brother smiled. "I'm afraid that, while you think like a husband in love, I always think like a politician. The politician who ever forgets to consider what the public knows or will find out about him or his conduct won't be a politician very long."

"Meaning?"

"Meaning if it gets out that my own sister-in-law tried to assassinate me, even if she changed her mind at the last minute, and regardless of her motive, that's about all the public will read or see or think about for the rest of my term in office. I'll be not only one of the few presidents someone tried to assassinate, but the only one targeted by a member of his own family. No, thank you, I'd much prefer this remain a case of a gun accident, a most unfortunate thing to befall the president's family, but the subject of sympathy and understanding instead of ridicule and scorn. Do you see my point?"

Adam nodded. "Yeah, I see," he said almost reluctantly. Although he realized it was far better for him and for Suzanne, should she survive—and for her friends and family if she did not—that her injury be labeled an accident, he couldn't help being put off by the cold calculation of political consequences his brother had made—and made so quickly—in the face of such a horrific scene. No wonder Pat was a great politician, whereas Adam could not even have run for dog catcher.

"So it's in the interests of both of us," Pat went on,

"even if for different reasons, to do what we can to save Suzanne. Besides, I really liked—sorry, like—Suzanne. Other than trying to kill me, she was always the model sister-in-law, and a helluva catch for you, dear brother. Most beautiful girl I ever met. Still don't know what she sees in you."

Adam smiled. He had to agree. "But one other thing. If you treat this as an accident, won't those bastards who planned the whole thing go free, so they can try it again?"

"Oh, I didn't say we wouldn't try to find and neutralize them, just that we wouldn't let on how far their little plan had gone. As we speak, the wheels of retribution are in motion. Don't worry—we'll find them, and when we do, we'll deal with them."

That was when it was agreed that the president would arrange to have Suzanne's mother brought out to DC, so she would be with Suzanne should she awaken from her coma. Nothing would give her more incentive to live, "other than seeing you there too, of course," the president said. Mary Sue would be at her daughter's bedside, for better or for worse.

They sincerely hoped it was for better.

Chapter 52

The Vigil

Between them, Adam, Marguerite, and Mary Sue set up a round-the-clock vigil by Suzanne's bedside. Of course, at times two or all three of them might be in the room at one time, but they made sure at least one of them was either in the room or within shouting distance at all times. Were Suzanne to awaken, they wanted to be certain it was one of them she saw first, and were she able to communicate, one of them should be there to answer her questions and reassure her about her future. Moreover, they took turns holding Suzanne's unresponsive hand and speaking quietly to her in reassuring tones, which they had been told could be very beneficial for a patient in a coma. Apparently, the subconscious mind received the messages, even if the conscious mind did not.

After three days, they realized their vigil was really a death watch, even if mixed with a modicum of hope. Suzanne's doctor broached the subject of removing life support.

"Have her chances of survival changed that much?" Adam asked the doctor, a young internist named Bradley.

"No, not really," he replied. "It's more a question of how long you want to wait. To be frank, Suzanne could survive in this state for months with no real change. Or her condition could suddenly deteriorate, at any time."

"Or she could come out of this and recover?"

"Yes, of course. We simply don't know in cases like this."

None of the three watchers was ready to give up, and the vigil continued.

It was ten days after she attempted to take her own life, at eight-thirty-one in the morning, that Suzanne opened her eyes.

****

When, after a few seconds, Suzanne was able to focus on her surroundings, the first thing she saw was the faces of two people. One was the nurse then on duty. The other was her mother, Mary Sue.

Suzanne's head throbbed and she couldn't think straight. She couldn't remember where she was or why. But she knew her mother, and seeing her caused her eyes to tear and her heart to pound.

Mary Sue, who had all but given up hope of Suzanne's recovery, rushed to her bedside and, leaning over to put her face next to Suzanne's, sobbed with relief and happiness.

The nurse immediately left the room to fetch the doctor on duty and to call Adam and Marguerite, as had been agreed in advance. They had been staying in one of the Fisher Houses on the grounds of the Medical Center, where families can live while their loved ones are receiving care at the hospital. Ordinarily, only military families are accommodated, but when the president had requested that a special exception be made in this instance, no one had demurred. Only one room was available, and it was a testament to the seriousness of the situation and Marguerite's affection for Suzanne that, for the first time in her memory, she had slept within an arm's length of a man without making the slightest suggestion of a sexual encounter.

When Adam and Marguerite arrived, the doctor was already examining Suzanne, as Mary Sue stood to the side and watched anxiously, tears in her eyes. The doctor was one of the senior members of the hospital's staff, and he had seen more than his share of bullet wounds and their consequences. Adam and Marguerite, both of whom wanted badly to embrace Suzanne as Mary Sue had done, waited until the doctor stood up and looked their way. When he saw them, he put down the instrument he had been holding and walked over to where they were standing, Mary Sue trailing behind.

He smiled and introduced himself as Dr. John Castillo. The visitors did not have to ask the obvious question; the doctor knew why they were there.

"I'm very encouraged by what I see," the doctor said. "In my experience, when a patient who has been through a violent incident and the shock following it falls into a coma and emerges on the other side, so to speak, her prospects are altogether different than they had been. In other words, her chances of recovery now are better than fifty-fifty, so long as she continues to make progress and there are no...no setbacks."

Dr. Castillo stepped back as the three visitors, after expressing their thanks to the doctor, walked quickly to Suzanne's bedside. All had tears in their eyes now, and Mary Sue was so overcome she started to collapse, Adam quickly pulling up a visitor's chair for her, and he and Marguerite then knelt on either side of Suzanne's bed and held her hands.

"Welcome back," Adam said softly. "We've missed you."

Marguerite, worldly and sophisticated Marguerite whom nothing phased, was too overcome with emotion to add more than, "What he said, honey."

"I have to emphasize," the doctor said when everyone had regained their composure, "that Suzanne is not yet out of danger. We'll continue to monitor her closely, and…well, we'll see."

Adam shook Dr. Castillo's hand. "Thank you, doctor. It's been a tough week or two, and we're just relieved that Suzanne is awake. We know you'll take good care of her from here on."

"We will, but remember how important it is that you, her family, continue to support her and to be here for her. I can't tell you what a difference that can make in a patient's will to recover and to live. In fact, even when Suzanne was unconscious, I really believe some part of her knew you three were here, and it made a real difference."

They thanked him again, and the doctor left the hospital room. Suzanne had closed her eyes and appeared to be sleeping. Mary Sue went over to sit next to the bed, and Adam did the same on the other side. Marguerite stayed back, realizing that, of the three, she was the least important member of the watch.

She would wait her turn.

****

As Suzanne gradually gained strength, the triumvirate of Adam, Mary Sue, and Marguerite gradually lessened the intensity of their vigil at her bedside. Most days only one of them was there at a time, and she was left alone at night. The third day, Patricia

Lee arrived at the hospital, having been alerted by Marguerite that Suzanne was awake. Suzanne was overjoyed to see Patricia, whom she had never thought she would see again.

One day about a week after she awakened from her coma, as Marguerite was sitting next to the bed and holding Suzanne's hand, Suzanne looked over at her and asked, very quietly, "Marguerite, tell me. Does Adam hate me for what I did? I mean, not just for almost killing his brother, but for how I deceived him? I certainly wouldn't blame him."

Marguerite didn't answer right away. Finally she said, dropping the upmarket speech pattern she had assumed around Adam, "Honey, I wish I could read that man's mind. There's no doubt he loves you and he wants the best for you. But whether he can 'forgive and forget,' so to speak, and stay married to someone who sorta tricked him into it…well, I just don't know. I mean, his ego's been kinda messed with, know what I'm sayin'? After all this time thinkin' he'd won this gorgeous, sexy lady fair 'n square, turns out he was just bein' taken for a sucker. Has to hurt a lot, even if you're in love, and no matter what happened afterward."

Suzanne nodded and tears welled in her eyes. Marguerite thought maybe she had been too honest with her answer, in light of Suzanne's condition, but it was too late for that.

Marguerite gave Suzanne a tissue from the box by her bed, with which Suzanne dabbed at her eyes. She sniffed. "Well," she said, sounding determined, "if I make it out of here, I'll just have to do whatever I can to make him understand. To make him forgive me. Marguerite, I don't—I don't want to lose him." She began to cry.

Marguerite handed her another tissue. "Listen, Honey," she said, "you just get yourself well. Concentrate on gettin' stronger every day. Then we'll take care of Mr. Adam McNeil."

Chapter 53

Aftermath

Adam pulled Suzanne closer to him as they lay together in bed. He was oblivious to the ugly scars that now marred her once-perfect skin and her once-perfect breasts.

Although her face was still as attractive as before, under her clothing Suzanne was no longer among the most beautiful of women, in an objective sense. The wound she had inflicted on herself and the operations that followed had left jagged red scars where there used to be only soft, pink flesh.

Neither she nor Adam could care less.

It had taken Adam several weeks of soul-searching—including many sessions with a counselor and earnest discussions with his brother and with Marguerite—but, in the end, he had realized that, in a strange way, and except for the fact that Suzanne nearly lost her life in the process, her deception had been the best thing that could have happened to him.

Characteristically, it was Marguerite who put it in the plainest terms—*sans* the Ivy League accent now that they were old friends. "Look at it this way, honey. Most men would give their left nut to have just one go at a woman like Suzanne. In fact, lots of men gave lots of cash for that privilege, for just one hour with her. You could've done the same, if you had the money and were so inclined. But to get it for free? And then marry her, to boot? You had about as much chance o' that as the pope did of marryin' Mother Teresa. Maybe less. And that's too bad, 'cause Suzanne's a wonderful girl and was gonna make some guy a great wife, someday. When the time came, she could have her pick. So what happens? These pricks set her up to fool you into marryin' her. You end up winnin' the prize that you could never've won on your own. You get yourself not only a gorgeous wife, but I'm sure some of the best sex you ever had. Am I right?"

She got no argument on that from Adam, who just gave her a sheepish nod, so she continued. "It's like you was a fisherman and hooked the greatest lookin' fish you ever saw. You had zero chance of landin' that prize fish, and here it just up and flops itself into your boat on its own. Are you goin' t' throw it back 'cause it caught itself instead of you catchin' it?"

Adam shook his head.

"Don't get me wrong," Marguerite said. "I know your pride's hurt, 'cause you've been taken advantage of. But sometimes good things happen in a strange way. Once you were married, Suzanne found out you were really just as much a prize catch as she was. Now all that deception, all that false crap she told you to get you to marry her, all that turns out to be true. Turns out she does love you, she does want you to be the only man in her life. It's true.

"Honey, you lucked out. If you love Suzanne, believe me that she loves you, and thank your lucky stars for the weird way you landed her."

****

Once Adam had reconciled himself to the fact that

his fish had caught him and the deceptive reason she had done it—in the words of his therapist once he "let it go"—he lost no time in letting Suzanne know how he felt. He wanted their life together to continue, just as if all that had happened had nothing to do with their future relationship.

And in a sense, the most important sense, it didn't.

Adam's decision not only put their marriage back on track, it surely hastened Suzanne's recovery. Within a few weeks, she was discharged from the hospital, and in time she was once again the vivacious bride of the president's younger brother.

Rumors did circulate about the circumstances of Suzanne's injury, which officially was put down to an accident suffered when Suzanne was showing the president the pistol she had purchased for self-protection. But then, conspiracy theories abound in Washington, and the vast majority of people put this latest one, about a plot against the president, in the same category as Kennedy's second shooter and Obama's Kenyan birth.

After all, who except the most gullible would believe that the president was going to be assassinated, not by some anarchist, or some terrorist, or some crazed political enemy, but— no, really…

By his stunning young sister-in-law?

EPILOGUE

All the while Suzanne was recovering from her wound, as Patrick McNeil had assured his brother Adam, the wheels of retribution were indeed in motion. The same day Adam related Suzanne's story to Patrick, the Federal Bureau of Investigation interviewed both Adam and Marguerite. From Marguerite, they learned about Lloyd Kilpatrick, and, by the next day, Lloyd was sitting across the table from two men from the Bureau's Knoxville, Tennessee, office in a minimally-furnished downtown conference room. The men had appeared unannounced at Lloyd's office, identified themselves as FBI agents Wagner and Soriano, and invited Lloyd to accompany them downtown. It was not an invitation Lloyd could refuse.

Lloyd was almost relieved to be there. "I'll be honest with you fellas," he said. "I've been regretting ever getting myself into this mess for quite a while, and when they changed their tune from embarrassing the president to killing him, I just wanted out—"

Soriano, in shirtsleeves and loosened tie, interrupted. "Just who is the 'they' you're referring to, Lloyd? We know you were just the messenger boy in this, and if you cooperate you might get off easy—well, easier than if you don't, anyway. What we want to know is who these men are who put you up to it."

"That's just it," Lloyd whined. "I don't know

anything, except their names. The names they gave me, that is. The first fella I talked to, the one who first approached me, was named Jamil Kahn, or that's what he said. Arab-looking fella." Soriano wrote the name in a notebook. "That's all I know is his name."

"Could you identify his picture if you saw it?" Wagner asked.

"I'm pretty sure I could," Lloyd said. "I mean a lot of them look alike to me, but I got a pretty good look at Mr. Kahn. I'd probably know his voice, too. Gave me the creeps."

"Good," said Wagner. "Any other names?"

"Oh, yeah. I only saw Kahn once. After that, I was picked up and driven 'round by a fella named John Smith."

Soriano almost groaned. "I see. That might not be too helpful, as I'm sure you can understand. Still, there are a lot of people in this country actually named John Smith…" His voice trailed off as he wrote down the name.

"I don't suppose you'd have any idea where we could find this John Smith?" Wagner said. He did not sound hopeful.

"Well, now, funny you should say that. Smith picked me up in his car, and I happened to notice the license number because it reminded me of my good ol' Remington 11-87."

Both Wagner and Soriano looked up, like two terriers that had just spotted a rabbit. "You know his license number?"

"Yep. New York plate. RHH 1187."

"Did you happen to notice whether it was a rental car?" Wagner asked. "If so, they probably gave the company false information—"

"Heck no," Lloyd said with a grin. "He came down two times, and it was the same car, at least the same license, both times. Unlikely he'd rent the same car twice."

Soriano wrote furiously in his notebook.

Even the most sophisticated criminal conspiracies could make a mistake, and, when they do, it's usually all the authorities need. So it was with Kahn, "Smith," and even Betsy Green. The license was traced, John Smith—actually William Schmidt—was arrested and interrogated, and the rest fell neatly into place. A search of Schmidt's computer yielded some very useful email messages, a search of his house a small arsenal of unregistered firearms.

The president was pleased when he learned the ring of would-be assassins had been broken up. He was especially glad to know that the conspirators seemed to be unaware that their plan had, in fact, been carried out, or at least carried to an abortive conclusion. Thus far, the president's attempt to keep Suzanne's actions and motives quiet and to keep her injury classified as an accident had been successful. It meant Kahn and Schmidt and the others could not be prosecuted for quite as serious an offense, having apparently only partially executed their plan. But the politician in Patrick McNeil considered the trade-off more than worthwhile for his sake.

As well as that of his sister-in-law.

A word about the author...

Mark Reutlinger is the author of several successful novels, including the "Mrs. Kaplan" cozy mystery series (MRS. KAPLAN and the MATZOH BALL OF DEATH, A PAIN IN THE TUCHIS, and OY VEY, MARIA!) and the award-winning caper crime story, MURDER WITH STRINGS ATTACHED.

Reutlinger is Professor of Law Emeritus at Seattle University. He and his wife Analee live in University Place, Washington.